PRAISE FOR *Stolen Time*

"**ENDEARING, EXCITING, AND VERY CLEVER**,
Danielle Rollins's *Stolen Time* is the kind of
time-travel story I'm always on the lookout for.
I know I can't really speak for him, but I feel like
Doc Brown would be on board with this one."
—KENDARE BLAKE, #1 *New York Times* bestselling
author of the Three Dark Crowns series

"The hauntingly evocative prose
seduced me, the compellingly nuanced characters
captivated me, and the twisting storyline ensnared
my thoughts in an infinite spiral that
REFUSED TO RELEASE ME UNTIL THE FINAL WORD."
—ROMINA RUSSELL, *New York Times* bestselling
author of the Zodiac series

"*Stolen Time* is an **EXPLOSIVE PAGE-TURNER**
set in a richly imagined new world,
with characters you can't help but root for, and a twist
I never saw coming. I couldn't stop reading!"
—MORGAN RHODES, *New York Times* bestselling
author of the Fallen Kingdoms series

DANIELLE ROLLINS

HARPER TEEN
An Imprint of HarperCollinsPublishers

For all the scientists in my life, but particularly Bill Rollins, Thomas Van de Castle, and Ron Williams, for helping me look like I know what I'm talking about

HarperTeen is an imprint of HarperCollins Publishers.

Stolen Time
 For information address HarperCollins Children's Books, a division of HarperCollins Publishers, 195 Broadway, New York, NY 10007.
www.epicreads.com

Library of Congress Control Number: 2018954401
ISBN 978-0-06-267994-9

Typography by Jenna Stempel-Lobell
18 19 20 21 22 PC/LSCH 10 9 8 7 6 5 4 3 2 1
❖
First Edition

PART ONE

Rapid space-travel, or travel back in time, can't be ruled out, according to our present understanding. They would cause great logical problems, so let's hope there's a Chronology Protection Law, to prevent people going back and killing our parents.

—*Stephen Hawking*

1

DOROTHY

JUNE 7, 1913, JUST OUTSIDE OF SEATTLE

The comb gleamed in the midmorning light. It was exquisite. Tortoiseshell, with a mother-of-pearl inlay and teeth that had the too-bright look of real gold. Far superior to the rest of the cheap costume jewelry scattered across the hairdresser's table.

Dorothy pretended to be interested in a loose thread at her sleeve so she wouldn't stare. It might fetch fifty, if she could find the right buyer.

She squirmed, her patience thinning. If she had *time* to find the right buyer. It was already past nine. The clock didn't seem to be on her side today.

She shifted her eyes from the comb to the full-length mirror leaning against the wall in front of her. Bars of light glinted in through the chapel window, bouncing off the glass and turning the air in the dressing room bright and dusty. Silk dresses and delicate ribbons fluttered on their hangers.

Thunder rumbled in the distance, which was odd. This part of the country rarely stormed.

It was one of the things Dorothy hated most about the West Coast. How it was always gray but never stormed.

The hairdresser hesitated, catching Dorothy's eye in the mirror. "How do you like it, miss?"

Dorothy tilted her head. Her brown curls had been beaten into submission, making a ladylike bun at the nape of her neck. She looked tamed. Which, she supposed, was the entire point.

"Lovely," she lied. The old woman broke into a smile, her face disappearing in a mess of wrinkles and creases. Dorothy hadn't expected her to look so pleased. It sent guilt squirming through her.

She feigned a cough. "Would you mind fetching me a glass of water, please?"

"Not at all, dear, not at all." The hairdresser set down her brush and shuffled to the back of the room, where a crystal pitcher sat on a small table.

As soon as the woman's back was turned, Dorothy slipped the gold comb up her sleeve. The movement was so quick and natural that anyone watching would've been too distracted by the row of delicate pearl buttons edging the lace at Dorothy's wrist to notice a thing.

Dorothy dropped her arm to her side, a private smile flitting across her face, guilt forgotten. It was unseemly to be so proud, but she couldn't help it. Her sleight of hand had been perfect. As it should be. She'd practiced enough.

A floorboard groaned behind her, and a new voice said, "Leave us for a moment, will you, Marie?"

Dorothy's smile vanished, and every muscle in her body tightened, like they were attached to slowly turning screws. The hairdresser—*Marie*—startled, sending a trickle of water over the side of the glass.

"Oh! Miss Loretta. Forgive me, I didn't see you come in." Marie smiled and nodded as a petite, impeccably dressed older woman stepped into the room. Dorothy pressed her teeth together so tightly her jaw began to ache. Suddenly, the comb seemed to bulge beneath her sleeve.

Loretta wore a black gown overlaid with a delicate web of gold lace. The high neckline and long sleeves gave her the appearance of a very elegant spider. It was a look more suited to a funeral than a wedding.

Loretta kept her expression polite, but the air around her seemed to thicken, like she had her own gravity. Marie placed the glass of water down and scurried into the hallway. Terrified, no doubt. Most people were terrified of Dorothy's mother.

Dorothy studied her mother's ruined hand out of the corner of her eye, trying not to be obvious. The hand was much smaller than it should be, with withered, wasted fingers curling in on each other like claws. Loretta grew her fingernails too long and allowed the edges to yellow. It was as though she wanted to enhance the look of decay. Like she wanted people to turn away from her deformity. Even Dorothy had a hard time with the small, wasted hand, and Loretta was her mother. She should be used to it by now.

Dorothy cocked her head and lowered her eyelids. Nerves crawled over her skin, under all the lace and frill of her dress. She curled her lips into a coy smile, ignoring them. She'd had a lot of practice ignoring her feelings during her sixteen years alive. She'd almost forgotten what they were for.

Beauty disarms, she thought. It'd been her mother's first lesson. She'd been prodded and poked since she was nine years old, her corset cinched tighter, her cheeks pinched until they were rosy red.

"Mother," she cooed, patting her curls. "Doesn't my hair look divine?"

Loretta assessed her daughter coolly, and Dorothy felt her smile tremble. It was foolish to try these tricks on her mother, but she was desperate to avoid a fight. Today was going to be difficult enough already.

"I thought you were thirsty." Loretta picked up the water glass with her good hand, withered fingers trembling. Someone else might think the muscles were failing. They might offer to help.

Dorothy knew better. She reached for the glass without hesitation, her spine going rigid. She'd been expecting it, but she still didn't feel the birdlike fingers of her mother's ruined hand slip down her sleeve and pull the expensive comb free of its hiding place.

The hand was Loretta's secret weapon, so grotesque that people had a hard time looking directly at it, so small and quick that no one ever felt it reach into their jacket or down their pocketbook. It was the second lesson Loretta ever taught her daughter. *Weakness could be powerful.* People under-estimated broken things.

Loretta tossed the comb back onto the table, one thin eyebrow arching high on her forehead. Dorothy fixed her face in a look of shock.

"However did *that* get there?" she asked, taking a sip of water.

"Shall I search the rest of you to make certain nothing else has crawled inside your gown?"

She said this in a flat voice that sent an unpleasant shudder down Dorothy's spine. Dorothy currently had a set of very expensive lockpicks tucked below the silk sash at her waist, nicked from her mother's underwear drawer before they left for the chapel. She could afford to lose the comb, but Dorothy needed those picks.

Luckily, Loretta didn't follow through on the threat. She lifted Dorothy's veil from its stand beside the mirror. It was a long, filmy thing, with a tiny row of silk flowers sewn across the crown. Dorothy had spent most of the morning pretending it didn't exist.

"What were you thinking?" Loretta spoke in the low, careful voice she used only when she was truly furious. "Stealing a thing like that, and minutes before your own wedding? Stand please."

Dorothy stood. Her skirts fell gracefully around her ankles, pooling at her feet. She hadn't put on her shoes yet, and, without them, she felt a bit like a girl playing dress-up in her mother's wedding gown. Which was silly. Her mother had never let her play.

"What would we have done if you'd been seen?" Loretta continued, lowering the veil to her daughter's head and jamming pins into place.

"I wasn't seen," Dorothy said. The sharp metal stabbed her scalp, but she didn't flinch. "I'm never seen."

"*I* saw you."

Dorothy pressed her lips together so she wouldn't argue. There was no way her mother had actually seen her take that comb. She may have guessed, but she didn't *see* anything.

"You put everything we've worked for at risk. And all for some silly trinket." Loretta pulled the silk sash at Dorothy's waist tight. Dorothy felt the lockpicks shift in their hiding place.

That "trinket" would have paid for her train ticket out of town. She could've been well away from this dreadful place before the ceremony even started.

Dorothy swallowed, pushing aside her disappointment. There would be other trinkets. Other chances.

"This is ghastly," she muttered, flicking a silk flower on her veil. "Why do people get married in these?"

"That veil belonged to Charles's mother." Loretta slid another pin into her daughter's hair, fastening the veil firmly into place. She was referring to Dr. Charles Avery. Dorothy's *fiancé.* The word still made her feel ill. Girls like her weren't supposed to marry.

Dorothy and her mother were confidence women. This time last year, they'd been running a marriage scheme. It had been easy enough money. Loretta would simply take out a classified in the local paper, claiming to be a lonely young woman seeking the correspondence of a single man with a view toward marriage. Then, when the letters began trickling in, they'd mail the poor sap Dorothy's photograph and he'd be caught like a worm on a hook.

After a few months of increasingly steamy letters and promises of true love, they'd reel him in, asking for money to buy medicine for a cough or to see the doctor about a twisted ankle. Then it was a check for the landlady, or a few hundred for a train ticket so they might finally meet.

They always ran the scheme on a few men at once, making sure to cut them loose before suspicion set in. Then Avery started writing, and everything changed.

Avery was rich, the newly appointed surgeon-in-chief at Seattle's Providence Medical Center. And he'd proposed the instant he saw Dorothy's photograph—likely wanting a trophy of a wife to go with his fancy new title. Loretta said it would be their biggest con yet. A wedding. A *marriage*. She said it would change their lives. They could have everything they'd ever wanted.

Dorothy twisted the engagement ring on her finger. She'd spent her entire life learning the art of the con. It wasn't all smiling in the mirror and tilting her head. She'd practiced her finger work until her hands had cramped, and taught herself to pick a lock with a few twists of her wrist and whatever she'd found lying around. She could read a lie in the curve of a mouth. She could slip a wedding ring off a man's finger while he freshened her drink. And now she was going to be sold to someone who'd spend the rest of her life telling her what to do and where to go. Just as her mother had always done. It was as though the two of them had conspired to make certain Dorothy never made a single choice of her own.

"You look lovely," Loretta said, examining Dorothy with a shrewd eye. She adjusted the veil so the silk flowers framed her daughter's face. "The perfect bride."

Dorothy stood up straighter, and the lockpicks shifted, poking through the back of her dress. She had no intention of being a bride, no matter how perfectly she looked the part. If her mother thought she was going to go through with this, she was a fool.

"Still missing something." Loretta took a small object out of her pocket. It glinted gold in the dim light.

"Grandmother's locket," Dorothy murmured as Loretta looped the fine chain around her neck. For a moment, she forgot about her escape plans. The locket was a thing of awe, like something out of a fairy tale. Loretta had unlatched it from her mother's neck right before the cruel woman tossed her out of the house and left her to wander the streets, pregnant and penniless. No matter how hungry Loretta had gotten, she'd never pawned it.

Dorothy touched the locket lightly with her fingertips. The gold was pale and very old. There'd been an image sketched onto the front, but it had long since worn away. "Why are you giving it to me now?"

"So you'll remember." Loretta squeezed her daughter's shoulders. Her dark eyes had gone narrow.

Dorothy didn't have to ask what she was supposed to remember. The locket told the story well. How mothers were sometimes cruel. How love couldn't be relied upon. How a girl could only trust the things she could steal.

But maybe not, something inside of her whispered. *Maybe there's something more.*

Her fingers went still against the cool metal. She'd never been able to name this feeling, but it nagged at her sometimes, leaving her strangely hollow. She wasn't even sure what she wanted, exactly. Just *more*.

More than men and dresses and money. More than her mother's life. More than *this*.

It was foolish, really. A shameful wish. Who was she to think that there *was* more than this?

"It's almost time." Loretta straightened the sash on Dorothy's gown again. She pulled the ends together in a bow. "I should find my seat."

Dorothy's palms had started to sweat. "The next time we speak, I shall be a married woman," she said, hoping with every breath in her that this wasn't true.

Loretta slipped into the hallway without another word, pulling the door shut. A lock slammed into place, making Dorothy jump. For a long moment she just stood there.

She'd expected her mother to lock her in. Loretta Densmore was not the type of woman to take risks, especially when it came to her valuable possessions. It made sense that she'd keep her daughter—her *most* valuable possession—safely stowed away until the rest of her wedding party came to fetch her. Loretta was pragmatic. She wouldn't leave something this important up to chance.

Dorothy fumbled for the lockpicks hidden beneath her sash, but her fingers found only lace and silk, and the hard fabric edge of her corset.

"No," she said, her search growing frantic. No no *no*. She dug her fingernails into the lace until she heard something rip. They were *just* here. She replayed the last few moments with her mother. How Loretta had smiled into the mirror. How she'd straightened the sash on Dorothy's gown.

Dorothy's fingers went still. Her mother must've slipped that dreadful little hand beneath the sash and stolen her escape plan. She inhaled, and the breath felt like a blade sliding between her ribs. She wasn't going anywhere.

Dorothy caught sight of her reflection in the mirror—the painted eyes and lips and pinned curls. Her gown had been custom-made; the lace hand-embroidered by the yard and as delicate as a spiderweb, affixed with freshwater pearls that caught the light when she moved. She'd spent her entire life learning to bend the truth and stretch a lie. But her own beauty was the biggest lie of all. She'd never asked for it. Never wanted it. It had nothing to do with the woman she yearned to be. So far, all it had brought her was pain.

Disgust twisted Dorothy's mouth, transforming her face into something ever so slightly ugly. She yanked the veil out of her hair. Pins tangled in her curls and pinged against the floor. Her hair flopped over her forehead, frizzed and ruined.

Dorothy smiled. For the first time all morning she felt like her outside matched her inside. Then, her eyes moved to the hairpins on the floor, and she froze.

Hairpins.

She dropped to her knees and grasped one, holding it up to the light. It was long and thin and pointed. She tried to bend it between her fingers. Strong, too. Probably real silver.

Her lips twitched. These would do nicely.

2

ASH

OCTOBER 14, 2077, NEW SEATTLE

Wing flaps up. Carburetor in the cold position. Throttle fully open.

Ash tapped the EM gauge, and the dial spun and then settled, twitching, on the half-capacity mark.

"Damn," he muttered, settling himself back in the pilot's seat. His nerves ratcheted up a notch. Half capacity meant there wasn't enough EM—exotic matter—for a safe flight. The ship he was sitting in could explode the minute he got her into the sky. He increased the airspeed indicator to 75 knots, ignoring the blood pulsing in his palms.

He was often told he could be stubborn. Back in the army, his commanding officer had once said, *Son, you make mules look easygoing.* His childhood Sunday school teacher had commented, *Persistence isn't always a virtue.*

But Zora—who knew him better than anyone—had put it best when she'd said, *Will you give it up already? You're going to die.* She'd started muttering stuff under her breath whenever he walked past. *Dangerous. Idiot. Suicide mission.*

It wasn't a suicide mission. Ash had already seen how he was going to die, and it wasn't like this. But Zora might be right about the other stuff. The trips were too dangerous, and Ash supposed he might be an idiot for attempting them. But the alternative was worse. He thought of black water and white hair and gave his head a hard shake.

It was an unsettling side effect of knowing exactly how and approximately when he was going to die. The visions haunted him.

Besides, there were worse things to be known for than stubbornness. He could be known for betrayal, like Roman. Or viciousness, like Quinn. Given the choice, he'd take suicidal idiocy.

"The *Second Star* is moving into position for departure." He spoke out loud, a leftover habit from his days learning to fly fighter jets during World War II. There wasn't anyone around to hear him, but it felt wrong to prepare for takeoff without announcing it. Tempting fate even more than he already was. He increased the throttle, eyes trained on the windshield, heartbeat thudding like crazy. His ship began to hover.

"Easy, darling," Ash murmured, speaking in a tone of voice most people reserved for puppies and kittens. Sweat had gathered between his fingers and the yoke. He wiped his hands on his jeans, telling himself he'd managed hundreds of takeoffs worse than this one. Thousands, maybe.

You won't die today, he thought. *You might be badly maimed. Blinded. Arms and legs might be ripped from your body. But you won't die.* The thought wasn't as comforting as he'd hoped it might be.

Ash crossed himself, a habit left over from hundreds of Sundays spent in the Church of the Sacred Heart back in his sleepy Midwestern hometown. He pulled back on the throttle. Smoke filled the air around him as his time machine shot into the sky.

3
DOROTHY
JUNE 7, 1913, JUST OUTSIDE OF SEATTLE

The hairpins had worked perfectly—better than real lockpicks. Dorothy's hand-embroidered gown was covered in burrs, and mud squelched between her toes. She carried a painful pair of heels in one hand, doubting she'd be desperate enough to put them on. She rather liked the feel of mud beneath her feet. Besides, the train station was only a mile away.

She started working on her sob story as she walked. *Please, sir, I was supposed to be married today, but I was kidnapped on my way to the chapel, and I only just managed to get away. Could you help me buy a train ticket?*

Or was that too dramatic?

Thunder rumbled ahead of her. Light flashed through the clouds.

Dorothy tilted her head toward the sky. She'd always loved storms. She and her mother had spent a few months in Nebraska when she was very young, and the thunderstorms there had been strange, monstrous things. Dorothy used to lie on her back in the grass, counting the beats of silence between the shock of lightning and the crash of thunder to guess at how long it would take for the storm to reach her.

This storm was different. The clouds directly in front of her were roiling, and near black. But when Dorothy glanced to the side she saw sunshine hitting a grove of trees beyond the churchyard, the sky above blue and endless. The storm—or whatever it was—seemed confined to the area above the woods, leaving everything else untouched.

More light flared behind the clouds, and then an object appeared, sleek and metallic against the black.

Dorothy's heart skipped. Was that . . . could that be an *airplane*?

She watched the metallic object streak through the clouds, awed. She'd never actually seen an airplane before, but the sketches she'd glimpsed had shown small, clumsy-looking structures with zipping propellers and wings that looked like a strong wind could break them in half.

This was different. Big. Sleek. It had no wings or propeller, but two huge, circular contraptions that roared from the back of the vessel, burning red against all the black and gray. Its nose dipped toward the ground, and Dorothy gasped, taking a quick step backward.

It was *crashing*.

The strange vessel zoomed toward the earth, disappearing beyond the tree line. Seconds later, smoke curled above the gnarled branches, just a few yards away from where Dorothy stood.

Dorothy's chest tightened. She hurried through the trees like she was in a trance, ignoring the twigs pressing into the bottoms of her bare feet. The smoke smelled odd, not earthy and familiar, like campfire smoke. This was acrid. It burned the skin inside Dorothy's nostrils and left the air dry and hot, like it was in danger of bursting into flames.

A voice echoed through the trees, cursing.

The voice had the effect of fingers snapping, breaking Dorothy's trance. She stopped moving, fear zipping up her spine. What was she doing? She needed to get to town. The road was just a few yards ahead, and from there it wasn't far to the train station.

Dorothy started to turn, but then a bit of metal caught the sun and glinted.

Damn it all, she thought. When was she going to get another chance to see a *real* airplane? She only wanted a glimpse, just to see what it was like. She gingerly picked over the brush and into the clearing where the airplane had crashed.

A man crawled out of the cockpit, his face creased in frustration. He didn't see her, seeming lost in thought as he bent over his aircraft.

Dorothy stayed hidden, her eyes roaming over his thickly muscled arms, the blond hair falling across his forehead, the reddened skin at his neck. A heartbeat passed and, still, she didn't move. He seemed so different from anyone she'd ever known before, rugged and windswept, like he'd just blown in from another world. He was attractive, sure, but that didn't matter much to Dorothy. She'd known many attractive men. Usually their looks were the only interesting things about them.

But the pilot was . . . odd. Fascinating. His rough hands hinted at days performing hard labor, and his red skin told Dorothy he'd spent a lot of time in the sun. She wondered what sort of life he must lead, that he was outdoors so often. Her mother had always steered her toward slim, gentlemanly types in fancy clothes, with the kind of soft hands that'd never done anything more strenuous than lift a pen to sign a check. She cringed, remembering the feel of Avery's smooth, perpetually damp palm resting on hers. She didn't like her mother's taste in men.

The pilot swore, loudly and colorfully, making Dorothy flinch. She shook herself and turned back to the airplane, her eyes widening. It was massive—twice the size of any drawing she'd glimpsed in a book—the aluminum siding gleaming beneath layers of dirt, the words *Second Star* flashing beneath the grime. The nose of the ship came to a sleek point, and someone had painted a face on it—a toothy smile, narrowed black eyes.

The face made Dorothy grin, and she found her eyes wandering back to the pilot, wondering if he'd been the one to paint it. She stepped out from her hiding place without really planning to do so. Seeing her, the pilot stood too quickly, knocking his head against the side of his airplane.

"*Jesus.* What are you doing out here?" he asked, rubbing

the back of his head. He was taller than he'd looked when he was all crouched over, and his eyes were a nice, light hazel.

Dorothy found herself staring, again. She wanted to ask him about his airplane and his odd clothes and the funny painted face but, instead, she blurted, "I-I'm getting married."

She regretted the words as soon as they were out of her mouth. The whole point of running away was that she *wasn't* getting married, and, for some reason, she didn't want this man thinking that she was. She lifted her chin as the pilot studied her, hoping her cheeks hadn't turned pink.

"You're getting married?" the pilot said. Dorothy was used to the way men looked at her, how they leered, like she was something to be possessed instead of a person with thoughts and opinions that she'd come up with all on her own. But the pilot only frowned at her wedding gown, which was torn and muddy from running through the woods. "Today?"

It was such a strange sensation, to be charmed because a man *hadn't* looked at her, but Dorothy was charmed anyway. She found herself talking too quickly, her voice oddly breathless.

"I mean, I *was* getting married today, but now I'm not. I'm leaving, actually. As you can see. The, um, train station is just over there."

The pilot blinked. "Well. Good luck to you," he said, and he gave a little nod, almost like he was bowing, or saluting, or something gentlemanly like that. If he'd been someone like

Avery, Dorothy might've giggled and batted her eyelashes at him, but he wasn't like Avery, so she just balled her hands up in the sleeves of her gown.

How was she supposed to talk to a man if she wasn't trying to con him? She realized she had no idea.

The pilot bent back over his airplane, muttering another colorful curse under his breath.

Dorothy watched him work in silence for a moment before asking, "Is this yours?"

"Yup." He maneuvered a bit of machinery back into place, hands black with engine grease. He seemed rather good at . . . whatever it was he was doing. It was quite impressive, actually. Avery could hardly be counted on to prepare a cocktail without spilling it all over himself. It was a wonder they let him cut people open.

"I've never seen an airplane in real life before." Dorothy peered over the pilot's shoulder. "Does it still fly?"

"Of course it flies." The pilot scrubbed a hand over his face, looking suddenly exhausted. "Listen, miss, I don't mean to be rude, but this isn't going to fix itself. And, well, you look like you have places to be."

Dorothy could tell she was being dismissed but couldn't bring herself to walk away. She'd heard stories of men going up to the Alaskan territories to mine for gold and wondered if that's where he'd come from, if he'd been trying to fly his airplane over the Pacific Ocean.

As the thought entered her head, church bells began to ring, the sound a haunting warning that echoed through the trees. A shudder moved up Dorothy's spine. The service was beginning.

She bit her lip, looking into the woods beyond the pilot's head. The train station was just past those trees. She could lift a pocketbook, buy a ticket, and be well on her way to . . .

Where? Another dusty frontier town? The thought had seemed thrilling that morning as she'd planned her escape, but now she couldn't believe she'd been willing to settle for so little. She'd lived her whole life in towns like that, and she always assumed she'd die in one, too. Something about this airplane had her dreaming of more.

The church bells stopped abruptly. Silence filled the air as Dorothy forced her mouth into a practiced smile.

"Actually, I was hoping you might be able to help me," she said, tilting her head. "I appear to be lost."

"Excuse me for saying so, miss, but it looks like you meant to get lost." As soon as the pilot said this, the backs of his ears turned pink. "Sorry," he muttered, shaking his head. "That was rude."

Dorothy smothered a grin. The pink ears were sort of cute. They didn't fit with his rugged windswept-pilot image. She could see how it might be fun to tease him, just to get him to blush.

She stared a moment too long, and the pilot looked up, meeting her eyes. His eyebrows drew together, questioning.

Focus, she told herself. Cute ears or not, she didn't have time for teasing right now. She needed to get out of here.

"It must be terribly frightening, flying through the sky all alone," she said, shivering in a way that she hoped made her look small and helpless. "You should consider taking someone along for company."

"Company?" He rubbed the bridge of his nose with two fingers, leaving a trail of grease on his face. "Why would I need company?"

"You don't get lonely?" Dorothy said this in a low, breathy voice, and any other man on earth would've picked up that she was flirting, but the pilot just blinked at her.

"Lonely? In the *sky*?"

"Or . . . other places?"

The pilot frowned, like the concept of loneliness was only just occurring to him. "I don't suppose I do."

"Right." Dorothy's lip twitched. This was not going well. She peered in through the airplane's front window. Shiny, brightly colored pieces of paper littered the floor, and there seemed to be half a sandwich sitting on the passenger seat. It was a mess. But there was room for two. "How fast does this thing go?"

"What? Oh, don't—I mean, *please* don't touch that." The pilot tried to step between Dorothy and the plane, but she moved around him before he could touch her, slipping a hand into his jacket pocket while he was distracted. She wasn't sure what she was looking for—a wallet, maybe, or something to sell—but her fingers closed around what felt like a pocket watch. She slid it up her sleeve with two fingers. Then, she inched toward the front of the airplane, wiggling the door handle behind her back. Locked.

The pilot no longer seemed amused. He crossed the space between them in just two steps, and Dorothy backed into the cockpit, her body pressed against the hot metal.

"I'm going to need to ask you to stay away from my plane, miss," he said in a huskier voice. He was leaning over her, close enough that Dorothy caught the dry, smoky smell of his skin. He looked a little brutish up close. All hard angles, like a beast from a fairy tale. Only his eyes stayed soft and golden.

Dorothy felt a strange sense of familiarity when she looked into those eyes. Right now they were tired and frustrated, but she could picture them bright with laughter as clearly as if she'd seen them before—

Then the pilot looked away from her, shaking his head. "What do you want?"

Dorothy's mouth suddenly felt dry. She wanted to get away from this place. She wanted him to take her somewhere she'd never seen. The strange, hollow feeling opened up inside her.

More. I want more.

Despite all her training in deception, she found herself telling the truth. "Please. I just need a ride. I can't stay here."

The pilot considered her for a long moment. Something in his jaw tightened, and Dorothy felt a flicker of triumph, mixed with something like disappointment. She knew that look. She'd seen it on the faces of dozens of different men, seconds before they handed over whatever it was she'd asked them for.

She had him. It was a shame, really. He'd seemed so different. He'd seemed better. But in the end he was just like everyone else.

And then the pilot said, "No," and Dorothy realized she had him all wrong.

He turned back to his airplane and pulled open the front door. Dorothy was trying to remember the last time a man had told her no, and it took her a moment to react.

She grabbed the edge of the door before he could close it again.

"Why not?" The desperation in her voice made her cringe. "I don't take up much room. I won't bother you."

The pilot sighed. "Believe me, you wouldn't like it where I'm going."

"How do you know what I'd like?"

"I don't." He wrestled with the door. Dorothy grabbed it with both hands, holding it open. "No one likes it," he grunted.

"I could surprise you."

The pilot stopped struggling with the door for long enough to level her with a steady look. "Where I'm going, there are entire cities hidden underwater, and gangs that steal little old ladies on their way to the market, and a girl who lives off human flesh."

Dorothy opened her mouth and then closed it again. The pilot's eyes flashed with victory. He'd meant to terrify her, she realized, and he thought he'd succeeded.

But Dorothy didn't feel terrified. She felt awed. The place

he spoke of sounded like something from a story. "There are *cannibals* where you live?"

"Only one," he said, and pulled the door closed before she could recover. Dorothy swore and fumbled for the handle, but a tiny click told her he'd locked it. He raised two fingers to his brow in a kind of mock salute.

So long, he mouthed.

A rumbling, whirring sound filled Dorothy's ears. The woods around her grew smoky and hot. She started to cough. This was it, then. Someone was sure to find her and drag her back to the chapel and her mother and Avery. It wouldn't matter that her dress was ruined or that her feet were muddy. She'd be marched down that aisle, her mother standing directly behind her to make certain she said "I do."

Dorothy stumbled away from the airplane. The life of a doctor's wife stretched out before her. Dull dinners and lonely evenings and boring women with nothing more useful to talk about than charity events and where they were planning to spend the fall. Her mother seated next to her, pinching the inside of her arm to make certain she laughed at the right times.

The air was too thick, her corset too tight. Dorothy slid her fingers down the neck of her dress and tugged the lace away from her throat. She couldn't breathe.

It'd never occurred to her that she might actually have to marry Avery. She always assumed she'd get out of it, somehow. But now the bells were ringing for a second time, and the plane was about to take off and—

Dorothy blinked, frowning. Wait a minute. Was that . . .

There, at the back of the airplane, was a door.

Dorothy cast a glance at the front window to make sure the pilot was distracted. He was bent over a sea of switches and buttons, worry lines creasing his forehead. She eased around to the door at the back of the airplane and casually tried the handle.

Locked. Of course.

Dorothy slid a single hairpin out of her curls.

ASH

JUNE 7, 1913, THE PUGET SOUND ANIL

Ash raked a hand through his hair, and his fingers came away wet. He looked at them and felt like he might laugh.

Was he really sweating? *Sweating?* And over a girl?

It was guilt, he told himself. And he did feel guilty, not for refusing the bride's request for a ride—a girl like her wouldn't last a day where he was going—but for taunting her with stories of Quinn Fox. The Black Cirkus assassin was rumored to eat human flesh and torture grown men without mercy and, as far as Ash was concerned, the less said about her, the better. There were already too many stories about her floating around his own time. It seemed wrong to allow her to taint another.

He forced thoughts of Quinn out of his head, and the girl from the woods crept back in. He pictured her tilting her head, asking, *You don't get lonely?*, and felt heat flare up at the backs of his ears.

"Dope," he muttered under his breath. He said a silent

prayer of thanks that Zora hadn't witnessed that particular exchange.

Did you find yourself a little bride?, he imagined his best friend asking in that condescending tone she reserved especially for him. And she'd probably make kissing noises.

As a general rule, he didn't flirt, so at least that explained why he was so bad at it. He knew *how* to flirt—he lived with three rather attractive people, after all—but he'd lost his taste for it, the way someone might lose their taste for steak after nearly choking to death on a hunk of meat. It was hard to enjoy something when he knew it could kill him.

Black water, he thought, remembering his vision. *Dead trees . . .*

Ash double-checked the EM readings, to keep his mind off the girl and the vision and the fact that a drop of sweat was now creeping down his neck. The EM gauge had dropped to 45 percent after the crash, which was . . . well, it wasn't great. Still not suicidal, but definitely entering maiming territory.

He'd been on his way to 1908, to see some dumb old clock get built on a sidewalk outside a jewelry store. The clock in question—the Hoeslich clock—didn't seem particularly special, but the Professor had once said it was cool how people used to build clocks in public spaces and pointed out this clock in particular, which was all the encouragement Ash had needed. He'd spent the last year following the thinnest leads possible, but, as he'd already exhausted all the obvious places the Professor might've gone, he was starting to get desperate.

Unfortunately, he'd crash-landed several years too late.

The EM was too volatile to attempt another trip now, so his only choice was to head back to the workshop and hope things stabilized enough to check the clock the next morning.

Which meant losing another day in his rapidly dwindling supply of days.

Ash tensed his shoulders and then released them again slowly, imagining each individual muscle going slack. His leather jacket shifted and settled with the familiar movement, like a second skin. It was a trick for stress relief he'd picked up during his first week at flight academy, back when the other guys joked that he'd treated the fighter jets like they might bite. He curled his fingers into fists and released them one by one, trying to ready himself for another unstable trip.

"You don't die today," he said out loud, and the words calmed him, some. The only good thing about knowing how and when he was going to die was that it freed him up to do whatever he wanted in the meantime, knowing it couldn't actually kill him. It was fairly lame as far as silver linings go, but still. It was something.

Ash pushed the throttle to 2,000 RPMs. The *Second Star* lurched . . . the engine made a wheezing noise. Ash held his breath, waiting for something to go boom.

After a tense moment, his ship began to rumble, and he took to the sky.

The Puget Sound anil's upper edge curved above the sea like the outline of a great reflective bubble. It looked like a glimmer of light dancing over the waves, a glare from the sun, or a trick of the eyes. Only when he was directly in front of it could he see that it was a tunnel.

No, not really a tunnel, Ash thought. A chasm. A nothingness. You couldn't look right at the anil without your mind skipping around, trying to make sense of the thing that clearly did not make sense. Sometimes it looked like a swirling mess of mist and smoke. Sometimes it looked like a sheet of solid ice. Sometimes it looked exactly like what it was—a crack in time.

He aimed the nose of his ship toward the anil. Everything in the cockpit began to shake. Ash's leftover sandwich trembled off the edge of the passenger seat and fell to the floor in a mess of lettuce and mayo. Candy wrappers whirled around him in an invisible wind. Thick sheets of water crashed toward the ship's windshield and then dissolved into a swirling mist.

Then, the *Second Star* leaped into light speed, shooting him into the future.

Before he'd started traveling through time, the closest Ash had ever come to experiencing a tornado crashing through a hurricane while hail and rain hurtled from the sky was when he'd once tried to maneuver an F6F Hellcat through a hot zone. It'd been 1945, his first combat mission, and the clouds had been thick as soup. He took a wrong turn somewhere and, all of a sudden, the sky filled with bullets. He'd spent twenty terrifying minutes dodging enemy fire, hands gripping his yoke so tightly he thought he'd never be able to pry them off again. It seemed to take forever to reach safe air.

Flying into an anil made that day look easy.

Lightning flickered from the curved edges of the tunnel, and winds howled outside the ship's thin walls. Ash struggled to hold the yoke steady. When he first became a pilot, his instructors all warned him never to fly in winds over 47 knots. Winds in an anil often rose above 100, but, when it was working properly, the EM formed a sort of protective bubble around the ship and its occupants, keeping the inclement weather from tearing their fragile human bodies apart.

The dial on the EM gauge began to spin.

"Hold on, *Star*," Ash muttered. He didn't dare take his hands off the yoke. Thunder rumbled behind him, and icy sleet thrashed around the edges of the EM's bubble of safety. Lightning arced past his windshield—much closer than should've been possible had the EM been at full capacity. Ash flew the ship closer to the stormy, misty sides of the tunnel, where visibility was poor but the winds weren't quite as strong.

Prememories flashed through his head. Like always, they came on so suddenly that he could do little to prepare himself for what he saw.

A rowboat surrounded by black water . . . Ghost trees glowing white in the darkness . . . A woman with a hood covering her head . . . White hair fluttering in the wind . . . A kiss . . . A knife . . .

His eyelids flickered, but Ash forced them back open, gasping. He premembered the feel of cold steel between his ribs, followed by pain like he'd never experienced before. Sweat lined his forehead. He groped for the spot where he felt the knife slide into his body, but his fingers found only fabric and hard, warm skin. No wound. No blood. None of that had happened.

Yet.

Ash doubled over, stomach churning. The pain faded, but the prememories remained, playing on an endless loop at the back of his head. A rocking boat, and a girl with white hair kissing him, and then killing him. They were always the same. Always terrible.

The Professor had explained prememories best.

In an anil, all of time exists at once, he'd said in that slow, quiet voice of his. *This confuses our fragile human brains, creating pathways in our memories where they shouldn't exist yet. As a result, you'll find yourself remembering things from days—sometimes up to a year—into the future, just as easily as you remember what you ate for breakfast this morning.*

Up to a year. Ash had started premembering the girl with the white hair and the dagger eleven months ago, and the prememories had only gotten stronger over the last few weeks. The Professor said that might happen as the event you're premembering draws closer. If that was true, it meant that Ash had less than four weeks left to live.

He blinked, refocusing on what was going on outside his windshield. The sleet had turned to hard rain, and the wind had calmed a bit, allowing Ash to fly the *Second Star* back to the center of the tunnel. Time had landmarks, same as anything else, and Ash recognized the familiar swirling pattern that marked the year 2077. His exit.

He tightened his grip on the yoke and pulled the ship

straight, toward a curl in the mist that was lighter than the smoky walls around it. It felt a bit like driving through the fog at night. Ash couldn't always find the exact minute and hour he was looking for, but he had a knack for breaking down the months and days.

Lightning flashed in the black, and the air around Ash grew thicker, wetter, until the *Second Star* was completely submerged in water.

Home at last. Ash rubbed his eyelids with two fingers, unsurprised to see that his hands were shaking. The prememories had rattled him this time, more than usual. He could still feel the phantom ache of the dagger. A warning of things to come.

He'd seen his own death a dozen times. Maybe more. He should be used to it by now.

"Pull yourself together, soldier," he muttered. He hadn't been a soldier in nearly two years, but the word still rolled off his tongue more easily than his own name.

He flicked on his headlights, and twin beams of light cut through the darkness of the water. He angled the nose of the ship upward and the *Second Star* bobbed to the surface. He glanced behind, eyes peeled for shadows passing across the water.

The waves stayed still. But that didn't mean he was alone.

OCTOBER 14, 2077, NEW SEATTLE

The Professor's workshop was half garage, half boathouse. The oddly shaped structure rose straight out of the water, the siding made of found bits of tin and plastic, the roof cobbled together from old tires and pieces of plywood. The workshop still had real glass windows and a door that functioned via remote control, a luxury Ash and Zora—the Professor's only daughter—allowed themselves even though powering it cost a small fortune. Ash hit the control, and the door rumbled away from the wall, leaving ripples in the water around it. There was enough room in the station for two or three ships at least as large as the *Second Star*, but the only other vehicle inside was Ash's motorboat. He flew the *Second Star* up next to it and pressed the remote to close the door behind him.

The time machine's headlights illuminated walls covered in hooks holding dirty tools, spare parts, and dozens—maybe hundreds—of designs, schematics, and maps of the world at various points in history. The maps weren't legible anymore. The moisture in the air had warped the paper and made the ink bleed, but Ash didn't take them down. He'd been to some of those places: the Fairmont hotel lobby to watch the moon landing in 1969; the Cubs World Series–winning game in 1908; the White House lawn for the inauguration of the first female president, in 2021. Zora said the maps hurt to look at, but Ash liked remembering.

He began his postflight check, hitting switches and turning knobs until the *Second Star* lowered down to the water and the engine sputtered off. The green safety light clicked on, telling Ash he was good to exit. He unlatched his seat belt and pushed the door open, a headache already pounding at his temples.

"Evening."

The voice came from the shadowy end of the dock, where the *Second Star*'s headlights didn't reach. Ash's hand twitched at his side, half moving for the navy-issued snub-nosed Smith & Wesson revolver he no longer carried. But then his eyes adjusted to the dark, and he could just make out the shape of a very tall girl sitting in a plastic patio chair, her long legs crossed in front of her. She was polishing a greasy bit of engine with a spare cloth.

Ash relaxed and lowered himself to the dock, leaving the door to the cockpit open. "What are you doing here, Zora?"

"Wanted to see whether you'd make it back alive." She said this with no inflection, as though she were disappointed that he'd managed the feat.

"Here I am. Alive, and still dead sexy." Ash tried for a smile. Despite much evidence to the contrary, he liked to think it was a winning sort of smile. Zora didn't look up from her engine.

Ash stopped smiling. "You mad?"

Zora spit on the cloth and worked it deeper into the crevices of a gear. She never yelled. Didn't have to. In the past two years, her silences had gone from unnerving to brutal. They took up space and energy. They made Ash think of a great hulking animal sitting in the corner of a room, and he wasn't supposed to look at it or even acknowledge that it was there.

"Come on," Ash urged. "Use your words."

Zora placed the engine in her lap and straightened, finally looking Ash in the eye. "You never listen to my words."

"That ain't true."

"Like when I said, 'Ash, please stop flying that piece-of-junk ship.'"

"It's *my* piece-of-junk ship—"

"And 'Ash, I'll never talk to you again if you keep risking your life in that ship.'"

"You're talking real good now—"

"And, *Ash*, I swear, if you die, too . . ." Zora trailed off. She was quiet for a moment, and then she picked up the piece of engine and threw it—not *at* Ash, but not exactly *away* from him, either.

It skidded across the dock and toppled into the water with a soft splash, leaving a trail of grease behind it.

Ash was just about to point out, again, that it was *his* damn ship, and he could die on it if he wanted to, but that one word stopped him.

Too, Zora had said. If you die, *too*.

He closed his mouth. Zora swore under her breath and lowered her head to her hands.

Zora liked to pretend she didn't have emotions. If she were in charge of these things, her insides would hum along just like the motors she loved to take apart and put back together. It was why they never talked about the real reasons she didn't want Ash going back in time. She'd already lost too many people.

Zora stood and released the *Second Star*'s hood, bending over the engine. "You flooded it again."

Ash had known Zora for long enough to hear that she was really saying, *We can talk about your damn feelings as long as we do it while fixing this engine.*

Ash wasn't particularly good at fixing things, but he knew how to make himself useful. He pulled a wrench off the wall and crouched beneath the hood, next to Zora. "It's not my fault. The throttle keeps sticking."

"If you didn't jerk it around so much, it wouldn't stick." Zora took the wrench out of his hands and worked in silence for a moment, Ash watching over her shoulder. He absently touched the spot below his ribs where the dagger had pierced his skin. It didn't hurt anymore, but his nerves hummed with premembered pain.

"Is that where she stabs you?" Zora asked, cranking the wrench to the left.

Ash nodded. He'd told Zora everything he could premember, from the girl with the white hair to the rocking boat to the stabbing itself, but she couldn't figure out a way to keep it from happening any better than he could. He patted his side. "Right about here, yeah."

"Is your kissing really that bad?"

"Want to find out?"

"Ha ha," Zora said, humorless. She lifted her eyes without moving her head. "Anything new?"

Ash opened his mouth and then closed it again. There wasn't anything new, but there was stuff he hadn't told her. Emotional stuff. Like how, when he first saw the girl with the white hair, he'd felt *happy*. He'd missed her. And how, when she pulled the dagger on him, he hadn't just felt scared. He felt heartsick. Like the sun had gone out.

That was the feeling that haunted him, more than the stab wound. He wasn't just going to kiss this girl. He was going to fall in love with her. And she was going to betray him.

This was where his avoidance of flirting, and girls in general, came in. He knew he was going to fall in love, that the girl he fell for was going to kill him, and that both of these things were going to happen in the next four weeks. It made dating anyone seem a little like Russian roulette.

He cleared his throat. "Nothing new. But they're getting stronger."

Zora cleaned the grease away from a bolt. Ash could see that she was working hard to keep her expression calm, like they really were just talking about fixing an engine. But it took her three tries to twist that bolt back into place, and, when she wiped her hands on the back of her jeans, they were shaking.

"We can search his office again." She didn't meet Ash's eyes when she said this, probably because she knew it was hopeless. "My father was a slob. There might be something in his notes, something we overlooked—"

"Overlooked?" Ash raised an eyebrow. Zora had spent nearly every day since her father disappeared in that office. If there were something to find, she'd have found it by now.

"It makes more sense than flying that broken-down time

machine back to 1908 because, once, my father mentioned a clock he kind of thought was pretty!"

She was right, of course. The Professor hadn't left any sign of where or when he might be. He'd simply left.

Twelve months ago he'd packed a duffel bag in the dead of night and disappeared in his other time machine, the *Dark Star*, along with a second container of EM—this one full. Ash waited a few months for him to come back on his own, and then, thinking he was being smart, he took the *Second Star* back to the morning when the Professor first skipped town, figuring he'd catch the old man before he left, warn him that something was going to go wrong, and stop this whole mess before it started.

Technically, they weren't supposed to go back in time to change things. But the prememories had started by then, and Ash was desperate. He wasn't ready to die.

It hadn't mattered, anyway. Ash's ship had broken down in the water on his way to the garage. By the time he patched the bird up and got on his way, the Professor was long gone. He tried again the next day and the same thing happened. And again. And again.

It took Ash an embarrassingly long time to figure out that he was never going to make it to the Professor before he left because, if the Professor hadn't left, Ash wouldn't have gone back in time.

It was a paradox—a causal loop. A person couldn't go back in time to change something that would prevent him from going back in time. For instance, if he went back in time to prevent someone else from leaving—and he succeeded—it would stand to reason that the person wouldn't actually leave. So he'd never have to go back in time to prevent them from leaving. Paradox.

Thinking about the logic of it made Ash's head hurt, like a riddle he understood in theory but couldn't explain to anyone else. Besides, Ash hadn't ever really expected to find the Professor on his own; he just had to *do* something. Doing nothing meant obsessing over his impending death.

Black water and white hair and a dagger in his ribs.

He scrubbed a hand over his chin, suddenly exhausted. He didn't even know whether it was possible to stop a prememory—it was a memory, after all, which meant that it already happened, even if Ash hadn't lived through it yet. But he knew that if anyone could stop it, it was the Professor. If the old man was gone for good, so was any chance Ash had of living past the age of eighteen.

"I have a new plan to keep the prememory from coming true," Ash said, slamming shut the cockpit door. "Unfortunately, it means we're going to have to become lovers."

Zora didn't look up from the engine. "You're going to break your no-dating rule?"

"Only for you. It's a perfect plan, see? You don't have white hair, for one thing. And you'd never stab me."

"And the thought of kissing you makes me feel carsick."

"Ours will be a chaste love."

"You're wrong, anyway," Zora said. "I can think of at least

three reasons to stab you. Four if you count the fact that you left dishes in the sink this morning."

"You're always so violent," Ash called back.

Zora stood, wiping her greasy hands on her jeans. She looked so much like her father—broad-shouldered, with dark brown skin and thick black hair that she wore in a braided bun at the base of her neck. They had the same strong nose and jaw, the same black eyes, the same way of frowning with half their mouths when someone was being an idiot. Ash had to remind himself that they weren't the same person. Zora didn't know where her father had disappeared to, either.

I swear, if you die, too—

Ash gave his head a hard shake. She hadn't meant it that way, he told himself. The Professor wasn't dead. He was just missing.

He unlatched the door to the cargo hold and threw it open, grunting. "Back in the war, we had a word for—"

The rest of his sentence got caught in his throat.

There, crouched in the *Second Star*'s cargo hold, was the girl from 1913, her wedding gown creased and muddy around her.

She pushed the sweaty hair off her face. "I think I'm going to be sick," she said.

And then she vomited on Ash's boots.

LOG ENTRY—OCTOBER 10, 2073

22:47 HOURS

THE WORKSHOP

I've done it.

I, Professor Zacharias Walker, am on the verge of what will likely be the biggest scientific accomplishment of my generation.

I'm not sure how to adequately convey my excitement here. . . . I love good old-fashioned pen and paper as much as the next history-obsessed mega nerd, but if I'd recorded my research notes on video or hologram I could include a badass clip of myself jumping up and down and pounding my fists in the air here.

As it is, there's just no way to adequately describe the brilliance of this discovery. But I'll try.

Here goes: I've built a time machine.

Just writing those words has every hair on my arms standing straight up.

I built a time machine.

In the last year, every single theoretical physicist and mathematician and engineer on the planet Earth has tried. Every day there've been new stories detailing their failures, their loss of funding, their embarrassments.

But I've actually succeeded.

I . . . I think I'm going down in history.

My wife, Natasha, says this journal will probably be published for posterity someday, so I should be a little more careful about what I write from here on. In fact, maybe I'll just go ahead and remove those earlier pages, making this the first entry. No one needs to know that I couldn't remember the exact calculation for channel flow (that's a little scientific humor for you).

In any case, let's get the boring stuff out of the way first: My name is Professor Zacharias Walker. I'm thirty-eight years old and an adjunct professor of mathematics at the West Coast Academy of Advanced Technology (WCAAT).

For the last few years, I've been researching the properties of exotic matter. For those of you who don't follow science gossip (and, seriously, how could you not?), the study of exotic matter was trendy in scientific circles around ten years ago, when a NASA mission called SIRIUS 5 managed to obtain a small sample of the substance from the outer rim of the black hole MWG2055, the first black hole discovered in our galaxy. As you know, exotic matter is matter that deviates from normal matter and has "exotic" properties or, in other words, properties that violate the known laws of physics.

Interest in the material waned for a relatively simple reason: lots of scientists, tiny little bit of exotic matter. Well, I shouldn't say *waned*. There's still quite a bit of curiosity around exotic matter, but the next mission to MWG2055 isn't scheduled until 2080, and, in the meantime, my research proposal was the only one approved for funding.

I was lucky, to say the least. The EM sample is currently being held at WCAAT, and I happen to eat lunch at the same sandwich shop as half the members of the board of trustees . . . but all of that is beside the point. I've spent the last year researching the properties of EM, and I've discovered that exotic matter *stabilizes an anil.*

You'll know all about the *anil*, of course. The discovery of the Puget Sound anil, on June 10, 2066, was compared to man's landing on the moon. Wormholes have always been thought to be these teeny, tiny little cracks in space-time, but the Puget Sound anil—a type of wormhole—is massive. Easily large enough for a human to travel through.

As of this writing, the Puget Sound anil is the only known anil in existence, and it's conveniently located right off the coast of Seattle.

Since its discovery, every theoretical scientist worth his or her salt has been trying to come up with a feasible plan to use the anil for space-time travel.

Unfortunately, it's volatile. Winds in an anil are so strong they make a hurricane seem like a light breeze. Only two men have entered the Puget Sound anil, to date. The first was killed instantly. The second is in intensive care. I believe his doctors are still looking for a way to reattach his skin.

But exotic matter keeps those pesky walls from tearing you to bits.

It's quite a bit more complicated than that, of course. You need a vessel, and the exotic matter needs to be very carefully incorporated into the structure of the vessel, or else it won't extend its exotic properties to the normal matter it's protecting. (Normal matter is a scientific way of saying everything that isn't exotic matter. Like, a person.)

I've spent the last twelve months restoring an old A-10 Wart-hog, and I believe I've come up with a way to fuse the exotic matter with the vessel without upsetting the overall integrity of the matter. If my theory is correct, then the EM should extend its exotic properties to me when I enter the anil. Which is just a fancy way of saying that I'll get to keep my skin on my body.

The anil is supposed to be a tunnel that leads backward in time. So if I'm correct, I should be able to fly my modified fighter jet *backward in time*.

I can't believe I just wrote those words.

I need to pause for a second here. Think this through.

Technically, the EM is the property of the school. It's to be used "for research purposes only." Which means that, if I want to test my machine, I'll have to steal it.

I'm not sure of the ramifications for stealing university property. Hefty fine? Jail? Death by a thousand cuts?

And that's if I actually survive the trip through the anil. No one has before. In addition to a wife, I also have a thirteen-year-old daughter, Zora. She's the one who named my time machine the *SECOND STAR*, after that line in *Peter Pan* that tells you how to get to Neverland by following the stars: "Second to the right and straight on till morning." In any case, I don't want to die before I have a chance to see her grow up. So I should probably take all that into consideration.

And, of course, I'll have to think about the earthquakes.

I know we all hoped they were just some weird anomaly, a strange effect of climate change, but they've been occurring more frequently than any of us expected. The last one was only a couple of years ago, and it was a 4.7. Still not terribly strong, but if I happen to be on the sound when an earthquake hits I'm going to have to deal with waves. Big ones.

I could be killed on impact. *Would* be killed on impact.

Really, this thing is only worth doing if I know I'll be successful. If I have a guarantee.

I'm going to need to think on this for a bit.

UPDATE—23:13 HOURS

I have an idea. It's a little out there, but what the hell? We're talking time travel, here.

The thing is, I want a sign.

And I think I know how to get one.

I'm going to call this mission Kronos 1, after the Greek god of time.

Objective: Tomorrow, October 11, at 0800 hours, I will pilot the *Second Star* into the Puget Sound anil. If the exotic matter keeps the anil stabilized, as I theorize that it will, I will travel back in time to October 10, 23:13 hours, and I will stand on the sidewalk outside my workshop. And I'll wave.

I'm sitting in my workshop now, of course. And it happens to be October 10, 23:13 hours.

Which means there should be a future me standing on the sidewalk outside. Waving like crazy.

I just have to look.

UPDATE—23:15 HOURS

I guess I'm going back in time.

5

DOROTHY

OCTOBER 14, 2077, NEW SEATTLE

The images moving through Dorothy's head were too vivid to be memories, too precise to be dreams. It was as though a silent film were playing back all the strange and beautiful moments of her life so far.

She was five years old and running barefoot through the overgrown field behind their small house in Nebraska. The sky was achingly blue and monstrous above her. She felt like she might run forever. . . .

And then she was twelve and standing in the cold outside a tavern in Salt Lake City. Her mother had pinched her cheeks to give them color, and they still smarted. . . .

She was sixteen and perched on the edge of a stiff chair in Avery's parlor. A young man with bright curls and a wicked smile was seated beside her. He reached for her hand. . . .

And then she was kneeling in a clearing outside the chapel where she was to be married. She was covered in blood, screaming. . . .

No, said a firm voice inside her head. *That hasn't happened yet.*

The images came faster now, a whir of colors and shapes that Dorothy could no longer pick apart. She began to feel dizzy. Her stomach clenched.

This must be what dying feels like, she thought.

And then she woke up.

A girl with brown skin and black hair swinging over her shoulders was leaning over her, holding a damp cloth to her forehead.

"You're awake," the girl said. The skin between her eyes crinkled as she adjusted her chunky black glasses. "Thank God. No offense, but I really didn't want to mop the sweat from your forehead all night. Zora thought you'd be out for *hours*, but I told her she was being insane and, anyway, she can get intense when she doesn't have control over every single aspect of a situation, you'll see. Hey, did you really *stow away* on the *Second Star*? Because that's *so* seriously badass. Ash barely even lets me *touch* it."

She said all of this very quickly, her voice tinged with an accent Dorothy didn't recognize.

Dorothy sat upright, heart hammering as she looked around. She was on a lumpy mattress, inside a small room with low ceilings and no windows. Distantly, she heard the hum of voices.

"Where am I?" she croaked, throat scratchy. "Who . . . who are you?"

The girl placed her cloth inside a black case that looked

an awful lot like Avery's surgical bag, only the leather sides were hard instead of soft and creased, the buckles a much brighter silver.

"My name is Chandra." The girl pushed her glasses up on her nose with one finger. "You rode in with my friend Ash. You remember Ash, right? Ornery? Nice eyes but sort of smelly? Like maybe try some cologne to cover the stink of engine grease once in a while?"

"Oh." Dorothy felt her cheeks color, remembering the pilot with the gold eyes. *Ash.* She thought of the dry, smoky scent that'd clung to his skin.

She'd planned to sneak out of his airplane before he noticed that she'd stowed away, but the flight itself had been such a blur. She could clearly picture crouching in the small, dark space, her stomach dropping as the airplane lifted off the ground—

And then there was nothing except for those haunting memories and dreams that seemed almost real.

Dorothy brought a hand to her head, cringing with embarrassment. "W-where are we?"

Chandra seemed to be avoiding her eyes. She took a folded pile of clothes out of her bag and placed them on the bed. "These are pretty hideous, but you obviously can't go around wearing that gown. They won't fit, but they were all we could find on short notice." She snapped the bag shut and headed for the door. "I'll let you change—"

"Wait!" Dorothy swung one leg off the bed. "You didn't—"

But Chandra had already left the room, the door settling shut behind her.

Dorothy glanced at the clothes she'd left behind. She wasn't fond of charity. In her experience, people didn't give things away for free; they always had a price in mind, even if they didn't say what it was. Dorothy much preferred to steal outright. At least that was honest—in its own way.

But Chandra was right; she couldn't go around wearing a ruined wedding gown.

She removed her gown and unfolded the clothes, finding a pair of pants and a thin white shirt.

She pulled the T-shirt on over her corset, and then moved on to the pants, frowning. She'd never worn pants before. She pulled them over her legs and waist, fumbling with oversize buttons. They were much too large, even when she rolled the waistband down three times and cuffed the hems. Standing, she held her arms out to the sides and took a few practice steps around her small room.

Pants were *shockingly* comfortable. It was a sin no one had told her. No skirts bunching around her legs, tripping her up. She ran her hands over the fabric, and her fingers brushed against a thick seam. *Pockets.* Just like in men's trousers. She jumped up and down a few times to make sure the pants wouldn't fall from her hips, but they stayed put.

There was a mirror leaning against the wall. Dorothy stopped in front of it, examining her new appearance. She looked lumpy and boyish and unkempt, the opposite of the gleaming, beautiful bride she'd been this morning.

A grin unfurled across her lips. Perfect.

She reached for the door and then hesitated, fingers twitching. Chandra wouldn't tell her where they were. It bothered her, the thought that she might walk out of this room and into . . . well, anything. She didn't know the first thing about airplanes. She didn't know how fast they could fly, or how far, and she hadn't the faintest idea how long she'd been crouched in that cargo hold. She could be anywhere in the world.

A thrill ran through her, delicious and terrifying at the same time. She could be somewhere *dangerous.*

But wasn't this why she'd climbed on board the airplane to begin with? To go someplace new? Until now, her life had been one dusty town after another, an endless line of well-mannered men with expensive clothes and hungry eyes. The airplane had been a sign. There was something more. There *had* to be.

Carefully, Dorothy eased the door open and found an equally dark and dreary hallway, empty except for the pilot, who sat in a metal chair a few feet away.

She frowned.

He hadn't seemed to have heard her open the door. He was crouched over, whittling, his forehead creased as he maneuvered a knife around a shapeless hunk of wood. He'd stripped down to his undershirt, jacket hanging over the back of his chair. He still smelled of airplanes, and the scent tickled Dorothy's nose as she breathed it in. Chandra was wrong; it wasn't a bad smell at all. Compared to the cloying cologne

Avery was always wearing, it was actually sort of nice. It made Dorothy think of adventure and far-off places.

But the man himself . . . Dorothy tilted her head, allowing her gaze to linger over the muscles flexing along his back and shoulders. Again, she thought of how different he was from the men she usually associated with. She'd taken it as a good sign, at first, but now she thought there might be a reason her mother picked gentlemen. This man had been perfectly content to leave her alone in the woods after she'd asked—no, *begged*—for help. He'd been unmannered. Rude, even. Avery might wear too much cologne, but he wouldn't have left a girl alone in the woods.

But Avery would've expected something in return, said a voice in the back of Dorothy's head. She shook it away. *Everyone* expected something in return. Help never came for free.

She slipped a hand into her pocket, curling her fingers around the cool metal of the pocket watch she'd stolen from the pilot. It looked like little more than junk, unfortunately.

More trouble than he's worth, her mother would've said. Dorothy hated to admit that she was right. Still, there was no way to get past without him noticing, so she cleared her throat.

"Jesus," Ash muttered, flinching. "Do we need to get you a bell? I nearly took a finger off."

He waved his finger at her for some reason. Dorothy frowned.

"Where have you brought me?" she asked, stepping into the hallway.

Ash tugged the jacket off the back of his chair and shrugged it on. "Where have I—?" He shook his head. "How about thanks for cleaning up my vomit and hauling me out of the garage after I passed out?"

Dorothy winced. She didn't remember vomiting *or* passing out, and the knowledge that she'd done both sent heat flaring through her cheeks.

Her eyes flicked down the dark hallway. There were still no windows, but the voices were louder out here. Grease stains crawled up the walls, and the air held the heavy smells of fried fish and beer.

She wrinkled her nose. "Is this a *bar*?"

"Not up to your standards?" Ash's voice was light, but his smile was all teeth. "A friend of ours rents out the spare rooms, and he doesn't ask a lot of questions. My place is all the way across town, so we figured you were better off here."

"He doesn't ask questions," Dorothy echoed drily. She'd known plenty of men like that, although she certainly wouldn't brag about associating with them. Her opinion of Ash was worsening by the minute. "So I take it you drag a lot of unconscious people through bars?"

"You're the first, darling."

"Don't call me darling," Dorothy said, lip curling. She hated cutesy names. *Darling* and *princess* and *sweetheart.* They were usually used by men who wanted to remind her that they were in charge and she was just a pretty face. "My name is Dorothy, not that you bothered asking."

"Call me crazy, but I don't actually care to know the name

of the *stowaway* who snuck on board my ship." He raked a hand through his hair and said, low enough that he could be talking to himself, "That part of the *Star* isn't even pressurized. You're lucky the ride didn't kill you."

Dorothy was growing tired of this conversation. She hitched her too-large pants up a little higher, feeling the stolen pocket watch shift in her pocket. It might not be worth much, but the fact that she'd taken it from this unpleasant person meant that it was worth something to her. The corner of her lip twitched, thinking about it. "Ah, but it didn't kill me. Does that make me special?"

Ash's eyes zeroed in on her twitching lip, and Dorothy knew he was wondering what she found funny. It made her want to dangle his watch in front of his face. *Look what I took.*

"You're lucky *I* didn't kill you," he said, frowning.

This, at least, was a topic that interested her. "Why didn't you? Kill me, I mean? I'm a stowaway, as you so kindly pointed out. Why bring me here?" She remembered Chandra mopping her forehead, offering her clothes. "Why help me?"

Ash hesitated, choosing his words. "The short answer is that Zora wanted to get you somewhere safe. I'm guessing she didn't want your blood on her hands."

Safe. The word seemed to zip through the air.

She *knew* they'd landed somewhere dangerous.

Swallowing her nerves, she said, "And the long answer?"

Ash scratched his jaw. "Honestly? I wanted to see your face when you realized what you'd landed yourself in."

"You mean cities underwater and disappearing old ladies

and cannibal girls?" She tried her best to sound casual, like she was in on the joke.

Ash smiled back at her—a real smile, not the scary, toothy grin he'd flashed earlier. He turned and started down the twisting hallway, chuckling to himself.

It *had* been a joke, Dorothy thought, confidence wavering. Right?

Gritting her teeth, she followed.

The hallway opened into a cramped, bustling tavern filled with mismatched tables and chairs, candlelight casting shadows over the laughing crowd. Dorothy felt a flicker of interest. It was a bar, clearly, but it didn't look like any bar she'd ever been to before. She saw a few tables and chairs made entirely out of metal and, scattered around them, a selection of stuffed armchairs that looked better suited for a living room. There weren't many windows, but an assortment of strange objects covered the walls—hubcaps and oil paintings and old dolls.

And there were women. Dorothy and her mother were usually the only women at the bar, but this place was filled with them—drinking like men, and dressed like men, in trousers and jackets, their hair scraped back in messy buns. Dorothy had assumed she'd look out of place in her lumpy clothes, her hair undone, but she fit right in. How odd.

Had they gone someplace where temperance laws were in effect? She'd heard of speakeasies cropping up in cities where alcohol sales were prohibited, but she and her mother tended to avoid those places. Men were harder to con when they were sober.

She cast her eyes around the room, searching for an exit. She had no intention of staying with this pilot. Now that he'd marked her as a stowaway, there was little chance he'd leave his pocket unguarded, and she'd need money. *Real* money, not whatever meager funds selling the cheap pocket watch might get her. She needed a much larger score if she were going to make it here . . . wherever *here* was.

Luckily, the bar was crowded, the people packed together tight. It would be easy to slip a watch off a wrist, a wallet out of a pocket. Dorothy's fingers itched.

But then Ash's hand was on her back, and he was angling his body between her and the crowd. He jerked his chin and said, "The rest of the team is over there."

"Team?" Dorothy's skin prickled. He meant to keep her from leaving, but he wasn't using force just yet. In fact, his fingers barely brushed her back, like he was afraid of touching her. "Team of what?"

Ash herded her through the crowd, shouldering past the people around them. She could step on his foot and make a run for it—but the bar was crowded, and she didn't see an exit. And there was the small matter of stowing away being illegal. Ash hadn't mentioned getting the police involved, but Dorothy didn't want to give him a reason to change his mind. She was still a minor, after all. They could call her mother.

Chewing on the inside of her cheek, she let him guide her to a table near the back of the bar. Chandra was already there, sitting beside a tall boy with even darker skin, tightly braided black hair, and a serious expression on his face.

Dorothy did a double take. Not a boy—a *girl*.

"See? What did I tell you? Isn't she absolutely gorgeous?" Chandra shifted to the side, making room for Dorothy on the bench directly opposite the girl who'd looked like a boy. "Ash, why didn't you tell us she was gorgeous?"

"Don't you two go making friends," Ash grunted, pulling a seat up to the end of the table. Dorothy noticed that his eyes flicked to her and away, as though checking to see if what Chandra said was true. "We're not keeping her."

"She's not a stray cat, Ash," said the girl who'd looked like a boy. "You can't decide what to do with her." Turning to Dorothy, she added, "I'm Zora. It's nice to meet you."

She held out her hand for Dorothy to shake, like they were gentlemen. Dorothy took it, an excited thrill moving through her. Zora sat like a man, too. Knees apart, arms slung lazily across her chest. Loretta would have called it unseemly, but Dorothy couldn't help but be impressed with how comfortable she seemed. Not like she wanted to *be* a man, precisely, but like she didn't care what a man might think of her.

Maybe she's a suffragette, she thought, sliding onto the bench beside Chandra. It wasn't until she was seated that she noticed a fourth person at the table with them. He was massive—easily the largest man Dorothy had ever seen—but he somehow blended with the shadows, his skin and hair pale beneath black clothes. The bones in his face slanted at sharp angles, causing the skin to pull too tight over his cheeks and chin.

"My name is Willis," he said, tipping his head toward

Dorothy. His voice was smooth velvet, like the voice of a jazz singer. "It's a pleasure."

"I'm Dorothy," Dorothy said, her attention sharpening. Four of them, one of her. Not exactly great odds, if it came to that.

Something hit her, then. She was *alone*. For the first time in her life, she was really and truly alone. Her mother wasn't waiting in the next room, her pearl-handled pistol hidden in the folds of her skirt. These people could do whatever they wanted with her.

But Zora only slid a glass of something clear across the table. "This is Dante's moonshine. He makes it in-house and it tastes like . . . well, it tastes like gasoline, but I think you're going to need it."

Dorothy looked down at the glass but didn't pick it up. Her mother had once slipped ipecac into a man's drink when he wasn't looking. He'd spent the next twenty minutes vomiting onto the floor while she dabbed at his face with her handkerchief to distract him from her hand slipping into his pocket. Dorothy had stopped accepting drinks from strangers after that.

"Thank you," she murmured, for pretense. She curled her fingers around the glass and waited to see what would happen next.

A silence fell over the table, interrupted by the clinking of glasses and muffled laughter elsewhere in the bar. They were all staring at her.

When no one spoke, Dorothy cleared her throat. "Is someone going to tell me where we are?"

Chandra laughed nervously. Under her breath, she said, "*This* should be interesting."

"Hush," Willis murmured. "She needs to know."

"Please, both of you, just be quiet so I can think." Zora scrubbed a hand over her face, looking suddenly exhausted. "I'm not exactly sure how to . . . my father always did this part."

"For God's sake," Ash muttered. He turned to Dorothy and said bluntly, "The question isn't *where* you are, but *when*. You're in the future. The year 2077, to be exact."

Whatever Dorothy had been expecting, it wasn't this. A surprised laugh burst out of her. "Pardon?"

"It ain't a joke, sweetheart," Ash said. "You climbed on board a time machine, not an airplane. We're still in Seattle, but we've traveled nearly two hundred years into the future. People call it New Seattle now."

Dorothy swallowed. "So when you said you were a *team* you meant you were a team of . . ."

She shook her head. She couldn't make herself say it.

Ash's eyes lingered on her. "Time travelers. Cool, right?"

"Ash," said Zora, teeth clenched. "You're not actually helping."

"Helping with what? She's a *stowaway*." His eyes flicked away, and he leaned back in his seat, arms crossed over his chest. "I don't see why we owe her an explanation." He wagged a finger at Dorothy. "Let this be a lesson not to climb on board strange ships."

Willis frowned, the ends of his mustache drooping. "That's cold, Captain. She just got here."

"Yeah, when I first got here, I thought those motorboats outside were rakshasas." Chandra turned to Dorothy. "Rakshasas are, like, these demons who consume human flesh. Zora had to stay up with me all night, holding my hand and promising me the boats weren't going to eat me."

"Flesh," Dorothy echoed. She didn't realize she'd brought the glass to her lips until the moonshine was halfway to her mouth. She put it down again, hard enough that a bit of drink sloshed over the side. She wasn't sure she trusted herself not to drink it.

Zora said, "I know it's a lot to take in, but I'd be happy to answer any questions you might have. And Ash—"

"Questions?" Dorothy spoke on an exhale, her voice breathy and incredulous. "About what? *Time travel?*"

She could hardly believe the words had come from her mouth. She'd heard some far-fetched stories in her life, but this—

Well. This was insulting. She pushed away from the table and, when no one moved to stop her, she said, "I think I've heard enough, thank you."

Chandra's face fell. "You're leaving?"

Dorothy's gaze lingered on Willis. "If I'm free to."

"No one's keeping you here," Ash said. But the corner of his mouth twitched, like he was disappointed, and when she took a step away from the table he caught her by the wrist. "Just promise me one thing, darling."

A shiver ran up her arm at his touch. "I *told* you not to call me that."

She pulled away and, to her surprise, his grip loosened immediately, sending her stumbling.

"*Dorothy*, then," Ash said. It was the first time he'd used her name, and it sent a strange thrill through her. Like butterflies but less pleasant. Moths, maybe.

It bothered her that this man could have *any* effect on her, pleasant or not.

Something in Ash's eyes seemed to soften. He nodded toward the back of the room and said, "There's a window in the bathroom over there. Promise me you'll take a look outside."

Dorothy lifted her chin, willing the moths in her stomach to be still. "Why?"

Ash was staring now, and it made her feel uncomfortable. He took a swig of her discarded drink. "Just trust me." Then, like an afterthought, "If you're capable of trust."

LOG ENTRY—OCTOBER 11, 2073
17:01 HOURS
THE WORKSHOP

Kronos 1 didn't go exactly as planned.

The thing is, no one has ever explored the inside of an anil before. We couldn't, obviously, because we didn't know how to stabilize it. I had theories about what I would find, but nothing concrete.

The EM worked exactly as predicted. Once it was effectively incorporated into the structure of the *Second Star*, it created a kind of protective bubble around the ship and its occupants (or, in this case, occupant). The gauge I installed in the *Second Star* showed the EM holding steady at 95 percent throughout the duration of my trip.

As such, I became the first man to successfully fly into the anil without the winds ripping my vessel to pieces.

(And I didn't bring a camera. I mean, I'm not sure whether a camera would work inside a crack in time and space, but still.)

In lieu of a photograph, here's a description of what I saw:

The anil is approximately twenty yards in diameter, with walls made out of what appears to be a kind of swirling smoke, or clouds. The color of the walls changes as you move through time, from dark gray to light blue to almost black. Occasionally, I saw lightning flash behind the clouds, or else I'd catch a brief glimpse of what appeared to be distant stars.

All was going well until it came time to leave the anil. As you'll remember, my mission was to travel back in time by one day, show up outside my office window, and wave. Sounds easy, right?

Unfortunately, like most monumental scientific achievements, it was not actually easy.

The first problem was trying to figure out how to travel back by just one day. The tunnel forks when you enter it, which makes sense. One direction leads into the past, the other into the future. I chose the most logical course of action, based on the Western understanding of backward and forward. Which is to say, I took a left.

Good choice! I mean, it was a fifty-fifty shot but still, I was feeling pretty confident with myself. My scientific intuition was helping me out!

Well, after that my scientific intuition failed me big-time. I made another "intuitive" guess as to how long I had to stay in the tunnel in order to go back in time a day. I figured I'd travel for an hour.

I admit, I landed on "an hour" somewhat arbitrarily. It seemed like a nice, round amount of time. A good place to start.

I wound up surfacing in the 1880s. I knew from the lack of electric lights on the shoreline that I'd guessed wrong. Seattle was a small port town in the 1880s, and all I could see from out in the sound were some small wooden houses and a dock crowded with a few sailboats. I would've loved to go out and explore the Seattle of almost two hundred years ago, but I'd been wearing jeans and a T-shirt, and I was a little worried someone might see my time machine and start worshipping me as a God. (That's a joke . . . sort of.)

In any case, at least this mistake provided me with a metric to use. One hour in the anil = approximately two hundred years.

Using that conversion rate, I was able to calculate a more appropriate place to exit the anil.

And I still missed my rendezvous by three weeks.

But I lucked out again, sort of. I was three weeks early, not three weeks late, so I ended up hanging around Seattle in a baseball cap, trying to remember exactly where "present-day me" had gone and hoping I wouldn't recognize myself wandering around the grocery store.

I know what you're thinking. Isn't *three weeks* a long time to spend wandering around a city, trying not to be seen by your wife and child and present-day self? And the answer is yes, of course it is. But it wasn't a total loss. I booked the cheapest motel I could find and used the extra time to put together a more robust theory for my anil stabilization technique, which I turned into a proposal for a series of "exploratory missions through space-time."

Monumental though this discovery might be, my findings are still in the preliminary stages. There's so much we don't know about the anil, about time travel, about the physics of space-time. Those additional three weeks were essential, as they allowed me the time to sort through my research without worrying that another physicist or mathematician might beat me to the punch.

As of this morning, WCAAT has approved my request for funding. They're allowing me to hire a small team for the next stage of my research. I have a whole stack of résumés on my desk right now.

First stop: assistant.

I really need an assistant.

ASH

OCTOBER 14, 2077, NEW SEATTLE

Ash watched Dorothy weave through the crowd, guilt creeping over him in a steady fog. He knew from experience that the time-travel conversation took a minute to sink in. He didn't have to be such an ass about it. A real gentleman would've—

His mind snapped shut on that line of thinking. He didn't owe her anything. He was just getting turned around because she was pretty.

But it wasn't just that. Ash had known beautiful women before. He'd turned his back on plenty of them in the last year, since deciding he wasn't going to date until he figured this pre-memory out. There was something else, something between him and Dorothy. Something that felt almost physical.

Familiarity, he realized. Even though they'd only met a few hours ago, she already felt like someone he knew.

But surely that was just part of the manipulation thing she was doing, right? He'd noticed it back in the churchyard, how she'd batted her eyelashes and tilted her head, trying to charm him into thinking she was a friend, someone he could trust.

And then, as soon as his back was turned—

He shook his head, feeling disgusted with himself. He wouldn't let his guard down again. If there was ever a girl who was trouble, it was one who snuck on board a time machine, wearing a wedding gown.

It was her own damn fault she was in this mess.

Zora didn't seem to feel the same way. She rounded on him, snarling, "What is *wrong* with you?"

Ash shifted his eyes away from Dorothy, pretending to study what was left of his—*her*—drink. "She's a *stowaway.* Did I miss the part where we owe her something?"

"She's all alone—"

"Explain to me how that's our problem." This conversation felt wrong. What did Zora care about some girl? Why bother fighting when they had so many other things to worry about? "I didn't *invite* her on board, Zor."

Zora rubbed her eyes. "I need a drink."

Ash lifted Dorothy's discarded moonshine. "You're in the right place."

She stood, glowering at him. "Make yourself scarce before she gets back. I really don't think you should be doing any more of the talking."

"Hey!" Ash called, but Zora was already shouldering her way through the crowd, and she didn't turn back around.

A nasty little shiver ran down Ash's neck as he turned back to his drink. Dorothy had him on edge, and it wasn't just because he'd accidentally stolen her from the past. Ash hadn't so much as spoken to a girl besides Zora and Chandra since the prememories started. He couldn't even *look* at one without thinking of a rocking boat and a kiss that ended with a knife ripping through his body. He'd thought that avoiding girls would keep the prememory from happening, that the woman he loved couldn't kill him if he never got around to falling in love with her. And then some bride from the 1900s had climbed onto his ship and inserted herself into his life without asking.

And now he couldn't stop thinking about her.

He raked a hand through his hair, trying to ignore the blood pumping in his ears. He wanted her gone. But that meant another trip back in time, another day wasted. The sand in his hourglass was already running low.

Willis was staring when Ash looked up again, the tips of his blond mustache trembling.

Ash's stomach gave an unpleasant twitch. "Are you *laughing*?"

"Sorry, Captain. I just never figured you for the type to take a bride." Willis smoothed the edges of his mustache with two fingers. "Mazel tov, by the way."

Chandra snorted so violently that she smacked an elbow into her glass, sending the remains of her cocktail into her lap. Willis slid her a napkin.

"Real funny," Ash muttered, frowning.

"Don't be like that," Chandra said. "He's just talking."

"Talk about something else."

"Okay." Chandra leaned across the table suddenly, her

voice low and conspiratorial. "Did you hear that Quinn Fox files her teeth into points?"

Now Ash's teeth were clenched. "Not her."

Chandra closed her mouth, looking stricken. "So I suppose we should all sit here in silence?"

"Would silence be so bad?" asked Ash, rubbing his eyes.

"Tell him about your new crush, Chandie," Willis said, flashing Ash a weary look. "That's what we were talking about before you got here."

Chandra sighed theatrically and looked across the room. Ash took another drink, following her gaze to the short bartender wiping down glasses behind the bar.

He started to choke. "*Levi?*" he coughed out, pounding his chest with a fist. The burning liquor carved a line down his throat. "You think Levi is cute?"

They'd all known Levi for ages. His father owned the bar.

"I already told her it was a bad idea," Willis said, studying a fleck of dirt beneath his thumbnail. "You're going to ruin the bar, Chandie."

"I will not!" Chandra said. She slumped back in the booth, pouting. She was the baby of the group by less than a year, and she seemed to think this meant she could get whatever she wanted with a trembling lower lip. "Couldn't we go back to a time period where dating wasn't so freaking *hard*," she asked. "Did you know that in the nineteen nineties, single women would go to bars and wear beautiful dresses and pick up men?"

"She found some old television show," Willis explained,

using the corner of a cocktail napkin to dab at his mustache. Chandra was obsessed with pop culture. She was originally from ancient India, and the Professor used to make her watch television to help with her English. It'd worked a little too well. Now she watched constantly, becoming fixated on a different decade in history every other week. Last week it was some anime series from the 2040s. Now, apparently, she was all about the 1990s.

"That's where these came from," Willis added, tapping the rim of his cocktail glass. The liquid inside was violently pink.

"It's called a cosmopolitan," Chandra said, pinching the stem of her glass with her fingertips. "Pretty, right?"

Ash frowned. He hadn't realized Dante owned pink liquor. "You're only seventeen years old," he said. "I'm not dropping you off eighty years in the past so you can drink and flirt with boys."

Chandra cocked her head to the side, studying him through her glasses. The lenses were Coke-bottle thick and left her dark eyes bugged. "So you're the only one who gets to use time travel to pick up dates?"

Willis's mustache twitched. Chandra's cheeks went pink.

"Zora was right," Ash muttered, standing. "I really should make myself scarce before your new friend gets back."

Chandra started to object, but Ash was already out of his seat and wading through the crowd, finishing his drink as he walked.

He knew he was being an ass, but he couldn't help it.

He had no interest in following this particular line of conversation just now. Willis and Chandra knew he didn't like talking about his love life, but Ash hadn't told them about the prememory, so they figured he was just prickly about mushy stuff.

Zora once asked him why he was keeping his best friends in the dark.

"And they're not just your friends," she'd pointed out. "They're your teammates. Dad brought you all back from the past to work together. They deserve to know what's going on with you."

She was right, obviously, but Ash just muttered something about not wanting to worry them and changed the subject. That was true, sort of, but there was a more selfish reason, too. Ash didn't want to spend his last weeks on earth dodging sympathetic glances, worrying that people were talking about him every time a conversation dried up when he entered the room. If the prememory was true, and he really had only a few weeks left to live, he wanted to enjoy every damn day.

Ash finished the rest of his drink and set the empty glass down on the bar, nodding at Levi.

Annoyingly, he found his thoughts returning to the bride. Had Zora found her and coaxed her back to the table? Did she believe her, yet, about the time travel? He couldn't help glancing at the bathroom door as he waited for Levi to make his way to his side of the bar, picturing her splashing water on her face, studying her reflection.

Had she looked out the window yet?

7

DOROTHY

Dorothy found the washroom and slipped inside, shutting the door firmly behind her. The noise of the tavern was instantly muffled. Exhaling, she switched on the faucet and gathered a handful of water to splash onto her face. She'd felt grimy since she got there. Everything she'd touched seemed layered with damp and mold.

Water dripped from her face as she straightened, her eyes landing on the window beside the sink. The curtains were tightly drawn.

Look outside, she thought. *Just trust me.*

She bristled, thinking of the way Ash's lip had curled as he teased her. It might have been charming if he hadn't been being such a rat. The moths started flapping around her stomach again. *Stupid moths.*

She wiped her face with the bottom of her shirt. Did he think she *wouldn't*? That she'd be so terrified by all their nonsense that she'd tremble at the thought of looking out a *window*?

She glanced at the bathroom door, imagining Ash back at the table with his friends, laughing about how gullible she'd been. *Time travel.* The nerve.

Steeling herself, she yanked back the curtains.

The ground seemed to tilt. She had to grab hold of the sink to keep her legs from going out beneath her.

She exhaled, her voice almost a sigh. "*Oh.*"

She saw light.

This wasn't the kind of light she was used to. It was stronger, *brighter*, and it took her a moment to realize this was because the setting sun was reflecting off glass skyscrapers and massive buildings with hundreds of windows—

All half-submerged in steely gray water.

She lifted a hand to her mouth, fingers trembling. The city seemed to be growing—weed-like—straight out of the water itself. She'd never seen anything like it before. She moved closer to the window, her breath ghosting the glass.

Something must've happened, some horrible disaster, to leave the entire city underwater.

But even as she thought this, she realized that the city was much more advanced than the one she'd just left behind. Buildings had been built closer together, and they towered over her head, seeming to stretch high up into the clouds. And there were so many of them! More buildings than Dorothy had ever seen in one place at the same time.

The city had been made into something extraordinary. And then it had been destroyed.

Well, not completely destroyed. Complicated-looking

bridges crisscrossed the water in an elaborate grid. Ladders stretched past her, and, when she followed them up, she saw that they connected to a second level of rickety wooden passageways just over her head.

While she was studying them, a man crawled out of a window in the building across the waterway, hurried over the bridge, and disappeared around a corner. Dorothy craned her neck to see where he was going, but he'd already gone.

She released a small, breathless laugh. What had happened here? Why had that man used a window instead of walking through the front door? She glanced back at the water sloshing up against the walls as a thought occurred to her—were the bottom floors of the building still *underwater*? That seemed impossible, but why else would the people living here need all the bridges and the docks and the ladders?

She pressed a hand to her chest. Her heart felt suddenly light and fluttery. *This must be what a near-death experience feels like*, she thought, giddy. Time slowed enough for her to notice small, seemingly insignificant details. A brightly colored wrapper floated past her. A ghostly pine tree grew straight out of the water. Its bark looked like it was covered in a layer of chalk.

Dorothy fumbled with the window latch. Part of her knew she should go straight back to their table and beg Zora and Ash to tell her what was going on.

But the other part was already pushing the window open.

ASH

"Another round?" Levi pulled a bottle of clear liquid out from behind the hubcap that served as a bar before Ash could answer, and filled his glass. Ash started to take out his wallet, but the bartender wrinkled his nose. "You better be reaching for a gun, man. You know my dad won't take your money."

Ash let his hand fall to his side. On the far end of the bar, a time-lapse version of Levi caught his eye and lifted a wrinkled hand in salute. Dante hadn't let Ash pay for a drink since he'd gifted the old man a boxy television set that now hung on the wall above the bar, mutely playing the nightly news. Ash had nicked the television the last time he'd flown through the tail end of the twentieth century. Well-made tech was near impossible to come by since the earthquake.

Levi slid the drink across the bar, sloshing clear liquid over the sides. Ash nodded in thanks. "Any noise tonight?"

"Heard a few boats earlier. They didn't get close, but it's early yet. You know the Black Cirkus doesn't get feisty until full dark."

The Black Cirkus was the local gang. They were either the hope of the new world or terrorist monsters, depending on who you asked. Ash tended to put his money on the latter.

Ash frowned, lifting the sticky glass to his lips. "A few?" Hearing even one boat used to be cause for concern.

Levi shrugged and pulled a dirty towel from his apron to wipe up the spilled liquor. "That's not the worst of it. Guess who Pop saw walking around the Fairmont this afternoon?"

Ash stifled a sigh. It seemed he would be unable to escape this topic of conversation tonight.

"Quinn Fox," Ash replied. The name tasted bitter on his tongue. He chased it with a sip of his drink. Dante's hooch burned all the way down his throat and settled in his gut like a tire fire, but Ash was careful not to make a face. Levi was known to throw a patron out for cringing at the taste of his father's terrible liquor.

"In the daylight and everything," Levi said, whistling through his teeth. "Did you hear that last week she killed a man with a *spoon*. She just . . ."

Levi mimed jabbing a spoon through someone's eye and made a disgusting *splurt* sound. Ash raised his eyebrows, trying hard not to grimace. He couldn't say exactly why he disliked hearing about Quinn so much. He knew people found her intriguing, that they gossiped over why she never removed the hood that covered her face (*disfiguring scar? lips stained with blood?*) and how she rose so quickly up the ranks of the Black Cirkus. He knew they secretly enjoyed telling stories of whatever newest horror she'd committed, even as they were disgusted by them. He knew it was their way of coping, but he couldn't join in.

Ash only ever found Quinn disturbing. A symbol of just how far their city had fallen.

"You know who they say she's hanging with, don't you?" Levi asked, watching Ash from the corner of his eye.

Ash jerked his head up in a half nod. He knew.

Dante suddenly raised a hand, motioning for the patrons to quiet. The old man was staring at the television behind the bar. The image on the screen skipped, then froze—then disappeared entirely.

Two shadowy figures appeared in its place. They wore hoods that covered their faces and stood in front of a tattered American flag. One had a sketchy crow painted on the front of his coat. The other had a fox.

"Speak of the devils," murmured Ash.

Levi's eyebrows went up. "That's her?"

"That's her," Ash said, dread pooling in his stomach. The Black Cirkus's nightly address had become famous, but he was never fully prepared to see the black-clad Cirkus Freaks on his television screen. "Do we have to watch this garbage?"

"Are you kidding?" Levi asked. Even those who were staunchly against the Cirkus found the nightly address morbidly fascinating. He turned up the volume.

"Friends," Quinn said. As always, her voice was heavily distorted, more machine than human. "Do not attempt to adjust your television. Our broadcast hack has taken over every channel. It cannot be traced.

"I am speaking to you at a moment of crisis. It has been over two years since the Cascadia Fault mega-quake devastated our once great city. Since that time, nearly thirty-five thousand people have died, our own government has turned their back on us, and violence and chaos rule our waters."

"*Your* violence," Levi muttered. He reached below the bar, and Ash saw his fingers tighten around the baseball bat he kept hidden there. The nightly address was prerecorded. The Black Cirkus was likely roaming the city already, looking for new recruits—that's what they called the people they kidnapped and forced to join their gang. They hadn't broken into Dante's Tavern yet, but it was only a matter of time.

Ash looked down at his knuckles. He tried to tune the Cirkus out, but Quinn's voice cut through his thoughts.

"Those deaths could have been prevented," Quinn said. "They can *still* be prevented."

Silence gathered in the bar as every face turned toward the television screen. Everyone remembered the earthquake. There wasn't a man or woman alive who didn't lose someone during that disaster.

A photograph of the Professor's face flashed onto the screen. Ash caught the edges of his mentor's salt-and-pepper hair and subdued smile out of the corner of his eye. It was the same photograph the Black Cirkus had been showing for the last year.

"This man has discovered the secrets of time travel," Quinn droned on. "He is capable of going back in time and reversing our fate. He could return to a time before the earthquake destroyed our city. He could save thousands of lives. But he refuses.

"The Black Cirkus does not think it's fair for one man to decide the fate of all of us. We believe that *everyone* should be allowed to change their pasts. Join the Black Cirkus, and we'll use time travel to build a better present, a better future. Join the Black Cirkus, and we'll create a better world."

The words hardened Ash's spine. For years people had been too distracted by the Cirkus's violent methods to take their message seriously, but they were starting to come around. Ash had overheard more than one conversation about how maybe the Black Cirkus had the right idea—maybe they *should* find the Professor and force him to fix their world.

But those people didn't know how dangerous time travel was, how volatile. How any change, no matter how small, could ripple through history, leaving even more devastation in its wake.

The Professor's photograph disappeared, and the image on the television screen froze. The two shadowy figures stared down at them. Hateful and haunting.

"So that's him, right?" Levi asked, squinting at the boy to Quinn's right. "That's—"

"That's him." Ash chewed the inside of his cheek, studying the slight, dark boy with the crow painted on his chest. It didn't matter that he had a hood pulled over his head, or that the angle of the lights left his face in shadow. Ash would always recognize Roman.

He was momentarily transported to another booth in

another bar. He'd just laughed so hard at some story Roman told that he'd spit beer across the table. He'd pretended he hadn't seen Roman move a finger along the back of Zora's hand, his touch lingering.

He'd been the Crow even then. Watching everything. Collecting secrets like scraps of colored paper. Before he'd joined the Black Cirkus he'd been their friend. Their ally.

And then he'd betrayed them all.

LOG ENTRY—DECEMBER 3, 2073
11:50 HOURS
FACULTY HOUSING—WEST COAST ACADEMY OF ADVANCED TECHNOLOGY

The good news is that we're all okay. Zora and Natasha are still a bit shaken, but no one's hurt.

They're saying last week's earthquake was a 6.9 on the Richter scale. That's the largest we've seen in Seattle in something like fifty years, at least.

I managed to make it out to the workshop this morning, and it looks like the *Second Star* is still in one piece. There were some overturned bookshelves, tools strewn around, but no major damage.

No word on casualties yet. The city's pretty torn up, though. A lot of trees and power lines have gone down, and a bunch of homes were ruined. WCAAT and the rest of the University District still have power, but we were lucky. I went downtown to donate blood, and all the buildings are dark. It was spooky.

I wasn't sure whether it made sense to continue my research in the midst of all this, but I had a conference call with Dr. Helm (the president of WCAAT) yesterday, and he seems to think we should keep going. The world needs hope! Science is our future! Et cetera. Dr. Helm has gotten in touch with NASA, and it looks like they'll take over the day-to-day operation of my missions from here on out. Dr. Helm thinks this project has gotten too big for the school to manage on its own.

"Working with NASA means real funding," he told me. "You'll be able to design an entire program for space-time travel with the most brilliant minds of our generation."

He's right, of course, and I must admit that I'm glad the project hasn't been canceled. But I think I'll feel better about all of this if I hire someone from the tent city.

I should explain about Tent City. The university put the tents up last week. Thousands of people lost their homes after the earthquake. The shelters filled up fast, but they didn't have the bandwidth to take in everyone who was displaced, so the university set up emergency purple pop-up tents on campus. There are dozens of them now. I look out my office window and all I see is purple.

I was walking through the tent city to get to a meeting in the main building the other day, and I saw this kid sitting outside one of the tents, messing around on his computer. He couldn't have been more than fourteen or fifteen years old, but he was already doing pattern recognition of tectonic-plate movement.

I asked him if he'd considered using neutral net to evaluate the data and he looked at me like I was ten thousand years old.

"I already did that," he said. "And now I'm using GPU-accelerated Python to make it faster, but my program can't exceed ten petaflops without better hardware."

I stopped to talk about his program for a while, I even tried to help him make it faster, but the kid is light-years ahead of me. He's trying to figure out a way to predict fault activity before it shows up on a seismometer. It's fascinating stuff. I told him that WCAAT has an entire department devoted to seismology and that he should consider applying after he graduated high school.

But he just looked at me like I was crazy and said, "I'm not graduating after this."

I think it really hit me, then, how these earthquakes are ruining people's lives. How are you supposed to play around in the past when the present is such a mess?

I don't know how to answer that yet. But I think I've found my assistant.

I realize that NASA might not be thrilled that I've hired a fourteen-year-old high school dropout to assist on what might be the biggest scientific achievement since the moon landing, but Roman Estrada is a better coder than half the people in the WCAAT mathematics department, so they're just going to have to deal.

I have a good feeling about this kid.

9

DOROTHY

OCTOBER 14, 2077, NEW SEATTLE

Dorothy remembered Seattle smelling of smoke and horses. Now, when she drew in a breath, she tasted salt on the air. She was on a narrow waterway between two half-submerged buildings, their walls covered in graffiti. Rickety wooden bridges arced over her head, raining debris as people hurried across.

Dorothy leaned back, shading her eyes against the setting sun. She could see the bottoms of people's shoes through the wooden slats, worn bags swinging next to hips, the tips of fingers. Everyone seemed to be in a hurry. She wondered where they were going. Did the people here have jobs? School? Families to get home to? She watched them for a moment, transfixed, and then leaped backward as an arc of water crashed over her feet. An odd-looking boat zoomed down the waterway past her, motor growling like an animal.

Her heartbeat sped up. *Remarkable*, she thought, despite her nerves. Nobody she knew would ever see anything like that boat. She wished she had another set of eyes on the back of her head. She kept turning in circles, desperate not to miss a thing.

More boats appeared as she wandered down the docks. Some were small and fast, zipping down the narrow waterways so quickly that Dorothy got an ache in her neck trying to follow them. Others were large and slow, and made of bits of found objects—a few old tires, half a door, a chest of drawers without any drawers—all bound together with thick rope.

She glanced over her shoulder, at the tavern window. She wouldn't go far, she told herself. Just around the corner. Down the block, maybe. She'd be back before anyone noticed she was missing.

The buildings huddled closer together as she moved deeper into the city. Light glimmered off steel and glass, so bright that Dorothy had to shield her eyes. Handmade signs hung from open windows, announcing hardware stores, groceries, and lunch specials. They reminded Dorothy of stories her mother had told of lawless frontier towns bustling with people who'd traveled to the edge of the country to make their fortunes. People bartered and haggled as she drifted past.

"Twenty dollars for a carton of milk!" she heard a man say. "That's absurd."

"You won't find anything fresher this far west of the center," the shop woman responded. The man grunted and handed over a crumpled wad of bills.

The sun was dipping low on the horizon now, sending fingers of crushingly bright light glimmering over water and bouncing off windows. The city seemed edged in gold. Dorothy climbed to the highest level of bridges and shielded her eyes, trying to see how far the maze of buildings and bridges and waterways stretched into the distance. She couldn't make out where they ended. Maybe they went forever.

When she lowered her head again, her eyes fell on a repeating pattern of crude black tents drawn over the brick walls beside her, words scrawled between the pictures.

The past is our right! Join the Black Cirkus!

Paint had dripped from the words and into the water below, where it spread like a flower.

Dorothy glanced down, wondering what lay beneath the waves. Weeds stretched up from the bottom, blossoming into ugly yellow flowers when they broke the surface. Ripples moved toward her, surely caused by one of the boats. She took a step closer to the edge of the dock and stretched out her neck, peering into the dark.

She could make out the hulking shapes of lost objects littering the ground far underwater. The tops of mailboxes. A stone bench. Vehicles that bore only a passing resemblance to the automobile in Avery's garage, weeds growing through their broken windshields. Street signs covered in algae.

Dorothy lowered herself to her knees and stretched over the edge of the dock, transfixed. There was an entire world lost below the waves. How horrifying. How fascinating.

She narrowed her eyes at something floating from one of the car windows. It was long and yellow—a plant, perhaps? Dorothy leaned forward. The water churned below her, making the object move. Shorter, thinner bits dangled from one end. She squinted. They almost looked like—

A sour taste hit the back of her throat. *Fingers.* She was staring at the few remaining bones of a human arm, the skin long dissolved in the water. All at once, she remembered her conversation with Ash back at the church clearing:

Believe me, you wouldn't like it where I'm going.

How do you know what I'd like?

No one likes it.

Dorothy balled a fist at her mouth to keep herself from screaming. She stumbled backward, nearly losing her balance in her hurry to get away from the side of the dock. There was a *body* down there. Perhaps even more than one.

She turned in place, trying to remember how to get back to the tavern. She'd taken a left at the first bridge, and then a right, and then . . . *blast.* It was useless. She'd gone too far. She'd never find her way back on her own.

Two girls were hurrying down the bridge just ahead of her, arguing. Dorothy sped up to try and catch them.

"Five minutes isn't a big deal," said one of them.

"Yeah?" the other snorted. "Tell it to my mom. She's convinced the Fox is going to, like, eat me if I stay out a minute after dark."

The first girl lowered her voice. "Come on, you know Quinn Fox isn't *really* a cannibal, right?"

"Um . . . Brian said the rest of the Cirkus Freaks won't even *talk* to her because her breath always smells like blood."

"Oh my God . . . that's so gross."

Cannibal, Dorothy thought, and a thrill of fear moved through her as she remembered Ash's story. Had he really been telling the truth?

"Excuse me," she called after them. The girls didn't turn, but their shoulders seemed to stiffen. They linked arms and started walking faster. "Wait!" Dorothy tried again, but the girls were already scurrying down a ladder, sending her dirty looks as they climbed through a window and then slammed it shut.

That wasn't very friendly, Dorothy thought, frowning. She followed the winding, rickety docks through the growing dark, fear prickling up her spine. The city had been crowded with people just a few minutes ago, but, now, it seemed deserted. Dorothy listened for voices and heard only waves lapping against the sides of buildings and wind rustling the white tree branches.

Then, a light appeared in the darkness, glimmering in and out of focus. Dorothy's heart leaped. She heard voices now, laughing and talking. And then a series of sharp cracks broke through the night.

She stiffened. She knew that sound. She'd often heard it late in the night, outside of the rougher bars she and her mother had sometimes frequented.

Gunshots.

The light grew closer. Dorothy saw the outline of a boat, but it was moving much faster than she'd ever seen a boat move before, practically floating above the water. She ducked into the shadows on instinct, pressing her body flat against the brick wall so she wouldn't be seen. Every nerve in her body sparked.

A small group of people stood on board the strange, motorized boat. They wore dark coats made of a puffy, shiny fabric, hoods rimmed in fur pulled low over their faces. There were weapons strapped to their backs—crossbows and axes and clubs. Dorothy couldn't make sense of them. Their weapons were like something from a history book, but she'd never seen clothes like that before.

A small figure stood near the front of the boat, one foot propped against the side. He held a lantern in one hand and a short, shiny gun in the other. The gun exploded again, and Dorothy flinched. The figure threw his head back and howled at the sky, waving the gun above him.

He was just a boy, Dorothy realized. No older than she was.

The boat made a rumbling noise as it grew closer, casting water in its wake. The spray hit Dorothy's face, but she didn't dare move, not even to wipe the wet from her cheeks. The hooded people didn't seem to notice her huddling in the shadows. Dorothy watched their light grow smaller and smaller as the boat vanished deeper into the city, but she still didn't move.

Cold fear gripped her chest, and her knees had gone watery. She'd never seen anything like that boat, or those people. They were something from a story, not real life.

Time travel, she thought, and an icy finger touched the base of her spine. For the first time since climbing out the window of the tavern she realized that this wasn't a game. It wasn't an adventure. She was a stranger in this dangerous world, and she had no idea what the rules were. She hugged her arms close to her chest. And she'd foolishly run away from the only people who'd wanted to help her.

She hurried quickly down the walkways, looking for a landmark or a sign—anything to tell her she might be going back the way she came. But the city was a maze.

A breeze picked at the curls on the back of her neck, making her shiver. In the growing dark, the white trees looked like cobwebs. In fact, this entire place gave the impression of something alive growing over the bones of a long-dead corpse.

Dorothy turned a corner and saw a boy standing at the far end of the dock, facing away from her, his dark coat flapping in the wind.

Her entire body seemed to sigh in relief. "Excuse me?"

The boy turned. His eyes were a deep, vibrant blue against his dark skin, and his black hair swooped away from his forehead in a mess of waves. A white crow stretched across the front of his coat.

Dorothy felt a flicker of something she couldn't name. Not quite fear, not quite recognition. She moved backward without making the conscious decision to do so.

But then the boy smiled, and it transformed his entire face. He looked like the romantic lead in a play. Dorothy had never been a particularly romantic person, but if she'd ever tried to imagine what sort of boy she'd want to fall in love with, he would've looked just like this, down to the tiny cleft creasing his chin. It was as though someone had plucked him straight out of a daydream.

"Hello." He took a step toward her, his heavy boots making the dock tremble. The corner of his lip twitched.

"Perhaps you can help me," Dorothy said. "I'm afraid I've lost my way."

"That's strange." The boy pulled a revolver out from under his coat. "I think you're exactly where you're supposed to be."

Cold hit the back of Dorothy's throat and trembled up the nerves in her teeth.

"That's a gun," she said dumbly.

"Why yes it is." The boy spoke in a lighthearted way, almost like Dorothy had just complimented him on his fantastic coat. "It's a snub-nosed S and W revolver, circa 1945, as a matter of fact. A dear friend lent it to me last year."

He cocked the hammer back with one finger.

Too late, Dorothy realized she should have been running. She should have started running the moment she saw this boy. She stumbled backward but, before she could utter a word, someone grabbed her from behind, covering her mouth and nose with a cloth.

She inhaled and felt instantly woozy. The dock spun beneath her feet. She clawed at the hand covering her face, but the strength was draining from her body. Her arm fell back to her side, useless.

In the second before she fell unconscious, she felt that strange feeling again—not quite fear, not quite recognition.

Déjà vu, she realized, eyes drooping. That's what it was.

She felt like she'd lived this moment already.

10

ASH

Ash was about to wave down Levi to see about getting another drink, when Willis slid his elbows onto the bar next to him. The hubcap creaked, ominously, beneath his weight.

"Captain," he said, frowning. "We have a situation."

"Situation?" As always, Ash was amazed by how many muscles Willis seemed to need for an expression as simple as a frown. Eyebrows furrowed and jaw twitched and mustache quivered.

A bar patron walked past, glanced at the massive teenager and swore under his breath, sloshing beer over the side of his glass.

"Did you see the size of that guy?" he muttered to his friend before disappearing back into the crowd.

Willis pretended not to notice this exchange, but Ash saw the way his fingers flattened against the bar, the muscles in his shoulders going tense. The Professor had found Willis working as a carnival strongman around the turn of the twentieth century. According to him, he'd been the largest, most intimidating man ever to live.

Willis's nostrils flared. Ash knew he hated the attention.

"What kind of situation?" he asked.

"Dorothy's gone," Willis said. "Zora went to bathroom to see if she was okay, but she wasn't there. Looks like she went out the window."

Ash studied a ring of moisture on the bar. "Good riddance," he muttered.

But something more complicated twisted through him. Wandering around New Seattle after dark was a death sentence. He thought of Dorothy's long, pale neck, her narrow shoulders. Manipulative or not, she was awfully breakable—and unarmed—at least as far as Ash knew. She seemed like the type to have a pistol shoved down her pants.

Willis fixed Ash with a steady gaze, and Ash grunted.

She deserves whatever she gets, he thought, pushing his concern aside. But he didn't want it on his conscience one way or another. He flashed the sharp edge of a smile and lifted his mostly empty glass to his lips. "Let me guess, Zora wants me to be decent and go out looking for her?"

Willis hesitated. Ash felt something cold slither down his spine and set the glass back on the bar. "What?"

"There's . . . something else," Willis said. "You should probably come with me."

Willis led Ash out back, to the docks that curved behind the bar, connecting them to the wider grid of walkways that spiderwebbed through the entire city. The docks beneath Ash's feet swayed, following the gentle rise and fall of the waves. Ash had lived here for two years. He would've thought he'd be past noticing the movement by now. But sometimes, when he stood very still, the rocking made him feel unsteady. Like a storm was bubbling up from below.

As they walked, Willis explained, "When Zora realized that Dorothy had left, she sent me out here to see if I could find her."

Ash tapped his fingers against his leg and then realized what he was doing and curled his hand into a fist to stop them. "She just assumed I wouldn't want to help?"

Willis raised one heavy eyebrow, his way of saying that Zora had clearly assumed correctly. "Found this."

He stopped, jerking his chin at something just ahead of him. The dock swayed and, once again, Ash had the feeling of being unmoored. Of things breaking and sinking and crumbling.

He squinted, and saw spray paint curled over the surface of the wood, the black still glistening and wet. At first, Ash thought it was just squiggles—run-of-the-mill vandalism wasn't at all unusual in the city—but, as he walked around the edge of the dock, his eyes began turning the slashes and loops into words.

Finders keepers.

Ash stared, feeling ill. The Black Cirkus took people at night. The city had a curfew to protect against it, but Ash still heard rumblings of friends disappearing on the way to the market, neighbors vanishing while walking around the block.

No one knew what they did with the people they took, but Ash had a feeling it was something along the lines of searching their pockets for valuables and ditching the bodies. Give or take a gunshot.

His mind spun. "You can't know it was her—"

Willis lifted his hand. A small silver locket dangled between his fingers. "I found this, just over there."

Ash bit back a curse. He recognized that locket. Dorothy had been wearing it.

It's her own fault, he thought, scuffing a boot over the still-wet paint. *She shouldn't have left the bar, shouldn't have gone off on her own . . .*

But hadn't he baited her? *There's a window in the bathroom over there. Promise me you'll look outside.* Hadn't he known she wouldn't be able to resist a peek? She probably only went outside in the first place to get a closer look, never dreaming of the danger that was waiting for her. Ash hadn't bothered mentioning the Black Cirkus when he'd dropped the time-travel bomb. He hadn't bothered telling her much of anything about this strange new world she'd landed in.

Damn it to hell. If she died, it would be on his head.

"What do you want to do here, Captain?" Willis asked. He still held the locket. It twisted between his fingers, catching the moonlight.

Ash chewed on his lower lip. *Son of a bitch.* This wasn't going to be fun. "We have to get her back."

Willis blew air out through his teeth. "That's a suicide mission."

Ash met Willis's eyes. He was right. No one came back from the Black Cirkus. Their headquarters was in the old Fairmont hotel, which they'd turned into a fortress. Guards at every entrance. Bars on the windows. Once they had you, you were as good as dead. But . . .

He thought of Dorothy standing in the woods beyond the churchyard. *Please*, she'd begged him, *I just need a ride*.

He'd been right to leave her behind then. But if he left her behind now it was almost like killing her himself.

He might be an ass. But he wasn't a murderer.

"On the other hand," Willis added, squinting down at the smudged words. "It might be fun to take something of Roman's for once."

He paused, smoothing his mustache with his thumb and forefinger. When he spoke again, his voice was deliberate. "I have a friend who used to run deliveries for the Cirkus. He told me about a parking garage that leads to the hotel's basement entrance. Isn't guarded."

Ash tensed. "Why haven't you ever mentioned that before?"

"Figured I'd save that information for an emergency. Didn't want you storming in all willy-nilly just because you could."

Ash bristled. He wasn't sure what bothered him more: the idea that he would do something so dumb, or the use of the phrase *willy-nilly*.

"This enough of an emergency for you?" he asked.

Willis cracked his knuckles. The sudden *pop* of his joints seemed a solid answer.

11

DOROTHY

Dorothy opened her eyes. The ceiling kaleidoscoped—first fracturing into a dozen dancing gray shadows, and then shifting back into place. She blinked, and pain flared up the front of her skull. With a groan, she pressed a palm to her forehead.

That's a gun, she heard herself say. She remembered the small black object in the man's hand, the soft click of metal as he cocked the hammer back.

No. She jerked the hand away from her face, nervous fingers running over the body beneath her loose-fitting clothes.

No bullet wounds, no blood, no pain. She hadn't been shot, then. She let her arm drop back to her side, fingers still. Well. That was something to be happy about, at least. It was important to appreciate the little things in life.

She opened her eyes again and, this time, the ceiling stayed put. Another small victory. She gingerly lifted her head, blinking hard against the fresh wave of pain. She was lying on a white quilt that had started to yellow around the edges. There was another bed next to her, covered in an identical, yellowing quilt, but it was empty.

This is a hotel, she realized. She and her mother had stayed in hotels on their way west. Hotels were nice, normal places, with doors and windows that any fool could open. There was no reason to panic.

Dorothy breathed in, her nose filling with cigarette smoke, and sat bolt upright, coughing. The scent brought memories with it, hateful memories that she'd tried hard to forget. This wasn't the first time she'd been kidnapped. Years ago, a drunken man had grabbed her while she'd been working a con with her mother. The bar that night had also reeked of smoke, the smell of rotten fish churning through the air beneath it. It'd been crowded, the sounds of laughter and shouting crackling through the air. Dorothy remembered screaming for her mother as the man dragged her out of the bar, her voice lost in the jeers.

"Real men take what they want," the man had growled, leering at her. He'd squeezed too hard, his fingers bruising her skin. He clearly had no intention of being gentle.

Beauty disarms, Dorothy had thought. She'd only been twelve at the time, but her mother had already drilled that lesson into her head. She wasn't strong enough to fight, so she'd looked up at the man and flashed her best smile, the one Loretta had made her practice until her cheeks cramped. Eventually, his grip had loosened.

Dorothy couldn't remember exactly how she'd gotten away. She seemed to recall landing a particularly well-placed kick to the man's nether regions and then running as fast as she could manage in her heavy skirts and tightly cinched corset. Her mother had been waiting at the bar when she returned, and she'd glanced up when Dorothy pushed through the door, her expression unreadable. Dorothy had still been breathing heavily when she took the seat next to her.

"Why didn't you come for me?" she'd asked. It had been the thought that circled her head as she ran back to the bar, anxiously glancing over her shoulder to see whether the ugly man was still following her.

Loretta had lifted a tiny glass of brandy to her mouth. "How did you know I wouldn't?"

Dorothy hadn't answered. She'd simply known, the way most children knew their mothers would be in to tuck the covers under their chins before they drifted off to sleep at night. She remembered screaming for her mother as the man dragged her away. Hadn't she heard?

Loretta placed the brandy back down on the bar, a drop of amber liquid slopping over the side. She pressed a finger into the spilled drop, and then lifted it to her lips. "There will always be men who want you. I had to know you could take care of yourself," she'd said. "Our world has no place for cowards."

There will always be men who want you. It was the first time Dorothy understood her beauty for what it was. A bull's-eye. A curse.

Now, she forced herself to focus on the room around her, to breathe past the smell of smoke and the memory of her mother's finger wiping at the drop of brandy. She felt powerless and alone and angry.

And something else, something that made her feel not quite human, but like she was a thing capable of being possessed. Like she was inanimate, an object that could be moved around according to someone else's will.

It was a hateful feeling. She promised herself that, one day, she would become strong enough that no one could just take her ever again.

For now, she had to get out of this room.

There were four doors in the room, two to Dorothy's left, one on the far wall, and one to her right. She crawled off her bed, nearly tripping over her own feet. She tried the door to her right—bathroom. The second was a closet. The third and the fourth were both locked. Of course.

Dorothy swore under her breath and turned in place. The room was intentionally nondescript. White walls, white bedspreads, blue chair, blue curtains. A dresser stood directly in front of her, its surface covered in a layer of dust. Hands trembling, she began yanking open drawers, not bothering to close them again when she saw they were empty.

In the last drawer, she found a small book bound in leather, the pages edged in gold. She picked it up and opened it. The journal didn't seem to know which page to open to, and flopped somewhere in the middle. Dorothy picked her way back to the beginning.

Blocky handwriting covered the creamy white page.

I built a time machine.

In the last year, every single theoretical physicist and mathematician and engineer on the planet Earth has tried. Every day there've been new stories detailing their failures, their loss of funding, their embarrassments.

But I've actually succeeded.

Time machine. For a moment, Dorothy forgot her plans to escape. She carefully turned the pages of the journal, finding sketches and jotted notes and scribbled numbers. And, though the handwriting was small and careful, there was a *yearning* to it. Want leaped off of every page. It left her breathless. She imagined crawling into the hotel bed, devouring every word.

The journal itself was tantalizingly elegant, all soft leather and heavy pages, the kind of book she would expect to contain delicious secrets. She would've wanted it even if the topic hadn't immediately caught her interest.

Dorothy flipped to the front cover, reluctant to put it down. A name had been written inside the leather.

Property of Professor Zacharias Walker

She touched a finger to the smudged ink. Then, making a quick decision, she tucked the small leather book into the waistband of her pants, pulling her shirt over the bulge to hide it from view. She wanted to find someplace quiet and spend hours poring over the pages. It gave her the same feeling that wandering through the city had: the sense of wonder and fear and amazement. Like something exciting was about to happen. She stumbled to the window on the opposite wall and tore the curtains aside. Crude iron bars had been fastened over the glass. She wrapped her fingers around one of the bars and tugged with all her strength. It held tight. They meant to keep her prisoner inside this tiny room. Like an animal.

No, she thought, jerking on the bar again. There would be a way out. There was no such thing as a room that couldn't be broken out of. She took a step away from the window, pressing two fingers to her forehead.

"Think, damn you," she muttered, tapping the space between her eyebrows.

She fingered the sleeve of her shirt, exhaling heavily when she felt the hard silver points of the hairpins she'd tucked inside the fabric. All was not lost.

She slid a pin from her shirt and knelt on the floor in front of the first door. The lock was odd. Instead of a keyhole, she saw only a narrow slit. She threaded her pin into the slit and wiggled it around but didn't feel a catch. She sat back on her heels, frowning.

There was one other locked door. Dorothy crawled over to it, and tried the handle. It didn't budge, but at least it had a normal lock. She squinted into the keyhole, and then slid her pin inside, her breath a solid lump at the back of her throat. She twisted to the left, and to the right. Something caught—

The lock clicked. Dorothy slid the pin back up her sleeve and pushed the door open.

It led to another room, exactly like the one she'd just broken out of. Two beds covered in white quilts. Blue chair. Blue curtains. Four doors. Dorothy quickly tried them: Bathroom. Closet. Locked.

"Blast!" she shouted, slamming a hand against the final, locked door. It had the same strange slit that the one in her room had. She dug a fingernail into the narrow opening, but it was no use. She had no idea how to work it. She was trapped. Really and truly trapped for the first time in her life.

Dorothy had never been inside of a room she couldn't find her way out of. It made her claustrophobic. The air felt thinner, and the walls seemed to creep closer whenever she blinked. She hurried across the room. She needed fresh air. She might be able to force the window open, even if the bars kept her from climbing out. She tore the curtains aside—then froze.

There were no bars on this window.

Dorothy squeezed her hands into fists, swallowing a scream of pure delight. She wedged her fingers into the edge of the window and pulled—it slid open an inch.

"Come on," she muttered through gritted teeth. She pulled again—

The door behind her clicked. Dorothy spun around in time to see a light above the odd lock flash green. She ducked on instinct, crouching behind one of the two beds. The door creaked open.

". . . why you even care what she does." The voice was a

low purr, like the lounge singers Dorothy had tried so hard to emulate when she was little. She ducked farther behind the bed, heart hammering. Shoes crunched against carpet as someone entered the room.

"Don't be jealous, Little Fox," came a second, deeper voice. Dorothy stiffened, recognizing it.

"God, Roman, you know I hate when you call me that," the first voice said. The mattress next to Dorothy's head creaked, rustling the blankets beside her ear. Dorothy tilted her face up. She felt her jaw go slack.

A girl sat inches from where Dorothy hid. Dorothy shifted, angling herself so she could see the girl's head and the tops of her narrow shoulders from her hiding spot at the side of the bed.

The girl was a slip of a thing, with pure white hair falling in tangles down her back. Dorothy had never seen such perfectly white hair before. It was like something out of a ghost story.

"Fine then. *Quinn*," Roman said. He sat on the bed beside her. Dorothy couldn't see much of him from her position, but she saw his arm as he draped it around the girl's shoulder.

Despite her better instincts, Dorothy kept her head lifted, staring at the back of the girl's head. *Quinn*. There was something magnetic about her. She seemed . . . regal. Small though she was, she took up space and energy. The room seemed to shrink as she moved through it.

Dorothy thought of her mother and a still iciness flooded through her. Loretta had the same effect on a room.

"Better," Quinn purred.

Roman cleared his throat. "Did you know they've written a song about us?"

Quinn tilted her head toward him.

"I don't recall the words exactly." Roman hummed a few notes, and then sang, "'Close your windows tight, little children, the fox and crow are scratching at the glass. . . .' And then something about being disemboweled. What rhymes with disemboweled?"

"Charming," Quinn said, her voice joyless. She stood, letting Roman's hand fall to the bed. She touched her neck with one pale finger. "Is everything ready?"

Dorothy lifted her head a fraction of an inch. She could see Roman's hand now. He curled his fingers toward his palm and then released them again. Dorothy had the impression of a chastened lover.

Roman murmured, "Stop worrying. . . ."

"Answer the question."

"Everything's ready."

"Good," Quinn said. She stared at the wall in front of her, and Dorothy stared at the back of her head. She narrowed her eyes, studying all that white. She'd heard of women dying their hair different colors, but this girl's hair seemed to grow straight out of her head that way.

Quinn flinched, like she could feel Dorothy's eyes on her head. She started to turn—

Dorothy ducked back behind the bed so quickly that a

burst of pain shot through her neck. She bit into her lip to keep from crying out loud. *Blast.* Had she been seen?

For a long moment no one spoke. It seemed that they didn't even breathe. Dorothy felt too scared to blink. She pressed her throbbing lips together. Waiting.

"What about our newest guest?" Quinn asked, after a long moment. "Have you checked on her lately?"

A pause. Then, "No."

She tutted. "Best make sure she's comfortable. Bring me whatever valuables you find, and get rid of the body. We need the room empty again by tonight."

There were more footsteps, and the creak of a door swinging open and closed as Quinn left the room. Alone now, Roman stood, the mattress creaking with the release of his weight.

Get rid of the body. Dorothy's ears filled with static. Quinn might not have seen her, but Roman would discover her missing the second he checked her room. She curled her fingers into the carpet, pushing herself into a slight crouch. She heard a shuffling sound as he moved toward the door that led to her room.

She wanted to leap out from behind the bed now, but she forced herself to remain still. She could feel blood pumping in her palms.

A door opened. Closed.

Dorothy raced for the window, her heart beating like a drum in her ears. She yanked the curtain aside with one hand, grabbed for the glass with the other. Muscles screaming, she pulled.

The window slid open and cool air swept into the room, blowing the hair back from her face. She stuck her head outside and looked down . . .

. . . and down and down.

Eight rows of sleek glass windows separated her from the ground below. *Eight* stories. From up here, the surface of the murky, brown water seemed hard and unbreakable. She'd die if she jumped from this far.

"Our world has no place for cowards," she muttered, lips numb with fear.

Her mother had left a moment after saying those words to her, crossing the bar to flirt with some businessman foolish enough to keep his wallet in his front pocket. She'd left her drink on the bar, and Dorothy had picked it up, throwing back the remains of her brandy in a single swallow.

Dorothy could taste that alcohol burning at the back of her throat now. She'd hated her mother then, but she couldn't help admiring her as well. Loretta wasn't the type of woman to be kidnapped. Men never looked at her and thought she could be possessed.

She would've been horrified to hear that her daughter had been taken again. That she'd trusted some man with a nice smile, even for a second. She'd taught her better than that.

Dorothy propped a foot on the windowsill and hoisted herself up, balancing on the edge. The world spun below her.

She hesitated, imagining her arms and legs going numb as she plummeted down and down, her neck snapping on impact with the hard surface of the water, losing consciousness as the icy liquid flooded her throat and lungs. Her fingers curled around the windowsill. It would be a painful death, drowning. Much more painful than a bullet in the back of the head.

Make a choice. Should be easy. Die jumping or die staying.

Roman shouted something from the other room. A door slammed.

Dorothy closed her eyes.

Make a choice.

LOG ENTRY—JANUARY 13, 2074
08:23 HOURS
WEST COAST ACADEMY OF ADVANCED TECHNOLOGY

It's been a little over a month since my first hire, and Roman is doing brilliantly. The kid is a genius (and I don't use that word lightly). He's already sorted through the résumés to weed out the most impressive applicants, upgraded my computer software, and helped me and Zora figure out what was causing the *Second Star*'s internal nav to go all wonky.

I'm satisfied that he'll be a great assistant, so it's time to start hiring the rest of my team. I've been given clearance for another three hires: a medic, in case of emergency; security detail; and a pilot.

(My own flight capabilities were deemed "subpar" after a particularly humiliating test with a NASA pilot, but that is neither here nor there.)

Natasha has pointed out that the brilliant minds at NASA didn't even consider that they might need an *actual historian* to research these "little jaunts through history," as she likes to refer to them.

Luckily, I told her, I had the good sense to marry a historian. Do you know what she said to that?

You can't afford me.

Ah, to have my beautiful, brilliant wife by my side while I make history! We're destined to be the Marie and Pierre Curie of time travel.

In any case, Natasha had an interesting idea for my dilemma. One evening, I was complaining that I couldn't find the qualities I was hoping for in the applicants the school provided, and Natasha said that it would make more sense to go back in time and find the most brilliant applicants in all of history.

I think she was joking.

But picture it: The strongest man in all of history. The world's most brilliant medical mind. The most talented pilot...

I'm going to have to ruminate.

Roman came to me with a curious question the other day. He asked whether it would be possible to go back in time and help some of the people in Tent City.

We can't go back in time and stop that 6.9 earthquake from happening, of course, but Seattle wasn't even set up with an EEW (earthquake early warning) like they have in California and Tokyo. If we'd had that in place, thousands of people wouldn't have died.

I desperately wanted to tell him yes. But I don't see how we can avoid a paradox.

Generally speaking, there are three types of time-travel paradoxes. I'm referring here to the first, a "causal loop," which exists when a future event is the cause of a past event.

For instance, if mass casualties from an earthquake convinced me to go back in time to set up an EEW, which then prevented the mass casualties from occurring, I'd have no reason to go back in time.

If there's no cause, there can't be an effect.

Of course, paradoxes are all purely theoretical. We can't really understand how the future will respond to changes in the past until we test them.

I'm not technically supposed to go back in time until I've chosen my team, but what could a really small trip hurt?

Causal loops are tricky, so I'll leave those for another day. Today, I want to tackle the big one: the grandfather paradox.

The grandfather paradox is a consistency paradox. It occurs when the past is changed in a way that creates a contradiction. For example, if I go back in time and kill my grandfather before he creates my father, my father won't be alive to create me, which would make it impossible for me to go back in time and kill my grandfather in the first place.

Disproving it'll be easy. All I'll need is an apple.

Let's call this mission Hera 1, after the Greek myth of Paris and the golden apple.

My objective, as stated, will be to disprove the grandfather paradox. I'll do this by taking an apple from the kitchen table and placing it in the bathroom. Then, I'll go back in time one hour, take that *same apple* from our kitchen, and eat it, thus making it impossible for me to place the apple in my bathroom an hour later. Brilliant in its simplicity, right? And absolutely no grandfathers will be harmed!

I'll update on my return.

UPDATE—07:18 HOURS

I have successfully eaten the apple. (This is kind of crazy, right? I take my journal with me when I travel through time, so I was able to write this update after the update from an hour into the future, but it looks so weird on the page!)

UPDATE—09:32 HOURS

Hera 1 has just hit an unforeseeable snag. Natasha has informed me that there were, in fact, *two* apples in our kitchen this morning. She set one aside for her breakfast. I ate *that* apple when I traveled back in time. Upon finding that apple missing, she found a second and placed it on the kitchen table. This was the apple that I hid in the bathroom.

Natasha has also expressed a wish that I no longer store fruit in the bathroom. Reasonable, I suppose.

UPDATE—16:40 HOURS

I've been thinking about this experiment all day. The thing is, I *looked* for additional apples when I placed the first one in the bathroom. I'm a scientist, after all. I have doctoral training in controlled experimentation. I wouldn't have left such an important aspect of the experiment up to chance.

There was only one apple.

But Natasha says there were *two*.

We've long theorized that space-time travel would cause massive changes to our *present*—a butterfly effect, if you will.

(A butterfly effect, of course, is the concept that small changes can eventually lead to bigger changes, e.g., a butterfly can flap its wings and cause a hurricane. Obviously it's a lot more complicated than this, but to get any more specific I'd have to go into chaos theory, which is a lot of theory for today.)

I wonder if this is the right question.

Or, would it be better to ask this: Can travel through time change the *past* as well as the future?

In other words, did I create a second apple when I moved the first?

Interestingly enough, this calls to mind the third time-traveler's paradox, the Fermi paradox, which posits, "If time travel were possible, where are all the visitors from the future?" If I changed the past by eating an apple I shouldn't have been able to eat, it stands to reason that time travelers can change the past upon showing themselves.

Put another way, there aren't visitors from the future yet.

But there will be.

12

ASH

OCTOBER 14, 2077, NEW SEATTLE

The parking garage outside the Fairmont hotel looked exactly like the photographs Ash had seen of old shopping malls in the late twentieth century. Ugly, concrete levels were stacked one on top of another. Long-rusted pipes ran along the walls, and busted light fixtures dotted the ceiling. A car stood several feet away, doors hanging open, but Ash got the feeling it was purely ornamental. Only the top few levels of the garage were still dry—the others sank deep into the murky water below.

"Shall we?" Willis asked, cocking an eyebrow.

Ash climbed out of their motorboat and crawled over a low concrete wall separating what remained of the garage from the water surrounding it. Several inches of water still covered the floor on the other side, making his boots squelch when he stepped down.

"You're sure this leads to the Fairmont?" he asked, lifting a sodden boot. "Because it looks flooded."

"That's the point." Willis held a flashlight in one hand, but the dusty beam was like a match in a black room. It only made it more obvious that the dark was winning. "Let's go."

They took a narrow staircase near the back of the garage. It must've been flooded once, but at some point the water had been cleared out and the area sealed, leaving the lower levels deceptively dry. The smell of something old and musty rose up from the ground, growing stronger the farther they descended, until it was almost like another person walking along beside them. Ash tried his best to breathe through his mouth.

After a while they reached a metal door, which led into a wide, open garage on one of the structure's lower levels.

The space was squat and long: the ceiling only a few inches above their heads; the far wall nothing more than a suggestion in the distance. Huge windows covered the wall to Ash's left, some of the panels old and clouded, others obviously new and made of thick glass. This level wasn't underwater, but it would look like it was from outside. Ash could make out the surface of the water glimmering beyond the glass, casting the whole space in blue.

"What is this place?" he murmured, stepping around an overturned trash can.

"Dunno," Willis said. He stopped beside a boxy automobile, its tires long relieved of air, cracks splintering its windshields. "Looks like they're trying to build something, though."

"What could they be trying to—" Ash stopped talking then, his question answered as his eyes snagged on something in the darkness. The shape shone silver in the dim light, it's body aluminum and bullet-shaped.

It looked awfully familiar.

"Ash?" asked Willis, frowning.

Ash walked past him without realizing that he'd spoken. It was dark, but he thought he could see the edge of a finned tail and the gleam of light hitting black stars.

A nasty shiver went down his spine.

It couldn't be.

Willis dropped a hand onto Ash's shoulder. "Is that . . . ?"

"It's a time machine," Ash said, his voice a rasp.

The first time he'd seen a time machine had been on February 25, 1945, at 0400 hours. He'd been fast asleep, and when he felt the tap on his shoulder, he thought it was Captain McHugh, coming to rouse him for the preflight briefing. He groaned and rolled over, reluctantly opening his eyes.

The man leaning over him wasn't Captain McHugh. He had black skin and hair, and a black beard speckled with gray. He was decked out in strange clothes, too, a badly fitting suit jacket and a stiff, striped tie. Almost like he was wearing a costume.

"It's time to wake up, Mr. Asher," the man said. He whispered, but his voice was so deep and rich that it boomed around them, anyway.

That voice had knocked Ash awake. There was a man in

the barracks. A man who'd somehow managed to get past the armed guards at the door. His heart jump-started, and he jerked backward, fumbling for the loaded .45 he always kept within reach.

The man grabbed his arm, holding him with a grip like a vise's. Ash tried to pull away, but he was strong.

"None of that now," the man said in that same vibrating whisper. "I'm not staying long, and you have no reason to be afraid. My name is Professor Zacharias Walker. I'm a time traveler from the year 2075."

Ash had stared at this professor for a long moment, still unconsciously reaching for his pistol. Then, the corner of his lips flicked upward. The boys were trying to pull one over on him, all right. *Time travel.* Well, that was something new, he had to give them that. He wondered where they'd found this old guy with the crazy voice and the weird clothes. He'd probably been some drunk from the pub down the street, looking to score a little free hooch.

The "professor" frowned. "I can see that you don't believe me. If you'll accompany me for a moment, I can offer you proof."

Ash swallowed, his throat still scratchy with sleep. "Proof?"

"I could show you my time machine."

Ash released a short laugh. But he sat up and threw his jacket over his long johns, trying to work his expression into something resembling seriousness. "Lead the way, old man."

The time machine was behind the barracks, in a secluded

area just past the trees. It looked like a miniature zeppelin, small and bullet-shaped, with otherworldly blue light leaking out of its windows. Ash realized later that it was the other time machine, the *Dark Star.* The one the Professor built after the *Second Star.* The one he'd disappeared in.

The light was what stopped Ash in his tracks. He'd lowered his hand to the side of the ship, dumbstruck. The metal was still warm.

"Why are you showing me this?" he'd asked, when he found he could speak again.

"Because I want you to learn to fly it," the Professor had said.

Now, Ash edged nearer, lowering a hand to the ship in front of him. He'd thought it was the *Dark Star* when he first saw it hulking in the shadows; it had the same bullet-shaped body, the same round windows.

But this wasn't the Professor's ship—it was a replica. The words *BLACK CROW* had been scrawled over the siding where the words *DARK STAR* would've been had it been authentic.

There were other differences, too. The *Black Crow* was a deep, charcoal color, quite unlike the bright aluminum of the *Dark Star*, and what Ash had taken for stars were actually crows, their black wings outstretched.

A cold shiver moved through Ash. It was a feeling like déjà vu—or a funhouse-mirror sort of déjà vu. The Professor was the only man in history who'd managed to build a time machine. Others had tried, back before the mega-quake, but they'd never gotten the finned tale just right; they didn't know what type of glass could move through an anil without cracking, or how to properly integrate the exotic matter into the structure of their designs.

Ash climbed in through the *Black Crow*'s main cabin. It was identical to the *Dark Star*. The seats in the cabin were set in the same circular pattern, all facing one another. The walls were the same deep, polished bronze. For a second, Ash imagined he could smell the Professor's peculiar mix of cologne and pipe smoke. He shook his head, and the smell faded. This wasn't the Professor's ship, he reminded himself. It was a copy.

He ducked into the cockpit. Unlike the *Second Star*, the *Dark Star* had an internal control panel to store its exotic matter. The Professor had built the bigger ship a year after completing the *Second Star*, when he knew more about time travel and had the funding to build the ship of his dreams. If the *Second Star* was a zippy little fighter jet, the *Dark Star* was a luxury cruiser. It had been designed to take a team of people back through time as comfortably as possible. Once the Professor had completed it, he'd gifted the *Second Star* to Ash so he'd have something to learn on.

The internal control panel was one of the key design elements the impostors had never gotten quite right, but the *Black Crow*'s was identical to the Professor's design, down to the tiny row of lights that would flash red in an emergency. Even the *Second Star* wasn't that advanced.

Swearing under his breath, Ash dropped to his knees.

The exotic matter was stored in a hidden compartment on a lower panel, back on the *Dark Star*. He moved his hands over levers and buttons, until a similar panel fell open, revealing—

Nothing. Ash exhaled, rocking back on his heels. That was a small relief. Without exotic matter, Roman wouldn't be able to take this ship back in time. Ash didn't know how he'd managed to so perfectly re-create the *Dark Star* but, without any EM, the *Black Crow* was a glorified tin can.

Gunshots cracked through the air, interrupting Ash's thoughts. He jerked around, squinting through the *Black Crow*'s windows. The shots had come from far off, echoing through walls and water, but there was no mistaking that sudden, horrible *pop*.

"Ash!" Willis shouted. "Hurry!"

Ash leaped to his feet and stumbled out of the time machine. Willis was standing in front of the wall of windows, staring out into the gloomy water that surrounded them. Moonlight slanted through the waves, drawing ripples across the floor.

"What's going on?" Ash could see the watery outline of the hotel towering over him, and what seemed to be movement far above.

"Fight, I think," Willis grunted.

More gunshots popped, sounding closer now. Bullets whizzed through the water outside their window, leaving trails like tiny shooting stars.

A shape pulled away from the hotel and began moving rapidly closer.

"Someone jumped," Willis said. The words had barely left his mouth when a body broke through the surface. Water churned and bubbled against the window and, when it cleared, Ash saw features he recognized: Wide, green eyes. Pale skin. Brown curls.

His entire body stiffened. "That's Dorothy."

13

DOROTHY

All Dorothy could see was white.

Then the white began to take form: white trees, white hair, white fingers attached to white hands, floating from the window of a long-rusted car . . .

Dead. Everything beneath the water was dead.

She blinked. *Water.* She was underwater. The white she was seeing was the cloudy glass pane of a window. A figure moved behind it, and Dorothy thought she saw Quinn's white curls and dark coat. But then she was gone.

Something inside of her screamed: *Swim.*

Physical sensations slammed back into her. The water was frigid enough to numb her skin and make her arms and legs feel stiff. It felt gritty against her eyes, clouding her vision. A deep ache stretched through her head. She kicked—*hard*—but her feet were too heavy.

Something whizzed past, grazing her arm. It felt hot—a match striking skin. Another followed a second later.

Bullets, she realized. Someone was shooting at her.

With stiff, half-frozen feet, she dug her toes into the backs of her shoes, prying them off. She kicked again.

The surface drew nearer. Moonlight glinted through the water. It took every last bit of energy she had to pump her arms, dragging her body up and up. Another bullet rocketed past, coming so close to her face that she could feel its heat on her cheek before it disappeared below.

Just three more feet . . . two . . . one . . .

Dorothy burst through the surface of the water, gasping. The air burned, but she gulped it down anyway. It tasted sweet. When her eyes focused, she caught sight of two things simultaneously: the narrow dock set against the outer edge of the hotel wall—and Roman.

Roman stood balanced on the windowsill eight stories above, calmly reloading his gun. Wind whipped his coat around his legs, causing the black cloth to billow and swell.

"That was very brave!" he shouted, but the wind ate snippets of his voice so that it sounded like ". . . at . . . wa . . . ery . . . brave!"

Dorothy ignored him. He was too high up to do anything but shoot at her. She kicked through the water, grasped the dock, and dug her fingers into the slats between the wood. She pulled—

A thud sounded above, followed by a grunt. She looked up.

Roman was two stories lower than he'd been a moment ago, climbing down the scaffolding, gun sticking out of the waistband of his trousers. Dorothy could see the muscles moving beneath his coat, flexing and relaxing easily, like this was something he'd done many times before. He dropped onto a patio on the fifth floor, and then whipped over the side of the ledge, holding on with one hand while the other reached for the windowsill beside him.

"You learn a few things growing up around here," he shouted. "Bouldering, in particular, is a useful skill. I hate getting wet."

He swung, fluidly, to the floor below and then crept along the narrow ledge, like a circus performer walking a tightrope, before dropping onto a third-floor patio.

Blast. Dorothy pulled with all her strength, scrambling onto the dock. She heard another *thump.* Roman must've leaped to the second floor. Limbs still stiff with cold, she pushed herself to her hands and knees and then up to her feet. Her legs wobbled, threatening to collapse.

Another thud—this one made the dock below her feet tremble. Dorothy lifted her head. Roman stood in front of her, gun hanging lazily from one hand.

He frowned and gestured with his gun. "You look nervous."

The statement was so ludicrous that Dorothy couldn't help the bitter laugh that escaped her lips. "You *kidnapped* me."

"Barely."

"You were going to kill me."

"Don't be absurd."

"You . . . you *shot* at me," Dorothy sputtered. Pain beat in her arm where the bullet had grazed her.

Roman shrugged with one shoulder. "How else was I supposed to get your attention?"

He took a step toward her, rolling his weight from heel to toes in a way that kept the dock from rocking. It was a slow, careful movement, and it made Dorothy feel like prey. She took an instinctive step backward as Roman lifted both hands, surrendering. The gun dangled from one thumb.

"Honestly, I'm surprised," he said. "I thought you'd be curious."

"Curious?" Dorothy swallowed, one eye still trained on the gun. She didn't know what he was talking about. She considered running, but her arm ached from her bullet wound, and her pants were so heavy with water they were slipping from her hips. "About what?"

"Don't you want to know why I took you?"

Dorothy thought of the drunk man who'd smelled of rotten fish. *Real men take what they want.* Her eyes flicked back to Roman's face. "I assumed you wanted to rob and kill me."

"Don't be ridiculous." Roman leaned toward her, like he was about to tell her a secret. His breath smelled of mint leaves. "The truth is, I've been watching you."

Liar, Dorothy thought. It was the sort of thing she could imagine saying to some foolish man to lower his defenses. *I've been watching you from across the room, and you're ever so handsome. Would you mind terribly if I joined you?*

"You can't have been," she said. "I just got here."

Something in Roman's face shifted, though Dorothy

couldn't have said exactly what it was. It was like he'd winked at her, but he hadn't. "I've been watching you for longer."

"How?"

"My darling, Alice. When you followed the white rabbit down the rabbit hole, you fell into a world where time is a circle instead of a line."

White rabbit? A chill spread over Dorothy's skin, raising the hair on her arms. "What does that mean?"

"Didn't you ever read *Alice's Adventures in Wonderland*?" Roman shook his head, twirling the gun around on his thumb. "Pity. It's one of the great works of literary nonsense. You should pick it up. I believe it was around in your time, but I admit I don't exactly remember when it was published."

He knows, Dorothy realized. Somehow, impossibly, he knew that she'd come from the past.

She remembered the feeling she'd gotten on the docks, right before Roman had kidnapped her. The feeling of having lived this moment before.

Her skin creeping, she repeated, "*Time is a circle instead of a line.* Are you trying to say that you've seen the future?"

A wolf's smile flashed across his face. "Perhaps. Perhaps I've even seen yours. Is there something you want to know?"

Dorothy took a step toward Roman, almost without realizing what she was doing. Questions blew through her head like so many colorful pieces of confetti.

Will I have to face my mother again? Is Ash going to send me back to 1913? Do I end up married to Avery? Will I ever see . . . ?

Her heartbeat was cannon fire. She blinked, refocusing on Roman's face. In the moonlight, his eyes were dark navy, not nearly as bright as they'd seemed before. In that moment, she would've given him anything he asked for if it meant knowing her future. She'd have handed over her soul like it was a forgotten scarf.

She shook her head, and the confetti questions blew away. Instead, she saw her mother's withered hand, yellowed fingernails tapping. She heard Loretta's too-sharp voice. *Everything's a con.*

Nobody offered something for nothing. If Roman was promising her future, he must want something in return.

A shadow crept around the edge of the concrete structure on the other side of the narrow waterway, saving Dorothy the trouble of considering his proposal any further. Roman was facing away and didn't see it, but Dorothy could follow the shadow's movement from the corner of her eye.

She didn't want to draw Roman's attention to it, so she blinked, letting her focus shift back to his face. "Why are you telling me this?"

"You've impressed me." There was something hungry in the way he looked at her. "You escaped your cell, listened in on a private conversation, jumped out of an eighth-story window. It would be a shame to rid the world of your talents. I'd like to offer you a job."

"A job?" This caught Dorothy off guard. She was momentarily at a loss for words—flattered even—until she remembered that Roman had kidnapped and shot her. Indignation took the flattery's place. "I'm not for sale."

Roman picked an invisible piece of lint from his sleeve. "Everything's for sale."

Dorothy was overcome with the sudden desire to slap him, a desire she might have given in to if he hadn't been holding a gun. Through her teeth, she said, "Sorry to disappoint you."

"I'm rarely disappointed." Now, he did wink. "In fact, I'm sure you'll change your mind."

In the background, the shadow grew closer. It looked like a bear, at first, but then he stepped into the light and Dorothy recognized the man from the bar. His name was . . . Willis, wasn't it? He caught her eye and lifted a single finger to his mouth. *Quiet.*

Stalling, she said, "Why would I do that?"

"Power." Roman smiled again, that same wolf's smile, all teeth and twitching lips. "*Money.* What more could a person want?"

Dorothy felt a pang somewhere deep inside her chest. He reminded her of her mother. *You put everything we've worked for at risk.* As though that was all there was. It made her feel strangely empty, that Roman would look at her and think she was the sort of girl who cared only for money and power. As in the chapel, she was again struck by the thought that her outsides and her insides didn't fit together. That there'd been some mistake.

Luckily, Willis chose that moment to leap for the dock. He seemed to hover in the air for far longer than physically possible before curling a massive forearm around Roman's neck. Roman choked out an expletive, and the two of them fell back with a splash, disappearing below. A spray of droplets cascaded onto the dock, soaking Dorothy's bare feet.

She hesitated for a fraction of a second, long enough to watch the ripples spread across the surface of the water as she contemplated how strange this all was. Why had this man she barely knew come to save her? What could he possibly expect in return?

Then, shaking the questions off, she picked a direction and ran.

14

ASH

Ash waited out of sight, back pressed against the grimy bricks of the Fairmont, cold wind nipping at his neck. He wanted to see what was going on around the side of the hotel but couldn't risk blowing his cover.

Snippets of conversation blew toward him.

"What . . . talents . . ."

". . . money . . ."

He strained to listen, but the wind was a roar in his ears, and the voices were low murmurs. Ash hunched down in his jacket, rubbing his chapped hands together to keep the blood pumping. Any second now . . .

A shout cut through his thoughts—followed by a splash that sounded like bodies hitting water. Willis had made his move. Ash whipped around the corner of the hotel and—

Wham. Something small and soft and smelling of wet denim slammed into him, knocking the breath from his lungs. He stumbled, hands clutching for his chest.

Dorothy flew back onto the dock, hitting the wood with a thud. She looked wet and pale, her sopping curls sticking to her face. Her legs were angled to either side of her, reminding Ash of a baby fawn just learning to walk.

But she was alive. Ash had a sudden flash of her frail body sinking through the water, bullets whizzing past her. He was unreasonably relieved that she hadn't been hurt.

He swallowed, struggling to catch his breath. "Damn it, woman," he croaked. "Where in God's name were you going?"

Dorothy pushed the sopping hair off her face, frowning. "What are you doing here?"

"I came to rescue you."

She propped herself up on one arm. "Why?"

Ash was pretty sure she wouldn't have asked him that if she knew how guilty he felt about baiting her back at the tavern. It was his fault she was in this mess. She must think he was a pretty terrible person if she thought he wouldn't come after her.

But, out loud, all he said was, "Because you needed help."

She looked skeptical. "Well aren't you a Good Samaritan?" Water splashed onto the dock, interrupting her. Roman and Willis had thrashed back to the surface and Roman seemed to be trying to lift his gun. Dorothy flinched and pulled her legs away from the edge. "He just *leaped* at him, you know. Was that the whole plan? Leaping?"

Ash felt the corner of his lip twitch, but he quickly bit the smile back, reminding himself that this was the second time he'd gone out of his way to help this girl, only to have his efforts thrown back in his face. "We would've had everything under control if you hadn't jumped out a window," he pointed out.

"I *had* to jump. He was going to kill me!"

Her voice caught on the word *kill*. Ash frowned, suddenly struck by the knowledge that she was scared and that it was only coming across as anger because she didn't like *admitting* that she was scared. He cupped the back of his neck with one hand, ashamed of himself for taking the bait.

She looked pretty pitiable right now, crouched on the dock, soaking wet and shivering. He remembered, again, the sight of her body sinking. The rush of relief when he realized she was okay. Heat climbed his neck.

"Here," he grunted, and reached for her arm, but she gasped and jerked away. Annoyance flared through him, and he snapped. "Do you want help or don't you?"

"It's not you," Dorothy gasped, nodding at her arm. "I—I was shot."

The idea that he'd hurt her made Ash feel even guiltier than he did already. Swearing, he knelt on the dock beside her, carefully folding her sleeve back. Her skin was a deep, ugly red, fading to purple, but at least it wasn't bleeding. The bullet had just grazed her.

"You'll be all right," he said, tracing the bruise with his thumb. "The shot didn't even break skin."

Dorothy's eyes fluttered closed, the pain clear on her face. But she didn't cringe, didn't gasp or cry out. Ash was impressed. The bruise had to hurt like hell.

"So it's a *good* bullet wound," she mumbled, standing. Again, Ash's lip twitched—almost a smile.

Willis was crawling back onto the dock, pulling Roman along with him by the collar of his shirt, like a kitten. Roman tried to lift his gun, but Willis swatted it from his hand and the weapon skidded across the dock, coming to a stop just feet from where Ash crouched.

Ash lunged for it, fingers curling around the familiar grip. It was his gun, after all. The navy-issue snub-nosed S & W revolver he'd had since 1945. Roman had stolen it a year ago, the night he'd left. Holding it now, Ash felt something shift into place. A wrong made right.

He knocked a boot into Roman's shoulder, and Roman lifted his head, eyelids heavy.

"Oh my," Roman droned, and Ash's shoulders went stiff at the familiarity of his voice. "Gang's all here."

Ash wasn't prepared for the revulsion that rose in his chest. He had his old gun in his hand and Roman, broken, on the ground in front of him. He'd expected to be angry but this was more than that—it was a force of nature. Everything in him wanted to grab his old friend by the collar and slam the butt of his gun into his temple. To hit him until he bled.

He leveled his gun at Roman's head. "How'd you do it?"

"How'd I steal your gun?" Roman coughed, spitting up water. "You used to keep the damn thing in your bedside table, and you sleep like the dead. It was like you *wanted* someone to steal it."

"The ship, Roman." Ash held the gun steady, though his

arm trembled with anger. He thought of the *Black Crow*, sitting in a garage below their feet. "You built a time machine. *How?*"

Roman gave him a withering look. "I worked alongside the Professor for much longer than you did. You think he never taught me anything?"

"He's lying," Willis said through clenched teeth. Ash thought so, too. The Professor wouldn't have taught Roman something so valuable. He hadn't even taught Zora, his own daughter.

"You need to train your monster better," Roman murmured, eyes flicking off Willis and then back again. "He speaks out of turn."

Willis lurched forward, grabbed Roman by the collar of his jacket, and lifted him into the air. The blood drained from Roman's face. His feet dangled inches above the dock.

"What did you call me?" Willis growled.

"Willis," Ash warned. His friend's eyes were molten, his mouth a savage crack in the stone of his face. It was a cruel twist of irony that he looked most like a monster when people called him one. "Put him down."

"Yes, Willis," said a new voice, one that sent a chill straight through Ash's bones. "Put him down."

Ash lifted his eyes from Roman's face, resettling them on a figure standing a few feet down the dock. Heavy coat. Dark hood. She lifted her arm, and Ash hardly had time to register the tiny, silver gun she was holding before the portion of dock directly in front of his left foot exploded in a mess of wood and water.

He stumbled backward, swearing. He could feel Dorothy shrink behind him, one hand dropping onto his arm.

"I saw her," she whispered fiercely. "She was in the room with Roman."

"That's Quinn," Ash spat, eyes moving over the sketchy white fox painted across the figure's coat.

Quinn cracked off another shot, and Ash felt the heat of it whizz past his leg.

"The boat's around the corner," he said. "Go wait there." Dorothy didn't argue. Ash heard the patter of her feet against the dock as she hurried over to where the boat was tied. Willis came up beside him, fingers curling into fists, his eyes on Quinn's gun.

"These are more difficult to aim than I thought they'd be." Quinn let the gun dangle from her fingers, sounding bored. "You should have told me."

She tossed the gun to Roman, who had just pushed himself to his feet. He caught it in one hand and said, "You always preferred knives."

"True." Quinn whipped two pencil-thin daggers out from the folds of her coat sleeves and struck them together. The sound of clashing metal was almost like music.

Ash caught Willis's eye and knew the giant was thinking the same thing. Every bar in New Seattle echoed with stories of what Quinn could do with those knives. Shredded skin and ribbons of blood. Ash was pretty good with a pistol but, just now, it felt like a toy.

"We're leaving," he said, raising both hands. He took a step backward.

"It's too late for that," Quinn said, cutting her blades against each other. There was something dark and brown crusted on the metal. An unpleasant emotion flipped through Ash's chest.

He leveled the gun as Quinn lunged—

A motor cut through the air, and Ash's boat jerked forward, Dorothy crouched inside, both hands over her ears. Ash was impressed for a fraction of a second, and then the boat shuddered past him, nearly passing the dock entirely.

Shit, he thought, moving his eyes away from Quinn. Quinn swiped at him with her dagger, catching the side of his face with the tip of the blade. Heat burned through his cheek, but Ash didn't have time to retaliate. The boat was leaving without them. . . .

He raced down the length of the dock and leaped for it, landing hard in the back. He heard a splash in the water and realized Willis had dived in after him.

"I didn't think it would keep going," Dorothy explained, breathless. "I pulled on that thing in the back there, and then—"

"It's fine." Ash curled an arm over her head, pushing her face down as another bullet whizzed past them. He glanced over his shoulder, catching one last glimpse of the dark figures on the dock. "Just keep going."

LOG ENTRY—JUNE 4, 2074
12:02 HOURS
THE WORKSHOP

I honestly never thought this would happen, but WCAAT and NASA have just approved the request, so it looks like we're moving forward.

I'm getting my team—and not just any team. Remember how Natasha suggested we go back in time and recruit the best possible applicants from all of history?

WCAAT and NASA are *actually letting me do that.*

The strongest man. The world's most brilliant medical mind. The most talented pilot.

I'm going to go back and find them all.

Natasha and I spent the night discussing how, exactly, we'll manage to do this. The thing is, taking people out of history—especially extraordinarily talented people—tends to muck things up. But, Natasha had an idea. She pulled up this old record of dead and missing pilots from WWII. The missing pilots were the ones she wanted me to pay attention to. You see, *missing* meant they'd just . . . disappeared. As in, no one ever saw them again. The US government assumed they'd been killed or captured.

But maybe not. Maybe they were taken by a mad scientist from the future.

I have to admit, this seems like the perfect method for recruitment. All I'll have to do is look for those special, talented individuals. And, if they disappear, I'll know that I already went back in time and found them.

Finding the rest of our team will be an exciting step forward, but it's not the only thing we're working on.

Roman and I have spent the past six months performing exploratory missions. This has mostly consisted of mapping the anil and coming up with some preliminary rules for how the time tunnel works. A little boring, true, but necessary. No one in history has been inside the anil before us and survived, so it was essential that we charted it.

Now that that's done, WCAAT and NASA have requested a more ambitious series of missions. Specifically, they want to know how we can use time travel to improve our current living conditions.

In other words, they want me to go back in time and change things.

Obviously, I'm not a fan of this idea. It completely ignores the scientific method. We don't just *change things* and then cross our fingers and hope it'll all work out for the best.

We observe. Form a question. Hypothesize.

And then we conduct a controlled experiment and come up with a conclusion based on the data.

You'd think NASA would be on my side about this, but they seem more interested in their press releases than anything else these days.

It's not like I don't understand where they're coming from. I haven't spent a lot of time writing about the state of our country right now, but things are pretty bleak. And it's not just the storms. Technology isn't exactly flourishing. We used to be the most advanced nation on the planet and now...

It's like the public has lost interest. They don't trust "science" anymore. I think NASA was hoping the time-travel experiments would bring the country together, sort of like the moon landing in the 1960s.

That's not what happened. Instead, the public has rebelled. They want to know why we're not using time travel to help people. To change things.

There've even been protests. Signs.

The past is our right!

Stuff like that.

The biggest protests have been in our very own tent city, right outside my workshop. Seattle isn't recovering from that last earthquake as quickly as we thought it would. Parts of the city are still flooded, and huge areas still haven't regained power. They've declared a state of emergency, but there's only so much the government can do. WCAAT wants to use these experiments to show the city that we're dedicated to helping. I can't fault them for that. I understand why people want to fix things. I do. But changing the past could make everything worse. We haven't even had this technology for a year yet. We can't start messing around with the past until we have a better understanding of how it all works.

In any case, I was explaining all of this to Roman last night. I expected him to take my side against the charlatans at NASA but, instead, we got into our first real fight.

I won't go into all the ugly details, but he did say one thing that struck me harder than I expected.

He said, "You haven't lost anything in the earthquakes. You still have your home, your family, your future. You have no idea how hard it's been for the rest of us to get up in the morning, knowing all of that is gone."

I admit, I didn't have a response to that. I can't help remembering the software Roman was building the day I first met him, how he was trying to find a way to predict earthquakes before they devastated entire cities.

Sometimes I forget that he's only fifteen years old. In the past year, I've started thinking of him as a real scientist. A peer, even. I'd assumed it was the research that drew him to our work on time travel.

It never occurred to me that he might have other reasons for doing this.

15

DOROTHY

OCTOBER 14, 2077, NEW SEATTLE

Fog clung to the surface of the water, leeching what little color remained of the city at night. Only the trees broke up the darkness, their trunks ghostly white and chalky. The moon must have been shining somewhere, because their bark appeared to be glowing.

Dorothy shivered, still damp from her fall in the water. She brushed her locket with one finger to make sure it was still there. Ash had just given it back to her, and she kept expecting it to slip away again, to be lost forever. She doubted she'd ever see that filthy wedding dress again, and so this was the only thing she still had from her own time period, and she found herself feeling oddly sentimental about it.

She shifted, feeling the heat of his body just behind her. They were still crowded in the tiny motorboat, so close that Dorothy could feel Ash's arm graze her lower back whenever he shifted in place. Briny, milk-white fog hung low on the water, carrying a smell of fish, but when the wind turned, Dorothy could still catch hints of the smoky scent of his skin.

She wanted to ask him about the white trees, but she held herself back. To be perfectly honest, she didn't really understand the dynamic between them. He wasn't a mark anymore—but he wasn't a friend, either.

And yet he'd come for her when she'd been kidnapped.

But not for free, she reminded herself. Everything had a price. Ash hadn't revealed his price yet, but she knew it was coming.

They seemed to have made it outside of the city. There were fewer tall buildings and bridges, but sharp, solid objects still jutted up from the waves. Dorothy touched the side of one as they rumbled past, and it was hard and grainy beneath her fingers, covered in a layer of slimy moss.

A rooftop, maybe? It was hard to tell in the night.

Finally, she couldn't take it anymore. She turned and asked, "Why are the trees all white?"

Ash pulled their boat up to a dock that appeared to run alongside the roof of a submerged building. It was hard for Dorothy to make out the details in the dark, but the roof looked slanted, with two cone-shaped turrets rising to either side.

Ash cut the motor, but the growling sound echoed in the silence.

"Because they're dead," he said as Willis brought a length of rope out from under his seat and began knotting it to the dock. "An earthquake hit the city two and a half years ago, and it caused a massive tsunami. That's why Seattle's underwater, in case you were wondering. Anyway, the salt water killed all the trees on impact, but they were big enough that they stayed standing. We call them ghost trees. Those trunks you see are just their corpses."

Dorothy hugged her arms close to her chest, fear prickling up her arms. *Ghosts. Corpses.* "Charming," she choked out.

Ash climbed out of the boat, shooting her a look. "Maybe not, but it's home," he said. "The people who survived spent the last couple of years trying to make this place livable again."

Home. Dorothy felt a hint of jealousy at how easily he'd said that word. She'd never stayed anywhere long enough for it to feel like home.

She stood, and the whole world swayed. She groped for something to grab on to and Ash took her elbow, steadying her. His hands were softer than she'd expected, his fingertips rough with calluses. The moths in her belly stirred.

Stupid moths, she thought. It took her a second to find her voice. "Thank you," she murmured, shrugging him off.

"Don't mention it," Ash grumbled.

Willis pushed a window open, allowing a thin crack of light to seep out into the dark around them. The light illuminated a white Gothic-looking facade complete with a clock tower and three small windows. Only the top story of the building appeared to be above water. A stone bell tower rose over it, making Dorothy think of the cathedrals in Paris. In the darkness, it looked spooky.

The two men climbed through first, and Dorothy

followed after them, grunting as she landed on the floor. "Is this your house?"

"It's an abandoned building." Ash fumbled with something Dorothy couldn't see. There was a hiss, and the smell of sulfur, and then a match leaped to life between his fingers. He pulled an oil lamp off the wall.

"Haven't you got electricity?" she asked, eyeing the lamp suspiciously. "How is it possible that there's no electricity in the future?"

Future. The word sent nerves prickling over her skin. She still couldn't quite believe it.

"The earthquake knocked the power out in most of the city," Willis explained gently. "Electricity is pretty hard to come by these days."

"It's not impossible to find, just difficult," Ash added. "Come on."

The dancing flame left deep shadows in the hollows of his cheeks. He lifted a massive hand, motioning farther down the hall. "Come on. We don't use light near the windows."

They made their way down twisting hallways and past darkened rooms, and Dorothy tried not to linger for too long near the photographs hanging on the walls. They were in color. Actual, real blues and reds and greens, like in a painting. She wanted to pull them off the walls and examine every perfect detail, but she held herself back. Her fear had become giddy, a strange mixture of horror and excitement and adrenaline. She wanted to skip down the hallway and cower under a large piece of furniture, all at the same time.

This must be what going mad feels like, she thought, and she had the strange urge to laugh again. Or, possibly, throw up.

They finally stopped in a large kitchen filled with more stuff than Dorothy had ever witnessed in one place at the same time. It looked like some mad inventor's laboratory, like something that had been dreamed instead of built. Books and maps and papers towered on top of every surface. A greasy pile of cogs and wires sat at one end of a long, beaten-wood table, beneath it a sheaf of newspaper that did nothing to contain the mess. Several layers of newspaper covered the floors, and moldy cardboard boxes towered up against the walls.

There wasn't an inch of space that wasn't already blanketed in scribbled notes. Papers were piled on top of each other, being used as coasters for greasy gears and rusted cogs. Some had been half crumpled into little balls and then flattened out again, the notes rewritten in a darker, messier hand. A rusted sink and strangely shaped oven slouched along one wall, almost like an afterthought.

Chandra was standing on an overturned bucket in the center of it all, rooting around inside a cabinet above the sink. "Jonathan Asher Jr., I know there's a bag of potato chips somewhere in this kitchen. If you've hidden it again—"

"Try behind the bread," Ash said. He moved a stack of papers off a wooden chair and motioned for Dorothy to sit. She stayed standing, out of stubbornness.

Chandra turned, shaking her head. "I already looked there and—" Her eyes shifted to Dorothy. "You found her!

Thank God." She hopped off the bucket. "I really didn't want Quinn Fox to eat you."

For a second, Dorothy's voice got caught in her throat. "Was that a possibility?"

"Chandra," Ash said. "Get your bag? She caught a slug on the arm."

Chandra blinked, eyes monstrous behind her thick glasses. "Slug?"

"Bullet."

"Bullet? Why was there a bullet? What happened?" Then, rounding on Dorothy, "Did you get shot?"

"Chandra?" Ash repeated, more harshly. "Your bag. And let Zora know we found her, will you?"

Chandra nodded and hurried from the room, casting one last, anxious glance at Dorothy.

"Zora was out looking for you, too," Willis explained. He glanced at a chair sitting next to the door, but seemed to decide that the skinny legs wouldn't hold his bulk and leaned against the wall instead. "We were all very worried. The city isn't safe after dark."

Worried. The word struck Dorothy harder than she thought it would. *Why* were they worried? In her experience, people didn't risk their lives saving strange women from gun-wielding maniacs for free. She didn't want to think about what they expected from her in return.

They gave you clothes, too, she reminded herself, and cringed as she added it to her mental tally. She'd never be able to repay all that.

She bit the inside of her cheek, pushing the thought away. "Where are we?"

"This building used to be part of the university," Ash said. "Before the city was underwater."

Dorothy was still having a hard time processing the idea that all of Seattle was underwater, so she focused on the part that felt familiar.

"The University of Washington?" she asked. Avery had taken her to see the university on their trip into the city a few weeks ago, but it had been grand then, all redbrick and climbing ivy. She frowned at the mold climbing the walls. This couldn't be the same place. "Are you sure?"

"It was the University of Washington up until about 2060," Ash explained. "Then scientists started taking the study of time travel more seriously and it became the West Coast Academy of Advanced Technology. For about a decade it was the best place in the world to study theoretical physics."

Dorothy blinked, saying nothing. It was far too much information. All at once the weight of one hundred years of history seemed to spin out around her, making her dizzy.

She sank into the chair Ash had offered without making the conscious decision to do so. "And all of you *live* here?"

"We do." Willis lit another match and lowered it to one of the burners on the stove. A red-orange flame leaped to life. "Would you like some tea?"

"Yes, thank you," Dorothy murmured. Her heartbeat had gone fluttery. She wasn't sure how tea was going to help, but she suddenly, desperately needed something warm in her hand. It was the sort of thing her mother would insist upon.

Her heart gave a lurch. *Her mother.* If they really had traveled over a hundred years into the future, then her mother was long dead. Everyone she'd ever met was dead.

"Oh God," she murmured. Had it really been just this morning that getting away from her mother had been her dearest wish? The idea that she was dead, that Dorothy might never see her again . . .

Ash cleared his throat. "I, uh, know it's a lot to take," he said. "But it gets easier after a few days. Trust me."

Trust? Dorothy almost felt like laughing, except that none of this was remotely funny. How was she supposed to trust a man she'd only just met? Loretta had taught her to trust no one but herself.

The teakettle started to whistle. Willis moved it off the stovetop, taking a couple of chipped mugs down from a cupboard.

Something suddenly occurred to her. "How would you know?" she asked Ash.

Ash frowned. "How would I know what?"

"You said that this gets easier, but how would you know that unless you did it yourself?"

He cocked an eyebrow. "I *did* do it myself."

Willis handed Dorothy a cup of tea, and she took it without thinking, absently lifting the cup to her lips. "*You're* from the past?"

"Born in 1929. Left in 1945."

"1929," Dorothy repeated. Sixteen years after she was supposed to be married. She released a small laugh. "You could be my grandson."

Ash's eyes flicked to hers. "But I'm *not*."

The tips of his ears had gone pink again.

Dorothy could feel a grin threatening. She'd been right. It was fun to tease him.

She swallowed, barely noticing that the tea had scalded her tongue. "But you *could* be. How would either of us know for sure?" The grin spread wide across her lips. "Maybe you should call me Nana?"

Ash's ears went from pink to red. He said, through his teeth, "Look, princess, maybe you thought it was appropriate to stow away on a strange ship, but the rest of us got here the old-fashioned way."

"My name is *Dorothy*, not princess," she said, grin vanishing. "And what does that mean? The old-fashioned way?"

"There used to be rules about how we did this. We were all recruited." Ash jerked his chin at something behind Dorothy's head. "See for yourself."

Dorothy swiveled around in her chair, sending a bit of tea sloshing over the side of her cup. There were pictures tacked to the wall behind her. A black-and-white of Willis wearing a teeny leotard that showed off every one of his great, bulging muscles. A sketch of Chandra looking strangely like a boy, her black hair cut very short. A color photograph of Ash with a pair of goggles propped on his forehead and grease smeared across his cheek.

That photograph was particularly jarring. Ash was smiling, happy. Much happier than Dorothy had seen him in real life. She itched to touch it, to run her finger along the edge of his smile. But she held herself back.

Someone had taped a handwritten sign above them. Dorothy straightened the corner, squinting to read it in the dim light.

The Chronology Protection Agency.

"What's a Chronology Protection Agency?" she asked.

"It was supposed to be a joke," Ash said, scratching his nose. "Some mathematician guy once said that, if time travel were real, we'd need to have a chronology protection law to stop people from going back in time and killing their parents."

Dorothy felt her eyes go wide. "Could you do that?"

"We don't actually know. Part of the Professor's research involved going back in time to see how changes to the past might affect the world now."

Something tugged at the back of Dorothy's brain. She said, "The Professor?"

"Professor Zacharias Walker," Ash explained. "He's sort of the father of time travel. He built the first time machine and discovered that you can stabilize an anil using exotic matter."

Professor Zacharias Walker. A shiver moved up Dorothy's arms. She'd seen that name before. It was scrawled inside the very journal that was currently stuffed down her pants.

"Cool, right?" Chandra interrupted, bustling back into the kitchen with a black medical bag tucked under one arm.

She dropped the bag onto the already messy table, sending a greasy-looking gear rolling to the ground. "Arm, please."

Dorothy held out her injured arm, while Chandra shuffled around inside her bag, pulling out a roll of gauze, a bottle of ointment, and some cotton balls. "Why would this . . . Professor person go back through time to find a bunch of kids?"

Ash started to answer, then stopped himself. He pressed his lips together, thinking for a moment before trying again.

"We were supposed to be part of a mission," he said carefully. "Well, a series of missions, back through time. We were a team, like I told you before. The Professor's always been a little, well . . ." Ash cleared his throat. "*Eccentric.*"

"He means crazy." Chandra popped open a bottle of ointment and began wetting one of the cotton balls.

"Whimsical," Willis added, mustache twitching as he sipped his tea.

"Whatever," Ash said. "The point is, the Professor thought it was a waste to have the most brilliant minds in all of history at his fingertips and not actually *use* them. So instead of hiring people from his own time, he took a time machine back to find the best of the best. You know, the greatest pilot, and the strongest man, and the most brilliant medical mind—"

"That's me," Chandra chirped. "Now hold tight, because this is going to sting like a mother."

She pressed the cotton ball to Dorothy's arm, and the bullet wound flared. Dorothy swore and tried to jerk away, but Chandra held tight to her wrist.

"Do you want your arm to get infected, turn green, and fall off?" she asked.

"N-no," Dorothy stuttered. The pain had made her eyes water.

"Good. Then hold still."

Dorothy clenched her teeth and nodded, looking back at the wall of pictures to distract herself from the pain. There was one last photograph, but it'd been ripped across the face so that she could see only the man's shoulders and the edge of his collar.

Below, it read, *Roman Estrada*.

"Roman," she breathed, momentarily forgetting the pain in her arm. She thought of the dark-haired boy with the wicked smile. *When you followed the white rabbit down the rabbit hole, you fell into a world where time is a circle instead of a line.* Her mouth felt suddenly dry. "*He* was part of this?"

"Yeah, he was." Ash's voice sounded thicker than it had a moment ago, and there was something complicated happening behind his eyes. "Roman was the Professor's first hire, but they got into this huge fight about a year ago. That's when Roman left to join the Cirkus."

Dorothy frowned, watching the emotion flick across Ash's face. *There's something he's not telling me*, she thought. But that made sense. They'd only just met, after all. Only a fool would blurt out all his secrets.

She sat up a little straighter. At least this explained why Roman had this Professor person's journal. He must've stolen it.

"What's the Cirkus?" she asked.

"The Black Cirkus," Chandra said. "They're the bad guys."

Dorothy remembered the images she'd seen painted on the walls back in the city. Repeating black circus tents. *The past is our right!*

"What do they want?" she asked.

"They want to go back in time," said Ash. "They seem to think that's the key to fixing all our problems."

"Isn't it?"

Ash shot her a withering look and said only, "No."

Dorothy bit her lip to keep it from curling. Ash threw out that *no* like it was obvious, but really, what sort of problems couldn't you fix with *time travel*? She was inclined to dislike these Cirkus people because of how they'd kidnapped and tried to kill her, but it sounded like they had the right idea.

Ash continued. "Time travel is . . . complicated. Mostly, if you go back and try to change something, you end up screwing things up even more."

"So you don't do anything?" Dorothy asked, disappointed. "Isn't that dull?"

"Yes," muttered Chandra.

"We're looking for the Professor." Ash shot Chandra a look that she pretended not to see. "We go back in time to places we think he might have visited. He took the *Dark Star*—"

"*Dark Star*?" asked Dorothy.

"It's another time machine."

"Like yours?"

"Better than mine. The Professor took it about a year ago and disappeared. He could be anywhere, in any time. The Black Cirkus is . . . problematic, but the Professor will know how to handle them. We just have to find him and bring him back."

Dorothy studied Ash's face, wondering if he knew about the Professor's journal. If it was this important to find him, they could probably use any help they could get. She could feel the slim, leather book shift beneath the waistband of her pants, soaking wet but otherwise intact. She only hoped it was still legible.

She didn't have to tell him she had it. But her mental tally flashed through her head, reminding her that she owed them. Chandra had already patched her up—*twice*—and they'd given her clothes and tea. . . .

She found herself glancing over at Willis. *We were all very worried*, he'd said. Like she was their friend.

Dorothy chewed her lip. She didn't have friends. They'd never stayed anywhere long enough for her to make one, and, anyway, her mother thought they were unnecessary. Loretta only ever trusted her daughter, and the people she could pay. Her circle of confidants had been small.

Dorothy's had been even smaller—she only trusted herself. These people weren't friends, but she didn't want to be in their debt, either. Handing over the journal would make them even.

Resigned, she tugged the book loose of its hiding place, dangling it between two fingers, like a dirty sock. "Would this help?"

16

ASH

Ash stared at the tiny black book, blood pumping in his ears.

Where did she get it? It was only the first of about a dozen questions racing through his head, but the others were mostly variations on the same theme.

Like, *How did she find it?* and *When?* and *What the actual hell?*

Then, Dorothy said, "I found this back at the hotel," and Ash felt like an idiot.

Of course.

Roman had ransacked the Professor's office the night he'd left to join the Black Cirkus. At first, it'd looked like he'd just torn stuff up. Bookshelves were overturned, boxes ripped open, books scattered across the floor. He must've stolen the journal then.

Ash thought of the time machine hidden in the depths of the Fairmont's garage, looking like a carbon copy of the *Dark*

Star. There was one mystery solved. The time machine's blueprints were in the journal.

He cleared his throat. "Where's Zora?" he asked, surprised by how normal his voice sounded.

Chandra said, "She was tying up her Jet Ski when I—"

"Get her."

Chandra grumbled something about saying please, and then Ash heard her footsteps in the hall. He didn't watch her go—didn't dare move his eyes from the journal in Dorothy's hand. They'd spent months sorting through scraps and scribbles, desperate, hoping for a forgotten note dashed off on a fast-food napkin, a date doodled into the corner of a notebook.

And now—this. Something that could lead them straight to the Professor himself. It seemed too good to be true. Ash half expected it to disappear.

And then—it *did* disappear.

Ash blinked. "The hell? Where'd it go?"

"Someplace safe," said Dorothy, stretching her fingers. "I want a bit more information before I hand it over."

He exhaled very slowly. "You have no idea how valuable that is."

Her eyes flashed. "So tell me."

Ash didn't like the look on her face. It was a look that said she already knew exactly how valuable the journal was, that she'd known long before she took it out and waved it in front of his nose. She meant to use it as leverage.

The muscles in his shoulders knotted together. It was

difficult for him to pinpoint how he felt just then. Excited about the journal, frustrated with Dorothy.

And—underneath all of that—light-headed, like he might actually faint if he didn't remind himself to breathe at regular intervals.

He thought, without meaning to, *I might not die after all.*

It was a raw, deeply personal thing to hope for, and he was embarrassed for thinking it in front of Dorothy. Which was ridiculous. Dorothy didn't know what he was thinking.

"Okay." He ran a hand through his hair and found that it was still damp with sweat and engine grease. Already, he knew that he couldn't tell her the real reason he needed to find the Professor. The thought of admitting to her that the woman he loved was going to kill him bothered him for reasons he didn't care to look at too closely. But he could tell her something.

"The thing about time travel is that so much of what we know is theoretical," he said. "Scientists spent centuries studying concepts and coming up with ideas, but they were never tested, because they couldn't be. Until the Professor came along."

Dorothy frowned. "Is this what the Chronology Protection Agency was for? You all were supposed to go back in time and do experiments and things?"

"Yes. But, before we came along, the Professor spent years performing experiments of his own, all of which he documented in that little book you found. One of the things he discovered was that time is infinitely more complex than anyone ever imagined. People always thought of it like a river that only moves in one direction—forward. But it's much more like a . . . well, a pond for lack of a better metaphor."

"Time is a circle, not a line," Dorothy murmured, almost to herself.

Ash blinked, surprised by this. Time travel was difficult to explain, and even more difficult to understand. It took most people a while to catch on.

His opinion of Dorothy shifted to include this new information. She was smarter than he'd given her credit for being. Possibly much smarter.

"That's it exactly," he said, studying her. "Time is moving all around us, all at once. The Chronology Protection Agency was supposed to figure out what happens when you go back in time and start changing things. But, before we could begin our mission, there was this massive earthquake."

"That's what flooded the city?" Dorothy asked.

"There were actually a bunch of earthquakes," Chandra cut in. "There was a 4.7 in 2071 and a 6.9 in 2073."

"Chandra's right," Ash said. "There were a few earthquakes leading up to it, but the Cascadia Fault quake, also sometimes referred to as the mega-quake, was the big one. It was a 9.3 on the Richter scale, easily the most devastating earthquake in US history. It completely wiped out the West Coast, taking something like thirty-five thousand people with it. It was so bad that the United States couldn't figure out how to fix the city afterward, so they decided to move the borders of the country."

Dorothy's eyebrows went up. "I'm sorry . . . move the borders? What does that mean?"

"It means that, officially, the United States starts near the Rocky Mountains and ends at the Mississippi River."

Dorothy was just about to ask what had happened to the East Coast when a larger question occurred to her. "We're not in America anymore?"

Ash shook his head. "This area is called the Western Territories now. It's a no-man's-land."

Dorothy chewed her lip, and Ash thought he saw a flicker of fear move across her features. It surprised him. She hadn't seemed capable of fear.

After a moment, she said, "That's terrible, but I don't understand what it has to do with time travel."

Ash hesitated, remembering. Before the Cascadia Fault quake, they'd all gone back to July 20, 1969, to watch *Apollo 11* land on the moon. It hadn't been their best trip—they didn't have a place to watch the footage, so they'd gathered in a crowded hotel lobby. It'd been too hot, and the footage was fuzzy, the reception terrible. But it had also been awesome in the truest sense of the word. Invoking of awe.

And then, only a few hours later, they'd exited the anil to find their world changed. Water covering the city. Destruction in every direction.

A lump formed in Ash's throat. He paused, trying to find a way to explain.

"The earthquake doesn't have anything to do with time

travel," said Zora, interrupting his thoughts. Ash hadn't noticed her hovering at the door to the kitchen, but now she pulled up a chair next to him and sat down, shrugging off her jacket. Her face was perfectly impassive, like she was wearing a mask, but Ash found himself studying it a little more carefully than usual, looking for some hint that she was thinking about the day her life had changed forever.

Zora seemed to intentionally avoid his eyes as she continued. "My father had a difficult time continuing his research after the earthquake. I mean, *everyone* had a hard time; we all . . . we all lost people we loved. But he just couldn't move on. He was supposed to be studying time travel, but he couldn't stop researching crustal deformation and fault slip rates."

"That's earthquake stuff," Chandra added. "He was obsessed."

Ash watched Zora, waiting to see if she'd say anything else. But she only stared ahead, eyes focused on nothing in particular, her expression stony.

There was more to the story, of course. But it wasn't Ash's story to tell, so he cleared his throat, moving on. "And then he disappeared, about a year ago. He took the other time machine and vanished. We think he went back in time to do something, but he didn't tell us where he was going—or *when* he was going."

"So this journal . . ." Dorothy stopped twisting her necklace at her neck, and the chain unraveled, causing the locket to twitch at her collarbone like a dead fish. Ash hadn't seen her pull the journal out of its hiding place, but it was suddenly in her hand. "You think he wrote down where and when he went?"

"The Professor kept meticulous notes," he said, watching her quick fingers flip through the pages. "If he were going somewhere, he would've explained why. We just have to read the final entry."

Dorothy paused to read something. She looked up again, and Ash felt a sudden jolt, but he told himself it was more about the journal than the intensity of Dorothy's green eyes.

She said, "I'll give it to you under one condition."

The adrenaline hit Ash then. He wanted to rip the journal out of Dorothy's hands, but he held himself back.

Did that mean there was something there?

"I could just take it from you," he said. But even as the words left his lips, he felt a flicker of doubt. Could he?

As though reading his mind, Dorothy's mouth curved into a small, private smile. "You could *try*."

"Fine. What's your condition?"

"I want a favor."

Ash's first impulse was to refuse. He didn't want to owe Dorothy anything, wasn't sure he trusted her to be reasonable with her request. But then his eyes landed on the soft leather cover of the Professor's journal, and he felt something inside of him shift.

Who was he kidding? He would have given her anything she asked for if it meant reading the Professor's final thoughts.

Heart hammering, he asked, "What kind of favor?"

"I don't know yet."

"I'm not agreeing to a favor unless you tell me—"

"Ash," Zora said, her hand suddenly on his arm. Ash stopped talking, ashamed of himself. Whatever he was feeling about reading the Professor's journal, he knew Zora must be feeling it times a hundred.

He lifted his eyes to hers. Of course, they would do anything.

"One favor," he said to Dorothy.

Something like triumph passed over Dorothy's face. She placed the journal on the kitchen table.

Holding his breath, Ash picked it up, and turned to the last entry.

LOG ENTRY—OCTOBER 23, 2076
04:43 HOURS
THE WORKSHOP

It's only been a few hours since my last entry, but I had to get this down.

I—I can hardly keep my hand steady enough to write, I'm shaking so badly.

These numbers can't be right. But they *are* right. I've run the calculations three times now. I know they're right.

And if they're right, that means . . .

Oh God. I can't make myself write it out. I need more data first. It would be irresponsible to posit this theory without the appropriate amount of research to back it up. I need to gather more information and . . . and develop a testable prediction and . . .

I can't do any of that here. The electricity is spotty, and half my books and notes are underwater. And I'll need access to some very specific information. Information I won't be able to find here—*now.*

This is a little out there, but stay with me. I read about an old army complex called Fort Hunter in a book Natasha gave me years ago, *Top Ten Secret Military Bases in the United States.*

I have the book in front of me now. The bases have all been shut down, so the book is able to go into incredible detail, telling you everything from how to get inside to what kind of research they were involved in to whether anyone ever successfully broke in.

Fort Hunter's security was incredibly tight back when the complex was operational, but according to this, they dropped to a skeleton crew between 0200 and 0600 hours. Their east wing was dedicated exclusively to the kind of work I'll need access to.

And someone managed to successfully break into the complex on the morning of March 17, 1980.

It all fits.

I have to go back. I have to do this. If I'm right, I still might have a chance to fix everything.

The state of the world may hang in the balance.

I only hope I'm not too late.

17

DOROTHY

OCTOBER 14, 2077, NEW SEATTLE

It was the handwriting that left Dorothy feeling uneasy. In earlier entries, the Professor's printing had been perfectly neat and uniform, like he'd used a ruler to get it just right.

But this was shaky, like he'd written it very quickly. It was smudged, too, although that was probably because it'd gotten wet.

"Oh my God." Zora covered her mouth with her hands. "Fort Hunter . . . I—I remember that book. We used to keep it on our coffee table, but I haven't seen it since he left."

"Do you think he took it with him?" Ash asked.

"He must've." Zora's eyes went unfocused, thinking. "If Fort Hunter is the place I'm thinking of, it's this military base hidden inside a hollowed-out mountain." She picked up the journal and started flipping through the pages. "There was top-secret research being conducted there, but I don't know exactly what it was."

"That's sort of the point of something being top secret, isn't it?" Chandra said, but Zora didn't seem to hear her.

"Nuclear bombs, maybe?" Zora flipped through the book, stopping every few moments to squint at her father's smudged writing, or peel two wet pages apart. "He must write something else . . ."

She paused for a moment, lips moving as she read. Frowning, she turned to an earlier page and then slowly shook her head. "There are only a few entries from after the megaquake, and they're mostly about Roman. This last one looks like the only place where he mentions anything about going back to Fort Hunter and this terrible thing he discovered. Damn it! Why wouldn't he just *say* why it was so important for him to go back?"

"There's another way to find out," Ash said.

Zora looked up, her eyes darkening. "Ash . . ."

"Zora, think about it. We know he's at Fort Hunter. He wrote down the exact date he wanted to go back to, the exact time. We could find him. We could *bring him home*."

"You of all people should know it won't be that easy," said Zora.

Dorothy pressed her lips together. Ash and Zora continued to argue, but she wasn't really listening. Her eyes flicked to the Professor's journal.

1980, the entry had read. Almost a hundred years in the past, but still the future, at least as far as she was concerned. It was dizzying to think about.

She leaned toward Chandra and asked, her voice low. "Do you know what the 1980s were like?"

Chandra's eyes lit up. "Oh, they were *awesome.* So many Molly Ringwald movies, and the fashion—" She shook her head, whistling through her teeth.

"Was the world"—Dorothy nodded toward the window—"like this? Flooded?"

"Um . . ." The skin between Chandra's eyebrows creased. "No, it wasn't. I think the eighties were pretty cool, natural disaster–wise. But most of what I know about that time period comes from watching old episodes of this show *Dallas*, which was *so good*, by the way. It was about these two feuding oil companies, and their kids are, like, in love? Sort of like Romeo and Juliet. And—"

"But were there any wars? Or gangs like the Black Cirkus? Or . . ." Dorothy trailed off, her mind going blank. She knew there were other, smarter questions she should be asking, but none came to mind. "Did women ever get the right to vote?"

"You're asking a lot of questions," Ash cut in, studying her.

Dorothy started. She hadn't realized he and Zora had stopped arguing.

"I'm curious," she said.

"Why?"

Dorothy wasn't sure how to answer. Ash had told her she wouldn't like this drowned world of his, but he'd been wrong. She found it fascinating.

Still, she didn't think she wanted to stay here, not when

she knew there were other places, other time periods to explore. She felt the same thrill of adventure she'd felt back in the clearing outside the church, when she'd first glimpsed Ash's airplane. *More.*

Time travel meant there were endless options, each filled with their own wonderful, terrible things.

Her heart thrummed inside her chest. She wanted to see them all.

"I have my reasons," she said finally.

Ash held her gaze for a long moment. There was something unfamiliar in his expression: confusion, maybe, or concern. It softened the hard lines of his face and made him look very young.

Young, Dorothy thought, *but still like himself.* Ash didn't seem capable of looking like anyone other than himself. In her mind, Dorothy pictured her own face reflecting back at her from the church mirror. That perfectly pinned hair, those painted lips. She felt a sudden, inexplicable twist of anger. That face had belonged to a stranger.

There was a part of Dorothy that felt like she could leave that girl—that *face*—behind, if only she kept running.

But these weren't thoughts she could put into words, so she didn't try.

Instead, she sat up straighter, looking Ash in the eye. "I've decided on my favor."

His eyebrows went up. "Already?"

"I want to go with you." She nodded at the Professor's journal. "I want you to take me back in time, to 1980."

18

ASH

Ash wasn't sure he'd heard her correctly. "What?"

"I said that I want to come with you." Dorothy spoke slowly, enunciating each word. "To 1980." And then, as if it had just occurred to her, she added, "Please."

He sputtered, "*Why?*"

She looked at him like she thought this was an odd question. "That's my concern."

Ash studied her, at a loss. In the short time she'd been here, she hadn't once asked to be returned to her own time. She hadn't mentioned a family or friends or the man who'd surely been waiting for her back at the church she'd snuck out of. Did she really have so little to lose?

Or was there something else? Something she was running from?

"Excuse me," Zora cut in. "But none of us are going back to 1980."

"I'm afraid I'm likely to side with Zora on this," Willis

said, as he set his empty mug back on the counter. "The Professor has the means to come back to 2077 on his own, if he should so wish. He has the better time machine and a larger store of EM. Why would we force him to return if he doesn't want to?" He nodded at the journal. "It sounds like he had reasons for going to 1980."

"Are you freaking kidding me?" Chandra said, rounding on him. "He's the one who took us from our homes and time periods in the first place!"

Willis frowned. "He gave us a *choice*, Chandie."

"Yeah, a choice between living in our lame old time periods and exploring all the mysteries of the past and future in his *time machine*." She made a noise in the back of her throat and motioned to the room around them. "Does this look like a time machine? Or does it look like a damp, boring room in the middle of nowhere?"

Willis straightened to his full height, the top of his head nearly brushing the ceiling. "Do you want to go back?"

Chandra scoffed. "That's not what I said!"

"After what happened, I would expect—"

"Stop," said Zora. Her voice was low, but Chandra and Willis stopped arguing at once.

Zora turned to Ash. "Can I speak to you in the hall, please?"

"Wait, what?" Chandra asked, annoyance leaping across her face. "Willis and I are part of the Chronology Protection Agency, too. Or did you forget?"

Willis didn't say anything but crossed his arms over his chest, looking menacing.

"And there's the small matter of my favor," Dorothy added. Ash was annoyed to see that she, at least, seemed delighted by this turn of events. She was watching their argument with interest, a smile curling her lips.

"This decision involves *all* of us," Chandra said. "We should discuss it together."

"There's no decision," Ash cut in. "The *Second Star* is *my* ship, and I'm going—"

"Give us a second." Zora grabbed Ash by the elbow and steered him into the hallway outside the kitchen. She pushed the door closed with her hip and spat, "What are you doing?"

Ash yanked his arm free but didn't step away. "What do you mean, what am I doing? You knew I'd want to go back for him."

"Yes, and if you were just risking your own life that would be fine—"

"That would be *fine*?" Ash felt his eyebrows shoot up his forehead. "I seem to recall many, *many* arguments with you that would indicate the contrary."

Zora pointed at the closed door. "*They* don't understand the risks of traveling through an anil with so little EM. I don't think *you* even understand the risks." She began ticking items off on her fingers. "We're talking skin being pulled from bones, eyeballs liquefying—"

"Yeah? And what about the risks of staying behind?" Ash drew closer to Zora and tapped the cover of the Professor's journal with one finger. "You read the same entry I did. I don't know about you, but I take phrases like 'the state of the world may hang in the balance' pretty damn seriously."

Zora opened her mouth. Closed it again.

"We always wondered why he didn't leave a note. What if *this* was his note? What if we were always meant to find the journal, but Roman just got to it first?"

Zora pressed her lips together. Ash knew she was replaying that last day with her father. Mining each word and gesture for hidden clues. Wondering.

Ash had spent two years talking Zora into doing things she didn't want to do, and he knew when he was winning. He lowered his hand to her shoulder, going in for the kill. "What if he needs us to come back for him? What if he's stuck somewhere, if that's the reason he never came home?"

Her eyes flicked back to his, flashing something painful. She said, in a small voice, "I can't lose anyone else. If something happened to you, or Willis or Chandra . . ."

"You keep saying that, but if I don't do this, I'll die for sure."

He saw it clearly. *Black trees. White hair. A kiss, a knife . . .*

Zora curled her hand over Ash's and left it there, the only sign she gave that she was bothered by this conversation. He wondered if she were picturing it, too.

And then, behind them, a small voice choked out, "What?"

Ash jerked around. The door to the kitchen was open a crack and, through it, he could see a sliver of Chandra's face, her eyes monstrous behind her glasses.

"You're going to die?" she said.

The door opened wider, and Willis appeared, mirage-like, from the shadows behind the door. He said nothing but kept his eyes fixed on Ash's face, frowning.

"Why didn't you tell us?" Chandra looked at Willis, like she was worried she might be the only one left out of this secret. "What's going to happen? Oh my God, will one of us die, too?"

"None of you are going to die," Ash said, and, with that, he gave them a quick overview of the prememory, telling them about the boat and the knife, the water and the trees. Something inside of him tightened as he spoke.

Now, he thought. Now was the time to tell them about the girl with the white hair. The kiss. Now was the time to admit to his friends that he was going to fall in love with his murderer.

"And then . . . um, it ends. It just ends," he finished, losing his nerve.

Zora raised one eyebrow when she noticed the omission, but she said nothing.

Ash wouldn't have been able to explain, anyway. He didn't want his friends to know how weak he was, how foolish.

"And you think the Professor will be able to help you avoid this future?" Willis asked. "How?"

"My father spent years studying time theory before the rest of you got here," Zora explained. "I can't say for sure that he can prevent the future from unfolding exactly as it did in Ash's prememory, but I know that he performed extensive experiments on that exact subject. If there's anyone in the world who can stop it, it's him."

Ash's eyes flicked up, meeting hers. He felt a cruel hope unfurling inside of him. Did this mean they were going?

"So that's it," Chandra said, as though reading his mind. "We *have* to go back."

Willis smoothed the edge of his mustache with two fingers. He said, "The risk would be worth it, if it meant there was a chance that you would survive." He nodded toward Ash. "I agree with Chandra. We have to go back."

"*We* don't have to do anything," Ash broke in. "I can go on my own. I can—"

"Don't be a fool," Willis muttered, voice low.

"He's right," Zora said. "Fort Hunter used to be one of the most secure places on the planet. Even if you were able to get inside on your own, you don't know how long it would take you to find my father, or what state he'll be in when you get to him."

Zora didn't hesitate, but there was something in her eyes, and Ash knew she was going over the possibilities, imagining each and every terrible thing that could have happened to her father.

"You're going to need backup," she continued, voice toneless. "And I think I'd feel better if we all stayed together. I couldn't stand for another one of us to disappear without knowing what happened."

"If the building schematics were indeed outlined in this

book the Professor refers to, I'm sure I'll be able to locate them online," Willis added. "I can use the dial-up connection to pull them up before we leave, help us find a direct route to this east wing area."

"My medical bag is already packed," Chandra said. "I can be ready to go in five minutes."

"We don't have to go right away," Ash started.

"But you don't know when this prememory will occur, correct?" Willis cut in. "It could happen at any time?"

"Technically, yes," Ash said.

"And you said they've been getting stronger. So chances are it's coming soon?"

Ash nodded.

"So we should go now," Chandra said. "Right?"

Ash looked at Zora.

Her eyes were wide and glistening, not crying but close, and the blood had drained from her lips, leaving them strangely pale. She wouldn't look at him.

"'The state of the world may hang in the balance,'" she said, repeating the phrase from the journal. She scrubbed a hand over her mouth. "You're right, it would be more dangerous to stay."

Ash's heart was thudding. "We're going?"

She looked up, finally meeting his eyes. "We're going."

19

DOROTHY

OCTOBER 15, 2077, NEW SEATTLE

Dorothy stepped into the *Second Star*, eyes wide as she dragged her fingers along the time machine's dusty aluminum walls.

The inside of this ship wasn't what she'd expected. It was bigger, for one thing. The photographs she'd seen of airplanes had shown tiny, toylike contraptions with a single seat for the pilot. They'd looked unsafe and rickety, like a strong wind might blow them apart.

But this aircraft—this *time machine*—was different. She looked around, at the leather chairs bolted to the floor, and at the strangely thick glass windows, and at the control panel affixed to the front of the ship, its buttons flashing red and green and blue. She itched to touch them but curled her hands into fists to help resist the urge.

She'd only just managed to convince these people to let her come with them. She didn't want to give them a reason to throw her off.

She lowered herself into one of the chairs as the others climbed on board, trying to keep the look of awe from her face. Belt-like straps dangled from the sides of the chair, and she gathered them in one hand, frowning. There were an awful lot of buckles.

"It's called a seat belt," Willis said, and the aircraft groaned as he settled into the seat beside her. He demonstrated slipping his arms through the straps, buckling them over his chest, and then clipping them shut.

Dorothy copied his movements. The buckles felt clumsy in her hands, and the straps were too big, but she was able to snap them closed after only a moment or two of struggle.

"I tried to tie it around my chest my first time," Willis explained. "And Chandra flat out refused to put it on."

Chandra was staring at Dorothy and didn't seem to hear what Willis had just said. "Does your hair actually *dry* like that?" she asked, pushing her chunky glasses up her nose with one finger. "You don't have to use any product or anything?"

Dorothy frowned and touched one of her damp curls. "How else would it dry?"

Ash climbed into the pilot's seat before Chandra could answer, grunting as he pulled the door shut.

"You're sure you want to sit up front?" he asked Dorothy. "I just made some room in the cargo hold."

"Are you trying to be funny?" Dorothy asked, voice dry.

"Or we could tie you to the windshield," Ash continued,

as though he didn't hear her. "You could really feel the wind in your hair that way."

Turning to Willis, Dorothy said, "Is he always so insufferable?"

"Ash has other virtues," Willis said.

"Such as?"

"He's a fair poker player," Zora called from the passenger seat.

The others laughed, but Dorothy shifted, restlessly, staring at the back of Ash's sunburned neck. As much as she hated to admit it, he reminded her of someone, a boy she'd met nearly two years ago.

She and her mother had been performing a variation on the fiddle game at a small bistro in Salt Lake City. The con was simple. The two women would enjoy their meals separately, pretending to be perfect strangers. Then, when she was brought the bill, Loretta would make a big show of looking for a wallet she clearly did not have. She'd promise the restaurant owner she'd run straight home and return with payment. As collateral, she left behind an old family heirloom—a gold broach worth little but valuable to her.

Dorothy's job had been to watch this exchange from across the restaurant. The moment her mother left, she'd approach the owner, pretending to be a fashionable young woman of means. She'd tell him the broach was a rare piece from an important designer, and she'd leave a (fake) name, promising some exorbitant payment should he decide to sell.

Inevitably, when Loretta returned moments later, the restaurant owner would offer her a few hundred dollars to part with the worthless piece of metal.

They'd performed the con a dozen times before. Dorothy could do it in her sleep.

But that night had been different. There'd been a waiter. Sandy-haired, with a wide, easy smile and shoulders that were . . . well, they were quite nicely shaped. He brought Dorothy an extra side of breadsticks and told her dumb jokes. He spent the entire night laughing at the witty things she said. He accidentally brushed his knuckles against the back of her hand when he took the menu from her. He never once told her how beautiful she was.

Dorothy missed her cue to approach the restaurant owner, and the whole con had been ruined. Her mother had been furious.

"You thought that boy really liked you?" she'd hissed, when Dorothy told her what had happened. "He was only flirting with you to get you to leave a bigger tip. How many times have I told you—men lie. *Everything* is a con."

Dorothy hadn't believed her. But when she'd gone back to the café the very next night, the boy had been laughing at some other pretty girl's jokes.

The memory sent something unpleasant flipping through her chest. Ash was like that. Joking, teasing her, pretending not to notice her beauty.

And she liked it, just as she'd liked it when the waiter at

the bistro had joked and teased her. But she knew enough now not to trust it. She touched a finger to the locket at her throat.

"The *Second Star* is moving into position for departure." Ash said.

The ship began to hover.

The anil looked like nothing more than a gathering of clouds, the beginnings of a tornado forming deep in the ocean. Lightning flashed inside, its faint reflection bouncing off the swirling gray walls of a tunnel.

Anil, Dorothy thought. And though she hadn't said the word out loud, she imagined she could taste it on her lips. It was a dry, acrid taste, same as the smoke that had filled the clearing where she'd first seen Ash's time machine.

It was mad that something so incredible could exist out in the open like this, just a few miles away from the city, where anyone might stumble upon it.

Its only protection was its *otherness*. Even now, looking at it for the first time, Dorothy could tell that it was powerful.

Ash brought the *Second Star* to the mouth of the tunnel and then stopped, his time machine hovering above choppy gray waves.

He raised his voice so it could be heard over the engine. "Everyone doing okay back there?"

He'd addressed them all, but he was looking at Dorothy, his eyes reflected in the mirror hanging from the *Second Star*'s windshield.

There hadn't been any more discussion over whether she'd come with them. Ash had simply come back into the kitchen and said, as though something crucial had been decided, "We leave now."

Dorothy had wondered what he'd been discussing out in the hall with the others, but she'd bit the questions back. If Ash wanted to keep his reasons a secret, that was fine—so long as he didn't keep asking after hers.

She wouldn't have been able to explain her reasons, anyway.

More, she thought, and something prickled over her skin. It was what she'd always wanted, the reason she'd run off on her fiancé and her mother and everything she'd ever known. But she'd never dreamed she'd find *this*.

Time travel. Other worlds. Entire cities underwater.

The possibilities set Dorothy's mind on fire. Did Ash really think she'd be content to stay here—or worse, return to her own time—when there was all of history to explore? She didn't think she'd ever be content again. Not until she'd seen it all.

Ash's eyes lingered on her for a second. Dorothy thought of the boy from the café and felt her pulse quicken. The moths in her stomach stirred, feeling more like butterflies than they had before.

She told herself she was ashamed of the memory, of her naïveté.

But this didn't feel like shame.

She curled her fingers into the sides of her chair, gathering her courage. “Ready,” she said.

As though waiting for her command, the *Second Star* shot forward, disappearing into the crack in time.

PART TWO

Dark Star: Noun. A starlike object which emits little or no visible light. Its existence is inferred from other evidence, such as the eclipsing of other stars.

—*Oxford Dictionary of English*

20

ASH

THE PUGET SOUND ANIL

Darkness closed around the ship. Ash felt the pressure change with a pop in his ears and a deep ache throbbing through his teeth. His world became very small: the black waves churning outside his windshield; the control panel's blinking red lights. Water crashed against the *Star*'s windshield in thick sheets, making the glass creak.

And then they were through the water, into the anil itself.

The waves thickened into gray clouds that broke apart as the *Second Star* hurtled through them. Lightning lit up the purple walls of the tunnel, but it was far off yet, not more than a flicker of purple in the mist. Ash didn't realize he'd been holding his breath, until the lights on the control panel seemed to dim. He gave his head a hard shake and sucked down a lungful of air.

It's fine, he thought. *Everything's fine*. Wind speed was only up to 45 knots, and the EM was holding steady at a quarter capacity. The exotic matter had stabilized the anil better than he could've hoped. This might even be a safe flight.

But nerves still prickled over his skin. Maybe it was because he could feel the prememory moving, shadowlike, around the edges of his mind, searching for a way inside. He saw a flicker of white and tightened his grip on the yoke, directing the *Star* to the center of the tunnel. He'd only ever experienced the prememory when he was alone, when he didn't have to worry that anyone might see him shake, or wonder why his skin had gone pale and damp with sweat. If he lost control now, with the rest of his crew and Dorothy here to watch . . .

His pulse beat in his palms, warning him not to let that happen.

Zora knocked a fist against his arm. "Everything good?"

"All clear," Ash said, his eyes still trained on the windshield. He tried to cover his nerves with a smile. "Don't worry. This'll be easy."

Zora leaned back in her seat. "It's going better than I expected."

"You expected us to explode into a thousand fiery pieces on entry. Anything's better than that."

"True."

Ash caught Zora's face from the corner of his eye, but she only stared straight ahead, her expression unreadable as ever.

He shifted his gaze back out the windshield, forcing himself to focus on the task at hand. Things seemed calm now, but weather inside an anil could change in the blink of an eye, especially when the EM reading was so low. They weren't out of the woods yet. The prememory should be the least of his worries.

Wind howled outside the windows, but it wasn't strong enough to break the protective bubble the EM had created around the *Star* and blow the ship off course. The roiling clouds that made up the sides of the tunnel flickered with lightning, but it never got close enough to the ship to cause trouble.

Ash gazed out the windshield without really seeing any of this. A thought had just occurred to him: they were going back in time to find the Professor. Maybe that meant he wouldn't get the prememory at all this time. Maybe the events they were setting into motion right now had already changed the future.

It was too much to hope for, and yet Ash could feel himself start to ease up, each of his muscles unclenching, one by one.

Maybe.

"I was able to find the book the Professor mentioned online so we should have all the same information he was working off of," Willis said. "I'm seeing building schematics, security details . . . whoa, there's even a list of the firepower the soldiers were packing before the place was shut down."

He was tapping the screen of a sleek, silver tablet. Ash had brought it back from the year 2020, when well-made tech was still easily obtained, and, as such, it was one of the most advanced models of tablet the world had ever seen—perhaps *would* ever see. Wireless internet didn't exist in New Seattle any longer, so Willis had used the crappy dial-up connection back at the school to download everything he thought they might need. The connection was spotty at best, but sometimes they got lucky.

Dorothy stared at the tablet like it was a strange and somewhat frightening animal. "What is that?" she breathed.

"Type of computer." Willis tapped the screen again. "I'll let you play with it when we get back." He paused, and then added. "*If* we get back."

"How about a little faith?" Ash called over his shoulder. "When have I ever gotten you into trouble?"

"Do you want an itemized list?"

"How long does it take to travel through time?" Dorothy asked.

She leaned forward, and Ash felt the sudden warmth of her body next to his arm. His skin prickled. He cleared his throat. "Half an hour, give or take a hundred years."

Chandra groaned. "Ugh. Total dad joke."

Ash's eyes flicked to the mirror hanging from his windshield and caught the tail end of Chandra's eye roll before his gaze moved to Dorothy. She was staring out the windshield, at the roiling purple clouds and distant sparks of lightning, and her smile was wide, childlike. Her eyes glistened.

The awe on her face brought her beauty into fuller focus, and Ash felt the corner of his lip twitch, unable to suppress a smile of his own. He'd forgotten this would be her first time seeing the anil. Not everyone got how amazing it was. Chandra had spent her first trip through time squeezing her eyes shut, too scared to look out the window. Willis didn't seem able to pick out the specific shades of purple and blue in the clouds and, as such, thought the experience underwhelming. But Ash had always seen the anil for what it was. Remarkable.

No, more than that: *holy*.

Staring at Dorothy's face just now, he wondered if she felt the same.

"Ooh!" Chandra squealed, clapping her hands. "Should we play a road-trip game?"

Dorothy blinked and shook her head, a spell breaking.

"This isn't a road trip, Chandie," Zora said.

"What's a road-trip game?" Dorothy asked. "Is it something to do with time travel?"

"No," said Ash. Dorothy caught his eye, and he quickly shifted his attention back to the swirling madness in front of him. "They're games you play while riding in an automobile. So you don't get bored."

Dorothy said, incredulous, "Who on *earth* could get bored riding in an automobile?"

Ash's lip twitched—almost a smile. He remembered feeling the same way when his dad bought their first family car, back in 1940. Just driving around the block felt like the most thrilling thing in the world. "Hate to break it to you, but cars get pretty boring after a few years."

Zora swiveled around in her seat. "How do you even know about road-trip games, Chandie?"

Chandra was practically bouncing. "I was watching old episodes of this television show about how this guy meets his kids' mom by drinking a lot of beer or whatever, and whenever they're in the car they play a game where they count how many dogs they see outside and then they yell 'zilch dog' really loud, and I think they punch each other on the arm."

"There are no dogs in here," said Willis. "We're in a tunnel hurtling through space and time."

"Duh. I *know* that, but we could count something else. Like how many times we see swirly gray clouds."

"Or lightning," added Ash. "We got a lot of lighting."

Dorothy was suddenly leaning past him, one hand gripping his arm, the other pointing at the windshield, "Zich lightning!" she called, breathless.

"It's *zilch*, not zich," Chandra corrected her.

"That's what I said!" Dorothy was still holding Ash's arm, her fingers soft and cool against the heat pulsing through his wrist. He could feel his attention shifting to the place where their skin touched. It wasn't entirely unpleasant.

Ash had always hated the types of guys who chased after pretty girls. He figured they were like dumb dogs with their tongues hanging out of their mouths, racing after a stick without ever stopping to wonder *why*. Did they really *want* the stick? Or did they just enjoy chasing it?

Ash would not be a dog. He reminded himself that, pretty though she might be, Dorothy was trouble.

And he was supposed to be avoiding girls, anyway, so what was he even thinking?

He shrugged her off. "Watch where you're grabbing,

sweetheart. I know I make this look easy, but one wrong move and the whole ship goes flying straight into the pretty lightning."

He heard the scowl in her voice. "I *told* you—"

"Don't call you sweetheart." Ash couldn't say why he didn't want to call Dorothy by her name, only that it felt like a truce, somehow, like admitting that having her climb on board his ship wasn't the worst thing in the world. He didn't want to give her the satisfaction—yet, anyway—so he grumbled, "Yeah, yeah. I know."

He pulled his eyes away from her and squinted through the darkness instead, searching the tunnel walls for the markings the Professor had grilled him on. Time had landmarks, same as anything. Slight discoloration marked decades, certain whirls in the smoke only occurred during certain years. Ash knew that the clouds at the side of the anil only got that bluish-gray cast to them in the mid 2000s. He'd know they'd entered the twentieth century when he saw darker whirls cutting through the gray. It was like following a map.

Zora's voice cut through his thoughts. "We could play the movie game."

"Movie?" Dorothy said. "You mean like a moving picture?"

"Yes," Willis said. "But they have sound now."

"Oh, I *love* moving pictures!" Dorothy said. "Do you know Florence La Badie? She's absolutely *divine*."

Willis's eyes lit up. "Did you see *Star of Bethlehem*?"

Dorothy, aghast, exclaimed, "It doesn't come to Seattle until next month!"

"Never mind," Zora muttered.

They sped past the 2010s. Ash decreased the *Star*'s speed to 2,900 knots. Wind slammed into the side of the ship. Everything trembled.

"What was that?" Chandra's voice sounded smaller than it had a few minutes ago. Lightning flared very close to their windshield.

Ash tightened his grip on the yoke. He tried moving the *Star* left, where wind speeds were weaker, but it listed right. He swore under his breath and pulled back, aiming its nose upward—

The *Star* plummeted. The sudden drop made his stomach flip.

Someone released a nervous yelp from the cabin. Zora was talking, but her voice seemed far away. The wind howled and screamed, sounding alive.

Ash dragged the yoke into position, shoulders and arms burning with the effort. Sweat broke out on his forehead. They'd just passed the early 2000s. They were getting close.

Something crashed to the floor, but Ash didn't dare turn his head to see what it was. He searched the tunnel walls. He could see the smoky clouds of the 1990s straight ahead. . . .

"What's happening?" Zora shouted. A gust of wind

slammed into them before Ash could answer, sending a tremor through the ship. The walls shook. Ash's knuckles went white around the stick. He tried to steer the *Star* over to one of the cloudy tunnel walls, but the winds were too strong.

The EM was failing—just like they'd known it would.

Lightning forked through the air in front of him—too close. The brief burst illuminated roiling purple and black clouds.

Chandra was shouting, but Ash couldn't make out her words over the roar of the storm. He glanced at the rearview mirror just as something slammed into the side of them, causing bits of metal to fly off the walls and scatter to the ground. One of Chandra's restraints snapped, and she lurched forward, an arm jerking before her limp body.

"Chandra!" Willis shouted. Chandra's eyes had rolled to the back of her head, her mouth gone slack. Her second restraint snapped in half, and she went hurtling against the curved metal wall of the ship. Ash heard a sickening crack.

He grasped for the yoke, relief flooding through him as his fingers closed around stiff leather. They were passing 1985 now. Ash could tell by the slight thickening of the clouds, the way the purple edges had dulled to gray. Only a few more minutes and they'd be in 1980. He started searching for the more subtle variations that hinted at which months they were passing. Thin, wispy clouds meant spring and summer . . . heavier clouds for autumn . . .

"Willis, don't!" Zora was shouting.

Ash glanced away from the anil, eyes flicking to the mirror. Willis was unsnapping his own restraints. Chandra lay on the ground in front of him, unmoving.

"Willis!" Ash warned.

"She's hurt, Captain." Willis's fingers trembled as he worked his buckle. It snapped open—

The effect was immediate. Willis seemed to be sucked out of his seat. He flew up against the ceiling, his head thudding against the metal.

"Hold on!" Ash shouted. He increased airspeed by 135 knots and the ship jerked forward. Every light inside the cockpit flashed on, filling the small, dark room with greens and reds. Ash thought he heard someone scream—

And then the prememory crashed over him, and everything went dark.

21
DOROTHY

Dorothy's eyes fluttered closed, images flickering beneath her lids:

She was walking down a dark tunnel, its brick walls coated with dirt and plaster. She ran her fingertips along the bricks and they came away damp.

The image changed. *She didn't remember walking, but suddenly she was standing in another corridor, looking at a door made of dull metal, the word* RESTRICTED *written across it in big, block letters. The handle was a black latch. She tried it, but it was locked.*

She looked down and saw a keyboard set into the metal just below the door latch. She lowered her fingers to the keys—

And then the hallway was gone and she was kneeling on the floor beneath a table, the light around her flashing. Roman was beside her, his face so close that she saw the muscle in his jaw twitch as he said, "You shouldn't trust them. The great Chronology Protection Agency will never deserve you."

Dorothy felt her lips part. "Why—"

Emergency lights blinked on, knocking Roman's face from Dorothy's head and bathing the ship in an eerie red glow.

She lifted one hand, wincing as her fingertips brushed a tender spot below her ear. Her head ached, even though she couldn't remember hitting it on anything, and her eyesight was all . . . fuzzy. She felt like she was looking at the world through opaque glass.

What was all that?

The images had felt familiar, like memories, only they couldn't have been. She'd never been that close to Roman, had never seen any of those places before.

But they weren't dreams, either. They'd felt too real to be dreams.

Dorothy blinked, and Ash's face swam into view. He was doubled over, his skin glistening with sweat, eyes barely open.

Nerves prickled up the back of her neck. She fumbled with her seat belt, the dream images forgotten. "Ash?"

Zora twisted in her seat, restraints bunched up around her shoulders. "He'll be fine."

"Are you sure?" Dorothy asked. She couldn't get her seat belt free. The contraption felt impossibly complicated between her fingers. "He looks—"

"Check the others. Can you reach them?" Zora was pointing at something on the floor now, but her finger became two fingers . . . and then three . . .

Dorothy blinked, fighting back the dizziness. Maybe she *had* hit her head. When she opened her eyes, Zora was only pointing with one finger, again. Dorothy followed it to the floor, where Willis and Chandra lay in a heap, debris strewn around them. They weren't moving. It looked . . .

Dorothy felt herself go bone still. It looked like they were *dead*.

"Check their vitals," Zora was saying. Her voice was steady. "See if they have a pulse. Do you know how to find a pulse?"

Dorothy nodded. She was staring at Chandra's hand, a sick feeling rising in her throat.

She'd never thought of herself as sheltered before, but she did now. She and her mother had no other family, and they'd never stayed anywhere long enough to make friends, so Dorothy's experience of death had always been limited. She'd never had to say goodbye to a beloved grandmother, or wonder why her pet bunny hadn't woken up.

It was a gift, sort of. If she never really loved anything, nothing she loved could ever die.

Dorothy didn't love any of these people, but she didn't hate them, either. Just a few minutes ago they'd all been talking and joking. Playing a game.

Now, Chandra's fingernails were broken to the quick, and there was a deep scratch along her palm. And—*oh God*—she didn't appear to be breathing.

Dorothy reached for Chandra's wrist, her fingers trembling. *Please don't be dead*, she thought.

Chandra's fingers twitched, and Dorothy jerked her hand back again, relief practically knocking her over.

"Are you okay?" she choked out.

Chandra groaned and sat up. She cradled one arm to her chest, her face contorting in pain. "I think I broke something."

"Willis?" Zora asked.

Dorothy shifted her attention to the giant unconscious man spread out before her. Willis still hadn't opened his eyes, but his chest was rising and falling, steadily. Dorothy pressed two fingers to his neck. . . .

Relief washed over her like cold water. "His heart's still beating."

Zora lowered her head to her hands, exhaling heavily. "Thank God," she murmured, her calm exterior cracking, just for a moment.

"I can revive him with the ammonia inhalants in my bag," Chandra said. She hesitated, glancing at the mess around her. "If I can *find* my bag."

Dorothy looked past her, at Ash. He was still doubled over, his face tight with pain, though he seemed to be managing to keep the ship airborne. Some instinct sprang up in her, to make sure he was okay, maybe, or to try to help him. She'd always hated pain, both experiencing it herself and watching it rip through others. Her mother used to tell her this was a weakness.

Pain can be useful, she'd say—another one of her ludicrous rules—but Dorothy had never listened. Her mother might have been smarter than her in many ways, but this was not one of them. Pain was always just pain.

She started to reach for Ash's arm, then thought of how he'd scolded her for having the nerve to touch him before and dropped her hand to the back of his chair, instead.

Rat, she thought. And he *was* a rat, but that didn't mean she wanted him to die.

She saw black leather nestled beneath the seat just in front of her and, recognizing Chandra's doctor's bag, pulled it loose with a tug.

"*Thank* you." Chandra unzipped the bag, and a mess of gauze, bandages, and bottles filled with brightly colored liquids tumbled out and began rolling around the ship. She ignored them and dug through the remaining objects in the bag, eventually producing a small vial of white powder.

"Here we go," she muttered, unscrewing the lid. She leaned forward and placed the inhalant under Willis's nose.

The giant twitched. His eyelids flickered open. He mumbled something that could've been "You're hurt" and frowned at the arm Chandra was clutching to her chest.

"How's your head?" Chandra asked. One-handed, she pulled a tiny, handheld light out of her overstuffed bag and flashed it in Willis's eyes. "Nausea? Dizziness?"

"I'm fine." Willis batted at the light like it was an insect, trying to sit up. "Why am I on the ground?"

"Because you are very large, and there's this thing called gravity." Chandra held his shoulders down. "Where do you think you're going? Lie *down*, you big oaf. Don't make me—"

The ship jerked and sputtered, reminding Dorothy of a dying animal.

She snatched at one of the restraints falling over the side of her seat, gripping so tightly her fingers cramped. She couldn't catch her breath.

She wasn't usually so easily frightened. Even climbing on the airplane had been an easy choice, though she'd heard stories of airplanes plummeting right out of the sky, killing everyone on board. It wasn't that she didn't fear for her life, it's just that she had a sort of block where her own safety was concerned. She could easily visualize terrible things happening. Just never to her.

But *this.* She was starting to realize that *this* might've been a mistake. Would it all be worth it? To see another period in time? She'd been so distracted by the idea that she hadn't bothered thinking of the possible consequences.

Death, for instance. And maiming. And falling from very high in the sky . . .

She covered her mouth with one hand, breathing hard.

22

ASH

Ash was standing in a small boat, easing his weight from leg to leg to keep his balance. Black water lapped at the sides, sending the boat rocking, but Ash moved, easily, with the motion. He'd grown used to the water over the last two years.

Trees seemed to glow in the darkness around him. Ghost trees. Dead trees. Water pressed against their white trunks, moving with the wind.

Ash counted ripples to pass the time while he waited. Seven. Twelve. Twenty-three. He lost track and was about to start again when her light appeared in the distant black. It was small, like the single headlight of a motorcycle, followed by the rumbling sound of an engine. He stood straighter. Part of him hadn't expected her to come. But of course she would. She always did.

Leave now, he told himself. There was still time. He felt sure that she wouldn't come after him if he left before she got there. He knew how this night would end if he stayed. He'd seen this exact moment a dozen times. A hundred, if he counted dreams. But he stayed still, his hand clenching and unclenching at his side.

He wanted to see her, even knowing what it meant. He had to see her one last time.

The boat drew closer. She was hidden by the darkness of the night. Ash wouldn't have known someone was standing there if it hadn't been for her hair, the long, white strands blowing loose from her coat, dancing in the darkness.

She pulled up next to him and cut the engine.

"I didn't think you'd come." Her voice was lower than he'd expected, practically a purr. She reached up, pushed those white strands of hair back under her hood with a flick of her hand.

Ash swallowed. He didn't see the knife, but he knew she had it. "It doesn't have to end like this."

"Of course it does." Her hand disappeared inside her coat. She leaned forward. "Ash—"

"Ash!"

The voice broke the prememory into a dozen flitting images. Ash straightened, gasping for air like a man drowning. He blinked slowly. The prememory was stronger than it had ever been before. He couldn't remember where he was, didn't know what he was supposed to be doing.

White hair dancing in the darkness . . .

. . . It doesn't have to end like this.

"Wake up!" Zora was clutching his arm, shaking him. He tried to move, but his limbs felt weighted down, like he was sinking through cold water. He could still smell the salty ocean air, the scent of fish rolling in with the fog, the spice-and-flowers scent of the girl's white hair.

So real. It had been so, so real.

Wind howled against the *Star*'s walls, making them appear to bulge inward. Ash thought he heard someone scream, but the sound might have come from the visions still flashing through his head.

White hair and black water and dead trees . . .

He held the yoke steady as the entire ship began to shake. The lights went dark.

"Come on, *Star*," he murmured. He aimed the *Star*'s nose at the tunnel walls and pulled back on the yoke, accelerating. The air around the ship grew wet and still. His headlights flashed back on, cutting through dark water.

A moment later, the *Second Star* bobbed to the surface, black night spread out around her.

They were here.

LOG ENTRY—DECEMBER 29, 2074
18:38 HOURS
THE *DARK STAR*

I'm writing this from the passenger seat of the newly built *Dark Star.*

A dark star is a star heated by the annihilation of dark matter particles. It's also an English psychedelic rock band, and a 1974 film by John Carpenter.

I thought it was a fitting name for the most advanced time machine the world has ever seen.

That's right. I've built a second time machine.

The *Second Star* can hold a crew of five, but it's a tight fit. There's also the problem of the external control panel. You see, when I was first building my time machine, my primary concern was incorporating the exotic matter into the design of the vessel without upsetting the underlying architecture.

To put it plainly, I stuck the control panel on the *outside* of the ship, because it was easier that way. But, now, it poses a problem. You can't tweak the EM midflight, which caused some safety concerns. Both WCAAT and NASA thought we needed something more advanced, and I have to agree that they're right. And, thus, the *Dark Star* was born. Not only does the new time machine seat eight, with legroom to spare, but it has an internal control panel, which makes midflight repairs much safer and easier.

First mission: pick up our new pilot!

Natasha's been teaching me all about the "golden age of aviation," which is this period of time between the 1920s and the 1930s, when Americans were absolutely obsessed with flying. I thought that sounded promising, but Natasha seems to think we'll find a more talented pilot by looking a few years later—at World War II fighter pilots.

I made a joke that we should just recruit Amelia Earhart and call it a day, but Natasha pointed out that Amelia is a bit old for our purposes. I hadn't thought about this before, but she's right. This isn't just *one* mission we're talking about. If things go according to plan, this will be a series of missions extending for years and years into the future—maybe even longer, if you take into account the fact that we'll be traveling back in time, possibly staying for quite a while before returning to our present.

In other words, we need to recruit them young.

We did some research. On September 27, 1942, the minimum enlistment age for the war was lowered to sixteen, so long as there was parental consent. And, of course, a bunch of kids lied about their ages and joined up when they were even younger. Natasha says the youngest was some twelve-year-old named Calvin Graham. Twelve years old! And fighting in a war! Zora's almost fifteen, and I won't even let her date.

I won't bore you with the rest of our research. The upshot is that we found a sixteen-year-old pilot from Bryce, Nebraska. His name is Jonathan Asher Jr. He lied about his age to get into the civilian pilot training program (known colloquially as flight academy, or flight camp), graduated early, and proceeded directly to pilot training. He was a rising star in the navy, right up until he went AWOL before a mission for no apparent reason.

I don't think this was a coincidence.

Asher is young, talented, and the fact that he went missing

means we won't muck up history too much by . . . well, *removing* him from it.

We go back for him first thing in the new year.

There's another thing I want to note before signing off for today. Something odd has happened the last few times I went back in time. I don't know how to describe it, other than "waking dream." I'll be flying the *Second Star* through the anil when a vision comes to me, kind of flickering through the back of my mind. It has the feel of a memory, only it's not *my* memory. In fact, I've never seen it before.

The vision is this: our city, entirely underwater. The tops of skyscrapers stick out of a sea of black. Waves lap against the sides of buildings. All the trees have turned white.

Then, all at once, I'm overcome with a feeling of intense, overwhelming sadness. Last time, it got so bad that I couldn't keep hold of the yoke. Roman had to steer the *Star* the rest of the way home while I took deep breaths and tried not to sob.

I don't know what to make of it.

Is it an omen? A dream? A trick of the time tunnel?

I haven't told Natasha yet. I want to know more about this vision before upsetting her with it.

Whatever it is, it scared me.

23

DOROTHY

MARCH 17, 1980, FORT HUNTER COMPLEX

It felt like another hundred years before the time machine settled on solid ground and the engine cut. The sudden stillness made Dorothy all the more aware of how the motor had trembled through her, shaking her to her bones.

Stupid, she thought. There was no reason to be afraid. But she slipped her hands beneath her legs so no one else would see that they were shaking.

"Zora, I need you under the hood." Ash was still flipping switches and twisting levers, even though they were on the ground. He looked better, though a thin film of sweat still clung to his forehead.

"On it," Zora said. She pulled a pair of goggles from her jacket pocket and slipped them over her braids, throwing her door open.

"I want a full report on how the EM is doing," Ash said, and Zora saluted, slamming the door shut behind her. Ash turned to Chandra. "How's the arm?"

Chandra was pawing around inside her bag again, her injured arm clutched to her chest like a broken wing. "It'll be fine once I find my sling . . ."

A small vial fell from Chandra's bag and rolled across the ship's floor, stopping at Dorothy's feet. She reached out automatically to pick it up. *Ipecac.*

"Aha!" Chandra shouted, pulling a bundle of white and blue cloth from her bag. Dorothy watched as she expertly fastened it around her broken arm. "See? Good as new."

"You sure about that?" Ash frowned. "You're no good to me if you can't patch up my crew."

"Nice to know you care," Chandra said. "But I can work one-handed."

"Good." Ash was nodding, oblivious to the sarcasm in Chandra's voice. "Willis, blueprints?"

"Pardon me, Chandie." Willis reached around Chandra and tugged the strange metal object out from beneath her medical bag. "We're offline," he said, tapping the object's brightly lit surface with one finger. "Definitely preinternet."

Ash was nodding. "The storm was bad, but I could tell from the clouds in the anil where we exited that we hit our date. March 17, 1980. Only—"

The door slammed open, cutting him off. Zora climbed back into the ship, her face pink from the wind.

"Tell me you have good news," Ash said.

"Engine's cooked," she said, collapsing into her seat. "Your boat needs a nice long nap."

"EM?"

"Shot." Zora pinched her nose between two fingers. "My father better be here, because we'll need the EM from his ship to get back home. I don't think the *Second Star* will survive another trip through the anil in the state it's in now."

"Not to pile on the bad news, but I don't think we exited the anil at the correct time," Willis said, nodding out the window. The sun was creeping below the tree line, sending fingers of gold light flickering through the woods. "The sun is only now setting, so it can't be later than six p.m. Fort Hunter will be fully operational for the next eight hours."

"That means armed soldiers guarding every entrance, security cameras following our movements, a locked gate at the perimeter, not to mention security codes to get through the doors." Zora ticked each item off on her fingers as she spoke. "Right?"

"Full staff, full security, yes," Willis confirmed. He shook his massive head. "Our best bet would be to wait here and try to enter the complex at two in the morning, when they drop down to a skeleton crew again."

"If we do that, we risk missing the Professor completely," Ash said. "According to his journal, he planned to arrive this morning, between two and six a.m. We have no way of knowing if he meant to stay here past that window, or head somewhere else once he got whatever he came for. We have to find a way inside, now."

"Haven't you been listening?" Zora said. "That's *impossible*."

Dorothy had been taking deep, even breaths to try to

calm herself after that flight, but now she tilted her head, her interest piqued. She'd spent a lifetime opening locked doors and slipping inside private rooms. If there was a building that was impossible to break into, she hadn't found it yet.

Ash said, "There's got to be a record of the old access codes somewhere in those notes Willis found."

Willis shook his head. "I didn't see anything like that, at least not in the materials I've already downloaded, and seeing as there's no internet in the eighties, we can't exactly double-check."

"Then we'll take out a guard. Get him to open a door."

"We're not breaking into a bank, Ash," Zora said. "These are trained soldiers at one of the most secure military complexes in the world. They're not going to let a bunch of civilians slip through the door."

Dorothy turned all this over in her head. Trained soldiers at every entrance. Doors held shut with access codes.

Yes, that did sound tricky. . . .

It was too bad they weren't trying to break into a bank. That was actually fairly simple. Dorothy had once needed to retrieve an expensive diamond broach from a bank that was supposed to be impenetrable. She chewed back a smile, remembering.

In the end, it'd been easy. The building had top-notch security, but it was the funniest thing. Once they caught you milling around outside—

Oh. Dorothy curled her fingers around the ipecac, a plan taking shape in her head. The others were still arguing and seemed no closer to landing on a solution of their own. She could help them. . . .

But she hesitated, eyes flicking to the time-machine door. *Why* would she help them? All she'd wanted was a ride back in time, and here she was. She doubted anyone would stop her from leaving. There was no reason for her to get involved.

And there was that strange vision. Roman leaning toward her, his face inches from her own. *You shouldn't trust them.*

Nerves prickled inside of her. But the vision had been nothing—just a trick of her subconscious. A dream memory, like the ones she had when she'd gone from 1913 to 2077. And the plan was already there, fully formed, and, if she could say so herself, perfect. She chewed on her lower lip. It would be a shame not to try it.

Tucking the bottle into her pocket, she leaned over, nudging Willis on the shoulder. "You have a sort of . . . map of this Fort Hunter place, right?"

Willis nodded. "All twenty-nine floors."

"May I see it?"

Willis tapped on his computer a few times and then handed it to Dorothy. "If you want to zoom in, just do this." He made a pinching motion with his fingers.

Dorothy didn't know what that meant, but she nodded like she understood, and took the device, squinting down at the image it displayed.

Tiny hallways and rooms spiraled out in front of her. It made her dizzy to look at them all. The words labeling them were too small to read, black blurs of ink on a too-bright surface. She'd never find what she was looking for.

"What are you doing?" Ash sounded wary, but there was something in his eyes as he looked at her. Amusement, maybe.

Dorothy said, "I thought I had an idea."

Now he grinned. "I hate to break it to you, but you ain't getting those doors open by batting your eyes at some soldier."

"I have other skills." Dorothy tried to say this in an offhand way, but she could feel the defensiveness seeping into her words. Men tended to assume that beauty and intellect were mutually exclusive. It was wearying.

Ash's eyebrow went up, making it feel even more like he was laughing at her. Dorothy could feel her neck heating.

"Is that so?" he said.

"Sometimes I do this little half smile. Turns men to putty." Dorothy kept her voice light, as though they were flirting, but her shoulders stiffened.

He kept underestimating her. First, back at the churchyard, when she'd snuck onto his ship, and then again after Roman had kidnapped her. She didn't know why it bothered her so much. He was nothing to her but a ride. She wasn't even particularly interested in the contents of his pockets.

And then she realized: she hadn't been trying to fool him. Every other man she'd known had only seen her pretty face. That was sort of the point of con work: she had to disappear long before anyone realized how talented she actually was. But she'd shown Ash who she was, and he didn't believe her.

The thought made her feel strangely lonely. She itched to pull the watch she'd stolen out of her pocket and dangle it in front of his nose, like a child. *See! See what I can do?* As though that might convince him that she had more to offer.

He was still smiling at her, a lazy sort of smile that said he didn't expect much from her, even now. "All right, sweetheart. Impress me."

Ugh, she thought. *Sweetheart.*

Luckily, that's when her eyes zeroed in on the room she'd been looking for. It was to the side of a tunnel leading in from the main entrance. She handed the computer to Ash. "*There*," she said, pointing.

He leaned in closer, frowning down at the tablet, one hand brushing against her back.

"You're joking," he said, in a very different tone of voice. His smile was gone.

"I'm not." This time, Dorothy was the one smiling. She tapped the device again, her confidence growing. "*That's* how we're going to get inside."

24

ASH

Twenty minutes later, Ash stood outside a chain-link fence, the massive mountain that hid the Fort Hunter complex towering over him. The only clue he had that he'd ended up somewhere special was the warning sign hanging above him.

WARNING. RESTRICTED AREA.

This installation has been declared a restricted area
according to a secretary of defense directive,
issued May 19, 1963, under the provisions of Section 31,
Internal Security Act of 1950.
All persons and vehicles entering hereon are liable to
search. Photographing or making notes, drawings, maps,
or graphic representations of this area or its activities
is prohibited unless specifically authorized by the
commander. Any such material found in the possession
of unauthorized persons will be confiscated.

Ash looked past the sign, fixing his eyes on a blinking red light hanging just over his head. Security camera. Someone was watching.

Nerves crept up his spine, warning him that this was probably a very bad idea. He wasn't sure he knew Dorothy well enough to place his entire crew's safety in her hands.

She got away from Roman, a small voice reminded him. That meant she was smart. And she'd stowed away on his ship, which meant she was sneaky. And she'd jumped out an eighth-story window, so she was brave, too.

Those were the reasons he'd agreed to her plan back in the *Second Star*, but now he was having doubts. He should have made her go over the details again, to check for holes. He should have tried harder to come up with an idea of his own. He should have waited. He should have—

Ash shook his head, forcing the concerns aside. The Professor was somewhere inside that mountain, past the security fence and the cameras, closer than he'd been in almost a year.

Ash would have to trust her. He lifted the walkie-talkie to his lips. "I've reached the perimeter. Over."

Zora's voice answered through the static: "You're clear. Over."

Ash clipped the walkie-talkie back onto his belt and glanced over his shoulder. He'd insisted the others hang back and let him go in first, as a pawn, just in case there were any trigger-happy soldiers hanging around the main gates hoping for a little target practice. Willis hadn't loved that idea, but Ash had pointed out that, of the two of them, he was the only one who knew exactly how and approximately when he was going to die. If he were shot, it wouldn't be fatal—it *couldn't* be. Willis had grudgingly agreed that was true.

Now Ash squinted, trying to make out the shapes of his crew spread out in the black. The moon hung full and silver in the night sky, but its light did little to break up the shadows of the woods. The gnarled tree branches looked too much like arms, the leaves twitching in the wind too much like fluttering hair.

Ash turned back to the gate. "Here goes nothing," he muttered, and said a quick, silent prayer as he cut straight through the fence. The link split with a *pop*.

Ash continued working in silence. After a few minutes, he'd created a vaguely person-shaped hole in the chains. He paused to wipe a hand over his forehead—damp with sweat, even though it was cold enough in these woods to freeze him where he stood—and then lowered the bolt cutters and ducked through the hole.

To the walkie-talkie: "I'm in. Over."

"We're right behind you," came the reply. "Over and out."

A bat flew above, casting a jerky shadow onto the already darkened ground. From somewhere in the distance came a sound like running water. Ash headed for the mountain, dry grass crunching under his feet. Every soldier worth his salt was taught to walk without making a sound, to move like a shadow. Ash felt like an idiot for ignoring his training, but he wanted to be seen. He'd spent enough time in the armed forces to know that there were always a few soldiers who fired first and asked questions later. If someone was going to get shot, it needed to be him.

His palms had started to sweat, his muscles gone tense. He tried not to think of the others creeping through the woods behind him, hiding in the shadows, ducking from tree to tree.

According to Willis's blueprints, the main entrance cut into the rock face about twenty yards ahead. The walk seemed to take longer than it should have. The dark playing tricks, Ash figured. Or maybe it was his nerves, drawing the seconds out, making every minute feel like three. He found himself speeding up, subconsciously hoping to shave a few seconds off the time it took to reach the Professor. He stopped himself when he realized what he was doing. Cutting corners would screw up everything.

They were so close. Now was the time for caution.

Finally, the trees parted, revealing a great metal tunnel protruding from the side of the mountain, like a mistake of nature. Barbed wire–topped fences stood to either side of the paved road leading up to the entrance. Soldiers waited at attention just before it, silent, their boxy guns carving lines across their chests.

Ash dropped to a crouch, fumbling for the walkie-talkie at his belt—

Cold metal pressed against the back of his neck.

"On your feet, civilian," said a deep, steady voice. "And keep your hands where I can see 'em."

Ash stood slowly, reaching for the sky. The gun didn't leave his neck.

"ID?" the voice asked. The gun vibrated against Ash's skin when he spoke.

Ash swallowed. He had a driver's license from 1945 tucked in a shoebox back home. Not that it would have done him any good now. He shook his head.

"Why don't you try explaining what you're doing around here, son?"

Ash's mouth felt dry. "Nature walk."

"In the middle of the night? Right. Want to tell me why you need a walkie-talkie for your nature walk?" The man removed the gun from Ash's neck and stepped around to where he could see him. He was a soldier, generic-looking in his army-green fatigues. He nodded at the walkie-talkie hanging from Ash's belt. "That looks military grade."

Ash didn't say anything. It *was* military grade. Stolen from 1997. He hoped the soldier didn't look at it too closely.

"Our cameras show you cutting a hole into our fence back there," the soldier continued. "Now that wasn't very nice. In fact, we call that destruction of military property around these parts. And then you went and ducked through that fence and started wandering around our base. We call that trespassing on military property. You're wandering around without ID, carrying what appears to be *stolen* military property." The soldier scratched his chin. "Well, that doesn't look so good. You and your little friends are in a hell of a lot of trouble, son. A *hell* of a lot of trouble."

"My friends?" Ash said. Before he could answer, Willis,

Zora, Dorothy, and Chandra shuffled out of the trees, hands over their heads, a line of soldiers fanned out behind them.

"You think you're the first group of kids we ever found messing around out here?" The soldier shook his head. "Happens practically every week. Doesn't mean we're letting you off easy, though. No, siree. There's protocol to follow in situations like this. In fact, I believe we're going to need to detain the lot of you back at the complex until we can get the local sheriff out here to pick you up."

The soldier nodded at a dirt path stretching through the woods, motioning with his gun to indicate that they should start walking. Ash forced himself forward, falling into line behind Dorothy.

She winked as he moved past, eyelashes flashing up and down so quickly he could've imagined it. He knocked his shoulder into hers when the soldier wasn't looking, smothering a grin. If they'd been alone, he might've grabbed her and kissed her.

Detain the lot of you back at the complex, the soldier had said. Which meant her crazy plan had actually worked.

They were in.

Dorothy's idea had been deceptively simple. Breaking into Fort Hunter was impossible. So they weren't going to try to break into Fort Hunter.

"You want us to get arrested?" Zora had asked, appalled.

"I got the idea when you mentioned breaking into a

bank," Dorothy had explained. "Breaking into a bank is actually quite difficult. There are guards to get past, and locked doors, and all this security. But once you're *caught* breaking in, they bring you right inside while they wait for the police to come pick you up. And if you're very lucky they leave you alone in an office, of all things, where you're separated from the rest of the establishment by a single door." She held up a finger. "*One* lousy door, and it's probably got a normal lock and everything. Any fool can get past that."

"Fort Hunter isn't a bank," Ash pointed out, skeptical.

"Of course it's not. But *this* room is clearly intended to detain people who aren't authorized to be on the grounds." She'd lifted Willis's tablet so that Ash could see it and pointed to a tiny room labeled *detainment*. "Notice anything special about it?"

Ash had squinted down at the blurry image. It was right inside the complex, off what appeared to be some sort of service road. He followed the twisting road with his eyes, understanding washing over him. It led all the way around the base.

"We can get anywhere we want from there," he'd said.

Dorothy had lowered the tablet, looking triumphant. "*Exactly.*"

Now the soldiers loaded them into a boxy, green jeep. Ash glanced at Dorothy as they all climbed in back.

She was already watching him, her brow furrowed, but she looked away the second their eyes met, her features smoothing over again.

He let his gaze linger for a second longer, wondering if she was nervous. Maybe, beneath the calm exterior, she'd been just as worried as he'd been that her plan wouldn't work. She always came across as so confident. Ash had never considered that she might be faking.

No one spoke as they drove. Trees and bushes and grass blurred together outside their windows, rocks and brush crunching beneath the jeep's massive tires. They followed a dirt path that curved out of the trees and deposited them onto a paved road lined by barbed wire fences. The entrance to Fort Hunter yawned ahead.

Ash swallowed. He'd spent the last eleven months telling himself that finding the Professor was the solution to all of his problems. And now that solution was *here*, in this building.

He couldn't help wondering if this was enough. Had his future already changed? Maybe he'd never meet the woman with the white hair, never climb into that boat, never feel the heat of her dagger.

Maybe just this—going back in time, coming here—was enough to alter everything.

A line of soldiers stood in front of the entrance, guns at the ready. Spotlights shone above them, and rain slanted in front of their faces, fracturing the yellow light.

Ash glanced at Zora and saw that she was watching the soldiers as well. Only her eyes were narrowed to slits, and a deep frown cut across her lips. Something was wrong.

Ash tried to catch her eye but she shook her head, nodding to the armed men sitting in front of them. *Not now.*

The soldiers guarding the entrance shifted aside, and their jeep rumbled through. The arched doors opened into a cavernous white space. Monstrous spotlights hung from the ceiling, pouring sterile light over blackened concrete floors. Dozens of identical Humvees filled the room, each surrounded by a unit of army-green-clad soldiers, rifles hanging from their shoulders. The hum of conversation buzzed around him, muted by the Humvee's thick glass.

The gateroom, Ash thought, remembering this point on Willis's map. He scanned the faces as they rolled past, his breath catching every time he caught a glimpse of salt-and-pepper hair. It was never the Professor—but it could've been. He could be anywhere. He could be close.

Ash turned his attention to the far wall, the only wall made of plaster instead of rock. Four separate seals stared down at him:

United States Northern Command

Northern American Aerospace Defense Command

Air Force Space Command

Defense Advanced Research Projects Agency

They were intimidating, all American flags and stoic eagles peering into the distance. They hung in a circle on the plaster, surrounding black block words that read: WELCOME TO FORT HUNTER COMPLEX.

Ash felt the nerves hit his gut just then. He was a soldier going against his country. He was committing *treason*. If he were still in the army, he'd be court-martialed for this.

It'll be worth it, he told himself. *It'll be worth it if I get to live.*

The jeep rolled out of the gateroom and continued down a dark tunnel with pipes and tangled wires crawling over its curved walls. The sound of its engine echoed off the grimy brick as it slowed. The lights down there were smaller, and they did little to keep the dark at bay.

Ash counted three security cameras before they finally rolled to a stop in front of a white station that looked like an oversize tollbooth. The soldier guarding the station ambled over to their jeep, gun at the ready.

Ash held his breath. *Here we go.*

The driver rolled down the truck window. The two soldiers looked identical, with close-cropped brown hair and cleanly shaved, unsmiling faces. They reminded Ash of the little plastic army men he'd played with as a kid. Generic. Interchangeable. He doubted he'd be able to tell them apart if the driver weren't wearing an army-green hat pulled low over his forehead.

"We found this group of civilians wandering around the grounds inside the perimeter," said Army Guy Number One. "No ID, and none of them can tell us what they were doing around here."

Army Guy Number Two tightened his grip on his gun, peering past the driver and into the back seat. Ash looked straight ahead so he wouldn't have to make eye contact. "Have they been questioned?"

"Negative. Procedure says we're to bring 'em straight to detainment."

Army Guy Number Two studied Ash for another long

moment, his eyes slightly narrowed. Finally, he nodded, stepping aside so they could drive past.

Ash exhaled through his teeth. *So far, so good.*

He resisted the urge to look back at Dorothy. He could feel her in the seat behind him, though. Her knee brushed against the back of his chair every time she moved. He thought, again, of that moment back in the woods, when he'd imagined grabbing her and kissing her, and felt a pang somewhere deep in his gut.

It was just the excitement, he told himself, pushing the thought away. But the image lingered.

The word *detainment* had Ash picturing barred doors and windows and grimy padlocks. But Fort Hunter's detainment area turned out to be a low-ceilinged white room with benches nailed to the floor, the walls made entirely of glass.

So they can watch us, Ash thought. The idea made his skin crawl.

The room was empty, but a soldier stood at attention outside the steel door. He didn't acknowledge the jeep, didn't so much as glance at Ash and his crew as they were led inside, hands behind their heads, eyes straight ahead. Three soldiers followed them as far as the door, guns flashing in the dim light.

No one dared speak until the door closed behind them, leaving them alone together in the small room. Ash watched through the glass until the soldiers climbed back into their jeep and drove away.

He sucked down a breath, trying to find some still, calm

place inside of himself. They were doing this for *him*, after all. To find the Professor; to save his life. And, so far, Dorothy's plan had gone without a hitch.

Maybe it hadn't been the worst thing in the world, having her climb on board his ship.

He turned around. Dorothy had lowered herself to the bench affixed to the far wall, hands folded in her lap, head tilted as she watched him.

"Ready?" she asked.

"Ready," he said, swallowing. "All right, Dorothy. Let's see what you can do."

25
DOROTHY

Dorothy. Ash had actually called her by her name.

It felt like a small triumph, though she couldn't say exactly why.

Something in her stomach tightened as she watched him move around the detainment unit, pacing and cracking his knuckles and jerking his shoulders up and down, like there was something caught in his jacket. He was acting too guilty. He was going to get them caught.

"Will you calm down?" She pretended to study a piece of dirt beneath her fingernail while watching the soldier outside their room from the corner of her eye. "He'll *see* you."

When her eyes flicked back to his, she saw that he was already staring at her. Heat prickled up her neck. His gaze lingered for a moment, and then he looked away.

"How am I supposed to calm down? We're in a military prison, in case you haven't noticed."

"It's a detainment room, not a prison. Stop being dramatic."

"We could be tried for *treason*."

Good Lord, she thought, biting back a laugh. "But we won't be. Didn't you hear them talking? They think we're kids playing around in the woods. The worst we'll get is a slap on the wrist. Haven't you ever been arrested before?"

Chandra gave a small laugh. "Ash? Arrested? Please, he's a total Boy Scout."

Dorothy frowned. Boy Scout?

"It's a saying," Willis explained. "Chandra is implying that Ash is a Goody Two-shoes."

Ash's eyebrows went up, challenging. "What about you, princess? You spend a lot of nights in a jail cell?"

Dorothy groaned internally. *So they were back to princess, again.* She should've known his use of her real name was just a fluke.

She said, "Define *a lot*."

"More than two."

She bit her lip. She'd been arrested four times (and two of those really hadn't been her fault) but she didn't want to give him the satisfaction of admitting it now.

"You really are a Boy Scout," she muttered, glad that now she had something unpleasant to call him, too. She knelt in front of the door. "Lucky for you, I'm not. Otherwise we'd never get out of here."

There was a twitch at the corner of Ash's mouth as he said, "I suppose that's true."

Almost a compliment. Dorothy smothered a grin of her own as she turned back to the door.

There was no lock on the handle—it must only be accessible from the outside. No surprises there. She hadn't really expected this to be as easy as fumbling with a few hairpins.

She glanced through the window, studying their guard's skinny, pink neck. He was younger than the other soldiers had been, the stubble on his cheeks still patchy. Had they been anywhere else, she would have had him eating out of her hand like an excitable puppy within the space of a few minutes. But she doubted even this boy would be foolish enough to flirt with a prisoner.

She chewed at her lower lip, studying him. He wore a giant key ring on a belt at his waist. Dorothy should have been able to relieve him of those keys with little difficulty, but there wasn't much she could do with a wall of glass separating them.

She flexed her fingers. That left only one option. She reached into her pocket, where she'd stowed the tiny bottle of ipecac that'd fallen from Chandra's medical bag, twisted off the lid, and drank.

It tasted sweet, like syrup. Dorothy made a face, and tucked the rest of the bottle away.

"Be ready to move when I get the door open," she said to the others. "I'm not sure how long—"

A thick, acid taste rose in her throat. She closed her mouth, swallowing it down. That was quick. Covering her mouth with one hand, she stood, and knocked on the window.

The soldier tapped his gun against the glass. "Miss, I'm going to need to ask you to step away from the wall there."

"I don't feel so well, sir." Dorothy curled her tongue around the word *sir*. She knew from experience that men were more likely to play the hero if they thought you respected them.

The young soldier glanced around, like he was looking for help. "The sheriff's department should be here shortly."

Dorothy moved her hand from her mouth to her stomach. She let her legs wobble beneath her, and collapsed against the glass wall, groaning. The soldier had his gun up in a second, the butt of the weapon propped against one shoulder.

"Miss, I'm going to ask you *again* to step away from the wall."

"I don't think I can stand."

"Don't make me use force!"

"Please—" Dorothy's stomach cramped. She groaned and hunched over. Her knees really were shaking now. She thought she might actually collapse. The soldier was shouting something, but she couldn't make out his voice over the blood pounding in her head. She doubled over, vomiting.

She heard keys clinking, followed by the grinding metal sound of a lock opening. Now seemed like a good enough time as any to faint. Being mindful of the mess, Dorothy swooned, falling into a heap on the concrete. This wasn't her first time, and she made sure it looked good. She fluttered her eyelashes and let her lower lip quiver. Beneath her shirt, her chest heaved.

A creak of a door opening, and the sound of footsteps as the soldier entered the cell.

"Back against the wall!" he barked. Dorothy had her eyes closed, but she imagined him brandishing his gun in a very manly fashion as Ash and the others backed up against the wall. She gave her lip an extra quiver.

"Miss?" His voice was closer now, just above her. "Can you hear me? Are you all right?" She didn't answer, her eyes still closed. She heard him fumble with something, and then, in a more professional voice, "This is Private Patrick Arnold down in detainment. We have a situation—"

Dorothy let her eyes flicker open, peering up at the soldier through the fan of her lashes.

He lowered the boxy device he'd been speaking into. This close, he looked like he was still a boy. Big brown eyes took up most of his face, and the beginnings of a scattered mustache clung to his upper lip.

"Miss?" He swallowed, Adam's apple bobbing up and down. "Are you all right?"

"W-what happened?" Her voice actually cracked. Mother would be so proud.

"You fainted. Do you—"

Willis slipped one arm around the boy's neck, easily lifting him off his feet. Dorothy wouldn't have thought it possible for a man his size to be so stealthy, but Willis had crossed the cell without a sound, his combat boots silent on the concrete floors.

Poor Private Patrick Arnold groped, desperately, for the

giant's arm. His fingers trembled. He lost his grip on his gun and the weapon clattered to the floor. His lips went pale.

"Shh . . . ," Willis murmured, his muscles bulging around the soldier's skinny neck. "Go to sleep."

Private Arnold's eyes drooped. Dorothy stood, cringing at the sour taste in her mouth. She wished for a mint leaf or something to cover the flavor of vomit.

"Do you think he has any breath fresheners?" she asked, as the soldier's eyes closed, his head nodding off to the side. The poor boy was going to be in a mess of trouble when he came to. She almost felt sorry for him.

Willis placed Private Arnold's unconscious body on the floor on the other side of the cell, being especially careful not to let his head knock against the concrete. He reached into the soldier's pocket, producing a small, red-and-white tin.

"Altoids?" Dorothy reached for the mints. "I've actually heard of these."

She popped a mint into her mouth, eyes moving over the soldier's pocket. He probably had a wallet in there.

Ash's hand was suddenly on her arm. "*Don't.*"

She bristled. "But he's already passed out. It'll be easy."

"It'll still be *stealing*."

The way he said *stealing* sent a prickle of shame up the back of Dorothy's neck. She let out an exasperated noise, muttering, "I think I deserve some sort of reward for breaking us out of here."

Ash's grip on her arm loosened, but he didn't pull his hand away. "I can't believe that actually worked."

He didn't sound like he was laughing at her this time. He searched her face, frowning. "Where'd you learn all this stuff?"

"Don't sound so surprised," murmured Dorothy, but she felt something warm curl in her stomach. She'd never actually been complimented for her con work before. "I already told you, I'm very skilled."

Ash cleared his throat and dropped his hand, but not before Dorothy saw the barest hint of red blossom across his cheeks. "Well," he muttered. "It was impressive."

Dorothy chewed her lower lip. That look he'd given her . . . it was like she'd finally earned his respect.

The thought caused a strange fluttering in her chest. She hadn't realized she'd wanted it so badly.

The talking device made a buzzing noise from its spot on the floor, and then a voice said, "Private? Are you there? Come in, Private—"

Ash snatched the device off the ground and lifted it to his mouth. "This is Private Arnold," he said, in a surprisingly passable imitation of the now unconscious soldier. "Sorry for the false alarm. We're all set over here."

More static. And then, "Roger that."

"He'll come to in a few minutes," Willis said, nodding at Private Arnold. "We should be elsewhere when that happens."

Ash grabbed the gun from the floor, next to the unconscious soldier, and handed it to Zora, who pulled out the magazine and held it up to the light, squinting.

"Full thirty rounds," she said, snapping the ammo back in place with a click. "Looks like our boy never got a chance to fire this thing."

Ash kept patting the soldier down. "Hopefully we won't, either. You catch the make?"

"SG 542. They all had them. Easy enough gun to handle."

"Why are we talking about guns?" Dorothy glanced through the door, fingers nervously tapping at her leg. "We shouldn't need—"

The words died before they reached her lips. There was a tunnel just next to the detainment room. Dorothy had known it would be there, of course. It had been a part of her plan. She'd seen it on Willis's blueprints, had followed the snaking path it made through the complex with her finger.

But she hadn't known that the walls of the tunnel would be made of brick coated in dirt and plaster. Just like in her vision.

"Dorothy?" Ash said.

But she was already moving toward the tunnel, lowering her hand to those walls. She knew, before she pulled them away, that her fingertips would be wet.

"Dorothy?" Ash touched her back so lightly that she thought it might've been an accident. She flinched.

"Yes?" she murmured. Ash said something about being ready to go, but she barely heard him. Her mind was elsewhere.

You shouldn't trust them.

The memory of Roman's voice made her pulse go jagged. Had that been real, too? A warning from the future?

Dorothy bit her lip. Even if it *had* been real, it didn't make sense to believe it. Roman had kidnapped her. He'd *shot* her. If anyone shouldn't be trusted, it was him.

But, still, something nagged at her. The sense of déjà vu she'd felt when she'd first seen Roman's face. The way he'd teased her.

Are you trying to say that you've seen the future?

Perhaps. Perhaps I've even seen yours.

She was missing something, she was certain of it.

But, try as she might, she couldn't figure out what it was.

LOG ENTRY—JANUARY 21, 2075
07:15 HOURS
WEST COAST ACADEMY OF ADVANCED TECHNOLOGY

Today's mission: find our bodyguard.

The bodyguard was a necessity everyone agreed on. Eventually we'll be traveling to some pretty frightening places, and the protection of our team has to be a top priority.

We went back and forth for a while over whether we should find the largest man, or the best fighter, but, in the end, we decided to work under the assumption that *large* will be a deterrent that'll keep him from having to fight at all. People can be taught to fight, after all.

Finding the largest man in history turned out to be easier than I expected.

Willis Henry was working as a circus strongman around the turn of the century. At sixteen years old, he's already over seven feet tall and weighs six hundred pounds. And he doesn't seem to be done growing yet. My guess is that he has some form of giantism. (Giantism is a rare endocrynological disorder that causes the body to secrete excessive amounts of growth hormone.) We'll have to get him checked out in 2075.

According to the information Natasha dug up, Willis worked at the circus starting in 1914 and then abruptly disappeared in 1917. There are dozens of pictures of him in our archives, but surprisingly little is mentioned about his mental and emotional state. The circus billed him as some sort of monstrosity, more beast than man. In any case, I thought it safest to leave Zora and Natasha behind for this trip. Roman, however, insisted on coming along.

"I've never been to the circus before," he told me.

The circus in question was a good one. The Sells-Floto Circus began in the early 1900s and ran up until 1929, when it became part of the American Circus Corporation. In the late twenties, the Sells-Floto Circus was considered one of the greatest acts on earth. When we arrived in 1917, it was clear that they were well on their way to that distinction. The air smelled of peanuts and popcorn. There were acrobats leaping around outside the tent, and a man breathing fire, and actual *elephants*. I was five years old when elephants went extinct, so I've only ever seen them in pictures. They took my breath away.

Roman was taken with the circus tents, oddly enough. Old circus tents were these monstrous white structures made entirely of stiff canvas. I didn't get the draw until Roman pointed out how they reminded him of the emergency tents back on campus.

I could tell he was nervous about bringing this up. Our arguments have only increased over the last few weeks. I've been trying to talk Roman into moving into our spare room, but he insists on living in Tent City. He says he likes it there, but I don't see how that could be possible. There've been more riots, more protests. No one knows how to help the people of Tent City anymore. The state has run out of money, and there's no chance of finding them new homes.

Most of the city pretends the tents aren't even there.

Anyway, I digress.

We found Willis in a trailer behind the main tent. If it weren't for his size, I doubt I would've recognized him. The photographs I saw showed a snarling beast man, but Willis wasn't like that at all.

He was sitting on an overturned barrel, playing a game of solitaire with dog-eared playing cards, and he looked . . . lonely, for lack of a better word. When we showed up, he just seemed glad to have someone to talk to.

I'm not sure he believed my story about time travel, and the future, but he agreed to come with us anyway.

"I don't care for circus life," he explained, as we made our way back to the *Dark Star*. "Everyone treats you like a freak, and the tents are cold at night. You get tired of people walking past and gawking at you."

I couldn't be sure I heard correctly, but I'm fairly certain that Roman said, "I know exactly what that's like."

Is that what living in Tent City feels like?

And, if he hates it so much, why won't he let us help him?

26

ASH

MARCH 17, 1980, FORT HUNTER COMPLEX

Ash peered down the service-road tunnel—empty. Whoever had been on the other end of Private Arnold's walkie-talkie had either bought the lie that everything was fine and dandy, or he wasn't in any hurry to come check things out.

"Willis?" Ash said. "Blueprints?"

Willis pulled the tablet out of the waistband of his jeans (where he'd stowed it so the soldiers wouldn't catch a glimpse of the newfangled tech) and tapped the screen, sending blue light dancing over the grimy brick walls.

"According to the Professor's journal, he was looking for something *here*, in the east wing." Willis tilted the screen toward Ash, motioning to a long hallway that ran down the side of the map. "The most direct route is down this service road, but it means walking through the gateroom, which is the most populated portion of the complex. That would have been fine had we arrived at two in the morning, as planned, but now—"

"Now it'll be busy." Ash chewed on the inside of his cheek.

"Is there another route we can take? One that avoids people?"

"We could try weaving through the complex and entering from another door. Here, perhaps." Willis motioned to a door on the other side of the wing. "But that could take hours, and I'm not sure it'll make much of a difference. There will be cameras between here and there. Lots of them."

Zora turned to Willis. "Can you find where they keep the security monitors on that thing?"

"Sure . . . looks like there's a control room two floors up, down the north hall." Willis nodded into the darkness. "There's a stairway about twenty-five yards that way."

"Ash and I will head there to see if we can find a way to get the camera feed to loop. That'll take care of the cameras, but the rest of you will need to find a way across the gateroom and into the east wing without being seen. We'll catch up with you there."

Ash frowned. She said all of this as though it were a plan they'd already agreed upon, but it wasn't. They were all supposed to go to the east wing together.

He opened his mouth to argue, but Willis beat him to it. "I'm not sure that will be possible."

"Have faith, Willis. I'm sure you'll figure it out," Zora said, clapping him on the shoulder. And then, abruptly, she broke into a run, stolen gun thudding at her hip.

Ash stared after her, his mind momentarily blank. Then, when he realized she wasn't planning on waiting for him, he swore and started after her. "Um, okay, see you all in the east wing."

He managed a single step down the tunnel before Dorothy caught his arm. Her grip was light, but Ash felt the heat of it burn through his skin.

"Should we really be splitting up?" she asked, voice tinged with fear.

His pulse sped up.

No, he wanted to say. *We shouldn't.*

But Zora was already halfway down the hall, the sound of her boots echoing hollowly off the walls. He didn't know what was wrong, but he couldn't let her run off alone.

He removed Dorothy's hand from his arm gently. "I've gotta go after her."

Dorothy's expression changed, but Ash couldn't say exactly how. For a split second it was as though a curtain had been pulled back and, beneath it, Ash thought he saw . . . concern. She was worried for him.

Ash couldn't remember the last time someone outside of his team had worried about him. There'd been a couple of girls during the war, but he hadn't been with any of them long enough for real feelings to develop. Sure, they'd made promises to wait for each other, and declared their devotion, but it'd all felt superficial. Like playacting.

This was different. Hesitant. Ash had the feeling of two predators circling each other, waiting for the other to blink.

"I'll be careful," he said.

Dorothy merely nodded and looked away.

But as he ran down the tunnel, Ash couldn't shake the feeling that something between them had shifted.

* * *

Ash caught up with Zora faster than he'd expected to. She wasn't running anymore, but walking with intention, her expression grim.

"What the hell?" Ash said. "I thought the plan was to stick together."

Zora's eyes slid toward him. Unbelievably, she looked frightened. "Plans change."

"You really think you can get the camera feed to loop?"

Zora shrugged, not answering. Ash studied her profile in the dim light. He'd never known Zora to be reckless. But he'd never known her to be afraid, either. He didn't know which one bothered him more, but it occurred to him that if Zora was scared, he should be, too.

"You saw something," he said, thinking of how her eyes had narrowed on the row of soldiers standing guard at the complex entrance.

Zora was chewing on her lower lip. She said, her voice unrecognizable, "Roman."

Ash didn't understand. "Roman what?"

"He was standing with the other soldiers guarding the front entrance." Her lips twisted. "Like he was one of them."

"That's impossible."

"You think I don't know that?"

"He doesn't have any exotic matter. Even if that time machine he built actually works, physically, he *can't* travel back in time."

"But it was him, Ash. I'd bet my life on it."

Ash swallowed. Putting aside, for the moment, the question of *how* Roman got back here, there was still *why*. With all of history spread out before him, why would Roman come to 1980? Why break into a military fortress in the middle of the woods?

But, of course, Ash already knew the answer to that. He thought of Quinn Fox's inhuman voice.

This man has discovered the secrets of time travel. . . . He could save thousands of lives. But he refuses.

The Black Cirkus had been looking for the Professor, too. And Roman read the same journal entry they had.

Something cold spread through Ash as the puzzle pieces started slotting into place. Over the last year, he and Zora had come up with dozens of reasons why the Professor hadn't returned. He could've gotten distracted by some experiment, or maybe he was in hiding, or perhaps he had some master plan to save the world.

Or the Black Cirkus could've found him first.

Ash glanced at Zora and saw that she'd already worked this out on her own. "We need to get to the control room," she said. She was holding her gun so tightly her knuckles had turned white. "If Roman's here, we need to find him before he finds my father."

They made their way down the tunnel and up two flights of stairs in silence. Ash paused once they reached the end of the hall, lifting a hand to indicate that Zora should stay back. He peered around the corner.

Dim yellow light shone from the control room. The door was ajar and, through it, Ash could see a single soldier studying a wall of boxy televisions, all displaying grainy images of black-and-white hallways.

The soldier wore bulky headphones that covered his whole ears, and didn't seem to hear them approach. Zora pulled the gun from her shoulder.

Ash moved quickly, sliding one hand around the soldier's mouth and using the other to grab his arm and twist it behind his back. The soldier stood and stumbled away from his chair, his headphones clattering to the floor.

Zora moved into view, raising the gun. "Evening, sir."

The soldier tried to say something. Ash tightened his grip around his mouth.

"Tab. Nice," he said, nodding at the pink soda can on the man's desk. He knelt, one hand still gripping the soldier's arm, and then removed his hand from the guy's mouth so he could rip an extension cord from the outlet in the wall. "I've always wanted to try that stuff."

"What are you doing here?" the soldier spat. "What do you want?"

Ash began knotting the cord around the man's bound hands. "Nothing of yours, so don't bother getting all heroic. I'm just going to ask you to sit here for a few minutes while we take a look at your system."

Ash forced the soldier back into his chair and then tied the cord behind his back, finishing with a square-lashing knot that Willis himself wouldn't have been able to pull apart.

“My commanding officer will be here any minute,” the soldier continued. Ash groaned and looked around. There was a wad of napkins on the desk, probably left over from whatever this guy had eaten for breakfast. “When he gets here, he’ll—”

Ash stuffed the napkins into the soldier’s mouth. “Sorry to do this, but we won’t be able to concentrate with you over here flapping your lips. Sit tight.” He swiped the can of Tab off the soldier’s desk and took a swig. “Not bad. Tastes like carbonated sugar.”

Zora rolled her eyes. “Start looking.”

They stared at the security screens in silence for a moment, studying the flickering black-and-white images. There were a dozen of them, stacked in four rows of three, and the images themselves showed hundreds, maybe even thousands of people moving down hallways and around corridors.

Ash didn’t see how they were going to find anyone in this mess. His eyes moved to the white labels at the bottoms of each screen. *NORAD Alternate Command Center*, one read. And another, *Global Strategic Warning/Space Surveillance Systems Center.*

His heartbeat ratcheted up a notch. He’d always known that the Professor must’ve gone back in time for a reason, to study something important, or prevent something terrible from happening. But now, staring at these security monitors, he realized how serious that reason might be. NORAD monitored incoming ballistic missiles and attacks on North America. And space surveillance was . . . what? *Aliens?*

Ash held his breath as he scanned the monitors for the east wing. *What was in the east wing?*

"So," Zora murmured, eyes never leaving the screens. "Dorothy's pretty."

Ash considered her from the corner of his eye. He knew what she was doing. Zora didn't know how to handle her own emotions, so, when things got tense, she made other people talk about theirs so she could pretend to be composed and above it all in comparison.

People tend not to notice that you're freaking out when they're droning on about themselves, she'd told him once.

He knew all this, and yet he still found his fist tightening around the soda can. "You really want to talk about this now?"

Zora had been gazing at the television screens, but now her eyes fixed on his face. She looked quickly away again, but not before Ash saw a flash of something raw and hollow. He felt a sudden flare of guilt.

He had a lot riding on finding the Professor. So much, in fact, that he sometimes forgot the man was Zora's father. That he was the only family she had left. Offering her this distraction was an act of mercy.

So he sighed theatrically and said, "Pretty? I hadn't noticed."

"Please." A small smile flickered over Zora's lips, the only thanks he'd get for offering up his personal life in sacrifice to the greater good. "I saw the way you were looking at her."

"I look at her like she's a girl. End of story."

"No, you look at her like she's a *girl*." Zora wiggled her shoulders in a way that made Ash decidedly uncomfortable.

He smacked her in the arm. "So she's pretty. Lots of things are pretty. Sunsets are pretty."

"It's not just that. It's the way you talk to her, baiting her with all that *sweetheart* crap. *Teasing* her. I've never seen you act like that around a girl." She shot Ash a sidelong glance. "You like her."

Ash grunted. "It ain't like that."

"She likes you, too."

"Yeah, like a snake likes a mouse."

"Come on, Ash, don't be an idiot. You have to have noticed. She flirts with you. She finds dumb reasons to touch you. She says things she knows will piss you off, just to get a reaction. She *likes* you."

Ash flushed, remembering the moment in the tunnel, the emotion he could've sworn he saw on Dorothy's face before she told him to be careful.

He considered that Dorothy might not be trying to manipulate him at all. That Zora was right. That she liked him.

Did he like her?

"You could think about this more strategically, you know," Zora said.

"Is your mouth still moving?"

"I'm serious. We know Dorothy isn't the girl from your vision. Aside from the obvious fact that she hasn't given herself an albino makeover, you weren't ever supposed to meet her. Bringing her to the future could've altered things." Zora glanced up again, studying him. "Maybe, if you fall for Dorothy instead of this girl with the white hair you could prevent the whole . . ."

Zora groaned, letting her tongue roll out of her mouth as she mimed getting stabbed.

"That was Oscar-worthy, really. You missed your calling."

Zora shrugged and went back to the television. "I'm still young."

Ash tried to stay focused on the screens, but his eyesight had blurred. For the past year, he'd avoided any girl who'd dared look his way. He told himself it'd make things easier. That his best chance of keeping the future from catching up with him would be to cut himself off. And if that happened to be a lonely existence, well, at least he still got to exist.

But Zora had a point. Dorothy wasn't supposed to be here.

Ash cleared his throat, pushing the thought away, for now. Zora was leaning forward, squinting at one of the many figures on the screen.

Ash's pulse jumped in his chest. *Here we go.*

She exhaled. "Ash . . ."

If she said something else, Ash didn't hear it. The man on the screen was too tall to be Roman. He had dark skin and short black hair sprinkled with quite a bit more white than Ash had seen in it before. He wore a familiar long black trench coat flapping open over a faded T-shirt and jeans.

Zora pressed her palm to the fuzzy, black-and-white image of the man on the screen and whispered, her voice cracking, "Dad?"

27

DOROTHY

Dorothy pinched her lower lip, trying very hard not to frown. She, Willis, and Chandra had spent the few minutes since Zora and Ash had disappeared down the tunnel trying to come up with a plan to get across the very crowded gateroom.

So far, Chandra was the only one with an idea. Dorothy wanted to be supportive, but the whole thing sounded . . .

Well, it sounded ludicrous.

Dorothy said, as politely as she could muster, "Come again?"

Chandra went back into the detainment room and knelt beside the unconscious soldier, struggling to unbutton his shirt one-handed. She seemed to keep forgetting that one of her arms was imprisoned inside a sling, which resulted in strange contortions of her body as she tried to use her fingers.

"Damn," she muttered, watching one of the soldier's buttons pop off and shoot across the floor. "Look, it'll be easy. You just have to put on this dude's clothes, pretend to be a soldier, and walk across the room like you belong. Simple. I'd do it myself, but I'm short and . . . roundish, and this guy is very much tall and not. And Willis can't do it because. Well. Duh."

Now Dorothy did frown. "Duh?"

"It means 'obviously,' but there's a negative connotation." Willis glanced down at the soldier. "He *is* a rather dainty little man."

"Thank you, Captain Literal," Chandra muttered. "Anyway, Dorothy can lead the two of us across the gateroom like we're her prisoners. See? *Easy.*"

Another button popped off of the soldier's shirt. Willis lurched forward, trapping it beneath a boot. "I don't know, Chandra," he said. "It seems . . . goofy."

Chandra tugged one of the soldier's arms out of his shirt. "Dressing as the enemy was a common movie trope in the eighties. They did it in *Star Wars*, remember? 'Aren't you a little short for a Stormtrooper?' You loved that scene."

Willis frowned. It was an expression that seemed to involve every muscle in his stonelike face. His brows were deeply furrowed, his jaw clenched. Even his mustache looked sad. "Yes, but this isn't a movie. People are going to notice us."

"And I don't see how that uniform is going to make me look like a man," Dorothy added. "My hair—"

"There are lady soldiers now," Chandra said. "Wait, 1980s . . . are there lady soldiers?"

"I believe there are a few," Willis said.

"Anyway, you don't have to look like a man, you just have to walk us across the gateroom without getting shot."

"Is there a high possibility of us being shot?" Dorothy asked, her throat strangely constricted.

Chandra pulled the soldier's shirt loose with a final grunt and handed it up to Dorothy.

"Not if you look like you belong. In the movies, it works best if you walk really confidently and don't stop to talk to anyone." Chandra shrugged, fingers fumbling with the metal prongs of the soldier's belt buckle. "And sometimes you have to make out with a guy against a wall so nobody sees your faces, but I don't think that's applicable in this situation."

Dorothy frowned. The soldier's shirt smelled rather strongly of body odor.

Chandra finally got the buckle undone, but couldn't seem to pull the belt loose. Willis was watching her with tightly clenched lips, one finger steadily tapping his chin.

"This is a highly problematic course of action," he said, after a moment. "And it has only a small probability of success—"

"What's *your* big plan, then?" Chandra asked. (Groan. Tug.) "Because you just said the only way to get to the east wing is by crossing the gateroom. And the only way to cross the gateroom is—"

"For me to put on this gentleman's trousers," Dorothy finished.

"Well. Yeah."

Willis watched Chandra struggle with the pants

one-handed for another moment before lowering himself to the floor beside her and taking over the job.

Dorothy felt a sudden pang, watching him. There was something resigned about the way he removed the soldier's trousers; he didn't approve, but that didn't mean he wasn't going to help. It was sort of touching, in a strange way. Nobody had ever done anything like that for her before.

"I don't think we'll be able to go with you. No one's going to buy that we're prisoners." Willis looked up at Dorothy, offering her the soldier's pants. "You'll have to cross the gate-room alone."

Dorothy frowned. "What about you? You can't just wait here for the sheriff's department to arrive."

"I think Chandra and I will have to make our way back to the *Second Star*. If I can get it in the air, we can find a closer spot to land and rendezvous with you, Ash, and Zora once they've found the Professor. I believe there's a helipad just above the east wing that should do the trick."

Dorothy swallowed. Nothing about this plan felt particularly smart. They were asking her to risk her life to save this Professor person, who she didn't even know. And why? Because she fit into a soldier's trousers.

Loretta would never agree to this, not unless she was getting something in return. She imagined her mother sitting stoically at the bar, waiting to see if Dorothy would make it away from her kidnapper, and felt herself stiffen. She knew exactly how much her mother was willing to risk for other people.

Did she really want to be like that? Trusting no one? Always on her own?

Dorothy looked over her shoulder, but it wasn't until she saw the empty tunnel spiraling out behind her that she realized she'd been hoping to see Ash in the distance.

She felt a strange, sudden rush of warmth, remembering how he'd raced into the darkness after Zora, refusing to let his friend go off on her own. Dorothy couldn't quite pinpoint why she found the image so comforting. It had seemed very brave to her, but it was more than that: it was the opposite of how she'd felt so many years ago, watching Loretta press a single finger into the drop of brandy on the bar.

I had to know you could take care of yourself.

She shuddered at the memory of her mother's words. Ash wouldn't leave Zora to take care of herself. They were a team. They helped each other.

Dorothy realized that she wanted that—to be part of a team. And if that meant walking across the gateroom alone because she was the only one who fit into the uniform . . .

Well, she supposed that was a small price to pay.

Resigned, she took the pants.

Willis said, "I'll turn my back so you can change."

You just have to walk across the gateroom without getting shot, Dorothy thought, pulling the soldier's trousers over her hips. *Small probability of success.*

By the time she finished lacing her boots, it felt as though someone was gripping her around the throat and squeezing the last bits of oxygen from her body.

"How do I look?" she choked out.

Chandra started chewing on her fingernail. Willis's mustache drooped.

"Walk fast," he said. "And don't make eye contact with anyone."

LOG ENTRY—FEBRUARY 6, 2075
17:01 HOURS
WEST COAST ACADEMY OF ADVANCED TECHNOLOGY

How do you determine who in history has the "best medical mind?"

We've been going over and over this question for the last few weeks. Do you go with the most technically advanced? Biggest IQ? Most experience? Pure genius? I have absolutely no idea which criteria I should be using here.

Last night, Natasha showed me the *Compendium of Suśruta*, which is this ancient Sanskrit text on medicine and surgery. It's so old that she had to get special permission just to take it out of the library. It's the foundation of the traditional Indian medical practice called Ayurveda. Apparently the ancient Indians were brilliant with medicine, way ahead of Hippocrates. They used plants to treat illness, and they were the first people on earth to perform surgery.

Natasha made a good point. "We're going to be traveling throughout all of history," she said. "So we won't have any way of knowing what medical equipment we'll have access to, or what sort of conditions we'll be facing. We need someone who can be prepared for *everything*. So wouldn't it make sense to find someone trained in the most primitive forms of medicine and get them up-to-date on modern technology here?"

Now the trick, of course, is finding someone capable of all that. Records from ancient India aren't exactly robust. We're working off of research that says things like, I kid you not, "We think he lived sometime between 1500 and 500 BCE."

That's a period of a thousand years. Not helpful.

Natasha found something interesting, though. There was a report of a girl attempting to study at the Taxila center of learning in 528 BCE. The Taxila was one of the first medical schools, but girls weren't admitted, so she'd cut off all her hair and tried to pass for a boy. The university found out, unfortunately, and threw her out at the end of her first year. She would've been fifteen. We looked and looked, but the girl is never mentioned again.

I have to admit, I have some reservations about this. It's one thing to get a WWII pilot or a strongman from the circus. But this is our doctor.

Natasha, on the other hand, won't stop talking about this fifteen-year-old girl who tried to fool the most brilliant medical minds in all of India. I asked her to explain what she found so fascinating, and this is what she said:

"This girl gave up everything when she tried to go to school. And all because she wanted to study medicine. Maybe she'll give up everything for us, too."

She won me over with that.

The girl's name is Chandrakala Samhita, and it took us three trips back in time to find her. As I mentioned before, records are spotty, and we couldn't figure out exactly when in 528 BCE she'd been expelled. Luckily, Taxila is a fascinating place to explore. We walked past Gandhara sculptures, endless reliefs of Lord Buddha, and stupas sitting atop green hillsides, all surrounded by lush trees and distant mountains. Over ten thousand students studied at Taxila, hailing from as far as China and Greece, and they flooded the primitive sidewalks, making it difficult for us to move around the campus. It was hotter than I expected, past ninety-five degrees though we arrived in mid-May, by the modern calendar. The air was heavy and wet.

We finally found Chandrakala at a reflecting pool outside a Buddhist monastery. Natasha had to do the talking, as Chandrakala spoke no English. Luckily, Natasha speaks both Prakrit and Pali. It wasn't long before she'd convinced the young girl to come with us.

Unfortunately, the success of our final trip to Taxila was hampered, somewhat, by another vision. The vision has been occurring more frequently (I catch glimpses of it whenever I enter the anil now), and it's always the same:

I see an entire city underwater, and then I'm hit with a feeling of deep, overwhelming sadness, like the sun has gone out.

It chills me to think of it, even now.

The scientific part of me wants to be logical about this. There's been endless research on the predictive properties of memory. It's possible that what I'm experiencing is a kind of "pre-memory," that entering a crack in space-time has created neuropathies inside my brain where none should exist, allowing me brief glimpses into the future.

It's a fitting hypothesis.

But I hope to God that I'm wrong.

28

ASH

MARCH 17, 1980, FORT HUNTER COMPLEX

He was here.

Ash hadn't realized how little hope he'd had left until this moment. But the Professor was really here. After almost a year of searching, Ash had found him.

Images flashed through his mind: a boat rocking on black water, white hair dancing in the wind, white trees glowing against the darkness.

He'd been counting down the months to that moment. And then the weeks, the days . . .

Now, he felt the sand in his hourglass freeze. Finding the Professor meant there was still a chance that he might keep it from happening at all.

Grinning, Ash moved in next to Zora, his eyes glued to the screen. The Professor appeared to be . . .

Whistling. He was walking down the hallway of one of the most secure military fortresses in the history of time and *whistling.*

Ash laughed, amazed.

Then, the security image flickered. The Professor moved quickly across the screen, stopping in front of a door. He hesitated for a moment, and then opened the door and disappeared inside.

It was a heavy metal security door, marked with a single word: RESTRICTED.

Zora dropped her hand from the screen. "Where does that go?"

"I don't know," Ash said. He searched the other security images, but there were too many other people crowded on the screens. He felt his heart sputter inside of his chest. *No.* The Professor was here. He was in this building.

He'd *just* seen him.

Zora pulled the gun farther up her shoulder. "You find Roman. I'm going after my father."

"Wait," Ash said, but she was already pushing past him and racing down the hall, her boots thudding heavily against the concrete floors.

He knew he should run after her, but he found himself turning back around, his eyes moving to the label beneath the screen where he'd just seen the Professor.

Environmental Modification.

Ash frowned. That was it? The mysterious east wing was devoted to environmental research? He raised a hand to the label and moved his finger over the words, as though that might help him understand.

Why would the Professor travel a hundred years into the past to study the *weather*?

As Ash contemplated this, another person stepped into the screen. He felt himself stiffen, expecting Roman. But it wasn't Roman. It was a girl.

She shifted toward the camera and Ash caught the sketchy, white curve of a foxtail painted over the front of her dark coat.

Quinn Fox. Ash stared, uneasy. If Quinn was here that meant they'd really done it. The Black Cirkus had found a way to travel through time without exotic matter.

Quinn lifted her hands, pushing away the hood covering her face.

She was turned away from the camera and, at first, all he saw was her scar. It carved up half her face, a misshapen, gnarled thing that made it difficult to focus on the rest of her. Ash cringed at the sight of it. It wasn't unusual to see bad scars and deformities in New Seattle—medical care wasn't what it used to be. But now Ash understood why Quinn hid her face. Her hair came out of the hood next, tumbling around her shoulders in a tangled mess of curls.

Ash's heart stopped beating. Somewhere deep inside his body, his veins were leaking acid.

He'd never seen Quinn's hair before. It had always been hidden under her hood, and now he felt stupid for not putting two and two together.

White. Quinn Fox's hair was white.

On the screen, a black-and-white Quinn Fox tugged

long fingers through her hair, pulling the last few strands loose of her coat. She wasn't looking at the camera anymore, so Ash stared at her hand, studying every detail he could make out on the grainy screen. Her short fingernails. The creases of her knuckles. A small black smudge that looked like a tattoo.

He raised a hand to his cheek, premembering the brush of her fingers on his skin, seconds before she slid a blade between his ribs.

She started walking again, heading deeper down the hallway before disappearing through the same door as the Professor.

Ash jerked around, scanning the other black-and-white screens as he waited for her to reappear. But she'd disappeared into the throng of people.

"Damn it to hell." His fist connected with the desk more violently than he intended it to. The screens trembled, and the bound-and-gagged soldier made a frightened grunting noise, like an animal in a trap. Ash flinched. He'd honestly forgotten the soldier was there.

"Sorry, man," Ash muttered, eyes on the screens. His brain was still struggling to catch up with what he'd seen. The woman with the white hair was Quinn Fox.

Quinn Fox, the cannibal of New Seattle. The girl whose lips always smelled of blood. The thought that he might kiss those lips made his stomach churn. It was impossible.

But the vision couldn't have been lying, not after all this

time. Ash was going to fall in love with a monster, and then she was going to shove a dagger into his gut. She was going to watch him die.

His heartbeat thrummed. He rolled his shoulders back, but the tension in his muscles wouldn't release. He felt like lit matches and rags soaked in gasoline and engines running too hot for too long.

This didn't make any sense. Quinn was the worst type of monster. She was violent and soulless. Ash didn't even think she was capable of love. Levi told him she'd killed a man with a *spoon*.

He thought of her gravelly voice on the Black Cirkus's nightly address.

Join the Black Cirkus, and we'll use time travel to build a better present, a better future.

She stood for everything he was against.

He would never—*could* never fall in love with her.

But bigger than that was this: he finally knew who was going to kill him. He knew her name, her face. He knew where she was right now.

Forget Roman—forget the Professor. Ash knew how to keep the prememory from happening.

He just had to find Quinn and kill her before she could kill him.

He calmly knelt on the cold concrete floor. He fished the pistol—a SIG Sauer P226—out of the holster at the bound soldier's belt and checked the chamber. Six rounds left.

Not bad. He hadn't been trained on this gun, but it looked straightforward enough. All he had to do was point and shoot.

The door marked RESTRICTED was down the same hallway that led to the east wing. Ash angled the tied-up soldier so that he could see the screen and pulled the napkins from his mouth. "I need you tell me how to get here," he said, pointing.

The soldier blinked. "The east wing?"

"I need to get to that hallway without crossing the gateroom or walking past any cameras. You got any ideas? There's got to be another entrance or something."

He rested his hand on the SIG Sauer, just in case the soldier needed incentive.

"Th-there's a stairway," the soldier said, swallowing. His eyes never left the gun. "Just down the hall. Goes down to the east wing, but there will be a guard—"

"That'll do. Sorry to leave you like this." Ash slipped the SIG Sauer into his jeans and pulled his jacket down over it. "But I gotta go see about a girl."

29

DOROTHY

Dorothy stood at the edge of the gateroom, trying not to look as uncomfortable as she felt in her stolen uniform. She could see the hall that led to the east wing on the other side of the room, maybe fifty yards away. Zora and Ash would be waiting for her there, and maybe this Professor person, too.

The problem was the hundreds of puke-green uniform-clad soldiers that filled the space between.

Dorothy watched them swarm, wary. Gun muzzles gleamed black in the overbright lights. Actual automobiles rumbled through the room; their engines sounded tinny echoing off the far walls and soaring ceilings. Almost like toys.

She inhaled as deeply as she could manage without drawing attention to herself.

You just have to walk across the gateroom without getting shot, she thought. *Small probability of success.*

Briefly, she considered leaving. She could probably walk

out the front entrance in this uniform. True, she didn't have any money or friends in this new time period, but that had never stopped her before.

But then she thought of Willis, kneeling to help Chandra even though he wasn't entirely sure of her plan. She thought of Ash racing after Zora in the dark.

"Team," she muttered, her lips barely moving to release the word.

Holding her breath, she stepped into the crowd.

This was just another con, and, like all cons, it could fall to pieces with a single misstep or poorly chosen phrase. Right now she was just another soldier in the throng. But she could already feel how the men's eyes lingered on her for a beat longer than they needed to. Their glances sent fear squirming down her spine. Beauty wasn't always an asset. Surely it wouldn't be long before they realized she didn't belong here.

Her legs itched to move faster—to run—but that would only draw more attention. She forced herself to move slowly. She was halfway across the room now, the hall leading to the east wing tantalizingly close. She didn't catch the other soldiers' eyes, but she could feel them traveling over her. She pinched the inside of her palm, her breath coming faster. The hall lay straight ahead.

Dorothy found herself starting to relax. Despite the long glances and the crowd, this ludicrous plan seemed to be working. There were simply too many people, and they all were in a rush. A few men spared a second glance for the too-small soldier in the ill-fitting uniform, but no one bothered with a third. They all assumed that she belonged there. That she was one of them.

No longer worried that she might be shot at any moment, Dorothy allowed her head to fall back, taking in the space.

It was, in a word, *extraordinary.* Nothing like the world she'd left in her own time, but familiar, somehow. Like a place she'd walked through in a dream. The ceiling arched high above her head, going up and up forever, and, though the walls started as craggy rock, they quickly morphed into flat, hard steel and wire and glass. The spotlights hanging from the ceiling were larger than anything Dorothy had ever seen before—the size of stagecoaches, at least—and so bright that she couldn't look at them directly.

And everywhere, *everywhere*, there were people. They were mostly men, but a few were women: straight-backed, serious women, wearing clothes that hid their figures, their faces scrubbed of makeup. These were not women trying to please the men around them. These were warriors. *Fighters.* Dorothy had to remind herself to keep her mouth closed as they walked past. Women like this didn't exist where she came from. Even her mother, who hated men, had built her life around them. These women were different.

Dorothy remembered the strange, hollow feeling she'd had on the morning of her wedding.

This, she thought, furiously. *This is what I was looking for.*

A grin threatened her lips, but Dorothy bit it back. Her fingers itched to reach into pockets, discover more treasures, but she resisted the impulse. If she really wanted to be part of a team, she needed to prove that she could be trusted. Which meant helping the others find this Professor person, instead of helping herself to the contents of strangers' pockets.

She was almost there—

"Private!"

Dorothy stopped walking, her spine rod-straight. Hadn't the soldier whose uniform she was wearing been called private something?

Did that mean that shout was directed at her?

Blast. She could just pick out the rapid approach of footsteps through the throng of thumping boots behind her. Fear prickled up her arms. The hall leading to the east wing was just ahead. Three yards, maybe. Less than fifty feet. The muscles in her legs tightened.

"Private!"

It was no good—he was too close. Running would only blow her cover. She turned slowly, shaking out her legs to release the tension. A man was pushing through the crowd of soldiers. He wore the same uniform she did, but without the hat. His hair was cropped so close to his skull that she could see the pink of scalp through the prickly brown strands.

"Do I—" she started. The man glanced at her, frowning, and then looked away. He lifted a hand to flag down a short, muscular woman with a long black braid who stood a few feet ahead of them both.

Dorothy jerked back around, relief and nerves flooding over her in equal measure. From the corner of her eye, she caught the soldier turning to look at her again. She kept moving, a little faster now.

Twenty more feet. Twelve . . . five . . .

The walls narrowed in as Dorothy stepped out of the gateroom and into a dark corridor. It was mercifully empty. She felt herself relax into her too-large uniform, her legs going wobbly around the knees as she glanced to her left. The corridor ended in a simple door, clearly marked with the words *East Wing.*

The Professor should be behind that door. She started toward it when a flash of metal caught her eye. She turned and saw that there was another door in the short, narrow hallway. This one was made of dull metal and marked with a single word:

RESTRICTED.

Her breath caught. Reality seemed to fold in on itself. She blinked, half expecting to find herself back in the *Second Star*, the anil swirling around her.

She'd seen this before, just as she'd seen the tunnel before.

Before she could stop herself, she stepped forward and tried the door handle—*locked.* Obviously. It'd been locked in her vision, too. Her eyes flicked down, finding the raised, metal keyboard below the latch. Just like before.

She looked over her shoulder. The east wing was just a few more feet away. The plan had been to go straight there. Meet the others. Find the Professor. Prove that she could be part of a team. This wasn't the right time for a detour.

You shouldn't trust them, she thought, remembering Roman's words. Something prickled inside of her.

She couldn't bring herself to move away. It was as though the door were whispering to her, urging her closer. She had to know what was on the other side.

She lowered a hand to the keypad. There were twelve keys, numbered one through nine, along with a pound sign, asterisk, and zero.

Her vision hadn't lasted long enough to show her a code. Although, she realized, if it really had been some sort of glimpse of the future it would've probably just shown her standing here now, confused.

She pressed the five, and a green light flashed—she flinched, jerking her hand away. The light blinked three more times, and then turned red, issuing an angry buzz. After a moment, it disappeared.

Dorothy bit into her lip, thinking. If this were a safe she'd have it open in minutes. But she didn't know how many numbers this code required, or what the purposes of the pound sign and asterisk keys were. Even if she could figure out the numbers used in the combination by studying their level of wear (the one and four keys looked particularly well scuffed), there were too many possibilities to account for.

"Blast," she muttered, pinching her nose between two fingers. This wasn't impossible. It *couldn't* be. She just had to think it through. Safe combinations typically had three numbers . . . but the numbers could be double digits, so, really, it was anywhere between three and six numbers. Or maybe—

"You there . . . Private!"

Dorothy froze. She recognized that voice. It was the soldier from the gateroom, the one she'd thought had been calling to her.

Footsteps thudded down the corridor behind her. She straightened, mentally flipping through every possible excuse she could have for being inside a military complex, wearing a stolen uniform, and trying to get through a locked door.

It didn't take very long, because there was only *one*, the truth, and she didn't think this soldier was going to believe that she had to get through this door because she was a time traveler who'd had a vision of it and now she desperately needed to see what was on the other side.

Oh God, those footsteps were coming closer. . . .

There was really only one thing left for Dorothy to do, the only thing besides picking locks that she was actually any good at. She relaxed her face, hoping that men in the 1980s were at least as big a bunch of fools as men from the 1910s, and turned around.

The soldier stopped walking, and that familiar leering, possessive look flashed across his face, twisting the corner of his mouth and narrowing his eyes.

Dorothy felt a hint of disappointment, mingled with her relief. *Every damn time.*

The soldier cleared his throat, the expression vanishing. "You're, um, new, aren't you? I don't think I've seen you around here before."

Chin down. Head tilted. Eyelashes lowered. Dorothy registered these commands without thinking about them. It was instinct—like a cat landing on its feet after a bad fall.

"Is it that obvious?" she asked, lip curling in a soft smile. The soldier swallowed, his Adam's apple bobbing up and down in his throat. She slinked toward him, a move made much more difficult by the too-large boots on her feet. "Perhaps you could help me. You see, I'm so silly and seem to have forgotten the code. . . ."

LOG ENTRY—MAY 9, 2075
16:42 HOURS
WEST COAST ACADEMY OF ADVANCED TECHNOLOGY

Now that we have a complete team, NASA and WCAAT have worked together to outline a training regimen. That consists of medical training and English language lessons for Chandra, flight school for Ash, and various martial arts and weapons training for Willis. WCAAT has agreed to bring Natasha on as the crew's historian, so she's been spending her days boning up on the few periods of history she's not already an expert on, and I've officially hired Zora as our backup mechanic.

NASA gave me some hassle for this, until I pointed out that, so far, my daughter has assisted on the construction of *two* time machines, compared to everyone else on earth's *zero*. She's more qualified than any other person alive.

The schedule is grueling for everyone. Hours of classes and training, followed by group sessions with Natasha where we study history. But not normal history. No wars and politicians and dates and things of that nature.

We study the price of milk in 1932. The proper way to greet a stranger in 1712. Makes and models of common automobiles in 1964. Popular music in 1992.

In other words, the boring bits of history.

We've taken a few small trips through time already, but these are mostly team-building missions. NASA wants to see how well we work together before they send us anywhere exciting. Last week we went to 1989 to watch the Berlin Wall come down, and, a couple of days ago, I took the whole team to Chicago, 1908, to watch the Cubs win the World Series.

But tonight's going to be even better.

Tonight, we get to watch a man land on the moon.

30

ASH

MARCH 17, 1980, FORT HUNTER COMPLEX

Ash found the stairwell right where the soldier had told him it would be. He checked over his shoulder to make sure no one was following him, and then he slipped inside. The door settled shut behind him with an ominous *thud*.

The soldier had said this entrance would be guarded, so Ash was careful to walk silently, breathing through his nose and rolling his feet to keep the soles of his boots from creaking. He checked over the edge of the stairwell every few minutes, eyes peeled for movement.

He was already several flights down when he caught the corner of an army-green uniform and heard a small sound, like someone clearing his throat.

Here we go. Ash stayed near the wall, letting the shadows conceal him. He waited until the soldier was facing away, and then he crept up behind him, pressing the SIG Sauer to the back of his neck. "Evening, sir."

The soldier jerked and reached for the walkie-talkie at

his belt, but Ash caught him by the wrist and twisted his arm behind his back, pushing his face into the wall. "Afraid I can't let you do that."

The soldier grunted. "Who're you?"

Just your friendly neighborhood time traveler, Ash thought. He tightened his grip on the soldier's wrist, pressing the gun deeper into his neck. The man flinched.

"We're going to take a walk," Ash said. "All you gotta do is stay calm, and everything will be grand. Does that sound okay to you?"

He kept his gun leveled against the back of the man's head until the soldier slowly nodded.

"Where are we going?" he asked.

"Just down the hall," Ash said. "Keep moving."

Ash pushed the soldier down the empty corridor, stopping when they reached the door Quinn Fox and the Professor had disappeared through only a few moments before.

He nodded at the door. "Get it open."

The soldier jabbed a few numbers into the keypad. The lights flashed green and a quick *beep beep beep* told Ash it was unlocked. He pushed it open with his shoulder, dragging the soldier with him. "I'm going to tie you up now," Ash told the soldier. "No hard feelings or nothing, I just can't have you alerting anyone to my presence. Got it?"

The soldier swallowed. Then nodded.

"Strong and silent type," Ash muttered. "I like that."

He pulled a bandanna out of his jacket pocket and began winding it around the soldier's thick wrists. When he finished,

Ash pulled the man's gun and walkie-talkie from his belt and added them to his own. "Now, I'm going to trust you to stay right here until I get back. Is that clear?"

Another shaky nod. Ash left the soldier where he was and headed through the door.

Darkness yawned before him. Ash took a step forward—and then paused. He couldn't see more than a few feet ahead, but the air felt thin, and his footsteps echoed. The smell of smoke and engine grease clung to his nostrils.

He inhaled, deep, tilting his head back. He had a sense that the room went up and up and up.

What was this place?

Slowly, his eyes began to adjust to the darkness. He could make out the silhouettes of objects hanging from the ceiling and jutting up from the floor. Something long and curved sliced through the black, and he could've sworn he saw the jagged halo of propellers, shadows blanketing their edges.

It was a hangar, he realized, and felt a hint of excitement, mingled with disappointment. He wished it were brighter. He would've liked to see the aircrafts the US government kept hidden in a secret bunker deep inside a mountain.

Not that he had the time to ogle planes just now, anyway. He eased deeper into the hangar, gun cocked, eyes peeled. No other shadows moved through the darkness, no other sounds echoed off the walls.

"Where'd you go, Quinn?" he muttered, surprised at the viciousness in his own voice. Adrenaline spiked through him.

Was he really going to do this? Was he really going to murder someone in cold blood?

He'd killed a person before. He'd been a soldier during wartime, after all. But those people had been armed. They'd been shooting at him.

He swallowed, picturing Quinn's dagger flashing silver in the darkness. The cold bite of a blade sliding into the skin just below his ribs.

It doesn't have to end like this.

Of course it does.

He didn't want to kill anyone. But he didn't want to die, either.

He tightened his grip on his gun, easing around an old fighter jet. His heart was thudding like a jackrabbit inside his chest. She had to be here. People didn't just vanish into thin air.

A finned tail cut through the darkness, catching his eye. He squinted, forgetting about Quinn for a fraction of a moment.

There was an aircraft hidden in the shadows. It was bullet-shaped, like zeppelins from the forties, but smaller. As Ash's eyes adjusted to the dark, he could just make out the shape of black stars gleaming from the metal.

He moved closer, his breath a spiky ball in his throat. He half expected it to be a copy, like the *Black Crow*. But, no. The ship was real, so real that it made him feel like a fool for mistaking it—even for a second—for the impostor in the Fairmont's parking garage.

The *Dark Star* was here.

His heartbeat sputtered. *Why* was it here?

The Professor wouldn't have taken the time machine into the complex with him. He would've left it in the woods, hidden, so that he could go back to it later. It being here now could only mean that the soldiers found it, that they brought it here. Which meant they knew the Professor had snuck into the complex.

Ash held the pistol before himself, approaching the ship like it was a horse that might spook. The door was already open.

He took the stairs two at once. His world had narrowed to a single point. No sound came from inside the ship, not a footstep, or a breath. Ash could practically hear his own heart pounding through the stillness, echoing, making the *Star*'s steel walls tremble.

The scent hit him first: pipe smoke and aftershave and burnt coffee. The Professor's scent. It was like seeing a ghost—or *smelling* a ghost—and it took everything Ash had not to drop his gun right there.

He tightened his fingers, the SIG Sauer's plastic creaking. The Professor had come this way, too, hadn't he? He could even be here, now, trying to get his ship the hell out of here before the complex guards found him.

"Professor?" Ash whispered, inching forward. The ship's control panel gleamed in the darkness, all well-oiled wood and shiny chrome. Professor Walker had style; no one could deny him that. The *Dark Star* was much larger than the *Second Star*, designed to carry a team comfortably. Ash eased through the three main rooms of the machine—passenger cabin, cockpit, and cargo room. All were empty.

"Quinn?" Ash tried instead. He imagined he heard a laugh—something faint, barely more than a release of breath—and he spun around, finger trembling against the gun's trigger. But there were only empty chairs and shadowy walls and nothingness.

Ash's eyes had grown tired from straining against the darkness. He relaxed for long enough to grope along the time-machine walls for the light switch. The darkness scattered, and he saw that the cabin was empty. No one was there but him.

Ash exhaled, lowering his gun. Perhaps he should be relieved, but he wasn't. He felt like something had been taken from him. He'd seen the Professor walk into this room, and he'd seen Quinn follow him. But neither were here.

It was as though they'd vanished. And, with them, any hope Ash had of keeping his prememory from coming for him.

He felt as though the air had changed—grown colder, more still. He slid his gun into the back waistband of his jeans, eyes moving to the *Dark Star*'s windshield. He hadn't noticed in the dark, but now he could see that it was covered in small, cramped numbers, written in the Professor's handwriting.

Curious, he drew closer.

2071–4.7

2073–6.9

2075–9.3

2078–10.5

2080–13.8

Ash felt his thoughts hitch. He thought he recognized those numbers. Didn't he? The first obviously seemed to be a year, and the second looked like a magnitude number, which was a number used to quantify the scale of an earthquake.

Ash hadn't gotten to New Seattle until 2075, so he had no memory of the 2073 earthquake though, of course, he'd heard the Professor and Zora, and even Roman, talk about it. He seemed to recall that it was somewhere around a 6.9. And of course he remembered the 2075 earthquake. That one had definitely been a 9.3.

"2078," Ash murmured, his eyes moving down the list. "10.5."

But that number couldn't be right. There had never been an earthquake over a 9.5, not in all of history. The devastation would be catastrophic. An earthquake of that size would destroy all of North America. Maybe all of the western hemisphere. It would cause a mass extinction event in line with what killed the dinosaurs.

And, below that,

"13.8," Ash read out loud. He almost laughed. The idea of an earthquake hitting 13.8 on the Richter scale seemed impossible.

A stair creaked.

Ash's body started working before his mind did: hands reaching, legs spinning, arms lifting. He tightened his hands around the grip of his gun, muzzle aimed at the *Star*'s entrance. The first nerves hit a second before his thumb pressed into the hammer.

Another creak, and a soldier appeared at the door.

Ash blinked; it wasn't a soldier, it was Dorothy. She wore an army-green uniform, her dark hair tucked into a boxy hat. The clothes were too big on her, and there was something suggestive about the way her pants hung low on her hips. Or maybe it was the way she stood. Or maybe it was the fact that Ash had never seen a woman in uniform before.

His fingers twitched. The backs of his ears grew hot.

"I thought I saw you come up here." Dorothy's eyes flicked down. "Are you planning on shooting me?"

Ash realized he was still pointing the SIG Sauer, one finger hovering over the trigger. He lowered his arm. "Where are Willis and Chandra?"

"They couldn't find a way across the gateroom, so I came on my own. They're going to get the *Second Star* and find a closer place to meet the rest of us."

Ash frowned. "How did you get here?"

"The normal way. Stole an unconscious soldier's uniform. Conned another soldier into giving me the password to the security door. He's still down there, by the way." She turned in place. "Is this the time machine?"

Ash nodded without hearing her.

She likes you, too, Zora had said.

"Ash?" Dorothy drew closer, frowning. "What is it?"

Ash swallowed. Some of Dorothy's hair had come loose from her hat, and it framed her face in soft brown curls, making her look—

"It's nothing," Ash murmured, looking away. Zora had

said they needed the *Dark Star*'s exotic matter to get back to 2077. She'd said the *Second Star* wouldn't fly without it and the *Dark Star* was currently locked up in a military hangar, so they couldn't take the bigger ship back instead.

He knelt, grateful for something to distract him, and felt beneath the control panel for the spare key the Professor kept taped there.

Dorothy crouched beside him, and now he could smell her skin. Old-fashioned soap and lilies. The scent still clung to her, even after everything that had happened. Ash's nose twitched. How was that possible?

She was close enough that, if he turned his face, they would touch.

His breath was a lump in his throat. It seemed an incredible distance.

She likes you, too.

He fumbled the key, and it fell to the floor between him. "Sorry," he mumbled, reaching for it. She reached, too, their hands brushing.

He jerked away, trying not to think about how soft her skin was.

"Is everything okay?" Dorothy wasn't smiling, but there was something about her lips that hinted at it. "Because you're acting very strange."

Ash nodded, but he didn't look away.

He'd come here expecting to find the Professor. To keep himself from dying.

And then he'd come here expecting to kill Quinn Fox

and—once again—keep himself from dying. And he'd failed. *Twice.*

He could feel the phantom pain of the dagger in his side. The soft press of lips against his own. Things that hadn't happened yet.

Things that didn't have to happen. *Maybe if you fall for Dorothy instead of this girl with the white hair . . .*

Ash wasn't sure whether Zora was right. But the Professor wasn't here, and neither was Quinn. But Dorothy was.

Maybe he could still change his future.

Dorothy released a short gasp of breath as Ash leaned closer, curling a hand around her neck. For a second, he forgot all about black water and dead trees and white hair. He forgot the feeling of cold steel sliding through his skin, and heartbreak ripping through his chest.

Instead, there was this: Dorothy's lips, warm against his. Her hand touching the back of his neck.

Then, she pulled away.

"Why did you do that?" she murmured, her eyes still closed.

Ash's voice felt thick. "I thought—"

Lights flashed on, filling the *Dark Star* with an eerie, white glow. Dorothy's eyes went wide.

The echoing sound of a hundred combat boots hitting concrete thundered through the hangar. There was a shuffling of movement, and then a sound Ash knew too well: hammers, dozens of them, clicking back.

"We have you surrounded," called a single, deep voice. "Please exit the vehicle with your hands raised."

LOG ENTRY—JULY 21, 1969
08:15 HOURS
THE *DARK STAR*, THE PUGET SOUND ANIL

My hands are still shaking. I'm sure you can tell—my handwriting's all over the place.

The moon landing was even more amazing than I thought it would be.

Let me take a moment to explain how we did this. It was quite a bit trickier than I'd expected.

Back in the 1960s, NASA went to a lot of work to make sure that the moon landing could be broadcast live. They went as far as sending an erectable antenna up with Buzz and Neil so they wouldn't have to wait for a tracking station to come within range.

I figured that meant it would be easy to find a place to watch the moon landing unfold. The whole country was watching, after all! Surely we would be able to find a spare TV!

I was incorrect, to say the least. Natasha kindly pointed out that the sixties were the golden age of television. Gone were the days of gathering on the sidewalk to catch a broadcast from a corner-shop window. Everyone had a TV in their own living room! They'd be watching the moon landing at home.

Which was all well and good, except that we are time travelers and, thus, we do not have access to a home in 1969.

This is where my brainstorming comes in. The Fairmont hotel in Seattle has been around since the 1920s. Their hotel guests must need a place to watch the moon landing as well, and I doubt there are televisions in all the private rooms. There would be a television in the lobby, though. I figured we could all sneak into the lobby and watch the moon landing there. I'd even be willing to pay for a room. In my opinion, it's a small price to experience one of the most scientifically important moments in history.

It worked brilliantly. There was already a crowd gathered around the black-and-white screen in the lobby, and they didn't seem to notice the presence of six time travelers among them. (This, thanks to Natasha, who spent the day perfecting our 1969 costumes but, sadly, had to sit the event itself out as she was home sick with the flu.)

I've never heard a silence so perfect. The image on the screen was fuzzy and hard to make out, but people waited with bated breath to watch Neil Armstrong bounce down those steps and utter his famous words:

That's one small step for man, one giant leap for mankind.

And then, the whole place broke out in cheers. People hugged. People screamed. It was magic.

I'm still buzzing. We're almost home now. I'm writing this in the passenger seat while Ash pilots the *Dark Star*, and I can see the familiar swirl of clouds that marks the year 2075.

That was . . . wow. It was really something else. I've written down everything I saw so that I can tell Natasha all about it. The clothes! The energy! The excitement! It was intoxicating!

Hell, now *I* want to be an astronaut!

We're exiting the anil now and—

Oh.

Something appears to be wrong. I can't see the lights from the bay, and there's something different about the shoreline. It looks flooded.

No. Not just the shoreline. The whole city's been flooded.

I . . . I don't understand what I'm seeing. We've returned just a few hours after we originally left. Was there another earthquake? What could have happened?

Everything's gone. The entire city is underwater.

I saw this. It's just like my vision.

Oh God—

Natasha.

PART THREE

Time is chasing after all of us.

—Peter Pan

31

DOROTHY

MARCH 17, 1980, FORT HUNTER COMPLEX

"We have you surrounded," shouted a voice. "Exit the vehicle with your hands raised!"

Dorothy couldn't quite register what was happening. Her mind was still on the kiss, reluctant to let the memory go even as circumstances demanded she act. Ash pulled away from her, his face a shadow blurred by white light. Dorothy felt cold air circle her waist where his hands had been.

"How many are there?" she asked. Her voice didn't seem to belong to her.

Ash was peering out the window of the time machine, his back to her.

"A hundred. Maybe more." He scrubbed a hand over his jaw. "They're armed."

Armed. That meant guns, a hundred guns aimed at them. Dorothy absently lifted a hand to her throat, a thrill of fear moving through her.

"You stay here," Ash was saying. "I'll go down. I'm betting

they don't know there are two of us. I can probably convince them I was alone up here. Then you can . . . get somewhere safe."

Safe. He said it like he thought he was doing her a favor. She opened her mouth and, at first, nothing came out. Then, sputtering, "You think I'm going to *stay behind*?"

"If we're both caught, we're screwed."

"Who said anything about being caught?" Dorothy frowned. "*I* don't get caught."

"Didn't you hear the thing about them being armed?"

"*So?*" She hated the idea of being left behind, like she was someone who needed protection from the big, bad world. She thought of the women she'd seen in the gateroom—strong women, *soldiers*—and felt a pang in her chest.

Not jealousy. *Want.*

She wasn't any different from those women, not in any way that mattered. Why did everyone insist on treating her like she was someone who needed to be protected?

She thought back to the moment in the bar, when Ash first told her about time travel. She'd thought he was being a jerk then, teasing her.

But, later, when she'd realized it'd been the truth, she appreciated that he'd just told her instead of dancing around the facts, acting like she might break.

She wanted to say something about that now, to explain, but Ash was already tucking the EM canister beneath his jacket. It made an odd bulge below his arm. He pulled the zipper up to his neck. "We don't have time to argue about this." His eyes slid back to the window and then narrowed. "Wait here for the others. Can you do that?"

No, Dorothy thought. Several insults filtered through her head, but none were quite what she wanted. "I'm not an object," she spat finally. "You can't leave me where it's convenient and expect I'll still be there when you return!"

Ash leveled her with a steady look. "*Please.*"

He said it with a hitch in his voice, like he was begging. Dorothy didn't mean to stop arguing, but the voice caught her off guard, and she didn't say anything for a beat too long. Ash seemed to take that as agreement.

For a moment, she thought he might kiss her again. He leaned forward, and she felt her chin lift, her lips rising to meet his without asking her brain whether it was okay.

She jerked back when she realized what was happening, her pulse fluttering. *Stupid lips.*

If Ash noticed, he didn't show it. He took a step back and lifted both hands over his head in surrender. For one confused moment Dorothy thought he might be surrendering to her, but then he stepped out of the *Dark Star*. And was gone.

With effort, Dorothy pulled her eyes away from the window. For some reason she thought of Zora, in her men's trousers, her expression unreadable as always.

Ash wouldn't have left her behind. The two of them would've walked down the stairs shoulder to shoulder, ready to take on the waiting army together. It made Dorothy feel strangely jealous. She wanted that, the chance to be someone's ally and not just their prize.

Something behind her creaked.

Fear was a funny thing. Dorothy had barely felt it when Ash had told her there were a hundred or so guns aimed at the too-thin walls of their time machine. But all it took was a slight groan and release of weight—almost like a footstep—and every nerve in her body sizzled.

That sound didn't belong in this room. She was supposed to be alone.

She spun around, feet nearly tripping over her too-large boots. She saw only shadows but knew better than to trust them. Someone was here. Someone was watching her.

The dark grew thicker. It began to move. And then someone said, "What's that thing they say in the movies? 'So we meet again'?"

Dorothy recognized Roman's voice before she saw his face. That low lilt, like he was laughing at her. His eyes came next, the bright blue slowly separating from the shadows surrounding them. They were tilted up at the corners. Amused.

For a moment, her reality seemed to fracture. She saw Roman standing in front of her and then, in a flash, another Roman layered over him—like a mirage.

This Roman was leaning toward her. A muscle in his jaw twitched as his lips parted.

You shouldn't trust them.

Something cold spread through her, but when she blinked she saw that the false Roman was gone and there was only this moment, this time.

The real Roman was holding a gun, its small black barrel aimed at Dorothy's chest. Whatever she just saw hadn't happened yet. But it was going to.

Breathless, she lifted her hands in surrender.

32

ASH

Ash hesitated at the door leading from the hangar, turning his head just enough to get the *Dark Star* back in his sights. A shadow moved at the window, and he flushed, remembering the feel of Dorothy's body curved against his, the way her fingers moved through his hair.

A gun jabbed into his back.

"Keep moving," grumbled the soldier behind him. Ash dragged his eyes away from the ship and shuffled forward, heat creeping up his neck. His lips burned.

He'd thought it would be so simple to avoid falling in love. He'd figured a few easy rules would keep him safe. No dating. No flirting. No kissing.

And it had *seemed* simple, when love had just been a vision of a girl with white hair and no face, just a feeling that disappeared once the prememory was over.

But Dorothy was blood pumping beneath skin and hair

tangled in his fingers. Her lips had been softer than anything he'd ever felt before. Her mouth had tasted like mint.

He wasn't in love with her. But he could feel something stirring inside of him, and he realized, suddenly, how stupid he'd been to think he could ever trick it or avoid it. This thing was a force. It was moving forward whether he wanted it to or not.

A thought occurred to Ash then. Had it been a betrayal to kiss Dorothy when he knew he was going to fall in love with someone else? It was misleading, certainly. Like making a promise he knew he couldn't keep. But that was only if the kiss hadn't changed anything. Surely kissing Dorothy meant he wasn't going to fall in love with Quinn.

Right?

The ferocious joy of the kiss was starting to wear off, and reality was creeping back in. Ash's head spun as he tried to work out what had just happened. What it meant.

Had his future changed at all? Or had he just pulled Dorothy down with him?

The thoughts haunted him as the soldiers led him down a maze of dark hallways, the only sound the uniform thud of their boots smacking concrete. Too late, Ash realized he should've been paying closer attention, marking when they turned left and right so he could figure out a way to escape, find the Professor, and rendezvous with Willis and Chandra. Instead, he'd been replaying a kiss, like some lovesick soldier back in the war.

"Dope," he muttered through gritted teeth.

The soldier behind him chuckled.

"You can say that again," he said, adding another jab of his gun for emphasis. "You don't even know how bad your day just got."

Eventually, they stopped outside a heavy, metal door. A soldier opened it with a quick jerk of his hand, revealing a small pitch-black room without any windows.

"Sit," said the soldier, his gun trained on Ash's back. "And no talking till he gets here."

"Talking?" Ash said.

The soldier flicked a switch. A raw bulb hung from the ceiling, humming gently. There were only two chairs in the room: one was empty.

Zora sat in the other.

Ash felt his stomach drop. She hadn't found the Professor, either. Somehow, they'd both failed.

Zora squinted into the sudden light, and then her eyes settled on Ash, and her face fell. "Aw hell, they got you, too?"

33

DOROTHY

Dorothy stood, rigid, eyes moving down the blunt barrel of Roman's gun for the second time in less than twenty-four hours.

Has it only been twenty-four hours? she thought.

It felt like more time than that. And, also, like less. It was as though no time and all the time in the world had passed since she'd first climbed into Ash's time machine.

"Are you frightened?" Roman's eyes were cold, but his voice was lilting, teasing her.

Dorothy didn't answer, but the bullet wound on her arm flared, reminding her that he wasn't always as careful as he should be with that thing.

"I only ask because you're trembling," Roman said.

Dorothy balled her fingers into a fist, furious with herself for giving him the satisfaction of seeing her scared. She remembered how Willis had leaped on Roman back at the dock, batting his gun away like it was a toy. Not for the first time, she wished she were a much larger person.

She shifted her eyes to the door. She was closer than Roman was. If she made a run for it—

"You'd be dead before you reached the staircase." Roman used his gun to gesture to the pilot's seat. He did this casually, like he was motioning with his own hand instead of a deadly weapon. "Sit down. There's no reason to be afraid."

Dorothy held his gaze. She doubted that.

"I promise, I only want to talk." Roman held his hands out, in surrender, and now the gun was dangling from his thumb. Dorothy knew better than to be fooled. A gun was still a gun, no matter how casually it was held. The men who treated their weapons like toys were the ones who really needed to be watched.

She sunk into the chair, hands knotting in her lap.

"See? That wasn't so hard, was it?" The corner of Roman's mouth twitched. He was laughing at her.

Teeth gritted, she asked, "What do you want?"

"She speaks!"

Dorothy tilted her head, saying nothing, and Roman released a deep, long-suffering sigh.

"I want to make a deal with you," he continued. "As you've surely noticed, our good friend *Asher* has gone and gotten himself captured."

His lips twisted around Ash's name, as though it had an unpleasant taste.

"I'm not sure Ash would call you a friend," Dorothy said.

"Probably not. But I'm here to help you rescue him, nonetheless."

Dorothy could tell that he'd meant this to be shocking, so she worked hard to keep the emotion from her face.

"Why?" she asked politely. "The goodness of your heart?"

The idea of there being any goodness in his heart seemed to delight Roman. "God no," he said, releasing a surprised laugh. "But why on earth should that stop you?"

Dorothy's eyes shifted to the shadows at the back of the time machine. Roman had been waiting there. Somehow, he'd known that she was going to come to the time machine. He'd known that Ash was going to be led away by soldiers. He'd known all of this before it'd happened.

Are you trying to say that you've seen the future?

Perhaps. Perhaps I've even seen yours.

A prickle went up the back of her neck as she realized what was bothering her. This felt planned. Dorothy didn't like plans she hadn't come up with herself.

She stared at Roman's gun. "What happens if I say no?"

"You won't say no."

"I already told you I didn't want to work with you."

"And I told you that you'd change your mind about that."

"Why would I do that?"

Roman grinned with half his mouth. It looked wrong. Like something he'd learned from a book. "I left you a little present, back at the Fairmont hotel. You remember, don't you? It was a small leather-bound book. Used to belong to Professor Zacharias Walker."

Dorothy blinked. "*You* left it?"

"The plan was for you to steal it and bring it to Ash and his friends, so that they could read the Professor's final entry and discover where in history their mentor had run off to."

"You meant for them to come back here?" Dorothy's voice sounded hollow.

"It was my idea, I confess, to use you," Roman went on. "I stole the journal the night the Professor disappeared. I've always known exactly when and where he was but, without any exotic matter, I couldn't exactly travel back in time and get him, could I? I needed Ash to do that for me. But Ash didn't know where to look, and he wouldn't trust any information that came from me. We needed someone to act as a go-between. So we kidnapped you, and we planted the journal where you were sure to find it. You performed splendidly, by the way."

"Stop," Dorothy said, but it was too late. His words had already wormed their way into her brain.

You performed splendidly.

She'd been played—they all had.

In a good con, the artist does his best to convince the mark that the game was all her idea. He dangles something tempting in front of her, something he tells her she can't have but knows she wants. In the end, the mark begs to be tricked.

Dorothy had found the journal and assumed it was valuable. She'd stolen it, and then she'd handed it over to Ash at her first opportunity, like the perfect little patsy she was.

Her eyes grew hot and she realized, horrified, that they'd

filled with tears. She blinked, determined to keep them from falling through sheer force of will. She'd never been conned before. She'd spent her whole life tricking others, getting them to trust her, to open up, and then taking them for all they were worth and leaving before they realized how foolish they'd been.

She'd never thought she might be on the other side of it.

"I still don't understand," she said carefully. "How are you *here*? Ash said you shouldn't be able to travel back in time, unless"—she thought of the cargo hold on Ash's ship, the one she'd hidden inside to get to the future—"did you sneak onto the *Second Star*?"

"Ah, that was a neat little trick but I'm afraid not." Roman's smile spread. "I had a much more elegant way of traveling back. Obviously I can't tell you how I did it now, but I expect you'll figure it out soon enough."

Dorothy's head was spinning. It was too much information, too many tangles to try to work out.

Voice steady, she asked, "So now what? You're going to find the Professor before Ash does and just leave us here?"

Roman gazed at her, amused. "Dorothy," he said carefully. "The Professor's already gone."

LOG ENTRY-MAY 10, 2075

23:47 HOURS

THE *DARK STAR*

Mission: Aphrodite 1

I'm writing from outside the anil, where I'm sitting in the pilot's seat of the *Dark Star*. I need to get this all down as quickly as I can before I take the ship back in time. I've left the rest of the team at home. They don't know I'm doing this. I don't want to get Zora's hopes up, in case I'm wrong.

Objective: Return to the morning of May 9, 2075, and retrieve Natasha Harrison from our home before it's destroyed in the Cascadia Fault mega-quake.

I'm aware of the causal loop. Of course I'm aware of the damn causal loop.

But this is different. Natasha's body wasn't found in the wreckage. There's a possibility that I've already traveled back in time. I've already saved her.

She's not really dead.

LOG ENTRY—JUNE 18, 2075

23:41 HOURS

THE WORKSHOP

Mission: Aphrodite ~~22~~ 27

So far, every attempt I've made to save Natasha has proven unsuccessful.

I honestly don't know what I'm doing wrong.

At first, I tried to return to the morning of May 9, 2075. I arrived sixty minutes before the earthquake hit Seattle, figuring that would give me enough time to locate Natasha, convince her to leave with me, and return to the anil.

On my first dozen or so trips back, I looked for Natasha in our home and around our neighborhood. She'd been sick that day, remember, so it would be logical to conclude that she wouldn't stray far. But she had not gone to any of her local haunts. Each and every time, I failed to locate her before the earthquake hit.

After those early failures, I stopped my search for a brief time to come up with a new plan. Looking for Natasha an hour before the earthquake hit was not working, so I should search earlier. The last time I saw Natasha alive was on the beach at Golden Gardens Park. She'd come to see us off. My new plan was to return to that moment, to intercept her in the few minutes between her saying farewell to me and leaving to an unknown location in her vehicle.

Unfortunately, when I attempt to exit the anil at this moment, I find myself surfacing in the sound approximately fifteen minutes after we leave, at which point Natasha has already climbed into her car and driven away from the beach.

It is an odd blip of the time tunnel, and, were things different, I might attempt to research the phenomenon further.

As it is, my only thoughts are of finding my wife.

LOG ENTRY—NOVEMBER 4, 2075

02:13 HOURS

THE WORKSHOP

Mission: Aphrodite 53

It's been four months since I last updated.

No, wait—five months.

It's strange that, for someone who's spent his whole life studying time, I have such a poor grasp of it. It seems like it's been much longer than that, and also like time is moving far, far too slowly.

I have since searched for my wife at the supermarket, the university library, the pharmacy, Natasha's doctor's office, and her mother's house. I went back hours earlier, and I stayed as late as I could possibly manage. Sometimes I only made it to the anil *seconds* before the earthquake hit.

I've gone over my original theory again and again, examining it from every angle. Even with the causal loop, it *still makes sense*. Natasha cannot be dead.

You see, I'm not actually saving her life, I'm taking her out of the past and bringing her here, just like we did with Ash and Chandra and Willis. I'm *removing her from the past* before the earthquake can kill her.

Why isn't this working?

LOG ENTRY—FEBRUARY 18, 2076
11:04 HOURS
THE WORKSHOP

Mission: Aphrodite 87

The downtown library is one of Natasha's favorite places in the city. I don't know why I didn't think of it before. When she isn't feeling well she always goes down to the library and finds the biggest, dustiest old biography or memoir she can and loses herself in its pages until she feels better.

I have now tried to get inside the library on five different missions, but I was prevented from reaching my destination each and every time.

During my last trip, I made it up the steps of the library and was just about to reach out and open the door, when a man ran directly into me, knocking me backward. I woke up inside an ambulance twenty minutes later, and I had to force my way back out and onto the street, and then race back to my time machine, all the while bleeding from a head wound, in order to get to the anil before the earthquake hit.

My current theory is that Natasha is inside that library. It's the only thing that makes sense. If I can just find a way to get inside without anything else going wrong, I'll be able to bring her home.

LOG ENTRY—MAY 9, 2076
19:07 HOURS
THE WORKSHOP

I don't know how I'm writing this.

I mean that literally. I'm staring down at my hand and I don't understand how it's moving. The words it's writing don't seem to be mine.

How could they be?

My mind is blank. Numb. Empty.

Natasha's body was found today. Some volunteers were clearing out debris from the downtown library in the hopes that the top few floors would be livable.

I—I can't write out what they told me about the state of her body. They were able to identify her from her driver's license, which was tucked inside the remains of her pocket and listed her home address. They brought it to me, and they told me where I could find her, if I would like to give her a proper burial.

I was right, all along. She was in the library. But I couldn't reach her. If only I could've reached her. It's been a year. I've tried to save my wife a hundred times, in a hundred different ways. But nothing works.

Natasha dies, every single time.

34

ASH

MARCH 17, 1980, FORT HUNTER COMPLEX

"Join your friend," the soldier said, with one last gleeful jab of his gun. Ash stumbled forward, nearly tripping over the metal chair bolted to the floor in the middle of the interrogation room.

He felt something jagged in his gut. Fear, or the beginning of it.

He sat down, careful not to look at Zora. The soldier knelt behind him, removed his handcuffs, and recuffed him to the bolted-down chair. Satisfied, he joined the other soldiers at the door and, without another word, they stepped back into the hall, pulling the door closed behind them. They were alone.

Ash's eyes slid to Zora. "Are you—"

The sound of footsteps cut him off. He heard mumbled voices in the hallway, and then the door opened, again, and a new, unfamiliar soldier walked into the room.

He wasn't dressed in fatigues but wore a green jacket over

a khaki shirt and tie, his hat tucked under one arm. He had the face of a bulldog, but his eyes were flat and black, like a shark's.

Ash's eyes flicked to the man's shoulder straps, checking his rank. Twin silver oak leaves stared back at him.

Ash's throat felt suddenly dry. Those leaves marked this man as the commander of the entire base.

"My name is Lieutenant Colonel Gross," the man said after a moment. "My unit has informed me that there's been a serious breach in our security."

He stared at Ash, as though he expected him to answer.

Ash stared back. He could feel blood pumping in his ears, hot and steady, and realized, in a detached sort of way, that this was panic. He was panicking.

Before he could come up with anything to say, there was a short knock, and the door opened, again. Two more soldiers walked in, pushing a boxy television on a metal cart.

"I aim to make this quite simple for you," Gross continued. "You all are barely older than children, and I don't like harming children. But, as this is a matter of national security, I may have no other choice."

He flipped a switch on the television and a grainy, black-and-white image flickered across the screen:

The Professor was racing up a flight of stairs, chest heaving. He reached a metal door and paused to look over his shoulder. The overhead lights glinted off his glasses, turning them white.

Gross pressed a button on the television set, and the image froze.

"This video was taken early this morning, at approximately 0400 hours. The gentleman you see on the screen broke into our facility undetected, somehow managing to procure top secret information on a weapon of mass destruction."

Weapon of mass destruction? Ash thought.

What did the Professor want with a *weapon*?

But Gross was already moving on, and Ash didn't have time to think about that too hard.

"It is our belief that he is working against the United States government and, as such, his actions constitute an act of war." Gross turned to Ash, black eyes narrowing. "You, young man, were discovered inside the gentleman's aircraft, which we found abandoned in the woods just outside the complex. You can see why that might lead us to believe that you, too, are working against the United States government. If you were to cooperate, if you were to tell us who this man was and which agency he was working for, we might be persuaded to be lenient, as far as your own punishment were concerned."

Ash's blood ran cold. He swallowed. "Was?"

Gross didn't blink. "The gentleman in question was found on the roof about fifteen minutes ago, trying to escape. He's been executed."

35

DOROTHY

"Gone?" Dorothy repeated, cold flooding through her. "How can he be gone? We're standing in his time machine!"

"Never mind that now." Roman leaned against the time-machine wall, arms crossed casually over his chest, gun dangling from his fingers. "There's something else that I need to obtain from this place. It's the last piece of a very specific puzzle, and, believe it or not, you're the only person alive who can get it for me."

Dorothy narrowed her eyes. "Why do you think I would help you?"

"Because I know how to free Ash, and you don't."

Dorothy hesitated, pulse fluttering. *Blast.*

She had a sneaking suspicion that she was being conned again. But Roman seemed to have a plan for getting Ash back, and she didn't even know where the soldiers had taken him. She needed Roman. For now, at least.

And there was the small matter of her vision. It felt . . .

close, if that made any sense at all. Her skin prickled with the anticipation of it.

You shouldn't trust them, Dorothy thought.

Why? she wanted to ask. *Why shouldn't I trust Ash and his friends?*

She had to admit that the vision had made it seem like they were working together. And it was easier to choose to work with Roman when it felt inevitable. A decision she'd already weighed and made. A future she couldn't avoid.

She studied his face. "And you'll let us go once we're through?"

Roman's eyebrow arced upward, pulled by an invisible string. "Naturally."

He was lying. But her eyes moved to the gun in his hand, and she realized she'd never really had a choice either way. Only the illusion of one.

"Okay," she said carefully. "So what is this thing I'm helping you get?"

Roman flicked the question away with a jerk of his hand. "Don't worry, you'll know it when you see it. For now, we need to focus on Ash. It's very important that we help him escape. He's the only one who can fly you all back."

Roman removed something from the inner pocket of his coat. It was a small contraption, not unlike Willis's computer, but bulkier, with bits of wire twisting off the sides and a metallic stick protruding from one end. Several of the panels were different colors, and a sort of shiny, silver fabric had been wound around the bottom.

Roman leaned forward, angling the device so Dorothy could see. Several dozen tiny films played across the screen at once.

"I rerouted the complex's security feed to send the images here," Roman explained. He tapped one of the tiny films, and it expanded to take up the entire screen. Now the image showed Ash and Zora sitting in the middle of a small room, apparently bound to their seats. "This is a few floors down, Room 321A."

Dorothy's nerves hummed. She itched to touch the screen but held herself back. "So let's go."

Roman gave her a pained look. "If it were that easy, do you think I'd need you?" He pulled up another image, this one of several dozen armed soldiers standing at attention in front of a door. "This is the scene right outside your boy's room."

Dorothy's lips burned, remembering their kiss. "He's not *my*—"

Roman lifted a hand, stopping her. "I don't actually care about your relationship status. In order to get past these men, we'll need to get to the control room and override the complex's central security system." He pressed a button on his device and a new image appeared: one soldier, standing at attention in an otherwise empty hallway. "With just a few lines of code, I can send this place into chaos. No lights. No locks. No cameras. I believe there's some sort of horrible buzzing sound, too." He lifted his gun, drawing circles in the air with the muzzle. "In any case, everyone will be running around, terrified. It'll be glorious."

"Glorious," Dorothy repeated, staring at the soldier. She touched the screen with one finger, her eyes flicking up to Roman's. "And how do you propose we get past him?"

Roman's smile was chilling. "That's where you come in."

A half an hour later, they were crouched at the end of a hallway, peering down at the flickering security image on Roman's device. The soldier in front of the control room appeared not to have moved.

"You understand the plan?" Roman asked.

Dorothy nodded. It was fairly simple, as far as cons go. She was still dressed in fatigues, so she was to walk up to the soldier on duty and inform him that she was there to relieve him of his post. Roman had even found a code word for her to use. Dorothy didn't know the slightest thing about army culture, but Roman seemed to think that saying the word *phoenix* would convince the soldier on duty that her orders had come from . . .

Well. Whoever was in charge.

"All right then." Roman jerked his chin toward the hallway. "You're up."

Dorothy stood. She didn't like this plan. It hinged on her ability to accurately impersonate a soldier, which seemed a rather large thing to expect of someone who'd never even *met* a soldier before today.

But she hadn't been able to come up with something better, and Roman seemed to think the code word was all they needed.

She hoped he was right.

She stepped around the corner, forcing a smile onto her lips as if she wasn't nervous. The soldier's eyes passed over her face without seeming to see it. In an instant, his gun was off his shoulder and angled across his chest like a warning. "Do you have clearance to be down here?"

Dorothy felt her smile falter. Was she supposed to say the code word now? Or would that look suspicious?

"I'm, um, here to relieve you of your post," she said. And then, remembering what the soldier in the gateroom called her, she added, "Private."

She took another step toward the soldier, and he tightened his grip on the gun. "This is a classified area. I'm going to need you to return the way you came."

Dorothy could feel Roman behind her, watching her fail. She wetted her lips. "Phoenix," she said, her voice barely a whisper.

The soldier didn't even blink. "You're going to need to go back the way you came."

Dorothy's heart started beating too fast. He didn't seem at all inclined to let her through. She took another step forward, and the soldier whipped the gun into his hands, pointing it directly at her.

She lifted both hands in front of her chest, horrified. Her

heart was vibrating, and she couldn't manage to catch her breath.

"Ph-phoenix," she said again, louder. "*Phoenix.*"

A black hole appeared in the soldier's forehead. Dorothy didn't register the sound of a gunshot until a fraction of a second later, when the soldier's expression went blank. He dropped to his knees and then lurched forward. Dead.

Fear crept over Dorothy in a cold fog. For a moment it obscured all other emotion so that her actions felt strangely disjointed, like she was performing in a play. She threw both hands over her mouth and staggered backward, gasping.

She replayed the moment the black hole appeared. The hollow expression that'd leaped to the soldier's eyes. The smack of his knees hitting concrete.

Oh God oh God oh God . . .

A thick pool of blood oozed out from beneath the soldier's head.

Roman lowered a hand to her shoulder, and Dorothy flinched, moving quickly away from him.

"You killed him," she said. She could taste something sour rising in her throat. "Why did you kill him?"

"We need to get through the door."

"But I *had* him." Even as the words left her mouth, Dorothy knew they weren't true. Her silly con wasn't working. The soldier would have killed her if Roman hadn't shot him first. She shook her head, not wanting to believe it. "I was working on him. I . . . I'd just said the code word!"

Roman knelt beside the soldier, lowering a hand to his neck to check for a pulse. Dorothy had the sudden, ridiculous urge to laugh. The bullet went through the man's forehead. How could he possibly be alive?

"There was no code word. I made that up," Roman said, wiping his hand on his coat. "This is the military. Their policy is to shoot first and ask questions later. There's no such thing as a magical code word that will get you through a locked and guarded door."

Dorothy opened her mouth and then closed it again as understanding settled over her. "This was your plan all along."

She didn't bother making it sound like a question. She already knew the answer. Roman looked up at her, something crafty in his eyes.

"You were meant to distract him long enough for me to get into position and take the shot. Without you here, he would've spotted me long before I took aim. You should be proud."

Proud.

Dorothy had always known she wasn't particularly moral. A person couldn't make her living lying and cheating and still believe herself to be the hero of the story. But Dorothy had never actually thought of herself as a villain before. Not until just now.

She stared at the dead soldier as a nasty shiver went up her neck. She'd never known someone who'd killed another person before. Her mother carried a tiny, pearl-handled pistol in her purse but, to Dorothy's knowledge, she'd never actually used it.

She felt like she'd crossed a line. Like something had changed and there was no changing it back again.

She tried very hard to ignore that feeling as she followed Roman around the body and into the control room.

They were greeted by a dizzying array of tangled wires, buttons, and cords. One entire wall was made up of screens much like the ones on Roman's device, all flashing black-and-white images of narrow halls and closed doors. A table curved beneath the wall of screens, covered in rows of metal switches and flashing red and green buttons. The remains of someone's meal sat in the corner.

"Take a seat," Roman said, nodding at a chair.

Dorothy felt like telling him no just to be contrary, but her knees were weak with nerves. If she didn't sit down she might actually collapse, like some ninny who'd tied her corset too tight.

Something sticky had dried on the floor, making her boots squeak as she moved toward the chair. The room was small enough that she and Roman were shoulder to shoulder, practically touching no matter where she stood. She perched at the edge of her seat, carefully angling her knees to the side. "Will this take long?"

"Not at all." Grunting, Roman pulled a screen away from the wall and began doing something complicated with a tangle of tiny blue and red cords. "During the late 2000s, a bunch of hacker kids got really into posting threads telling you exactly how to dismantle old military security onto the internet."

He peeled the blue bits of the cords away, revealing even smaller, copper-colored wires below. He did the same to the red ones, and then twisted a few copper wires together. "Cover your ears."

Dorothy had just managed to press her hands over her ears when Roman reached for a switch at the upper right-hand corner of the desk and flicked it. The lights in the control room all switched off immediately, and a distant, whooping alarm began to blare.

"God, I love the eighties," Roman said.

36

ASH

"Executed?" Zora's voice sounded hollow, and it chilled Ash more deeply than if she'd yelled. "What do you mean, executed? What did you do?"

Ash's eyes shuttered closed. He didn't think he could listen to the details.

Did they shoot the Professor in the back as he was running away? Was it just one bullet? Did the greatest scientific mind in history say anything before he died?

Ash was overcome with the desire to hit something. It was all he could do not to stomp his feet and slam his cuffed hands against the back of the chair, just to make some noise.

When he opened his eyes again, he found Gross studying him, his mouth twisted in a sneer that Ash longed to knock right off his face.

Gross said, "As I've already explained, the gentleman was apprehended on the roof, just over fifteen minutes ago. He—"

"*What* did you do to him?" Zora pushed the words

through clenched teeth, and Ash felt his heartbeat ratchet up a notch.

"Zora—" he said, warning.

Gross's eyes slid back to Zora. "You, young lady, are in no position to—"

"You're a liar!" Zora threw herself against her restraints, and the sound of metal biting metal filled the small room. Gross didn't flinch, didn't blink. "He's not dead! What did you do to him? *What did you do?*"

A soldier stepped forward and drew his arm back—

Ash saw what was going to happen a second before it did. "No!" he shouted, trying to stand, but he was still cuffed to the chair, and the chair was bolted to the ground. Metal dug into his wrists, yanking him back down.

The soldier's fist came down hard across Zora's cheek, and her head whipped violently to the side.

Anger exploded in Ash's chest.

"You son of a bitch!" He lunged forward, not caring that the cold metal dug into his wrists, or that something wet clung sticky and hot beneath them.

They hurt Zora. He was going to kill them.

Zora was shouting again, but her words didn't register. Ash couldn't hear anything over the blood pumping in his ears. He was dimly aware that Zora was thrashing against her restraints in the chair next to him, screaming—

Gross's voice cut through the noise: "Get her out of here."

It wasn't a request.

One of the soldiers moved toward Zora, one hand resting on the butt of his gun.

Ash didn't know what they were going to do with her, only that he couldn't let them take her, couldn't let her out of his sight.

The soldier knelt behind Zora's seat. Ash heard the click of her handcuffs opening—

And then the lights flicked off, bathing them in darkness.

For a fraction of a second it was like everyone in the room was holding their breath. And then a siren began to howl, the low, whooping sound reminding Ash of wind in an anil.

A red light flashed on and off, on and off.

Ash saw, as though in slow motion, Zora pull her arm loose and whip around, one fist connecting with the kneeling soldier's temple.

Ash couldn't hear anything over the wailing alarm, but he saw the soldier blink, dazed. His fingers loosened their grip on the gun, and then the weapon was falling. It clattered to the floor but didn't go off, and then Zora was stopping it with her boot, and crouching, and the gun was in her hand. The handcuffs dangled from her wrist.

The second soldier fired. The bullet whizzed close to Zora's face, and Ash sucked in a breath, certain it was a hit, but Zora moved out of its path a second before it landed. She charged forward, grunting as she slammed the top of her head into the soldier's chest. She hit him again as he struggled to regain his balance.

"Don't move!" Gross slid the gun from the belt at his hips in one motion, easy. "I said don't—"

He fired and Zora ducked, the bullet exploding into the wall behind her. She tucked and rolled across the floor, one leg flying at Gross's shin and then jerking upward, into his knee. Her foot connected twice—*pop, pop*.

Gross's face crumbled and he stumbled backward, dropping his gun.

Zora stood, her own gun leveled at his head.

"Keys," she said.

Gross eyed her like he might a wild animal. "You listen here, girl. Every soldier in this base will be looking for you after this. You don't stand—"

Zora slammed the butt of the gun against his temple and he crumpled to the ground with the others.

"That was impressive," Ash said, but he wasn't sure Zora heard him over the wailing of the alarm.

She knelt beside Gross, glancing at the door as she rifled through his pockets, as though she expected soldiers to come pouring through at any moment. She removed a silver key from his pocket and got to work on Ash's handcuffs.

Ash jerked his chin at the unconscious Gross. "He's right, you know. The entire base is going to be on lockdown after this."

The cuffs snapped off and Ash groaned, rolling his wrists. "If we want to get out of here alive, we'll need a plan."

Zora lifted her chin. Red lights danced across her face,

gathering in the shadows under her eyes and along her cheekbones.

She said, bitter, "Do you honestly think any of us are getting out of here alive?"

37

DOROTHY

Boots thudded outside. Dorothy couldn't hear them over the wailing siren, but she felt the floor tremble. She inched the door open a crack and squinted into the hallway. Several soldiers had appeared, already staring down the sights of bulky, black guns. The flashing red light painted their faces with deep shadows. They looked like devils.

"I thought the idea was to keep the soldiers from finding us," she whispered, irritated. "Not shout our location to half the base!"

Roman was staring down at the images on his device. "The idea was to move them away from the room where they were holding Ash and Zora. Look."

He angled the screen toward her, but she was too distracted by what was going on in the hallway and waved it away without looking. She had her face pressed so close to the door that she could feel the wood creasing her skin.

The soldier at the front of the group froze when he saw

the dead man lying across the floor at the door to the control room. He lifted one hand to alert the men behind him, and then his eyes moved from the dead man to the door Dorothy was peering out of.

She felt herself go still. It was impossible, but it seemed, for a moment, like he was able to see through the flashing red lights and the shadows to locate her on the other side of the cracked door. Her breath caught.

Then, Roman's hand was on her arm and he was yanking her down to the floor, one finger pressing to her lips.

His eyes shifted to the crack in the door. Shadows moved beyond the sliver of open space. Roman swore silently and motioned for Dorothy to hide beneath the desk. He crawled in beside her.

They were close now, their faces just inches apart. Dorothy could smell the mint on Roman's breath. She could count the freckles that dotted the skin between the bottom of his nose and his upper lip. It was all achingly familiar and, for a moment, she just stared, her pulse fluttering inside of her chest.

This is it. The moment from her vision.

Now that she realized what was about to happen, she found herself impatient to get it over with. How did it start again? Roman was going to lean toward her, a muscle in his jaw twitching. He was going to say, *You shouldn't trust them.*

The memory felt so real that Dorothy could almost believe it had just happened. The word *why* lingered on her lips. . . .

Roman turned to her, and Dorothy felt something inside her chest catch. Her heart thudded with anticipation.

His body was pressed against her arm, the warmth of his skin spreading through the fabric of her stolen uniform.

A muscle in his jaw twitched.

She couldn't take it anymore—

"*Why* shouldn't I trust them?" she blurted out.

It was such a small change—*her* saying the words instead of Roman—but Dorothy felt it ripple through the air. Now, the moment she'd seen wouldn't happen, *couldn't* happen.

She'd stolen Roman's line.

Roman blinked at her. "How did you know what I was going to say?"

"I—I saw it," Dorothy admitted. "On the way here, in the time machine. It was like a vision."

He frowned. "And it happened just like this?"

"Well, no, not exactly. In the vision you said that I shouldn't trust Ash and the others, and I asked you why, but it ended before you could explain. But just now I could tell it was about to happen and, well, I suppose I got impatient."

"Fascinating," Roman said, his eyes glittering.

Dorothy didn't care much about whether she'd succeeded in changing a future she knew nothing about. People changed the future all the time, just by living.

But Roman's warning still haunted her.

"Are you going to tell me why you would say something like that?" she asked.

"But I *didn't* say it."

Dorothy studied him for a long moment. He stared back, his smile sharp. She was hit again with the strange déjà vu feeling. This moment felt like the echo of another, one she might remember if only she tried hard enough.

"Tell me why I shouldn't trust them."

Roman shook his head, relenting. "You're an outsider. They're a team, one for all and all for one, and all that crap. But you aren't on the team, and you never will be. You haven't proven yourself."

Dorothy thought of the ripped photograph on the wall in Ash's kitchen. *Roman Estrada*. "Is that why you betrayed them? Because they didn't think of you as part of the team."

In an instant, all the careful charisma and lighthearted mischievousness drained from Roman's face. "No," he said. "It's not."

"Then why?"

"I'm afraid we haven't been acquainted long enough for that story," he said, clearing his throat. "But who knows? Maybe one day I'll let you in on all my secrets."

He pulled something small and black out of the pocket of his coat. "This is a smoke bomb."

Dorothy frowned down at the object. She'd never heard of a smoke bomb before, but she knew what smoke was, and she knew what a bomb was, and the thought of the two things together didn't seem entirely pleasant.

"I'm going to throw the smoke bomb as a distraction. As soon as I do that, you need to run."

"Where do you suggest I go?"

"The roof." He said this as though it were obvious. Dorothy frowned, vaguely remembering discussing this with Willis just a few hours before. He'd told her he'd meet them on a helipad just above the east wing. Was that near the roof?

"Your friends will be up there." Roman continued, "Trust me. I'll stay here and deal with"—he flicked his hand toward the door—"*that*."

Dorothy felt something in her chest go tight. "Why are you helping me?"

Roman looked irritated. "I've already told you—"

"You need me to bring you something," Dorothy said, remembering their conversation back in the *Dark Star*. "Something only I can get."

But that didn't make sense. She didn't *have* anything, and if she did, she certainly wouldn't just *give* it to him.

What was she missing?

Roman touched a button on the side of the small black bomb, and a ribbon of hissing smoke drifted into the air.

"You better hurry. Don't want them leaving without you." He winked and then rolled the smoke bomb through the crack in the door, directly between the legs of the nearest soldier.

The soldiers all looked down, coughing as the stream of smoke quickly became a gray cloud, obscuring them all.

LOG ENTRY—SEPTEMBER 15, 2076
07:07 HOURS
WEST COAST ACADEMY OF ADVANCED TECHNOLOGY

I haven't kept this log up-to-date.

I admit, it seemed pointless once the Chronology Protection Agency disbanded.

Did I ever mention that's what we'd decided to call ourselves? Natasha was the one who came up with it. It's based on an old quote from Stephen Hawking.

Not that any of that matters, anymore.

I suppose we haven't officially disbanded, but I see no reason to continue. The West Coast Academy of Advanced Technology is almost entirely underwater. I managed to clear out a few of the topmost levels, and we've been squatting here for the past few weeks, but as for the board of trustees, and Dr. Helm . . .

They're all dead.

NASA hasn't fared much better. There was an earthquake in Washington last month, an 8.2. It hit the New Madrid fault line, which hasn't seen an earthquake over 5.4 in a hundred years. From what I hear, the city is in ruins.

This is harder than I expected it to be. In these few sentences, I have already set my pen down several times, too distraught to continue. But I think Natasha would've wanted me to keep an account of what's happening here. It's what she would have done.

I'll try to stick to the facts.

The Cascadia Fault mega-quake was a 9.3 on the Richter scale, the largest our country has ever seen.

And then the tsunami hit.

For those of you who don't study seismology for fun, the earthquake itself is just an appetizer. When tectonic plates shift beneath the ocean floor, they displace a colossal amount of seawater, which then surges upward at an outstanding speed. Imagine a mountain of ocean striking a city that's already been beaten and broken by the earthquake. That's what the tsunami did. When the shaking stopped and the water receded, Seattle was past saving. The city that used to be here was gone.

At least, that's how the United States government saw it. The destruction was so great that they'd never be able to rebuild, so they did the noble thing and kicked us out of the country. Moved their borders in and started calling us "the Western Territories." Assholes.

That all happened a year ago.

There are people here who haven't given up yet. They're trying to rebuild, make the city into . . . something. I don't know why they bother. Even if we were to construct a new city on top of all this water, the next earthquake will just knock it down again.

The West Coast is lost. All of America might be lost.

Sometimes I think of that day so long ago, when I first met Roman. He'd been sitting outside of Tent City, trying to build a program to predict earthquakes. I wonder what happened to that program. I assume he forgot about it once he started helping me with my own research. What a shame. That program would have been infinitely more helpful to our current reality than a time machine.

I suppose I could ask him about it. But he doesn't come around much, anymore. I think I've disappointed him. Not that I can blame him for that. I've disappointed myself.

I should probably sign off for the night. It's not good to keep the electricity on after curfew.

The lights attract vermin.

38

ASH

MARCH 17, 1980, FORT HUNTER COMPLEX

Zora tried the door. It was unlocked. She eased it open as Ash whipped his gun up to his shoulder and aimed, finger trembling near the trigger. They stepped into the hallway.

Empty.

Ash lowered his gun, frowning. There'd been a dozen or so soldiers standing out there just a few minutes ago. He turned to Zora, but she was already halfway down the hallway, hurrying toward a door marked STAIRCASE.

Cupping a hand over his mouth, Ash shouted, his voice just audible over the sirens, "Zora, wait!"

When she didn't turn around, Ash swore and chased after her. The empty hallway bothered him. *Too easy*, he thought. His stolen gun thumped against his hip as he ran, though he kept one hand curled around the strap, waiting for the missing soldiers to appear, guns blazing, bullets flying. But no one showed.

They made it to the stairwell, and the metal door slammed shut behind them, cutting the sound of the alarm.

Ash cringed and rubbed his ear. The wailing still echoed through his head.

Zora was already racing up the stairs. She hadn't slowed, hadn't even turned to make sure Ash was still behind her. She hadn't shouldered her gun, either, but carried it crossed in front of her chest, like a shield.

"Where are you going?" Ash asked, chasing after her. They needed to get back down to the *Dark Star*, find Dorothy, and figure out where they were supposed to meet Willis and Chandra. They didn't have time for a detour.

Zora said, "The roof."

A heaviness dropped through Ash's gut. He didn't want to go to the roof. He didn't want to see anything that proved, definitively, that the Professor was dead.

It made it all too real.

"They're lying," Zora called over her shoulder, as though reading his mind. "Dad isn't dead. He can't be."

Dad. Zora hadn't used that word in months. Now she'd said it twice in one day.

Ash felt the hairs on his neck crawl with something he couldn't name. He wanted to tell Zora to wait. To talk to him. Even if Gross had been lying about executing the Professor (and Ash didn't know why he would do that), it made no sense for them to go to the roof.

What did she expect to find up there?

But they were pushing through another door before he could put those thoughts into words, and then light was spilling into the stairwell, and Ash was stumbling back, squinting.

Floodlights, he thought, thinking back to the east wing hangar and the hundreds of soldiers waiting to cart him away.

But he blinked and saw that it wasn't floodlights. It was the moon hovering low in the sky, stretching pale silver fingers across the roof.

Ash shielded his eyes with one hand, squinting. This kind of light made it impossible to see. Everything was in shadow. He could just make out Zora standing in front of him, her body all silhouette, her chest rising and falling, rapidly.

"See?" she said, turning in a circle. "There's nothing here. So they couldn't have . . ."

Ash approached her slowly. "Zora."

"If they really shot him, there'd be a body, or blood, or . . . or . . ." Her voice was small and terrible. "I can't lose him, too. Not after what happened to my mom."

Ash didn't know what to say. He had to remind himself to breathe.

Zora didn't talk about her mother. Ever. Natasha died in the Cascadia Fault mega-quake, along with thirty-five thousand other people. After that, Zora changed. She stopped talking about her emotions—stopped, it seemed, feeling her emotions at all. It was almost like she thought that feeling anything meant she'd have to feel everything.

Ash had tried to talk to her about it, once. The second the word *mother* left his lips, Zora's eyes had unfocused, and her fingers had gone slack. The gear she'd been holding had tumbled to the floor, but Zora hadn't moved to pick it up.

It was like she'd gone catatonic. Like he'd broken something inside of her.

He never mentioned her mother again.

Now, Ash grabbed Zora by the shoulders. He expected her to pull away but, instead, she became very still. She'd always been a still sort of person, but now it felt unnatural, like the air before a storm hit, how the wind stopped moving, and all the leaves turned over, showing their underbellies to the wretched sky.

With effort, he said, "We can try again. We'll come back before they execute him." He patted the canister of exotic matter still tucked inside his jacket. "We have more EM now. We can come back as many times as it takes."

Zora was nodding against his shoulder, but Ash could tell that she didn't believe him, either. Time travel couldn't bring someone back from the dead. The Professor had proven that when he'd tried to go back and save Zora's mother.

Whatever happened here, it was unchangeable. It was over.

Which meant Ash's prememory would eventually come true, no matter how hard he tried to fight it. In just four short weeks, he was going to die.

Something deep inside of him began to ache. He couldn't put it into words, this knowledge that his death was close, that he wouldn't be able to avoid it, even after months of telling himself he'd find a way. It was too big a feeling, something that couldn't be contained by skin.

Zora pulled away, as though this thought had just occurred to her, too. She grabbed Ash's arm.

"We'll find a way," she said furiously. "I'm not losing you, too. I promise you. We'll . . . we'll research. We'll go through his journal. There has to be something . . ."

She brushed a tear away from her cheek with an angry twitch of her hand.

Ash took a breath, trying to be strong for her. "Don't worry about that now. . . ."

He trailed off. He heard a motor sounding in the distance and, though he couldn't say exactly when it started, he was suddenly aware that it was closer.

Zora tilted her head toward the sound. "What's that?"

Ash's eyes flitted to the horizon. He couldn't see the source of the motor yet, but that didn't mean it wasn't close.

He looked around. This wasn't a roof so much as a small landing area in the middle of the mountain—probably a helipad, if he had to wager a guess. Rocks rose all around them, blocking most of the woods below.

"We should go," he said, heading for the door. He lowered his hand to the doorknob—

And then froze, frowning. There was a sound echoing inside the stairwell as well, muffled by the door. Ash pressed his ear to the cold metal.

"Ash!" Zora was peering over the side of the roof, her back to him. "Something's coming."

Ash's palms had started to sweat, leaving the door handle slick against his hand. He could hear propeller blades cutting into the sky, a motor whirring. And, below that, something thudding up the stairs. Echoing off the concrete walls below.

It's the alarm, he told himself. But it wasn't. It was footsteps. Someone was running up the stairs.

Ash stumbled away from the door, hands reaching for his gun.

"*Ash—*"

"I got a bit of a situation here!" He turned and, at that moment, a ship appeared at the side of the roof.

Not just any ship. *His* ship. The *Second Star*. Her toothy grin looked dirty in the early-morning light, and a crack had spread across her windshield. But it was his ship, all right. He lowered his gun, squinting at the cockpit to see who was flying it. The massive shadow hovering behind the windshield could only be one person.

Ash stumbled backward as Willis set his ship down on the roof. The giant opened the front door and leaned outside, flashing Ash a salute. "Morning, Captain."

Chandra climbed out of the cabin. She'd started speaking before she'd gotten the door all the way open, and Ash missed the first half of her sentence. ". . . was supposed to tell you that Willis and I couldn't go across the gateroom with you, but we figured you could get into plenty of trouble or whatever all on your own and, like, you might need our help? So we went back through that creepy-ass tunnel, and wow are those guards easy to sneak past if you're trying to get *out* of the base instead of *inside* of it, and then we got the *Second Star* and Willis was all like, 'I bet I can fly it,' which, hey he totally did. We weren't sure you'd all make it up here, though. That's convenient. Hey, where's Dorothy? Did you find the Professor?"

"I think I just got whiplash," Zora said. Her face had closed off, her feelings hidden again.

Ash cleared his throat. "Dorothy's in the east wing hangar with the *Dark Star*, and we need to—"

The door to the stairs slammed open, cutting him off. Ash turned as figures spilled onto the roof, instantly surrounding them. *Soldiers.*

Their guns flashed in the dying sunlight. Their faces were hard with anger.

"On your knees!" one of the soldiers shouted. The others spread into a half circle around them, neatly, blocking them in. "And get your hands in the air!"

LOG ENTRY—SEPTEMBER 20, 2076
21:00 HOURS
WEST COAST ACADEMY OF ADVANCED TECHNOLOGY

If this is to be an accurate account of Seattle after the Cascadia Fault mega-quake, I suppose I should explain about the curfew.

For any of this to make sense, you have to understand that most of the people living in Tent City died during the Cascadia Fault mega-quake. The shelters were too flimsy, and the water got so high. Women, children, families—they were all wiped out.

There were a few survivors. A small group of kids hijacked a boat and moved into the old Fairmont hotel. Roman lives with them now. He says he knew them from before the earthquake, that they were friends of his, back in Tent City.

I don't know what he sees in them. They're angry kids. Violent. There have been rumors of muggings and theft and looting. The curfew was put in place to keep people safe from them.

Roman isn't like that.

He stopped by the school last night. Zora must've told him I've been having a hard time moving on, because he came by with a box of these individually wrapped chocolate brownies we used to snack on while doing research, probably to try and cheer me up.

(I have to admit I'd forgotten how good those brownies were. I wonder where he found them—food in the city has become scarce.)

We talked for a while. I asked him about the program he'd been building years ago, the one that was supposed to predict earthquakes, but he said that someone nicked his computer before he could finish. Apparently lots of things got stolen in Tent City.

I explained my theory that he would've been better off continuing work on that project than helping me with my useless research. I tried to explain, at least. I'd had a drink or two by then, so I'm not sure I made myself clear.

In any case, Roman just gave me a very strange look.

"Are you joking?" he asked, and he motioned to the underwater city outside the window. "This isn't over. We can go back. We can fix all of this."

He went on to say that he knew I had issues with using time travel to alter the past, but that surely *now* I must see how important it was. We could keep thousands of people from dying. We could save the world.

I think I started laughing when he said that, which, in hindsight, was a poor choice. It's just that I couldn't help myself. My emotions have been so strange over the past year. So close to the surface.

And, of course, there was the fact that I'd been drinking.

I told Roman that I'd already tried. I'd gone back a hundred times. I'd tried to save Natasha in a hundred different ways, and it never worked. Never.

I don't think I would have told him as much had I been sober. In any case, Roman was furious. The little punk overturned my desk.

"Why do *you* get to go back?" he'd yelled at me. "We all lost people we loved. Why do you get to save them?"

I sobered up pretty quickly after that. I pointed out that I never actually succeeded in saving anyone. I'd tried, and I'd failed. My grief had clouded my better judgment but, in the end, I'd only succeeded in proving my original hypothesis.

Time travel is not magic. It can't be used to change the past or bring people back from the dead.

I'm not sure Roman really heard me. "The Black Cirkus is right about you," he'd said. "You're either completely pathetic, or you're a selfish bastard! You have all this power, and you don't even use it."

Naturally, I was confused. "Who is the Black Cirkus?" I asked.

He wouldn't answer, but I supposed he didn't need to. I could already imagine the kids from Tent City calling themselves the Black Cirkus, thinking that ridiculous name would make people take them seriously. It was only a matter of time before they became an official gang instead of just a band of thugs. Ha. Just what this ruined city needs.

There's no government in Seattle anymore. There's no police force, no rule of law.

If this Black Cirkus wants to take over, all they'll need are some guns.

Later, after I'd sobered up a bit, I couldn't help remembering our trip to collect Willis, how enthralled Roman had seemed with circus life. How he'd asked Willis questions, related to him.

Roman, I'm certain, is the one who gave the Black Cirkus their name.

I wonder if that means he's joined them.

39

DOROTHY

MARCH 17, 1980, FORT HUNTER COMPLEX

Dorothy threw the control room door open and raced down the hall.

The alarm screamed in her ear, a low wail that reminded her of howling wind.

She held her breath as she plowed through the gray smoke, dodging the swinging elbows of confused soldiers, stumbling around heavy boots. A man grabbed for her, but the smoke made it easy to hide. Dorothy saw him lunge past, hands grasping nothing but air.

She veered right at the fork without considering why she knew to go that direction. She was somehow certain there'd be a staircase at the end of the hallway. She rounded the corner, and her eyes fell on a steel door—

Her breath caught. There it was. Almost like it had been waiting for her.

She raced down the hallway and tugged the door open

with a grunt. A concrete staircase spiraled in front of her. She knew without knowing *how* she knew that it would lead to the roof.

This wasn't just déjà vu. It was something else. Something stronger.

It felt like an omen.

Time flowed around her like water and, for a moment, it was as though the past and the present and the future existed together, at the same time.

She was still running down the hall, but she was also standing with Roman in the *Dark Star*, hands raised as he pointed his gun at her chest.

There's something else that I need. . . . Believe it or not, you're the only person alive who can get it for me.

Then Dorothy's thoughts hitched, and she was just running again.

No, she thought, desperate, and pushed herself faster. Each step she took shuddered through her, rattling her bones and making her knees ache. Roman was wrong on this point, at least. He might need something from her, but she didn't have anything to give him.

And, besides, the future wasn't a set thing. Hadn't she just proven that? She'd had a vision of one thing and lived another. She'd rewritten the script, and maybe the change had been small, but it still meant something.

The future wasn't something that just *existed*, regardless of the decisions she made now. She had a choice.

And her choice was this: She was going to go back to 2077 with the Chronology Protection Agency. She was going to be part of a team.

Roman was on his own.

Her legs were already feeling weak beneath her, quivering with each step she took up the stairs. She dragged a hand over her forehead, and her sleeve came away damp with sweat. Her chest was starting to feel tight. Every breath was work.

Voices echoed down the stairwell, growing louder the higher she climbed. Shouting. Gunshots. Dorothy froze. Nerves prickled up her skin and, for the first time, she considered that Roman might've led her into a trap. Those voices didn't sound like her friends. They sounded like soldiers.

Then, "Everybody on the ship!"

Ash. Dorothy steeled herself and kept moving. *Please don't leave.*

It was funny, just the day before, all she'd wanted was a ride, the chance to run farther away, to disappear in history. Now, all she wanted was to be on the *Second Star.*

She pushed through the last door and stumbled outside. Sunlight hit her full in the face. She shielded her eyes, squinting into the glow.

40

ASH

The soldiers didn't wait to open fire.

The air filled with bullets. Ash felt their heat cutting through the sky, so close. He had his own gun off his shoulder in an instant. Finger on the trigger, eyes squinting through the sight.

"Everybody on the ship!" he shouted. He aimed for a leg—these men were innocent after all—and fired.

A soldier fell to his knees, swearing, and three more surged forward. Ash struggled to find the still place inside of himself that usually only came to him when he was flying. He couldn't get to it. This was chaos. He aimed again. Fired again. Another soldier fell.

"Zora!" Ash chanced a look to his left. Chandra had climbed back inside the *Second Star* and was hovering near the door in the back cabin, a look of grim horror on her face. Zora crouched beside her, using the time machine door as cover. It was too thin. One bullet punched into the metal. A second tore a hole straight through it.

"I think it's time to leave!" Zora called back. She peered around the edge of the door and cracked off a shot—she seemed to be trying to scare the soldiers more than hit them—and then swore and pulled back as a bullet whizzed past her face, coming within a hairbreadth of her nose. "Get us in the air!"

Ash's palms had started to sweat. They couldn't leave yet. They still had to change out the EM—

And they didn't have Dorothy.

The thought of her waiting for him back in the *Dark Star* sent something raw and guilt-stricken twisting through his gut. He shouldn't have left her there, alone. God, he hoped she was okay.

He glanced at the cockpit. Willis was already climbing out and lumbering toward them. He wasn't armed, but Ash saw how the soldiers all stumbled back a few steps as they took him in, eyes bulging like cartoon characters.

"Here!" Ash tossed Willis his gun—the giant caught it easily, frowning like he didn't know what it was for. A soldier raised his own gun to shoot, and Willis knocked him back with one hand, sending him stumbling into the others like a bowling ball into a row of pins.

Ash crashed into the cockpit, and that stillness he'd been searching for a second ago fell over him in a curtain. He started flipping switches, taking comfort in the familiar motions, even as a bullet flew into the passenger seat window, cracking glass. Ash didn't look away from the ship's control panel. *This* he knew how to do.

From the corner of his eye, he saw the roof door swing open and closed.

Damn, he thought, his stomach dropping. *Reinforcements.*

"Everybody in!" he shouted. He wasn't sure how, but they'd have to find a way back to the hangar after they got clear of the soldiers firing at them.

Then, once they were out of the woods, they could find a place to land for a bit while Zora installed the EM he'd taken from the *Dark Star.*

Something prickled in Ash, uncomfortable. If he took the EM from the *Dark Star*, the Professor wouldn't be able to come back to 2077.

The Professor's dead, he reminded himself. *He won't be able to use it*, *anyway.*

Willis slammed the butt of his gun into a soldier's temple—the man dropped like a rock—and leaped into the cabin. Zora was about to crawl into the ship after him, but a bullet pinged off the metal an inch from her hand. Swearing, she jerked back.

"Get her airborne!" she shouted, firing. "I'm—"

A voice rose above the gunfire. It sounded like it called, "Wait!"

Ash frowned, glancing at the window. All he saw were soldiers. He pulled back on the throttle and the *Star* lurched off the ground.

Zora tried, again, to lunge for the cabin. Again, a bullet

pinged off the metal, blocking her way.

The voice shouted, "Wait! Please!"

Ash dropped the stick and the *Star* crashed back to the roof with a thud that made the whole ship shudder. He twisted around in his seat, squinting through the cracks spiderwebbing across his window.

One of the soldiers was smaller than the others. He didn't have a gun that Ash could see, and he was pushing through the armed men, *against* them, head ducked like he didn't want anyone looking at him too closely.

Ash recognized the dark curls escaping from the sides of the small soldier's hat. *Dorothy.*

A feeling roared up inside of him, a happiness so similar to how he'd felt in his prememory, when he'd first seen the girl with the white hair, that he flinched, like he'd been hit.

But the feeling remained, pulsing beneath his breastbone like a second heartbeat. He couldn't deny what it was. Not love, not yet. But something like the beginning of it.

He swallowed, confused and embarrassed. What was happening? He'd seen Quinn Fox's white hair. He knew Dorothy wasn't the one he was supposed to be falling in love with.

"Zor!" he shouted, and jerked his chin at Dorothy. Zora cracked off a few shots at the men surrounding her, clearing the way.

Gasping, Dorothy leaped for the ship. Willis grabbed her by the arm to haul her on board.

She looked up, finding Ash in the cockpit. "I thought you'd leave . . ."

Ash felt something complicated twist inside his chest. Relief at seeing that his girl—and he was already thinking of her as *his* girl—was safe. Disappointment that she didn't trust him to find her. He cleared his throat and turned back around, trying to keep his voice even.

"Another second and we would've missed you," he said. "Didn't I tell you to stay put?"

"Yes, well, I've never been good with orders." Dorothy smiled, and he smiled back, unable to help himself.

Zora was climbing in behind her, still shooting one-handed as she reached to pull the door closed. Fingers tightening around the throttle, Ash pulled back on his ship, coaxing it into the sky. The *Second Star* popped off the ground, easy.

Atta girl, he thought.

Zora shouted, "Get us out of here, Ash. We've got—"

Another gunshot. This one was louder.

And then Zora was stumbling backward, dropping to one knee. Ash had a second to think that was weird, because Zora wasn't clumsy. Then she clutched at her chest as blood appeared beneath her fingers, blossoming across her shirt like a flower. "Zora!" Ash shouted. He released his hold on the yoke without realizing what he was doing. The *Star* was hovering mere feet above the roof, and it started to dip—

"Jonathan Asher, you get this ship in the air!" Chandra dropped beside Zora, two fingers going for her neck, looking for a pulse. Willis pulled the cabin door closed. His face was monstrous.

Zora closed her eyes.

Ash's throat felt thick, but he grabbed the yoke and pulled back before the *Star* could crash into the roof. "Is she—?"

"Do your job and let me do mine!" Chandra shouted.

Ash wanted to tell her to go to hell. He wanted to climb back into the cabin and hold Zora's head in his lap. He'd never seen her look helpless before. Not once.

Shaken, Ash turned back around.

"*Second Star* preparing for takeoff," he muttered, like an afterthought.

The ship lurched forward, bullets pinging off its wings.

The outside world raced past his windshield, but Ash didn't see it. He didn't know where he was taking them. Just away.

He was vaguely aware of the mountainous Fort Hunter disappearing behind him, the bullets chasing them becoming fewer, and then none.

He reached for the state of perfect calm flying usually brought to him, but he was like a child reaching for fireflies and grasping only air. His mind raced, playing and replaying the few seconds before they left the roof: Zora climbing into the cabin. The gun shot. Blood appearing on her chest. And him, acting too slowly. Doing too little.

He didn't chance another look back at the cabin until they were clear of Fort Hunter. When he did, he saw Zora's eyelids fluttering, her breath reedy and thin. Chandra crouched over her body, face pinched in concentration, and Dorothy was beside her, arms filled with bloody towels. Willis was a shadow behind them, praying. Ash had never seen him do that before.

He turned back around, blinking, and finally saw the world around him. Trees. Water. Fields of nothing but grass. The danger had passed.

"I'm going to land," he said, searching for a place clear enough to put the ship down. He needed to install the fresh canister of EM, and he could only do that with his ship on the ground. At least he'd have something to occupy his hands while Chandra patched Zora up.

"No!" Chandra didn't look up from Zora's body. "You have to keep flying."

"You can't fix her in the air." Ash knew he sounded like a crazy person, but he didn't care. Chandra was a genius. That's why the Professor went back a thousand years to find her. She could fix anyone. "We need to land, find supplies or . . . or medication . . . whatever you need."

"I *need* a clean operating table, and an ultrasound machine, and more gauze—"

"A hospital, then."

Ash looked at the mirror hanging from the windshield. Zora's chest rose and fell heavily. Her body began to shake. Chandra's hands went still, and she lifted her face, finding Ash's eyes in the reflection.

"*Time*," she said desperately. "That's what I need. I have to get the bullet out of her chest before she crashes, but she's losing too much blood. By the time I dig it out, she'll be . . ."

Ash swallowed and tore his eyes away from Chandra's.

Gone. That's what she'd been about to say. By the time she digs the bullet out of her chest, Zora will be gone. It was like some horrible riddle, one without any real answer. *How many time travelers does it take to make time stand still?*

Ash tightened his fingers around the stick.

A thought came to him, out of nowhere: *In an anil, all of time exists at once*. It felt like another riddle: *If all of time existed, did any time exist?*

He checked the EM readings: 15 percent. It wasn't safe to take the *Second Star* into an anil with the EM readings so low. He needed to land, to install the new EM. But, if he did that, Zora would die.

Ash suddenly felt short of breath. He wasn't the right person to work this out. They needed Roman, whose mind was slippery, always looking for loopholes. Or Zora, and her infallible logic. But they only had him. His hunch. He hoped it would be enough.

"Hold on," he shouted. He increased the throttle to 2,000 knots, and the calm he'd been grasping for settled over him like a blanket draped across his shoulders. "I've got an idea."

41

DOROTHY

Avery's hospital had a viewing area off the main operating theater where medical students would gather to watch the doctors perform miracles. Avery had invited Dorothy to attend once, insisting that she take a seat on the hard wooden benches to see him do what he did best. Thinking, perhaps, that she'd be impressed.

Dorothy was not impressed. The way her fiancé had spoken about his own abilities made it seem like he was more God than man. He'd never mentioned the team of other nurses and surgeons who surrounded him at all times, handing him equipment and mopping his brow.

He'd saved a life that day and, yes, Dorothy had to admit that was moving. But she couldn't help feeling disgusted at how he'd insisted he'd done it alone.

Chandra was his opposite. There was no team, no army of people to help her bring Zora back to life. There was only her and her talented hands, which seemed to manage the extraordinary feat of being in six places at once. She was taking Zora's pulse, and holding a cloth to her gushing wound. And then she was pressing a stethoscope to the girl's chest, and grasping for a pair of forceps. There was blood in the creases of her knuckles, and dried beneath her fingernails. There hadn't been time for gloves.

"Cloth," Chandra said. Dorothy took the bloody cloth from her hands and handed her a fresh one. She noticed that Chandra's forehead was damp with sweat. Without thinking, she leaned forward, as she'd seen Avery's nurses do, and dried it.

"Her pulse is weak," Chandra muttered. "And she's bleeding right here, by her right ventricle. I don't think I can make it stop—"

Zora's back arched. Her eyes rolled to the back of her head. She started coughing up blood.

Dorothy's heart seized. *Please don't—*

It had only been a day. Two days, maybe, and already these people felt like they might be friends. Zora had been so nice to her, had taken her into their group and given her a place to belong. Dorothy had never had that before. Zora didn't deserve to die, especially not here, like this, when she'd been trying to save her.

Darkness overtook the ship. Everything became very still and quiet. Except for the air. The air hummed like it was alive.

Dorothy looked up and saw roiling black clouds pressing against the shattered windows. Lightning flashed, turning the clouds purple. They'd entered the anil.

She looked at Ash. From her position on the floor of the time machine, she could see only the back of his neck, and the tense muscles along his arms.

What was he thinking? The trip through the anil had nearly killed them last time. She remembered how he'd doubled over, his skin going green. They couldn't go through that again. Not with Zora—

"Dorothy."

Dorothy jerked at the sound of her name. She heard a moan and heavy breathing and leaned over Zora, fresh cloth in hand. "What is it? What happened?

"She stopped seizing," Chandra said.

Dorothy stared at Zora's closed eyelids. They'd gone still. *Please don't be dead*, she thought. Out loud, she said, "What does that mean?"

Chandra looked shocked. "It means she's stable. She's not bleeding anymore. I . . ." Chandra shook her head, a nervous laugh escaping her lips. "I can remove the bullet now."

"How's she doing?" Ash shouted from the cockpit. He didn't turn to look at them but kept his eyes trained ahead, piloting his ship through a darkness so thick Dorothy couldn't make sense of it.

He'd known, she realized. Somehow he'd known that flying into the anil would save Zora's life. And he'd done it without a second thought, even after the last trip had nearly taken his own.

Dorothy thought of her mother, only trusting the people

she'd paid. And Avery, who could save a life in a room full of people and see only his own hands.

All her life, Dorothy been taught to rely only on herself. She'd been told that trust was a luxury that people like her couldn't afford.

But it wasn't true. It had simply been a consequence of the life her mother had chosen.

For the first time since it'd happened, Dorothy thought of their kiss back in the *Dark Star.* The warmth of Ash's lips pressed to her own. His heart beating against her chest.

She'd spent sixteen years being told she was only worth what she could steal, that her only value came from her pretty face and flirtatious smile. She'd always wanted something more. She'd always wanted to *be* more.

She lifted a finger to her lips. *This* was more.

Men lie, her mother warned.

You aren't one of them, added Roman.

Dorothy pushed their voices aside. She didn't want to listen to anyone else anymore. She knew exactly what she wanted.

LOG ENTRY—OCTOBER 22, 2076
01:14 HOURS
WEST COAST ACADEMY OF ADVANCED TECHNOLOGY

Nicked, he'd said.

The last time we spoke, Roman's exact words were, "Someone *nicked* my computer before I had a chance to finish the program."

I can't believe I didn't think of this before.

I must've been the one who nicked it. I must've gone back and stolen the damn thing.

I knew he'd never finish the program. Even with his computer he wouldn't have had the time, not with how hard we worked over the last few years. So I went back, and I took the computer so I could do it myself.

I'd told myself no more time travel. But this is different. This is for the greater good.

This could be the key to everything.

I'm leaving tonight.

42

ASH

THE PUGET SOUND ANIL

Ash focused on the path directly in front of his ship, letting the rest of the anil grow hazy and dark around the edges. Years passed him by, the changes in the quality of the smoke the only signs guiding his way.

1989 . . . 1992 . . .

Dorothy crawled into the cockpit and settled herself in the seat beside him.

“How’s she doing?” Ash asked.

“Chandra was able to remove the bullet. She’s stable.” Dorothy shifted so that she was facing him. Ash caught the movement from the corner of his eye.

She wasn’t touching him, but there was something about the expression on her face that made his skin prickle.

He kept his eyes trained on the windshield. “Is she awake?”

“Yes. She and Chandra are talking a little.” She touched the locket at her neck with one finger, an unconscious gesture.

Ash realized she often did this when she was thinking, and it scared him, a little, that he already found things like this familiar.

Ash leaned forward, pulling the EM out from inside his jacket. "Hold on to this for me?"

Dorothy frowned, turning the canister over in her hands. It was a glass cylinder filled with liquid sunlight. Then a shadow passed overhead, and the substance turned the color and texture of steel. "What is it?" she breathed.

"Exotic matter. Pretty, right?"

She nodded, her eyes going unfocused as she stared at what was now a swirling blue mist. "I saw you take this out of the *Dark Star*," she murmured, and then her eyes focused again, flicking to the *Second Star*'s control panel. "Wait a minute . . . isn't this supposed to be inside the ship somehow?"

"Yeah, well the *Second Star* doesn't have an internal control panel, like the *Dark Star* does, so you can't change the EM midflight."

"Is that safe?"

Ash's eyes flicked to the EM gauge. The dial still twitched near the 15 percent mark, taunting him. The new EM would only protect them if it were correctly installed inside the time machine. Sitting in Dorothy's lap, it was useless.

"I hope so," he said.

There was a moment of silence, and then Dorothy sighed and removed a small brass pocket watch from her pocket. "I should probably give this back to you."

Ash glanced at it, but it was a moment before he recognized

the thick gold chain and the familiar grooves around the edges of the face. His hands flew to the pocket where the watch generally lived. "Hey!"

"It's a little old-fashioned, isn't it?" Dorothy asked, turning the watch over in her fingers. The metal chain spilled from her palm. "The men in my time all have watches like this."

"It was my pop's," Ash said, as she placed the watch in his hand. Earlier, he might've been annoyed that she'd stolen a precious family heirloom. Now, he found it weirdly endearing, the way a person's faults could sometimes become endearing. "He was, well, I guess he would have been alive around the same time as you."

"I have to admit, I was expecting something much more exciting and expensive from a time traveler." Dorothy's lip twitched, like she was teasing him. It was a different sort of teasing than when they'd first met. Then, it'd felt like she wanted something from him. Now, it seemed more like she wanted to make him laugh.

"Pick a richer time traveler next time."

"Do you know any?"

Ash laughed out loud, the sound surprising him. He shouldn't feel this way so soon after Zora had been shot, but the knowledge that she was safe, at least for a little while, had left him light-headed and giddy.

That and the smell of Dorothy's hair, so close.

He cleared his throat. "You're one to talk," he said, nodding at Dorothy's locket. "You steal that off some nice little old lady's throat?"

"As a matter of fact, yes. But she wasn't nice, and I wasn't the one who stole it."

Ash waited, hoping the silence would get her to offer up the whole story, but she didn't take the bait. He took a second to squint at the engraving. "That a cat?"

"A dog, I think. It was like this when I got it."

"Right." Ash swallowed and shifted his gaze back to the windshield. He dropped a hand into his jacket pocket, fingers closing around his old man's watch.

The watch was its own kind of time machine. All Ash had to do was hold it in his palm and he'd be transported to a cornfield in 1945, the Asher family farm a dusty gray against the setting sun. The day he got this watch, he'd been standing at the edge of a dirt road, duffel bag at his feet, watching the speck of black in the distance rumble closer. That speck would turn into a bus, eventually. And that bus would take him to the flight camp over a thousand miles away, the farthest he'd ever been from home.

Before the bus could reach them, Ash's pop had placed his old watch in Ash's hand.

"Don't die," Jonathan Asher Sr. had said, closing his own hand around his son's. "Promise me."

Ash let go of the watch and pulled his hand from his pocket. Maybe that's what he'd been looking for when he asked Dorothy about her locket. A story. Some small sign of who she'd been before she found him in the woods and climbed into his ship.

He cast her a swift glance. "You religious?"

Dorothy began braiding her hair over one shoulder. Her fingers were quick, like she'd done this many times before. "I never saw the point. You?"

"I was Catholic."

"Was?"

Ash shrugged. He'd never lost his faith, exactly, but he'd gradually replaced it with science. The Professor's workshop had felt like church to him, the *Dark Star* and *Second Star* his altars.

"There's this passage in the Bible," he said, after a moment. "I don't remember it exactly, but it basically says that God knows the time of your death before you're even born. That it's fated."

"Do you believe that?"

Ash swallowed.

Did he believe it?

He thought of white hair and black water. A knife sliding into his gut. He'd tried so hard to believe there was still a way to keep all of that from happening. But that hope had died when they'd lost the Professor, when he caught a glimpse of Quinn Fox's white hair.

He couldn't explain it, but he felt like he knew that future was coming for him, no matter what he did to try to stop it. He could see it approaching like a bus on a dusty road. Just a speck in the distance now, but crawling closer with every moment that passed.

"It's kind of like time travel, isn't it?" Dorothy said,

interrupting his thoughts. "If God knows the day that you die, then he must know everything that's going to happen. It would mean our futures were set, and there's nothing we can do to stop them."

Black water. Dead trees. Ash nodded, not trusting himself to speak.

Dorothy laughed, but the sound was bitter. "What would be the point of any of this then? If our futures were already written, why bother living at all?"

"Aren't you curious about how this all ends?"

"Not if I can't change it." Dorothy's fingers went still, leaving several inches of perfect brown spirals at the end of her braid. Ash glanced at them. He wondered if he could pull the curls straight, or if they'd be like springs, bouncing back into shape as soon as he let go.

Dorothy licked her lips. "Are you taking me back? To 1913, I mean?"

Ash shifted his eyes from her hair to her face, and then away again. It hurt to look at her. It seemed like she was waiting for him to say something, but he couldn't speak. Pain flickered below his ribs, but it was the memory of pain, not the real thing.

"I could belong here." There was no seduction in her words. They fell out of her mouth in a rush, tripping off each other like puppies. "You said I wouldn't like it, but I do. I really do."

Tell her, Ash thought. But how was he supposed to tell the girl he'd only just kissed that he couldn't be with her because he was destined to fall in love with someone else? Someone horrible.

Lightning flicked in the distance. The dial on the wind reader twitched. Ash kept his attention on those small things until he could stand it no longer. And then, he looked at her.

She looked like hell. Her hair was a mess, with curls frizzing around her face and falling loose of her braid. Grease and sweat covered her face. Her shirt had ripped along the collar, showing faint smudges of dirt along her neck.

She looked real. She looked more beautiful than he'd ever seen her.

"I could stay here," she said. "I could be one of you . . . I could be with you."

Black water, Ash thought. *Dead trees.*

Zora said that falling for Dorothy would stop his horrible future from coming true. But this wasn't a curse that could be broken. It wasn't a prophecy that might not be fulfilled.

It was an actual, honest-to-God *memory*, and memories are fixed things that you can't change after the fact. Ash didn't understand before, but he thought he understood now. If he was remembering something that happened in the future, it was because that thing *happened*. He wasn't going to stop it by finding the Professor, and he certainly wasn't going to stop it by kissing pretty girls from the past.

Which meant he had to find a way to face it like a man. Like his father would have. A man wouldn't drag someone else down with him just because he was scared of the fall.

Dorothy's hand was on his arm, her fingers featherlight. "Ash—"

"I can't—" He'd been planning on telling her about the prememory. He wanted to tell her, but he lost his nerve half-way through. He shook his head, shrugging off her hand. "I just can't."

43
DOROTHY

Dorothy stumbled back to her seat, careful to keep her head lowered so no one would look at her. She felt like she'd been hit. Her cheeks flared with humiliation, as painful as if Ash had actually slapped her. She lifted a hand to her face, fingers trembling. She almost wished that were what happened. Physical pain seemed so much easier to endure than this . . . this burning.

What had she done?

She couldn't even pretend she hadn't been warned. Her mother had taught her the dangers of placing her trust in other people since she was old enough to walk, but she'd done it anyway. Why?

Because they'd been *nice* to her. Because she'd wanted to be part of a team.

And because she'd been lonely. She might not have wanted to admit that was part of it, but she couldn't ignore it now.

She'd been alone in this strange new world and desperate for a family to replace Loretta. She was ashamed of it now.

She sunk into her seat, looking out the window. The cloudy sides of the anil flew past in billowing blues and grays and purples. They were beautiful. Probably the most beautiful thing she'd see in this lifetime. But she found she couldn't focus on them.

She clutched the locket at her neck, closing her eyes against the gathering tears. God, she'd been a fool.

Not true, whispered an insistent voice in her head. She wasn't a fool. She knew exactly what she wanted. Perhaps she couldn't have it here, with these people. But that didn't mean she couldn't have it.

There were other people. Other futures. She didn't believe in destiny. She could still change things.

She tightened her grip around the locket, ignoring the cut of steel against her fingers.

You're an outsider. Roman had said. *You aren't on the team, and you never will be. You haven't proven yourself.*

Dorothy pressed her palms under her eyes to stop the angry flow of tears. This time, she had a harder time pushing his voice away.

A howling started outside the ship. It sounded far off at first, like a dog baying at the moon. Dorothy managed to ignore it for a while. But then it grew louder. It became a fire-engine siren, racing closer. She covered her ears with her hands.

Something slammed into the ship, making everything tremble.

Chandra knelt on the floor, holding Zora down by the shoulders. She jerked her head up. "Ash!"

"Storm's getting worse," Ash shouted back.

Rain began to fall. It started light, barely pricking at the windows. Over the course of a few minutes it grew steadily heavier, until it was hammering into the glass, making the walls of the *Second Star* shake.

"I can't keep her steady," Ash said. "It's getting—"

A window burst—filling the air inside the ship with wind and glass. Chandra screamed, throwing herself over Zora to shield her wound from the debris. Zora released a hacking cough. Her face had taken on an ashy, gray cast. Despite her restraints, Dorothy felt herself being sucked toward the window, pulled outside by the force of the storm. She wrapped both hands around her belt, gasping as the wind hit her.

Slowly, like he was walking through mud, Willis lumbered across the ship. He pressed against the broken window with his massive body, blocking the wind. For a moment, there was quiet.

"Change . . . the EM," Zora moaned from the floor. She tried to sit, but Chandra held down on her shoulders.

"You've been *shot*," she said. "What are you thinking?"

"We can't risk exiting the anil," Ash called back to them. "The tunnel's too unstable. The entire ship could break apart."

Zora sucked down a deep breath, her eyes fluttering

closed. "I know how to change the EM midflight. I've . . . done it before."

"Not with a bullet wound to the chest, you haven't."

"The anil . . . will keep me stable."

Chandra closed her eyes. She appeared to be counting to ten to calm herself down. After a moment, she said, "Let me be very clear. If you do this, you will die."

The ship dropped. Dorothy felt the fall in her stomach, like something twisting and pulling at her gut. Willis lost his balance and dropped down to one knee. Wind whirled through the ship again, tugging at their hair. Chandra's doctor's bag slid across the floor and slammed into the far wall. A few tiny vials spilled out and were immediately whipped into the air, twirling in the window.

Willis pushed himself back up to his feet, and positioned his body in front of the window, again. "Sorry," he murmured.

Zora groaned, one hand going to the bandaged wound at her chest. "If I don't do this, we'll *all* die."

"I can install the EM," Willis said. "I've done it before."

Zora turned her head without lifting it from the floor, studying him. "You're too big. The ship won't hold."

The sides of the ship creaked. Dorothy lifted a hand to touch the buckling aluminum. She had the feeling of being inside a paper bag that someone was slowly crumpling.

You haven't proven yourself, she thought.

She said, without thinking, "I'm not big."

Every set of eyes turned toward her.

"You don't know how," Zora said.

Dorothy sat up straighter. *Reckless*, her mother would have called her. *Foolhardy*. The knowledge that she wouldn't have approved made her all the more determined. "Willis can tell me how."

Willis frowned, appearing to turn this idea over in his head. "It's not terribly complicated if you know which wires go where. And she has steady hands."

"You can't be considering this!" Ash shouted. But he was flying the ship. There was nothing he could do to stop her.

They're a team. Roman had said. *You're an outsider, and you always will be.*

Maybe not, Dorothy thought. If all she had to do was prove herself, then this should do it. She didn't see how they could think of her as an outsider after she'd saved all their lives.

She made her way over to the window where Willis was standing. Outside, a flash of lightning set the anil ablaze. *Zilch lightning*, she thought, as the tunnel walls lit up with shades of orange and red, a hellscape of fire and smoke. Dorothy felt tension move through her shoulders, tightening her muscles, but at least she didn't flinch. A small victory.

She should be nervous, she realized. But she wasn't. She felt an eerie sort of calm. This was right. It was what she was meant to be doing.

"There's a harness in my bag, right there." Zora tried to lift her arm, but it trembled and fell back to the floor. Her eyes fluttered closed. Chandra unwound the stethoscope from her neck and leaned over Zora's body, pressing the diaphragm to her chest.

"That one there," she said, nodding at a bag near Dorothy's feet. Dorothy knelt and dug around inside the bag until she located the thick harness. She handed it to Willis, who began knotting it around her waist.

"You don't have to do this." Willis pulled her tether taut, testing the knot connecting the thick rope to the harness at her waist. It didn't give, and he nodded, satisfied. "We can find another way."

"Don't be a ninny." Dorothy tried for a smile. "It'll be fine."

He didn't look convinced. "I'll be in your ear the whole time." He tapped the headset he'd strapped over her curls. "I'll walk you through everything."

Dorothy swallowed, tasting acid at the back of her throat. She'd heard everything he said but the words seemed to evaporate the moment they reached her ears. She touched the contraption he'd made her wear. *Headset.*

Lightning knifed through the sky outside her window. Thunder roared.

"Ready?" asked Willis.

Dorothy jerked her head up and down in an approximation of a nod. She supposed she had to be.

Willis took a step away from the busted window and cold air gusted into the ship, blowing the hair away from Dorothy's face and forcing her back a few steps. He unlatched the window and pushed it open. Steeling herself, Dorothy lurched forward, propping one hand to either side of the window to hold herself steady.

Don't look, she told herself. But she was already turning, her eyes finding the back of Ash's head where he sat in the cockpit. She studied the place on his neck where soft, blond hair met sunburned skin. But he didn't turn around to watch her go.

She shoved the EM down the back of her trousers, tightened her fingers around the window, and crawled out the ship.

44

ASH

Ash looked up a second after Dorothy climbed out the window, then looked quickly away again.

He wanted to tell her to stop. He wanted to tell her he'd changed his mind. But he couldn't do either of those things, so he stayed quiet until she was gone.

Lightning flashed outside, and there was another shuddering slam against the walls.

Their conversation gnawed at him. He'd thought telling her they couldn't be together would feel noble, or at least brave. He was doing it for *her*, after all, so he wouldn't hurt her. Wasn't that supposed to feel good?

Well, it didn't. Ash couldn't quite put a name to the feeling crashing through him, but it was dangerously close to cowardice or shame or some terrible mixture of the two. He'd seemed to hurt her, anyway, no matter how hard he'd tried not to.

Wind pressed hard on the ship's windows, making the

glass creak so badly that Ash braced himself for a shatter. A small object flew past his face, pinging off the time machine's walls and then zipping, bullet-like, across the cockpit again.

He couldn't believe Dorothy was climbing into *this*. The ship was rocketing around the anil like a pinball in a machine.

He felt suddenly restless. He wanted to climb out after her. To *help* her. But he could only sit and steer and ask favors of a God he no longer believed in.

Don't let her die.

45

DOROTHY

It was cold in the anil. Dorothy's fingers went instantly numb, and the moisture on her lips froze into a thin veneer of ice. Her limbs felt clumsy and stiff.

"Dorothy? Do you copy?" Willis's voice spoke directly into her ear. *Copy?* She frowned, and the ice coating her lips cracked.

"Copy?" she repeated, confused.

"Great! You're coming in loud and clear," Willis said. "Can you look to your left and tell me what you see?"

Dorothy inhaled so much icy air that her lungs burned with cold. Wind tugged at her back, threatening to peel her away from the *Second Star*. She turned her head, pressing her cheek into the side of the ship.

A ladder hung beside her, its lower rungs just a few inches from the top of her head.

"There's a ladder," she forced out.

"Good," came Willis's soothing voice. "Now, reach up and grab that lower rung."

Cold fear seeped through her. Grabbing the rung meant removing one of her hands from the side of the ship. But the wind was so strong. It picked at her pants and shirt, making the fabric flap wildly around her body. If she made one wrong move it'd blow her off into the tunnel like a piece of tissue paper.

She tightened her grip, shaking her head. "The wind . . ."

"The harness will keep you from falling."

A voice in Dorothy's head screamed, *Don't! He's wrong! You'll die!* She was quite comfortable listening to that voice, actually. But another, equally insistent voice kept breaking through it. This voice sounded like her mother.

Our world has no place for cowards.

The fingers of her left hand relaxed, just a little. She removed them from the side of the ship and reached over her head, grasping for the ladder rung at the same time that she inched to the side. The wind pulled at her body, lifting her legs away from the ship and sucking her backward. The breath left her chest—

Then there was cold metal beneath her fingers. She curled her hand around the ladder rung, muscles screaming as she dragged her body closer.

"All right." She held tight to the ladder. "I've done it."

"Good. Now climb."

The climb was brutal. Dorothy would no sooner release one hand from the ladder before the wind was picking at her again, trying to pluck her off the side of her silly little ship like a child might pluck an ant off a log. And if that wasn't bad enough, the cold had made her arms and legs stiff and hard to maneuver. Her fingers were so frozen she could hardly manage to curl them around the icy ladder rungs. Harsh winds bit into her eyes, causing tears to stream down her face, blurring her vision. She didn't dare lift a hand to wipe them away.

"Dorothy?"

"Nearly there," she grunted, hauling herself up one final rung. She lifted her head—and gasped.

Seeing the anil through the *Second Star*'s dirty glass windows was nothing compared to seeing it like this, up close, with nothing separating them except for the tears still pooling in her eyes.

The tunnel walls were made of smoke and cloud and mist. At first they looked gray and purple, but the longer Dorothy stared at them the more color seemed to be woven in the whorls and tendrils. A flash of orange. A curl of red. Pinpricks of light flashed deep within the smoke and, for a moment, they made Dorothy think of stars. Dozens, and then hundreds, and then an entire galaxy waiting beyond the mist and smoke. A breeze blew a cloud across the walls and the stars all winked out at once, like they'd never been there in the first place. A deep rumbling echoed from somewhere inside the tunnel.

Dorothy had never been religious, but she imagined this must be what people felt when they prayed. She was suddenly deeply grateful for the chance to see it.

"Dorothy?"

Dorothy blinked. She didn't know how long she'd been staring at those mesmerizing walls. She shifted her eyes back to the ship.

"I'm here," she gasped.

"You should have reached the control panel by now. Do you see it? It'll look like a crack in the metal of the ship, almost like a door."

Dorothy studied the side of the ship until she saw the crack Willis was talking about. "Yes."

"You'll need to wedge your fingers into the crack to open it."

Dorothy did as she was told, and tugged. The door creaked open a half inch. Dorothy stuck her hand all the way into the opening and pulled—

The wind caught the edges of the door and jerked it backward, sending it shuddering into the side of the ship. The *Second Star* gave a frightening lurch and then shot toward the opposite side of the anil.

Dorothy flattened herself against the ship, clenching her eyes shut so she wouldn't see what was happening. She had the sensation of being spun like a top. The world around her became a dizzying blur of colors and lights. An acid taste climbed her throat, making her feel that she might be sick.

And then it stopped. The ship stopped spinning and the wind calmed. Dorothy didn't lift her head right away. She kept her check pressed to the cool metal and breathed.

"Dorothy? Dorothy are you there?" Willis sounded frantic. "Are you okay?"

Dorothy exhaled. "I'm here. I'm okay—"

A chunk of ice the size of a tennis ball separated from the cloudy walls and slammed into the ship, hitting inches from Dorothy's hand. Another followed, and then another.

"It's hailing," Dorothy said, flinching as a shard of ice pricked her ankle.

"I need you to listen to me. The anil is about to collapse. You need to install the EM and get the hell out of there. *Now.*"

"What do I do?"

"Look at the control panel. Can you locate the existing container of EM?"

Dorothy inched toward the control panel. The winds were still blowing the panel door back so that it was pressed firmly against the side of the ship, but Dorothy trembled to think of what might happen if the wind turned. She imagined the door snapping shut on her hands, cutting her fingers off at the knuckles. Fear rose in her throat. She let her eyes travel over the odd, brightly colored wires and greasy bits of metal before—

There! She located the EM in the far corner. A crack splintered down the side of the canister, and the material inside was charred and black. Dorothy didn't need to be an expert in time travel to know that was a bad sign.

"I found it," she said.

"Good," came Willis's voice. "Now, there will be a wire attached to one end. A thick, blue one."

Dorothy crept closer. She located the wire. "Got it."

"It should be attached to the EM by a three-pronged—"

A shard of hail the size of a golf ball slammed into Dorothy's arm. She heard a sickening crack and her fingers lost their hold on the ship.

46

ASH

The dashboard was on fire.

Ash didn't know how it had started. He'd been too busy squinting through the nightmarish scene unfolding outside his windshield—hail the size of fists, lightning so close he could smell the sizzle of ozone—desperately trying to catch a glimpse of Dorothy's leg, or a lock of her hair, or *anything* that might indicate that she was okay.

A flame unfurled from beneath the wind gauge, singeing his finger. He jerked back, and the *Star* began to plummet. . . .

Ash grasped for the yoke and pulled the ship level again, tears gathering in his eyes as red-hot curls of fire licked the backs of his knuckles. But he wouldn't let go, not even when the heat made his skin crack and blacken. They were too close. He chanced a look outside, at the roiling dark of the tunnel walls. They were flying past the 2040s now. . . .

"How's she doing?" he shouted, gritting his teeth against the burn. Willis had been leaning out the window, both hands clutching the tether attached to Dorothy's waist. He pulled back inside at the sound of Ash's voice.

"She was doing great out there, Captain, but I—" Wind punched into the side of the ship, blowing straight through Willis's words. The *Second Star* trembled violently, and Ash heard a great *thunk* that sounded an awful lot like a very large man being tossed to the floor. "Willis!" Ash swerved to avoid an arc of lightning. Willis didn't answer.

Ash moved his eyes up to the mirror. For a long moment, no one stared back at him. Then Willis pushed himself to his feet, still holding Dorothy's tether.

"I'm here, Captain," he groaned, wrapping the thick rope around his hand a third time. He lifted the walkie-talkie to his mouth and, despite the screaming wind, Ash heard the words, ". . . Dorothy . . . read? Come in . . ."

"What's happening?" Ash shouted.

"I lost contact," Willis called back. He was staring down at the tether wrapped around his hand, a deep frown creasing the skin between his eyebrows. "Ash—"

"Pull her in!" Ash's heart was beating too quickly. He pictured Dorothy clinging to the side of his ship, her hands gripping slick metal, her body blowing in the violent wind.

He tightened his grip around the yoke. Out of the corner of his eye, he saw flames dancing closer to his fingers, but he didn't even feel them. They could make it without the EM. Only another decade to go. "Do it now!"

"That's the—"

The windshield exploded inward with no warning, filling

the air with glass like sand, tiny and razor-sharp. Ash felt it on his face and hands, and he closed his eyes on instinct. Someone was screaming—hell, it could've been him.

He blinked, trying to force his eyes open again, but the wind was too strong. He thought he saw 2074 fly past. 2075 . . .

He opened his eyes a little wider. Wind and glass gusted around him. The smoky tunnel walls had formed a familiar orange crest. 2076. Almost there. He aimed the *Star*'s nose for the darker curve just beyond.

He shouted, "Pull Dorothy in!"

"Captain, I—"

A jagged piece of metal flew off the wall, slicing into Ash's arm as it hurtled past. A hole appeared in the floor of the cockpit, the haunting black and gray of the anil swirling below. Ash yanked the yoke to the side and it came off in his hands. He fell backward, head cracking into the seat. They were flying through the tunnel walls now. Everything was smoke and fire and mist. . . .

Ash opened his mouth to tell the others to hold on tight when—

Black water and dead trees. A kiss . . . a knife . . .

He felt the steel point of the dagger slide into his body, cutting through muscle and skin, making his nerve endings scream. He groped for his belly, and his hands came away bloody.

Real blood. A real wound.

The *Star* slammed into something, shuddering. A roar filled Ash's ears. More screaming, he thought. Or maybe it was the wind. He kept his hands pressed against his wound, trying to stop the bleeding. The world blinked in and out of focus.

Of course it does, someone said.

And then the darkness took him.

47

DOROTHY

"Dorothy? Dorothy, do you read?"

Willis's voice sounded very small and far away. Dazed, Dorothy lifted a hand to her head and found that the headset was no longer propped over her ears. It'd been knocked askew, and now it was tangled in her curls.

She blinked, groaning. Her other arm was pinned beneath her, somehow tangled in the ladder rungs. She was fairly sure it was the only reason she hadn't blown off the ship.

"I'm coming, Willis," she murmured. She groped around for something to grab hold of and felt nothing and more nothing before her fingers finally brushed against the control panel door. It flapped against the side of the ship like a fish on dry land, attached by a single remaining hinge.

Dorothy curled her hand around the door and pulled—

The door broke away with a snap and came hurtling toward her. She felt a slash across her face and then pain like she'd never experienced before—white-hot and burning. She grasped for something to hold on to but felt only air—

And then she was flying backward, the tunnel walls billowing toward her. Smoky tendrils curled around her arms and legs, like a hand grasping. She tried to scream, but the smoke filled her mouth and seeped into her lungs. She blinked, and her eyesight turned bloody.

Distantly, she heard something snap. With her one good eye, she watched the tether break away from the *Second Star* and come whipping toward her.

LOG ENTRY—OCTOBER 23, 2076

02:13 HOURS

THE *DARK STAR*

I've only just returned. I had to check my earlier entries to jog my memory, but it seems that Roman and I met on December 3, 2073, right around noon. I didn't want anyone else to steal his computer before I got the chance, so I traveled to the very next morning, in the early hours, while he and everyone else in Tent City slept. There's no real security in Tent City, no locks or guards, and so I was able to sneak in unnoticed.

The computer was relatively easy to locate. Roman kept it just beside his bed. I slipped it out from beneath his fingers without waking him, but something fell to the floor as I was tucking the computer into my bag. It was a small white scrap of paper.

I knelt to pick it up and saw that it wasn't a scrap of paper at all but a photograph. An actual, printed photograph of a young girl with Roman's dark hair and blue eyes. A sister, perhaps? The photograph looked like the sort of thing schools printed out for parents, as a keepsake. But a quick look around the tent revealed that there were no parents. No sister. No one but Roman and his computer.

I would've left the computer behind at that moment. I'm not a monster.

But Roman said someone nicked it.

If I don't steal it now, someone else will just steal it later.

So I took it.

Roman was waiting inside my workshop when I brought the *Dark Star* back. He had a gun, Ash's gun, from the look of it, and he aimed it at my chest as I climbed down from the ship.

"When were you?" he demanded. I remembered wondering if there had always been so much rage in his voice, or if it had crept in recently. If I hadn't noticed him changing.

I told him what I'd done, how I'd gone back to retrieve his computer, so that we might predict future earthquakes before they occurred.

I expected him to be angry. I hadn't expected that he wouldn't believe me.

"You're a liar!" he'd said. I assumed he would shout and yell and throw things, as he'd done in my workshop the last time we fought. But his voice was calm and collected. "You went back to see your wife again. To save her."

I tried to deny it. I even tried to grab the computer, so I could show him, but he shoved me when I went to reach for it. He actually *shoved* me.

"The past is our right," he'd said, repeating the Black Cirkus's horrible slogan. "You might be the only one capable of traveling through time now, but that won't always be the case."

And then he'd left me there alone, without once firing his gun.

48

ASH

OCTOBER 16, 2077, NEW SEATTLE

"*Ash . . . Ash . . . .*"

The voice swam toward him from somewhere deep down in the black. Ash needed to find it. He swam hard, but the current was strong. It dragged at his feet and pressed down on his shoulders.

Black water, he thought, kicking. *Dead trees . . .*

"Ash, you've been sleeping for a really long time. You need to wake up."

A kiss . . . a knife . . .

Pain slammed into him, and Ash jerked. He felt the sticky warmth of blood on his fingers and the cold bite of metal slipping between his ribs. He woke up gasping.

"Quinn," he choked out, trying to sit, "it's—"

"No, you don't," said another, deeper voice. Something pressed down on his shoulders and he realized that it wasn't water but two hands trying to hold him down.

The fight drained out of him all at once. Ash allowed

himself to be pushed back into what felt like his bed. Someone had propped a ridiculous number of pillows behind him and tucked a blanket so tightly around his body that he felt as though he were wearing a straitjacket.

He had to blink a few times before the rest of his room took shape. Rough plaster walls and beat-up wooden floors. Willis and Chandra were leaning over him.

Ash didn't have the energy to ask how they'd gotten home. The pillows were soft beneath his head. It would be so nice to sleep again. He shifted in place, and pain moved through his lower ribs.

Suddenly, he was wide-awake. That was real pain, not premembered pain. He lowered his hand to his belly and felt thick bandages beneath his fingers.

He tried to speak, but his tongue was dry, and too big for his mouth. "She . . . stabbed me."

"What was that now?" Willis asked, leaning closer.

"The girl . . . white hair," Ash managed. Willis frowned.

"Do you mean the bandages?" Chandra asked. "Those are from the crash. The *Second Star* exploded before we could get out of the anil, and a piece of the ship got lodged right below your ribs."

"You were bleeding pretty badly," Willis added. "We weren't sure you were going to make it."

"Yeah, and we were, like, stranded outside the anil without a boat or anything, and Willis was freaking brilliant. He grabbed part of the ship that had, like, exploded, and then he somehow managed to get both you and Zora on top of it—even though I thought it was way too small—and then, you won't believe it, he pulled the thing through the water like a freaking horse or . . . is there a horse that swims? Like a dolphin, maybe—"

"Zora?" Ash choked out, cutting Chandra off.

"Zora's fine," Willis said. "Or, she will be fine. She was pretty banged up but our Chandie pulled her through."

"Best doctor in the history of the world," Chandra said, with a shy smile. "I keep telling you all, but it's like you don't listen."

"Atta girl," Ash said. He looked down at his hands, surprised to find burns blackening his skin. The sight of them unnerved him. He didn't remember getting burned. Didn't remember anything about the crash.

He curled his hands into fists. The burns made it feel like they belonged to someone else. "Where's Dorothy?"

A heavy silence was all that answered back. Ash closed his eyes. He had the vague feeling of a little kid hiding beneath the blankets on his bed, thinking that the monsters wouldn't come for him if they couldn't see him. He was old enough to know that trick didn't work.

With effort, he asked, "What happened?"

"I don't know for sure," Willis said. "One moment, everything was fine. I had her tether in my hands, and I was walking her through the job. She didn't even seem scared.

"And then there was a sound. Like a crash. I lost contact with her, but the rope was still taut, so I knew she was out there. I figured her headset got knocked off in the storm, and I gave her a few minutes to fix it but she never came back online, so I started to reel her in. . . ."

Willis said all of this like a soldier giving his report to a superior officer. It was soothing, somehow. Ash could almost pretend it'd happened to someone else. That it didn't affect him.

"The tether . . . snapped." Willis's voice cracked, breaking the illusion. "She was gone."

Ash squeezed his hands until the burns on his knuckles flared. He was the reason she'd been lost.

He suddenly felt very tired. His ribs hurt, and the burns on his hands stung, but these things were just distractions. Eventually they'd fade, and he'd have to think about the thing that was really killing him. Dorothy was gone. Forever.

He asked, "The EM?"

"Dorothy had it when she . . ." Chandra cleared her throat, unwilling or unable to finish her sentence. "It's gone, too."

Ash nodded, relaxing his hands.

They were right back where they started. They'd failed, utterly and completely. This had all been for nothing.

Suddenly and intensely, Ash wanted to sleep. The exhaustion seeped into his muscles and pulled at his bones. His eyes drooped but, before they closed, he thought he saw something odd behind Chandra's left ear. He blinked, trying to focus.

A lock of her hair had turned white.

OCTOBER 17, 2077, NEW SEATTLE

Ash knew Zora was beside him before he was fully awake. He drifted in and out of sleep, listening to her shift in the chair next to his bed.

"I know you aren't sleeping." Her voice sounded weak.

Ash opened his eyes. "How could you tell?"

"You stopped snoring." Zora's skin was ashen, and dark circles colored the area below her eyes. Her chest had been wrapped in thick, cotton bandages that made her tank top bunch.

She caught him staring and shrugged. "Looks worse than it is."

Ash swallowed. He didn't believe her, but he could smell engine grease and burnt coffee clinging to her skin, so at least she was well enough to make it to the workshop. Chandra wouldn't have let her fumble around with wrenches and gears if she was about to die.

"Besides, you look like shit," Zora said without smiling. "We make a good pair."

She took his hand and squeezed. The burns on Ash's knuckles stung, but he didn't let go. He tilted his head back, staring at the ceiling. A crack ran through the plaster.

He thought about Dorothy. And, when that hurt too much, he thought about the Professor, instead. It hurt just as bad, but at least it was a hurt he was prepared for.

"I'm really sorry about your dad," he said, voice cracking.

The skin around Zora's eyes tightened, just a little. "Yeah. Me, too."

For a while, they were both quiet. Ash thought he heard Willis and Chandra out in the kitchen. Willis said something in his low, deep voice, and Chandra laughed.

Zora cleared her throat. "I read the rest of his journal. Cover to cover."

Ash felt his eyebrow go up, curious despite himself. "Did he write anything useful?"

"Yeah, actually. There was a lot of stuff about Roman and about . . ." She paused to take a deep breath, eyelashes briefly flicking closed. "And about my mom. That was really hard to get through, but I found something interesting near the end. Apparently, when my dad first met Roman, Roman was working on some sort of computer software that was supposed to predict earthquakes before they happened. Roman never finished, though, so Dad went back in time and took his computer. I think he wanted to finish the program himself, to see if he could predict the next big earthquake before it messed everything up more. Before anyone else's mother died."

Ash remembered the Professor walking out of the room labeled *Environmental Modification*, and the list of numbers scrawled across the *Dark Star*'s windshield in the Professor's handwriting. The numbers that had looked like predictions of earthquakes to come.

He told Zora what he'd seen.

Zora frowned as he spoke, turning this over. "That makes sense with what he wrote in his final entry. Remember how he said the state of the world hung in the balance? He must've been thinking about those two earthquakes to come, the 10.5 and the 13.8. Those wouldn't just destroy the West Coast. They could potentially destroy the world."

Ash pushed himself up to his elbows. "But why go back to 1980? What does Fort Hunter have to do with any of that?"

"They used weather-modification techniques to extend the monsoon season during the Vietnam War back in the seventies. In 1980, the program was probably at its peak . . . maybe Dad thought he could look at their research?"

"That Lieutenant Gross guy said he'd stolen information on a weapon of mass destruction," Ash said.

"Environmental modification would've been considered a weapon of mass destruction, so that fits. Dad must've taken whatever they had on changing the environment in the hopes that he could modify our current environment enough to keep the earthquakes from happening."

"But he failed," Ash pointed out. He felt suddenly and overwhelmingly tired.

The Professor had rescued him from a life of war. He'd shown him things he never would've imagined. He taught him to fly a time machine. And then he'd died, for nothing.

And then Dorothy had snuck into his life and made him feel like he could change his future. And she'd died for nothing, too.

And now it was his turn to die.

It was too much to think about.

Zora said quietly, "My father didn't fail."

This answer startled Ash. Ordinarily she was the

pessimistic one. Or maybe *pessimistic* wasn't the right word. Realistic was closer. Or hesitant. Or cautious.

But, now, she stared at Ash with eyes like lit coals.

"He died before he could do anything with that research," Ash said. "These earthquakes are going to happen."

"Maybe," Zora said. "Or maybe not."

Groaning, she leaned over, one hand pressed over the bandages at her chest as she dug something out from beneath the bed. Without a word she straightened, dropping it on Ash's lap.

It was a small black laptop.

Ash exhaled through his teeth. "Is that . . . ?"

"Roman's laptop," Zora said. "I found it in Dad's office, beneath a pile of junk. And before you ask, yes, the program is still there. I ran it before coming here, and it spit out the same information you saw written on the *Dark Star* windshield. A bunch of dates and some seriously terrifying-looking magnitudes."

Ash was shaking his head. "But what are we supposed to do with it?"

Zora shrugged. "My parents went back in time to find the smartest, most talented people in all of history."

"Your parents went back in time to find a pilot, a circus strongman, and a girl who was expelled from medical school."

Zora's look was withering. "You were all trained by NASA, and I'm the only daughter of the greatest scientific mind the world has ever seen. And, besides, there's still all of my dad's research to go through, and now Roman's program.

I think Dad left this computer here for a reason. I think he wanted us to do something with it. Which means there's still a chance to change things."

She held Ash's gaze in a way that made him think she wasn't just talking about the earthquakes.

She was talking about the prememories, and his impending, early death.

Ash nodded. "We'll try."

Satisfied, Zora pushed herself to her feet, her face twisting in a grimace, and hobbled to the door.

She paused before stepping into the hall, one hand resting on the doorframe.

"For what it's worth, I don't think Dorothy died. I think she's still out there, somewhere."

Ash closed his eyes. Hoping hurt almost more than not hoping had. Hoping meant there was still more to lose.

"Yeah," he murmured. "Maybe."

"There's a lot that we don't understand about the structure of the time tunnels. Flying through one stopped me from bleeding out, and we're not entirely sure why. And Dorothy had the EM on her, didn't she? It might've kept her safe. Maybe she only missed us by a few months."

Zora pushed a braid behind her ear. Ash frowned, staring at it. The braid was white.

"What's that," he asked, pointing.

"Oh." Zora shrugged. "It was like that when I woke up. Chandra has one, too. And so do you, right here."

She leaned forward, touching a lock of hair below Ash's ear.

"I think it has something to do with the energy in the anil, and how it interacts with melatonin, but I need to do a little more research to be sure. Strange, right?"

Ash's hands had started to shake. Something was taking shape in the back of his mind, but he didn't understand. Not yet.

Black water and white hair.

"Strange," he echoed.

LOG ENTRY—OCTOBER 23, 2076

04:07 HOURS

THE WORKSHOP

I can't stop thinking about what Roman said to me.

You might be the only one capable of traveling through time now, but that won't always be the case.

Roman knows almost as much as I do about time travel. He helped me build the *Dark Star.* He has access to all my notes—to this very journal. He's been back in time with me more than any of the rest of the team combined. If anyone other than myself were capable of traveling back in time, it would be him.

But he doesn't have any exotic matter.

A human being absolutely cannot go through an anil without exotic matter. There's no other way to stabilize the tunnel. He'd be killed, instantly.

I double-checked the EM in the *Second Star* after he'd gone, thinking he may have stolen it. But it was still there, what little there was, exactly as it should have been. And, of course, I have the EM from the *Dark Star* with me now, so there was no way for him to take that, either. Those two canisters are the only two stores of exotic matter that exist in the world.

I need to get back to the school. I need to see what Roman has on this computer, to see if I can finish the work he started three years ago and predict the next earthquake before it's too late to do anything about it.

I know this, and yet I can't make myself leave the workshop. I can't stop replaying our last argument.

Something changed in the past few days. Something happened since he saw me last, something that convinced him he didn't need me anymore.

So what was it?

PART FOUR

It's no use going back to yesterday, because I was a different person then.

—Alice's Adventures in Wonderland

DOROTHY

OCTOBER 22, 2076, NEW SEATTLE

Damp wood pressed into her cheek. Crisp air nipped the back of her neck.

Dorothy groaned, which sent pain pumping through the left side of her skull. It felt like someone had taken a knife and sliced clean through her face, from the corner of her mouth, up past her eye, and over her eyebrow. She lifted a hand to the pain, felt something sticky beneath her fingers.

She forced her eyes open.

No. She forced her *eye* open. Something was holding her other lid shut. *Blood*, she realized, tiptoeing fingers around tender edges of ragged skin. She must have a bad cut on her face. It had bled heavily, but the blood seemed to have stopped and dried into a sticky paste on her cheek. That's why she couldn't open her eye.

This all came to her in strangely detached clarity, like it was happening to someone else.

She lowered her hand to the wood beneath her cheek.

Water crept over the sides, inching toward her fingers. *I'm on a dock*, she realized. She turned her head, and a pair of black boots appeared in her line of vision.

"You're lucky I pulled you out," said a voice. "There are very bad people roaming around here after dark. They'd have let you drown."

"Roman?" Her voice was a beast with dirty claws, crawling up the inside of her throat. She swallowed, cringing. "Is that you?"

The boots moved closer. Dorothy turned her head. Pain beat against her cheek, turning her eyesight foggy, but she could still make out Roman's dark hair and cleft chin. He held Ash's old pistol in one hand, but it was resting at his side, not pointing at her.

"Have we met?" he asked.

Dorothy's good eyelid flickered closed again. The cut on her face actually hurt very badly. She was having a hard time thinking through the pain. Roman seemed to be playing some sort of trick on her. Pretending they didn't know one another.

It was sort of funny, she supposed. She started to giggle—

Something jostled her shoulder. "Focus, girl. How do you know my name?"

The trick didn't seem so funny the second time. Dorothy's laughter became a hacking, painful cough. She tried to open her eyes—*eye*—again, but the cut on her face really hurt. It was going to get infected if she didn't clean it soon. She didn't want to touch it, but she didn't like the feel of the wind brushing against the raw skin, so she cupped a hand over the injury. She used the other hand to push herself to her knees.

Roman took a quick step backward, lifting his pistol. "Easy."

"What do you think I'm going to do? Bleed on you?" Dorothy blinked and Roman's face came into stronger focus. A scraggly, black beard covered his chin and cheeks. It was a sad sort of beard, the kind that only grew in patches.

Hold on. How had he grown a beard so quickly? When she'd last seen him, he'd been clean-shaven.

Are you trying to say that you've seen the future?

Perhaps. Perhaps I've even seen yours.

With effort, she asked, "What day is it?"

Roman frowned. "October twenty-second."

Understanding hit her all at once.

She asked carefully, "What year?"

Roman paused, and then said, "2076."

"2076," she repeated. When Roman told her he'd seen her future, she'd assumed he'd traveled ahead and seen what was to come. But she'd been wrong. He knew her future because she'd landed a full year too early. Her future had been his past.

If there was a feeling beyond fear and hopelessness, that's what hit her now. No one in this time knew who she was. Ash and Zora and Willis and Chandra wouldn't meet her for another year. She was nothing to them now. Just some stranger. She had no friends, no family, no money.

Slowly, Dorothy stood. They were on a narrow dock wedged between two grimy brick buildings. The windows were mostly smashed and boarded up, but a few slivers of glass remained in the frames, reflecting herself and Roman back to her a hundred times. She caught sight of her face in the window directly across from her.

At least she thought it was hers. The girl staring back at her might've been beautiful, once. Not anymore. Half her face had been shredded, and blood leaked through the fingers cupped over her eye. And her hair, her beautiful, brown hair . . .

It had turned completely white.

"I'm waiting for a name," Roman reminded her.

Dorothy barely heard him. She took a step closer to the window, amazed. For the first time that she could remember, she saw her reflection and didn't feel like it was a lie. The broken, ugly girl in the window was more *her* than she'd ever been before.

Everything's a con, she thought and, for a moment, she felt like laughing.

It was so simple. Roman really had set her up. She thought of everything he'd done back at the complex—breaking Ash out, making sure she got into the time machine, baiting her with all that nonsense about proving herself—it had all been meant to get her here, to this moment, standing on the dock with Roman a year earlier than anyone expected.

He'd known that the ship wouldn't make it through the anil, that she'd offer to change the EM. That she'd be lost.

Despite her pain, Dorothy felt herself start to grin. It was just an elaborate con. *Her* con. She'd told Roman everything that happened. She'd told him exactly how to manipulate her.

Hand trembling, she patted down her jacket, calming when her fingers found the small, cylindrical shape inside her pocket.

She heard Ash's voice in her head: *He doesn't have any exotic matter. Even if that time machine he built actually works, physically, he* can't *travel back in time.*

And then Roman: *There's something else that I need. . . . Believe it or not, you're the only person alive who can get it for me.*

"I'm beginning to get impatient," Roman said. He raised his gun.

Time is a circle, Dorothy thought. She fumbled for her jacket pocket, fingers closing around the container of exotic matter.

"Quinn," she said, turning away from the window. The name tasted like honey on her tongue, instantly and completely right. She stood up straighter, mimicking what she remembered of Quinn's regal posture back in the hotel room. "My name is Quinn Fox. If you let me live, I can help you."

Roman hesitated. "Help me? How?"

Dorothy pulled the EM out of her pocket. It flashed beneath her fingers: purple and oily, and then thick, like white lava.

She held it out to him. "I have something you need."

ACKNOWLEDGMENTS

It seems fitting that my tenth published novel should also be the one that was in the works the longest. When I go into my email account and do a search for this novel, the earliest reference I find is from 2011, but that's misleading—I came up with the idea for this book long, *long* before that, only then it was called *Time Traveling Monster Hunters.* And, uh, there were actual monsters involved, and not just metaphorical ones. (The monsters were cut for good reason, believe me!)

And so it stands to reason that I have a lot of people to thank, starting with my first agent, Chris Richman, who also happened to be the second person I told about this strange little book. Any writer can tell you that we have about a dozen story ideas floating around in our heads at any time. There are all sorts of reasons we decide to pursue the ideas that we do, but early encouragement is a big one. Chris's reaction to this idea was one of the reasons I decided to keep tinkering with it, even if I wouldn't get around to actually writing it for another five years. So, thank you, Chris. I hope you pick it up and recognize that idea I told you about years and years ago.

If Chris's encouragement helped me start this book, Mandy Hubbard's continued enthusiasm and support is what helped me finish it. From cheerleading me through early drafts, to doggedly helping me seek out the very best home, to holding my hand as the pub date inched ever closer, Mandy has been a better advocate for my career than I ever could've wished for. I reread the email she wrote me after I sent her the first pages of this book whenever I need a pick-me-up, or to remember what I'd hoped this series could be. Thank you, thank you, thank you times a million.

No book is published by just one person, and *Stolen Time* benefited from having a truly fantastic team of people supporting it behind the scenes. I want to thank everyone at HarperTeen for everything they did to bring this book out into the world, but, particularly, thank you to my editor, Erica Sussman, who has been championing *Stolen Time*, and me, from the beginning. Huge thanks, also, to Louisa Currigan; Bess Braswell and Sabrina Abballe in marketing; Gina Rizzo in publicity; Michelle Cunningham, Alison Donalty, and Jenna Stempel-Lobell in design; Alexandra Rakaczki in copyediting, and finally, to Jean McGinley, Alpha Wong, Sheala Howley, and Kaitlin Loss in subrights for taking care of the Chronology Protection Agency abroad. Also, thank you to the entire Harper sales team for helping this book find its people.

This book was heavily influenced by early reads from a bunch of brilliant writers and good friends. Thank you so much to Leah Konen and Anna Hecker for helping me bring Dorothy to the future (and getting her into a pair of pants). And to Wade Lucas, Becca Marsh, Lucy Randall, Julia Katz, and Maree Hamilton, a resounding thank-you for so enthusiastically cheering me on from the very beginning. Anne Heltzel gave me brilliant notes on an early draft. Thomas Van de Castle helped me sneak into a military base (but, you know, not a real one) and provided invaluable details on the US government—which I promptly ignored so I could make up my own. And, Bill Rollins, your name is in this book because you spent years making me think about math and science even when I didn't want to (and I never wanted to). So thanks for that. I don't think I would've understood any of the theory if not for those early discussions. And, of course, a huge thanks to my husband, Ron Williams, who let me read him chapters while he was cooking, and who asked great questions and pointed out dumb mistakes and read the whole damn thing at least five times and still pretends it's his favorite book ever. Thank you.

And, finally, I'm going to finish these acknowledgments with a story. A long time ago, in the backyard of one of my favorite wine bars, I was sipping rosé with one of my favorite people. *Stolen Time* was still my shiny new WIP, and I couldn't help gushing about how excited I was to finish it, and how great it was going to be when it was done. Somewhere between the second and third glasses of wine, Jocelyn Davies—who, in addition to being one of my favorite people, was also an editor at HarperCollins—told me she wanted to buy it. And then, six months later, she did. Jocelyn is the reason that all the good parts in this book are so good, and all the bad parts aren't quite as bad as they might've been. Jocelyn fixed the pace and made the love story steamier and helped me untangle the time-travel logic. The reason this book has entries from the Professor's log is because of Jocelyn. It, quite simply, would not be the same book without her.

Thanks, J. Drinks soon?